PARADISE PARK

Rhiannon is alone in the world after Bull Beynon,
her   She
wo   hen
as   s a
liki   ays.
He   reat
unl   uns
aw   b or
a h   nds
bet   nds
her   cely
mo   ged
har   ing
gra   ute
int   only
thi   Bull
Be   ears
tha

PARADISE PARK

Iris Gower

PARAGON

CHIVERS PRESS
BATH

First published 2002
by
Bantam Press
This Large Print edition published by
Chivers Press
by arrangement with
Transworld Publishers
2002

ISBN 0 7540 9172 4

British Library Cataloguing in Publication Data available

Printed and bound in Great Britain by
BOOKCRAFT, Midsomer Norton, Somerset

To Tudor
with thanks for all his love and support

CHAPTER ONE

'I want you out and as quick as you like—you're not staying here now my brother's dead!' The voice was harsh, and Rhiannon Beynon shivered as she looked at the thin-faced woman standing in the doorway of her bedroom.

She could hardly believe this was happening. Her employer, Mr Cookson, had assured her there would always be a place for her in his house. His sister, it seemed, had other ideas. Rhiannon tried appealing to her. 'But, Miss Cookson, you can't throw me out into the street—where will I go?'

'I don't know and what's more I don't care. My brother might have harboured a whore but I will not have your sort living under my roof.' Her lips narrowed into a thin line and her eyes held such scorn that Rhiannon knew there was no point in continuing to plead with her.

Fear clutched at her heart. She wanted to ask for a little more time but before she could frame the words Miss Cookson spoke again. 'You call yourself Mrs Beynon but that is just an assumed name,' she shook her head in disgust, 'a name you shamelessly took from a previous lover. I pray that the Good Lord above will protect me from such evil.'

'Please, Miss Cookson, give me a chance. I've learned to be respectable now, I promise you. I've lived with Mr Cookson for the best part of a year and he was pleased with my work. If you'll trust me, I'll prove to you that I'm a reformed woman.'

Miss Cookson stared at her in icy silence and Rhiannon knew that her words had been in vain.

1

She looked around the room, with its thick curtains and good bedclothes, and tears welled in her eyes. This room was her home now: how could she bear to leave it? 'Your brother wouldn't have wanted this,' she said, her voice almost a whisper.

Miss Cookson inched a scrap of lace from her sleeve and dabbed her dry eyes with it. 'My brother was too generous for his own good but now that he has departed this world your life of ease is over. I own this house now and I want you out.'

'But he said I'd always be provided for—and I was a good servant, anyone will tell you that.'

Miss Cookson sniffed. 'You were nothing more than a common harlot who happened to keep house for my brother. That's what you were, my lady. I know all about you, so don't think you can pull the wool over my eyes.' She looked down her long nose at Rhiannon. 'The new maid I employed this morning has just told me you were a camp-follower before my dear misguided brother took you in.'

Rhiannon fell silent. What could she say? Miss Cookson was speaking the truth.

'And as for remuneration you won't get a penny piece from me. Now shift yourself before I have you thrown out.'

Rhiannon opened her mouth to ask if she could at least stay the night but closed it again quickly: Miss Cookson's expression told her that any request would be flatly refused. 'I'll pack my things at once.' Rhiannon stood up, suddenly angry, first with Miss Cookson for being so harsh then with herself for having pleaded with the woman.

She dragged open a drawer and took out her neatly folded clothes. She packed quickly, aware that Miss Cookson was standing over her as though worried she might steal something. Rhiannon glanced up at her. 'I won't rob you of the family silver. If I'd been a thief I'd be a rich woman by now.'

As she fastened her bag Rhiannon felt a deep sense of loss: she had been fond of Mr Cookson, who had been a kindly, considerate employer, and she would miss him.

'Come along, girl, I haven't got all night.'

Rhiannon straightened and faced Miss Cookson squarely. 'How could a kindly man like Mr Cookson have a harridan of a sister like you?'

'What?'

'You heard, you miserable old hen!' Rhiannon said. 'No wonder he never asked you to visit him, not even in the last days of his illness. You haven't a compassionate bone in your body!' She moved closer and Miss Cookson backed away nervously. 'Who sat with him day and night, seeing him through the long dark hours?' Rhiannon resisted the temptation to slap the woman. 'I did! You should be grateful to me, not throwing me out into the night like this. What are the neighbours going to make of it, do you think?'

Evidently that had not occurred to Miss Cookson because she looked startled. 'I don't know, I never thought . . . Well, perhaps you could stay here until daylight. I suppose another night here wouldn't do any harm.'

'You can keep your bed,' Rhiannon said. 'I wouldn't stay here now if you begged me to.' She knew she was being a fool: in daylight she could look for another job and arrange some cheap lodgings, but who would bother with her in the

3

middle of the night?

Miss Cookson smiled thinly. 'That settles it for me, then, doesn't it? I'll just inform all who wish to know that when I asked you to stay until morning you refused.' She laughed spitefully. 'In any case, who would give your sort the time of day? No one respectable, I'll wager.'

'May God forgive you because I won't.' Rhiannon picked up her bag and pushed past Miss Cookson. 'Oh, and I shouldn't worry about what the neighbours think of you. Tales of your meanness have travelled before you.'

Miss Cookson looked as if she had swallowed a lemon as she folded her arms across her thin chest. 'Get out at once, you insolent upstart!'

'I'm going! I wouldn't stay here another minute. You're a miserable dried-up spinster and I'm not surprised you couldn't get a man.' Rhiannon hurried down the stairs—her bag bumped against her legs, but she was too angry to notice.

Out in the street she looked around her, wondering which direction to take, then began to make her way through town uphill towards the Stryd Fawr. Even at this time of night the high street was thronged with people. She saw several affluent gentlemen in good coats and tall hats step out of a carriage and make for the brightly lit entrance of the Paradise Park Hotel and knew what sort of business they would be conducting in such premises. Prostitutes lurked in doorways, knowing that the time to ply for trade was later when the gentlemen, fortified with a hearty meal and a great deal to drink, would want to round off the evening with a good wench.

Rhiannon paused, and a great sadness washed

over her as she saw a young girl, little more than a child, rubbing one bare foot against the other in an attempt to keep warm. That had been the way she had lived once but she would never again sell herself to any man. She squared her shoulders. She must look on tonight as a new beginning. Now, having worked as maidservant to a respected gentleman of the town, she would be more likely to find another position in service. Perhaps with a newcomer who'd never have heard about her past.

'What you looking at, missus?'

Rhiannon realized that the girl was talking to her. 'Evening,' she said. 'Sorry, I didn't mean to stare.'

'That's all right, then. Now, push off—there's enough of us working the Paradise Park as it is.'

'I'm not here to do business,' Rhiannon said. 'I'm just looking for somewhere to stay the night.'

The girl shrugged.

'Look, why don't you give up this life?' Rhiannon said impulsively. 'It's no good for you, not in the long run.'

'Just go away. I don't want no sermons preached to me, thanks.'

'No, you've got it wrong. I used to do what you're doing and I know what life on the streets is like. Why don't you get out of the trade while you're still young enough to find a decent position somewhere?'

'Had one once,' the girl said, 'till the master got 'old of me. Ruined me, he did, and I was thrown out into the street like a stray dog.'

Rhiannon tried again. 'Something like that happened to me but I had a bit of luck and got out of it.'

'I won't have no luck.' The girl pushed back her tangled hair. 'I 'aven't never 'ad any.'

'Things can change,' Rhiannon said gently, 'like they did for me.'

'Well, you had all the luck going, then, didn't you? You 'ad my share as well, by the look of it.' She glanced at Rhiannon's good clothes.

'I'm Rhiannon Beynon. What's your name?' Rhiannon tried a different tack. 'And how old are you?'

'Sal Evans is my name and I'm twelve, though what it's got to do with you I don't know.' She shifted position and rubbed the other foot against her leg.

'Why don't you come with me?' Rhiannon said. 'I'll find us somewhere to sleep, and in the morning I'll fit you out with some of my clothes and we'll look for work together.'

Sal was silent for a long time and then she nodded. 'All right, then. I'm that tired I could sleep for a week.'

Rhiannon led the way along the high street towards the station. Once she had lived there in a rough shack as woman to one of the navvies who had built the railway running into Swansea. It had been a poor enough place but Rhiannon had been happy there; happy because she had been with the man she loved. But that was a long time ago, almost a year. Now her man was married to a respectable girl and lived in a proper house in a nice part of the town.

'Where the 'ell are we going?' Sal said mournfully. 'I was tired before I started and now me legs are killing me.'

Rhiannon thought quickly. 'We'll go to the

station,' she said. 'It's only a little way further up the track. We can sleep there for the night and then tomorrow I'll see what I can do to find us a position in some nice house where we'll have a decent bed and food to put in our bellies.'

'Sounds too good to be true,' Sal said doubtfully.

Rhiannon took her arm and led her over the rough ground. 'I'll give you a pair of my boots too. I'll make sure you're all right.'

'Will you? Why?' Sal asked.

'Because I was like you once and I know that the older you are the worse it gets.' She stopped for a moment and pointed. 'Look, there's a light on at the station. Come on, it's not far now.'

Spurred on by the thought of shelter Sal seemed more cheerful. 'Oh, I could kill for a little lay-down with no man to pester me.'

'We'll go in the ladies' waiting room and keep warm till the morning,' Rhiannon said.

Inside the small room a pot-bellied stove burned brightly, issuing a comforting warmth. Rhiannon sank down on a bench and sighed with relief. 'It's not the Mackworth Hotel, Sal, but it will do us until morning.'

Sal lay across the bench and tucked her feet under her skirt. Lying there in the dim light she looked more of a child than ever. Rhiannon felt pity tug at her: she herself had been little more than a child when she lost her virginity to an unscrupulous lodger in the rented house where she had lived with her mother. No wonder Sal had little time for men. Still, there were some good men around and for a time she'd been lucky enough to live with one.

Rhiannon was almost asleep when the door

7

opened. She sat up quickly, holding her bag tightly. She had few enough possessions and had no intention of losing them.

'What's this, then?' A uniformed station-master came into the room and looked from Rhiannon to Sal, his sharp eyes taking in every detail of their appearance. Rhiannon had never seen the man before and realized he would know nothing about her previous life.

'You.' He prodded Sal. 'Out of here now, we don't want your sort cluttering the place up.'

'She's with me,' Rhiannon said.

The man's eyes narrowed. 'Well, I took you to be a respectable lady but if she's with you then I suppose you're both harlots. This room is for respectable ladies only.'

'Surely you could let us stay for the night. No one's going to come along until daylight, are they?'

He stared at her sternly. 'I said, out of here. Now, get going before I call the constable. Unless . . .' He moved closer to Rhiannon. 'You look clean enough and a fine handsome woman into the bargain. What if you stay with me for the night and the girl can sleep in by here? How would that suit you?'

Rhiannon swallowed her anger. 'I'm sorry, you've made a mistake. I'm not a street woman.'

He fell back, uncertain now. 'Well, I don't know . . .' He lifted his cap and scratched his head. 'You seem respectable enough, but if you are, why are you out at this time of night with this little whore for company?'

'I was employed by Mr Cookson, the railway engineer. I'm sure you've heard of him.'

'Aye, I have that. Didn't the poor fellow pass on

a week or two ago? Clever man knew the great Mr Brunel personally, so I hear.'

'Yes, that's right. I nursed Mr Cookson on his deathbed and now his sister has taken over the house and dispensed with my services without giving me notice.'

'That wasn't very nice of her, was it?' He paused. 'All right, you can stay but the girl goes.'

'If she goes I go,' Rhiannon said flatly.

For a moment it looked as if the man would give in but then he walked to the door and opened it. 'That's up to you, then, isn't it?'

'Come on, Sal, let's get out of here,' Rhiannon said, and swept past the station-master, her head high.

'Lot of good being respectable's done you,' Sal said. 'I'm going back to town. I should pick up a good customer at this hour and then at least I'll have a roof over my head for the night.'

Before Rhiannon could argue, Sal had disappeared like a shadow into the darkness. Rhiannon looked about her: this was the second time tonight she had been thrown out but she would sleep rough rather than go back to her old trade.

Slowly, she walked away from the station, feeling desolate as the glow of the gaslights faded from sight. She followed the railway line as it wound outwards from the station and a feeling of hope gripped her. Perhaps she would find the hut where she had lived with her man.

Her man. She thought of Bull Beynon, strong and handsome, with a good head on his broad shoulders. For a few short months she'd been so happy; even the rough surroundings of the shanty

9

town had not diminished the joy she had felt when she was with him. Bull had gone up in the world, become a manager on the railways, with the job of overseeing the maintenance of the line from Swansea to Chepstow. And he had married a respectable girl from Greenhill. She only hoped Katie Cullen appreciated what a fine man she had.

The edge of the railway was dark and deserted— the camp-women had gone with their men, following the web of rail track through the countryside—but the hut was still there. With a sigh of relief Rhiannon let herself in. The place smelt of damp as no fire had been lit in the brazier for a long time. Could she really sleep here? What choice did she have? Rhiannon rummaged on the dusty shelf until she touched a stub of a candle. Carefully she felt around until she found some matches and a smile curved her lips. Now she could make herself comfortable for what remained of the night.

As she lit the candle a warm glow filled the small hut. Now she could light a fire. She knew that Bull used to keep a bundle of sticks under the bed and she bent down to slide her hand beneath the frame. Good! Some kindling had been left behind when the hut had been abandoned. At first it refused to light and Rhiannon thought of the warm room she'd grown used to. Still, she was here now and she just had to make the best of it.

At last, she had a good fire shooting flames and spitting sparks through the bars of the brazier. Rhiannon held out her hands, enjoying the warmth. Suddenly she felt weary, and stretched out on the bed she had shared with Bull. It was then that the tears ran fast down her face, but she had learned that crying did no good. Life was full of ups and downs, and she had weathered them all, hadn't she? But she had never felt so despairing as she did now, alone in the damp hut to which she'd thought she'd said goodbye for ever.

The candle flickered and died, and Rhiannon stared into the flames, which danced in a blur before her tear-filled eyes. Then she heard a rat scratching and drew her shawl closer to her face. She thought of chasing it out of the hut but she was too weary to bother. Perhaps the creature needed warmth and shelter as much as she did. She was almost asleep when the whistle of a train woke her again.

As the train thundered past she wondered briefly whether it would be better to go back to her old life touting for custom from the rich men of the town. Then she decided she was too tired to think clearly now. She lay down again and in a few minutes she was asleep.

*　　　*　　　*

Sal Evans thought she had found some of the luck Rhiannon Beynon had told her about. Next to her in the bed was a young buck, a clean, good-looking man who had taken her into the Paradise Park with him to spend the night. He had been very drunk but now he was sleeping like a baby.

Sal stretched her legs enjoying the warmth of the bed and the cosy feel of the blankets around her shoulders. This was better than sleeping on an old bench in a railway station. Her eyes grew heavy and she drifted off to sleep.

A heavy slap across her face woke her. She sat

11

up, wide awake. The young man she'd slept with was kneeling before her, his face red with anger. 'You whore!' he said. 'You dirty stinking whore!' He hit her again, this time with his clenched fist. Sal reeled back from him in horror. Gone was the nice young buck of the night before: the man hitting her looked like a demon.

He lashed out again and his fist connected with her jaw, sending Sal sprawling on to the floor.

'How dare you sleep in my bed, you dirty slut!' He climbed down and aimed a kick at her face. Sal curled up into a tight ball trying to protect herself. 'I'll teach you to take advantage of a decent young man.' He kicked her again, his foot connecting with her stomach. Sal gasped in pain and tried to crawl towards the door. He caught her ankles, turned her over on her back and hit her across the face again. Sal thought she must be in a nightmare—how could this be happening to her? He continued to slap her until she gave up trying to protect herself. How long the beating went on she didn't know: a kick connected with her head and she lost consciousness.

When she came to, Sal's eyes were swollen so badly she could hardly see. Her body ached, and as she struggled to her feet she felt a trickle of blood run down her legs. The bastard! He must have raped her after the beating.

She staggered out of the room. She knew there was little point in complaining: no one would listen to a cheap whore. In the back-street she felt the early light touch her bruised face and it was then that she began to cry.

CHAPTER TWO

A cock crowing outside the hut woke Rhiannon and she sat up, her heart pounding as she was transported back to her childhood. She was living in the tall, gloomy house and the lodger downstairs was keeping chickens in the back garden. One day she had asked him where the fluffy chicks that huddled in his kitchen near the fire had come from. His reply had been to lay her down in his room and demonstrate how they had been conceived. Rhiannon had lost her childhood innocence for ever.

She took a deep breath, shook away the painful memory and stared around her at the damp hut. The fire was low in the brazier and Rhiannon realized that she had not come very far since the days of her childhood. At least then she'd had a roof over her head and enough to eat. Now she had nothing but the memories of her sordid past to keep her company.

She swung her legs off the bed and pushed some sticks into the fire, shivering in the chill of the morning. She went to the window and looked outside. It was barely daylight and a thin mist hung over the silver of the railway track.

She returned to the fire and poked another batch of sticks into the flames. Soon the store would be gone and then she would have no means of keeping herself warm. She opened the battered cupboard door and searched inside, hoping to find some tea-leaves, but the cupboard was bare. Anything left there had doubtless been taken by

13

one of the other camp-women.

She returned to the bed and sat down. She had been so settled here once, respected by the navvies because she was Bull Beynon's woman. She had loved him desperately. She pushed these thoughts aside. Looking back never did any good. She must find a job, however humble, or go back to the streets.

When daylight came Rhiannon looked about for her bag: she needed to dress in clean, fresh clothes if she was going to find employment. There was no sign of it. Someone must have crept into the hut during the night and taken it with her few possessions. It seemed as if the whole world was against her.

She twisted her hair into a knot and wrapped her shawl around her shoulders. Her skirt was creased but there was nothing she could do about it now. Slowly, the sun was coming up, bringing the landscape into full colour. Suddenly, in spite of her empty stomach, Rhiannon felt better. She would find some respectable work if it took her a month of Sundays.

She walked away from the railway line and down the hill towards the Stryd Fawr. A baker's van stood in the high street at the entrance to the Paradise Park Hotel and the smell of fresh bread made Rhiannon feel faint. She leaned against the window of the hotel and waited for her head to clear; she was just hungry, she had been hungry before but not in a long time.

'Rhiannon!' The voice was familiar. 'Rhiannon, are you all right?'

'Katie Cullen, it's you.' Rhiannon rubbed her eyes, remembering that Katie was married now so

14

she was no longer a Cullen. She had taken Bull Beynon as her husband. Rhiannon knew she should hate Katie for that but she'd always known Bull would leave her one day. 'I'm all right, really. How are you?' She scarcely needed an answer because it was clear Katie was blooming. The soft swell of her stomach revealed that she was expecting Bull's child, and Rhiannon burst into tears.

'Rhiannon, you don't look all right! What's wrong?' Katie touched her arm. 'Come on, you can tell me. Perhaps I can help?'

'What's wrong?' Rhiannon repeated flatly. 'I'll tell you what's wrong, you've taken my man from me.' Katie's cheeks flooded with colour and Rhiannon held out her hand. 'I'm sorry, that was stupid of me.'

'I'm sorry it still upsets you about Bull and me,' Katie said. 'I thought you might have got over it a bit by now.'

Rhiannon forced a smile. 'Oh, I have, I was just being silly and childish. You heard that poor Mr Cookson died, didn't you, Katie?'

'I heard, and I'm sorry. I'm sure you were very fond of him and it's only natural you miss him.'

'I'm not that unselfish,' Rhiannon said. 'I'm crying because I'm out of work, I'm hungry and I've spent the night in a damp hut with the rats.'

'Oh, Rhiannon, I'm so sorry. What happened? Didn't Miss Cookson want to keep you on?'

Rhiannon shook her head and sagged against the window. Katie took her arm and glanced up at the windows of the Paradise Park Hotel. 'We don't want to go in there. I'll take you up to the Mackworth. It's only a little way up the road and when we've eaten we can talk about finding work

15

for you.'

Rhiannon allowed herself to be led into the softly carpeted foyer of the hotel, and here the smell of bacon made her mouth water. She was grateful when the waiter led them to a table and she could sit down—she felt as if her legs were about to collapse under her.

'Tea and toast for two, please,' Katie said, and the waiter slid away. 'Shouldn't be long bringing the food,' she went on. 'There's hardly anyone in here besides us.'

'Good.' Rhiannon made an attempt to smile. 'If he takes too long I might just start to eat the tablecloth.'

By the time the food was put on the table she was hard put not to cram her mouth with the hot buttered toast. When she had finished, Katie pushed her plate across the table. 'Go on, I've had enough breakfast as it is. I'm eating like a starving horse, these days.'

Rhiannon did as she was told, then leaned back in her chair. 'I feel almost human again,' she said, wiping her lips with a thick damask napkin marked with the crest of the hotel.

'Now we must find you a job,' Katie said. 'We can't have you sleeping rough again tonight.'

'Finding jobs is not so easy,' Rhiannon said, 'not when you used to be a street-walker like me.'

'That was a long time ago,' Katie said quickly. 'Now, I heard my cook talking about a position going vacant at Mrs Buchan's place. How would that suit you?'

Rhiannon shook her head. 'You know what a name Mrs Jayne Buchan's got for herself. I can't see her taking me on.'

'I know she can be a bit of a Tartar,' Katie said, 'but if you worked in the kitchen you wouldn't see much of her, would you? And it's a start.'

'I know, and I'm grateful for the suggestion—but look at me.' Rhiannon gestured to her rumpled skirt and the bedraggled shawl around her shoulders.

Katie smiled. 'Aye, you do look a bit like a rag-and-bone girl! How about we go up to my house and I find some fresh clothes for you?'

'Oh, I don't know,' Rhiannon said quickly. Could she bear to see Bull as the master of his own home with his wife at his side?

'Bull isn't in at the moment.' Katie had read her reluctance well. 'He's up the railway line with the men checking the track. Come on, we can't sit here for ever and we must find you some work.' She paid the bill and they left the hotel.

'Why are you being so kind to me?' Rhiannon asked. 'We haven't seen much of each other over the last year, have we?'

Katie looked at her. 'I know, but I felt so guilty about finding my happiness at the expense of yours. I'll never forget how you looked the day the Great Western Railway opened.'

'How did I look?'

'When you saw Bull take me into his arms in front of all those people you were so sad. I know you loved him, but so do I,' Katie said. 'I'm sorry, Rhiannon.'

'Don't be, I'm well over Bull Beynon by now.' Rhiannon knew that Katie wasn't convinced. 'Being with Mr Cookson helped. He was a fine man and so kind to me. He'd be angry if he knew his sister had turned me out of the house.'

17

Katie's steps slowed as she came to the hill leading up to her house. She leaned on a wall and took deep breaths. 'I'm as heavy as a cow at milking-time,' she said. 'This baby is going to be a big one.'

Rhiannon felt a stab of jealousy that Katie had everything she wanted: Bull for a husband, a baby on the way and a nice house to live in.

'Did you know Bull and I have a new home?' Katie asked. 'His employers thought so much of him they bought him the house by way of a bonus.'

Rhiannon looked at the large gates and at the square, solid house behind them. 'No, I didn't.' She had often heard Mr Cookson talking about Bull, of course. The two men had worked together until Mr Cookson retired, but he had never discussed matters of business or finance with her. 'Bull has done well,' she said proudly. 'I always knew he would.'

Katie looked at her quickly, 'He speaks highly of you, too, Rhiannon. And I hope you don't think I'm showing off about the house because I wouldn't hurt your feelings for the world.'

'Why are you such a nice person?' Rhiannon asked, in exasperation. 'I couldn't hate you however hard I tried.'

'I suppose it's easy to be nice when you're happy,' Katie said simply.

They entered the large hallway and Rhiannon looked round in appreciation. 'What lovely colours you've got in here,' she said, unaware that she sounded wistful. 'The pale blue silk paper on the walls and the deep blue of the carpet go so well together.'

A young maid hovered around them, taking

18

Katie's shawl and waiting politely for Rhiannon to take off hers. Rhiannon was impressed. 'Imagine having a maid of your own! You have gone all posh, Katie. And you've got a cook too now. You never have to light a fire or bring in coal or spend time in a hot kitchen. It must be so nice.'

'I suppose I've got used to it,' Katie said. 'I never had such luxuries at home, mind, and then when Mam died I worked as a maid myself. You know that, Rhiannon, you came to work with me for a while.'

'I remember it well,' Rhiannon said. 'I more or less pushed you into asking Mr Morton-Edwards to take me on. He thought a lot of you, didn't he?'

'Aye, but only because he nearly ran over me with his coach and horses! It was then I met Bull. I used to think the navvies a rough lot and I never thought I'd end up marrying one.'

'Well, Bull's hardly a navvy, is he? He's a posh manager with a respectable wife and a lovely home. It's what you both deserve, though,' Rhiannon said, 'and I don't grudge you any of it.' And she didn't, but she would have lived with Bull in a shabby, rat-infested hut for ever and been the happiest woman alive.

'I'll get you something fresh to wear.' Katie's voice broke into her thoughts. 'If you're going for a job we have to make you look nice, don't we?'

'It would be nice to work here.' Rhiannon regretted the words as soon as they were spoken. Of course she couldn't work in Katie's house. How could she live under the same roof as Bull and not pine for him every moment of the day? 'But I can see you've enough staff as it is,' she added quickly, 'and I know it wouldn't work me being here. In any

19

case, you've been kind enough as it is.'

'Sit down, make yourself comfortable,' Katie said, 'and I'll see we're brought a nice cup of tea.'

She left Rhiannon alone in the sitting room and Rhiannon stared around her at the pictures, the curtains and the cheerful fire burning in the grate. One day, she decided, she would have a place like this, somewhere of her own. She smiled ruefully. Right now she needed to get a job. Then she could think clearly, make plans for her future: she did not intend to be in service for the rest of her life.

The maid brought in a tea tray and smiled pleasantly at Rhiannon. 'Like sugar in your tea, miss?'

Rhiannon nodded. 'Please—milk too.'

The girl handed her the cup and Rhiannon looked at her curiously. 'Do you like working here?'

'Oh, yes, miss. It's my first job and though I did miss my mam and dad at first I soon settled in. Mrs Beynon is so kind, Mr Beynon too. I'm very lucky.'

The girl seemed young, little more than sixteen. She had an air of innocence about her that Rhiannon envied. When she had been sixteen she had known nothing about kindness. All she knew was the dark underworld of street-walking. By seventeen she had lost count of the men she'd been with. Some were kind but some were rough, handling her as if she had no feelings. Even now the indignity of it all made her feel ill.

Katie came back into the sitting room and sat down slowly, adjusting her legs to accommodate her belly. 'I swear I'm getting heavier by the minute.' She smiled. 'Now, I've laid out some clothes on my bed. First we'll have our tea, then go up and see how they fit you.' She pointed to the plate of dainty cakes the maid had put on the table. 'Go on, help yourself. I expect you're still hungry.'

Rhiannon took a cake to please her rather than because she wanted it. She felt uncomfortable, as though she was an intruder in Katie's house. As soon as she could, she rose to her feet. 'You sit here by the fire and I'll go and find the clothes for myself. I don't want to drag you upstairs again, do I?'

Katie smiled and nodded, and eased off her shoes. 'Go on, take anything you fancy. All my clothes are far too small for me.'

Rhiannon went up the stairs, holding on to the polished banister. The sunlight poured in through the window giving the house a glow of warmth, and Rhiannon stood on the landing wondering which room she should look in. She opened a few doors and knew at once which one Katie shared with Bull. There was the scent of him here, the unmistakable, pleasant odour of a man. Her memories rushed in. She was in Bull's arms, clinging to him, kissing him, being loved by him. He was the one man who had aroused any feelings in her; with Bull she'd learned that making love could be a beautiful, magical thing.

She must get out of here quickly: knowing that Bull lived in this house, that he slept in this bed, was too much for her to bear. The pain of him leaving her for Katie was as raw as it had ever been.

Quickly, she selected some clean, pressed clothes, a good woollen skirt with red and black stripes, and a jacket to match. When she was dressed she drew a red shawl around her shoulders and looked at her reflection in the mirror. Her hair

21

was tangled over her face and, in spite of the fresh clothes, she still looked a sight.

On the table was a silver-backed brush and Rhiannon picked it up and brushed her hair until it shone, then twisted it into a knot at the nape of her neck and pinned it into place. That was better. She looked like a respectable woman now, not an outcast from the workhouse.

With a last look round, Rhiannon left the bedroom Bull shared with Katie—and heard the maid opening the front door for the master of the house to enter.

'Bull!' Rhiannon murmured his name, but he seemed to hear her because he looked up and their eyes locked. Rhiannon took a deep breath: she must get a grip on herself—she couldn't let Bull know that she was still in love with him. 'Hello, Bull, I haven't seen you for ages but I must say you're looking very well.' Her voice was light, and gave no indication of her inner turmoil. She went downstairs and then she was standing close to him, so close she could have touched him. But he was no longer her man. Bull belonged to Katie.

'Rhiannon, it's good to see you and looking so beautiful too.' He spoke impersonally as if they had never been lovers.

Rhiannon summoned up a smile. 'You can thank your wife for the way I look because she's just lent me some of her clothes. I'm hoping to find work this morning and Katie's determined I'll look my best.'

'I meant to get in touch with you and tell you how sorry I was about old Cookson. He was a fine man and I owe him so much.'

They stood in silence for a moment. Then Bull

spoke again: 'I caught a glimpse of you at the funeral but you left before I could offer my condolences.'

They were speaking to each other like strangers and Rhiannon knew then that whatever Bull had felt for her in the past had dissipated.

Katie came into the hallway and smiled as Bull took her in his arms. They looked so happy, so much in love, that tears came to Rhiannon's eyes. 'I'd better be off then,' she said quickly. 'Thank you, Katie, for your kindness. I won't forget it.'

'Oh—take this,' Katie said. 'I've written out a reference for you. I know I'm far below the Buchans in society but I thought it might do a bit of good.'

'I'm sure it will.'

'Come back and let me know how you get on,' Katie said. 'I'd like to know you were safely settled somewhere.'

'I will.' Rhiannon smiled and left. She closed the front door behind her and began the long walk across the hills to where the élite of the town lived. She was alone now, but she was strong and one day the whole of Swansea would know that she was a woman to be reckoned with.

CHAPTER THREE

Jayne Buchan was a pretty woman with pale blonde hair and a fine complexion. She had been born to wealth: her father Eynon Morton-Edwards was one of the most influential men in Swansea. She appeared to have everything a young woman could

23

want: a handsome, successful husband, a fine home and a doting father. But Jayne's pale beauty was marred by the downward droop of her full lips, which revealed that she was an unfulfilled woman.

She was in need of a new maid—maids were inclined to come and go from the Buchan household in quick succession. She looked now at the girl standing before her. She seemed sensible enough, clean and neat, and willing to work. 'So, you kept house for Mr Cookson, the engineer, then, for almost a year.' Jayne pursed her lips consideringly. 'Why haven't you a reference from him?' She might be in desperate need of new staff but she would not take just any girl who chanced along.

'He died suddenly, Mrs Buchan,' the girl looked down at her feet, 'and when his sister came from England to take over the house she dismissed me.'

'Wouldn't she give you a reference?'

'She felt she didn't know me well enough, Mrs Buchan.'

Jayne studied the girl, who looked familiar, but couldn't place her. 'Have I seen you before?'

'I worked for your father for a time, and Mr Morton-Edwards was always very kind to me.'

'Ah, that's it.' Jayne made up her mind to take on the girl. 'I'll give you a month's trial. I haven't many rules, except that I don't like my maids encouraging callers. If you want to go courting, do it on your days off. Is that clear? And remember your place especially when Mr Buchan is around. He's inclined to be too lenient with the maids.' Jayne felt it wise to offer a warning: this girl was good-looking in a world-weary way, with a full figure and luxuriant hair. Not that Dafydd Buchan

24

had resorted to bedding the maids yet but Jayne did not mean to take chances. 'Do you understand me?'

The girl nodded. She seemed grateful for the job and that was all to the good: she would work hard to keep her position.

Jayne rang the bell and almost at once the maid appeared in the doorway. 'Yes, Mrs Buchan?'

'Show the new girl to her room. The one in the attic, please, Vi.' Jayne smiled: Violet had only been with her for a few weeks but she had a sweet nature and, so far, they had got on well. 'Go with Vi now. She'll show you where you're to sleep. What's your name again?'

'It's Rhiannon, Mrs Buchan.'

'All right, Rhiannon. I hope you're going to be comfortable here. And, Rhiannon,' Jayne smiled, 'I can sometimes be a bit crotchety but you mustn't take any notice of that.'

'Yes, Mrs Buchan, and I'll do my best to fit in, I promise.'

When the two maids had left the room Jayne returned to her writing table and picked up her pen. She had one invitation still to write. The rest had been no problem but this one was to Llinos Mainwaring. Jayne swallowed hard, tasting the bitterness of jealousy. Llinos had had an affair with Dafydd, and however hard she tried, Jayne couldn't forget it. Llinos had even borne Dafydd a son. How her poor husband, God rest his soul, had put up with it, Jayne failed to understand.

Llinos was quite an old lady now, past her fiftieth year, yet she remained irritatingly beautiful. Jayne had often caught her husband staring at Llinos. It seemed that even though their affair had ended long ago Dafydd still had feelings for her. 'Damn him!' she said aloud.

She rose and looked at her reflection in the mirror over the fireplace. She was much younger than Llinos and owned a fortune in her own right. She and Dafydd should have been soul-mates and ardent lovers but the marriage had gone wrong almost from the first moment she and Dafydd were alone together in the intimacy of their bridal suite.

She remembered it now, the disappointment she'd felt when Dafydd had made love to her. It was not the wonderful, earth-shattering experience she had believed it would be, and when her husband had turned his back on her and gone to sleep she had known instinctively that something was not right about their union.

It had taken several months and clear signs of Dafydd's faithless ways before Jayne realized she had made a mistake. All Dafydd wanted was a young bride who would bear him plenty of children. Well, in that *he* had been the disappointed one.

Jayne returned to the table and looked down at the name she had written on the card, resisting the urge to tear it to tiny pieces: that would only show that she saw Llinos as a threat, which she could not allow.

Jayne hastily signed her name to the card and put it with the others, wondering about the hold Llinos had on any man who came her way. Jayne's own father had always been dazzled by her and would only make a fuss if she wasn't invited. Another thing: there would be enough of a crowd to distract Dafydd's attention. Jayne knew he would flirt with all the young ladies present—that was his nature and he would never change now.

Jayne rang for the maid and Violet came into the room, bobbing a curtsy.

'Get these invitations sent out, there's a good girl. Oh, and do you think Rhiannon has the makings of a good maid?'

'I think so, Mrs Buchan. She's knuckled down straight away, doing all that Cook wants of her. She's very quiet, don't talk much, but Cook will soon alter that.'

'I suppose so. Cook's the nosy sort—she'll have the girl's life story before bedtime tonight. That's all—you may go now.'

Jayne shuffled her papers and put them into some sort of order. Life as Mrs Jayne Buchan had not turned out as she had hoped it would. Perhaps if she had had children things would be different. She must put that idea right out of her head: there would be no children because Jayne would never again allow Dafydd Buchan into her bed.

*   *   *

That night Rhiannon was glad to crawl into bed and stretch her tired limbs. She had worked hard in the kitchen, which she didn't mind except that she had become used to an easy life with Mr Cookson and her hands had grown soft. Today she had peeled potatoes and scrubbed the kitchen flags, carried coal and water upstairs until she thought her back would break.

She looked up at the small window: the curtains were open and she could see the clear night sky through the glass. One star seemed to burn brighter than the rest and Rhiannon smiled.

27

Someone up there was looking out for her. She turned over and snuggled under the blankets. She must sleep—tomorrow was going to be another busy day.

*　　*　　*

'Come in, Father, it's lovely to see you,' Jayne said, as the drawing-room door opened and her father was framed in it. As usual, Llinos was not far behind him but Jayne had to force herself to smile at the older woman. 'Llinos, how kind of you to come. You're not getting any younger and being social can be such a chore.' She was fully aware of the sting in her words and glanced quickly at her father, but her comments had gone over his head. She kissed Eynon and brushed cheeks with Llinos. 'The other guests haven't arrived yet so we can have a quiet drink before they come.'

Jayne tensed as her husband came into the room. 'Good evening, Eynon,' he said, his eyes resting on Llinos. 'I hope you're well.' He did not wait for a response. 'And Llinos, as lovely as ever. You must have learned the secret of eternal youth.' He bent over her hand and held it to his lips for a moment longer than was necessary.

'So, Buchan, have you heard that the Great Western shares have gone up two shillings again?' Eynon said, seating himself in the most comfortable chair near the fire.

'Oh, Father, there's no need to talk business now,' Jayne said hastily, knowing that he was taunting Dafydd: he had wanted shares in the railway but by the time he had decided to buy some it had been too late. How it must irk him that three

28

of the shareholders were seated there before him! Her father, Llinos and Jayne herself had seen the wisdom of buying into the railway in the early days.

'But I'm sure Buchan is interested in anything that affects the town and its inhabitants, aren't you, Buchan?'

Dafydd inclined his head. 'Of course.' He turned to Llinos, curtailing the conversation with Eynon. 'How is Sion? Well and strong, I hope.'

Jayne bit her lip, afraid that she might blurt out her thoughts; Dafydd was reminding them that he had a son, an illegitimate son but still a son.

'He's well, enjoying school now that he's older. It seems he's quite the scholar.'

'And your other son,' Jayne said quickly, 'my dear friend Lloyd, is he still living among the savages in America?'

Llinos looked at her coolly. 'That's unkind of you, Jayne. The American Indians are not savages.'

'I'm sorry, but all the pictures one sees in the papers show the Indian people as half-naked heathens who kill for the pleasure of it.'

'Jayne,' her father spoke sharply, 'keep your ill-informed opinions to yourself. Llinos's late husband was half American Indian, as you well know. Have you no sensitivity?'

Jayne pressed her lips together. She'd known that the evening would turn out badly—it always did when Llinos was present. She glanced at Dafydd, whose eyes were still resting on Llinos. Couldn't he see her grey hairs and the suggestion of a double chin? Llinos was old, and still Dafydd pined for her.

Jayne was relieved when the other guests began to arrive and the talk became more general. She sat next to Dafydd and whispered, 'Will you stop looking at Llinos like that?'

'Like what?' He was infuriatingly calm.

'As if she was a feast and you were starving.'

'I am starving, though, aren't I, Jayne? What man wouldn't look at other women when his wife won't allow him into her bed?'

'Keep your voice down!' Jayne wanted to slap him.

He rose and moved away from her, and she saw him greet one of the younger ladies with a wide smile. Priscilla was the daughter of Admiral Grenfell, very rich and beautiful. Jayne scrutinized her. The girl was besotted with Dafydd and made no attempt to conceal it.

Jayne thought of going over to them and putting a stop to the flirting but she changed her mind: let Dafydd make a fool of himself—the girl was too cosseted to become mistress to a mere businessman, however rich and handsome he might be. 'Dafydd's enjoying himself with the ladies as usual.' She leaned towards Llinos, wanting to hurt her. 'He'll never grow up, will he?'

'Well, flirting is harmless enough, isn't it?' Llinos said. 'And you are the one wearing his wedding ring so I wouldn't let a bit of harmless fun worry you.'

Jayne subsided in her chair. Evidently Llinos did not care any longer what Dafydd got up to. And neither should I, Jayne told herself. She had long since given up her ideas of romantic love. Dafydd was a philanderer who had enjoyed many mistresses and, no doubt, would enjoy many more.

Jayne watched him, trying to be dispassionate about him. He was good-looking still, although his hair was touched with grey, and he was as slim as a boy. He also had enough wit to charm the birds from the trees.

'Oh, look, Jayne,' Llinos said, in a low voice, 'the little madam's coming to talk to you. She has plenty of nerve, I'll give her that.'

'Hello, Jayne.'

'Hello, Priscilla. You're looking very well.' The girl kissed Jayne's cheek. 'Perhaps you've put on just a little weight.'

'I don't think so, my waist is so tiny that Dafydd can encompass it with his hands.'

'He's given a demonstration, has he?'

'Well, only in fun, of course.'

'When was that?' Jayne asked casually, but her heart was beating so fast she thought she would choke.

'At the summer ball in the assembly rooms. I was surprised you didn't come, it was such fun and Dafydd was the star of the occasion.'

'I can imagine,' Jayne said drily.

'But, then, perhaps you were too tired to cavort around the dance floor,' Priscilla said. 'I suppose as one gets older the prospect of staying at home near the fire becomes more inviting.'

'But, Priscilla, I'm only two years older than you, and Dafydd, well, he's quite a few years older than both of us.'

Priscilla glanced at him over her shoulder. 'But men age beautifully, don't they?'

Jayne tried desperately to think of a suitable reply but it was Llinos who broke the uncomfortable silence that had fallen on the small group. 'How is your father, Priscilla?'

'Very well indeed.' Priscilla's voice was frosty and Jayne half smiled. However hard Llinos tried, she

31

would never be accepted among the élite of the town: in marrying a heathen she had put herself outside polite society.

Jayne looked across the room to see what her husband was up to—perhaps trying to charm some other girl. But he was talking earnestly to a man who was a stranger to Jayne. He was younger than Dafydd and very good-looking: his hair was crisp and dark and he stood a good six inches taller than her husband. Jayne felt a stirring of interest. It was a long time since anyone new had joined the social set of Swansea. Why didn't Dafydd bring him over and introduce him? 'Who's that?' she asked.

Priscilla turned to look. 'Handsome, isn't he? His name is Guy Fairchild, and he's an entrepreneur from London.' She touched Jayne's shoulder. 'No good staring at him, Jayne. You're married, remember?'

'I remember,' Jayne said, 'but there's no harm in looking.' She got to her feet. 'I'd better go and check the dinner. I think it should be ready.' As she threaded her way through the guests she glanced towards her husband. He was smiling affably and it seemed that he was getting on well with Guy Fairchild. Just then, the man looked round and his eyes met and locked with hers. Jayne felt an unexpected thrill of pleasure run through her. He nodded to her and, hastily, Jayne left the room. 'You silly little fool!' she said to herself. She was far too old and sensible to be mooning over another man. In any case, he was probably married, too, with a tribe of children at his coat-tails. But then she thought of those lovely eyes looking into hers, and her heart beat a little faster.

'Do you really want me to seduce your wife, Dafydd?' Guy asked, in a low voice. 'She's such a beauty, and if she was mine I wouldn't let another man within a mile of her.'

'No, not seduce,' Dafydd Buchan said sharply. 'What I want is for you to worm your way into Jayne's good books. She'll trust you, and you're such a genius with money you can't fail to impress her.'

'But these shares you want her to sell, are they so very important? You've already got more money than you can spend so why do you need shares in this railway venture?'

'It's not so much need as want,' Dafydd said. 'She and her father never stop rubbing it in that they have plenty of shares while I have none.'

'And why should she agree to sell them to me?'

'Because you're a charmer, Guy. Why do you think half the women in London are chasing after you?'

'But your wife looks like a lady with a good head on her shoulders. I shouldn't think she'd let her heart rule her head in matters of finance.'

'No, but money talks and if you offer her enough I'm sure she'll accept—especially if you turn on the charm.'

'Do you trust me to charm your wife?' Guy smiled. Couldn't Dafydd Buchan see that Jayne was not only the most beautiful but the most intelligent woman in the room? She had almost touched him as she went into the hall, and on the way back she had smiled at him. Her pale hair gleamed like spun gold in the candlelight and she had an intriguing innocence about her.

'I'd trust her with anyone.'

'How touching.' Guy felt a dart of disappointment. 'Is she so much in love with you that she won't even look at another man?'

'No, I don't think Jayne's in love with me at all. She might have been once, but things were never good between us.' He paused, leaning closer to Guy as one of the guests brushed past him. He looked up and saw Priscilla smiling at him as she pressed herself against him.

'Ah,' Guy said. 'Your wife discovered you had a roving eye, is that it?'

'Something like that.'

'Then why do you trust her so unquestioningly?'

'She's frigid,' Dafydd said.

That was a challenge to any red-blooded man. 'In that case, why should you think she'll listen to anything I've got to say?'

'Jayne is not impervious to charm and good looks, Guy, and she likes intelligence in a man. I think you might be the right one to persuade her to sell.'

'Well, if you really think so, Dafydd, I'll do my best. Come, everyone is going into dinner and the last thing we want is for your lady wife to think that we're plotting anything.'

He followed Dafydd across the wide hallway and a smile curved his mouth. The seduction of Jayne Buchan would be pleasurable—very pleasurable indeed.

CHAPTER FOUR

'Rum lot, these Buchans.' Mrs Jones was kneading dough with vigour, pummelling it within an inch of its life. 'Mrs Buchan is enough to try the patience of a saint, and as for that husband of hers, he's a ne'er-do-well. I've only been here six months and already I'm thinking of finding myself a new position.'

Rhiannon looked up from the sink and saw that the cook was flushed from her neck to her hairline. Something had really got her temper up.

'*Duw, duw*, it's enough to turn an old woman silly—all these rows and all the banging of doors. I thought the master and mistress were supposed to show *us* how to behave.'

'I suppose they have off days too,' Rhiannon said. 'And Mrs Buchan did warn me not to take any notice of her little moods.'

'That's all well and good but when it comes to having my honesty called into question I draw the line.'

Rhiannon shook the water off the last of the plates and stacked it on the wooden table beside her. 'I'm sure no one doubts your honesty.' She dried her hands on her apron. 'In any case, you'd think with their sort of money a few more pounds spent at the grocer's or the butcher's wouldn't make any difference.'

'Well, it does! Called me into his study, Mr Buchan did, and asked me to explain the accounts for the last month. I told him Mrs Buchan likes things done proper and if he didn't want to spend

35

the money not to give so many lunches and dinners to a gaggle of disagreeable folk who turn up their noses at good home cooking.'

Rhiannon was intrigued. 'What did he say?'

'He looked as if he would dismiss me on the spot at first but then he burst out laughing. Told me I was quite right.'

'Good for him, then.' Rhiannon pushed the kettle on to the fire. 'Cup of tea, Mrs Jones?'

'Aye, good idea. Let's sit down a while.' She placed a cloth over the dough and set it down in the hearth. 'Just let that breathe.' She smiled. 'Have I been going on a bit?'

'Of course not. I think you're right to say what you think to folk.'

Mrs Jones sat in her rocking chair and kicked off her shoes. 'Ah, that's lovely, that is. Couldn't do me a favour, could you, *cariad*?'

'Just ask and I'll see what I can do.'

'Fetch me a bowl of nice warm water to soak my feet in and you'll be my friend for life.'

Rhiannon nodded. 'I'll push the kettle on the side of the fire and warm some more water. Shall I put a bit of mint in the bowl? It's supposed to be refreshing.'

'Aye, go on, then.' Mrs Jones had been good to Rhiannon: in the few weeks she'd been there, Mrs Jones had made her second-in-command in the kitchen. The other girls were younger than Rhiannon, more scatter-brained, and didn't do half the work she did.

'You was a lucky find, you know,' Mrs Jones said, pushing her stockings down over her varicose veins. 'These young 'uns haven't got an ounce of elbow grease between them.'

36

Rhiannon nodded, grateful that she no longer had to scrub floors and carry coal and water upstairs. Those jobs had been delegated to the 'young 'uns'. She smiled to herself. Violet and Hetty were only a year or so younger than she was but they had lived the life of the innocent while she had been a harlot.

She made the tea and prepared the bowl of warm water for Mrs Jones. 'There we are, then. Put your feet in that while you drink your tea. You'll soon feel better.'

'Oh, it's heaven on my corns, that is.' Mrs Jones swished the water between her plump toes. 'I'm that grateful to you for your kindness.'

'I'm sure Hetty or Vi would have done the same if you'd asked them, they're not bad girls.'

'No, but they would have pulled a face. Last time I asked Hetty for a bowl to soak my feet in she told me it wasn't part of her job, cheeky dab.' She watched as Rhiannon built up the fire. 'Sit down, girl, you're looking tired yourself.'

'I think I will, Mrs Jones.' Rhiannon sat at the table and rested her elbows on the white-scrubbed top. 'I am tired, but I'm enjoying the work much more than I thought I would. Sometimes I can pretend I'm keeping house for myself.'

'Some hope, Rhiannon. You'll never own a house like this, unless you get a rich man for a husband.'

'I won't ever depend on any man,' Rhiannon said. 'Sometimes I feel sorry for Mrs Buchan. She's not happy, is she? She never shares a room with Mr Buchan.'

'Don't blame her neither!' The cook fanned her face with her apron. 'That man has bedded more women than we've had roast dinners.'

'Well, we don't know that for sure, do we?'

'Yes, we do.' Mrs Jones smiled wickedly. 'The girls come back to me with plenty of gossip from the maids of other big houses. And I've heard the pair of them quarrelling. Mrs Buchan was telling him to sling his hook one day, but he won't go—not him! He's too keen to get his hands on Mrs B's railway shares, whatever they are.'

'How do you know that?'

'Because he keeps on about them. He asks her all the time to give him some and she always refuses. In a ladylike way, mind.'

The cook leaned closer to Rhiannon and lowered her voice. 'That Mr Fairchild's been round here a lot.' She nodded, and her chins wobbled. 'I think he's got a liking for Madam and she for him.'

'Oh, I don't think Mrs Buchan would do anything improper,' Rhiannon said. 'She's a nicely brought-up lady, isn't she?'

'Aye, well, a woman gets lonely when she goes to an empty bed every night. Mrs Buchan's got hot blood in her veins, I'll wager.'

Rhiannon sipped her tea. It was hot and sweet and she savoured the taste as she tried to imagine Mrs Buchan in bed with a fancy man. Rhiannon wouldn't blame her: she had seen for herself how the woman's husband treated her. It was strange how fate wove its web: she had known many men and Mrs Buchan only one—perhaps it would do her good to find a lover.

'Doesn't Mr Buchan notice that this Fairchild man is interested in his wife?'

Mrs Jones shook her head. 'Don't seem to care. I wouldn't be surprised if he planned it all.'

'Why would he do that?'

'I don't know. Perhaps it would ease his conscience if Mrs Buchan was to fall from the straight and narrow like he's done.'

Rhiannon doubted it: men were not made like that—at least, not the men she had known. They guarded their women with a ferocity that had nothing to do with love. It was all about holding on to what was theirs.

A sudden clanging of saucepans from the scullery made Mrs Jones jump. '*Duw*, those girls are noisy.' She chuckled. 'Just as well, mind. I was about to drop off.' She pushed the bowl of water away gently with her foot. 'Get Hetty to empty that out the back then give it a good scrubbing. Oh, and pass my shoes and stockings. It's time I got back to work.'

'Have another cup of tea and rest yourself for a while longer—you deserve it.' Rhiannon took the bowl into the scullery. 'Hetty, will you throw the water out in the yard then wash the bowl, please?'

'What's wrong with you doing it, then?' Hetty said sharply.

'Because I've other work to do.' Rhiannon's tone was just as sharp.

'Funny that, isn't it, Vi?' Hetty's voice was full of mock-innocence. 'Funny how doing housework is harder than lying on your back all day.'

Rhiannon stared at the girl, who had the grace to look away. 'If you've anything to say to me just say it. Don't make sly remarks.'

'Well, you was one of them loose women living by the railway track, wasn't you?'

Rhiannon went closer to Hetty and looked her in the eye. 'And what if I was?'

39

'Well, then, you're no better than you ought to be, is she, Vi?'

Rhiannon took a deep breath. 'That was a long time ago and I want to forget all about that life now.'

'Well, I don't think other folk can forget that easily, see? How could you do it, Rhiannon, sleep with all those awful men?'

'If you'd ever gone without food for days you might not be asking me that.'

'Go on.' Hetty smiled spitefully. 'I expect you like having a different man in your bed every night.'

Rhiannon grasped the girl's apron straps and pushed her up against the wall. 'I hated it. Some of the men treated me like dirt under their feet. Now, if you breathe a word of this to anyone else I'll give you a damn good hiding. Do you understand?'

'All right, I didn't mean any harm.'

'Just as well I learned how to look out for myself when I lived in the shanty town. If it meant laying a woman out flat with my fist that's what I did.' She released Hetty. 'Now, hold your tongue or you'll learn just how nasty I can be.'

'All right! Don't get so mad—I was just teasing you.'

Rhiannon walked to the door. 'Remember this, Hetty. If I'm suddenly dismissed I'll know who to blame.'

As she went back into the kitchen Rhiannon was trembling. Mrs Jones was still barefoot but her head was on the table and she was snoring like a bull. Rhiannon smiled. Poor woman, the work was too much for her. She took a cushion from one of the chairs and put it under Mrs Jones's feet. 'Can't

40

have you getting chilblains, can we, old dear?'

Quietly, Rhiannon went on preparing the food for the evening meal. She opened the oven and the smell of the meat roasting made her mouth water. She looked at the clock. It was a long time until supper—and then she smiled. There had been a time when she didn't eat from one day to the next, but that was long ago.

Rhiannon filled the big pan with water, put it on the fire and waited for it to boil. The pudding was ready to be cooked and she lowered it carefully into the water.

The two younger maids came into the kitchen. 'There,' Hetty said, 'that's all the work in the scullery done. Anything in here we can help with, Rhiannon?'

'No, thank you,' Rhiannon said easily. 'I don't want to be accused of overworking you, do I?'

'Look, Rhiannon, I'm sorry I picked on you about the shanty town. It's none of my business and I won't go running to Mrs Buchan carrying tales, I promise.'

'Let's forget it, shall we?' Rhiannon said.

'Is there any tea in the pot?' Violet asked, and Rhiannon nodded. 'Aye, help yourself. Though I'd top it up with boiling water if I were you. It might be cold by now.'

The girls sat at the table with their heads together and Violet giggled over something Hetty said. Rhiannon had the feeling they were talking about her, but they were just children, really, still tied to their mothers' apron strings.

Mrs Jones woke as suddenly as she had fallen asleep. 'Trust you two!' She frowned. 'I might have known you'd be giggling as soon as I took my eyes off you.' She sighed and looked down at her feet. 'Rhiannon, there's kind of you to put a cushion on the floor for me. You've saved my toes from dropping off, with the cold coming up from the flags. I suffer enough bone ache as it is.'

'How do you know Rhiannon did it?' Hetty asked. 'It might have been me or Vi.'

'No fear of that.' Mrs Jones pulled on her stockings. 'Neither of you would think of anything so kind.'

'Oh, I forgot,' Hetty said. 'Our Rhiannon is perfect, isn't she? How can we hope to live up to her?'

'No,' Mrs Jones said severely. 'Rhiannon is not perfect but she's a kind, thoughtful girl and you two would do well to learn from her.'

'How to please the men, you mean?' Hetty said, and Violet nudged her arm in an effort to shut her up.

'Oh, you've heard, then?' Mrs Jones's voice was heavy with sarcasm.

'Heard what, Mrs Jones?' Hetty was grinning.

'Heard that Rhiannon was once Bull Beynon's woman and lived in a hut on the side of the railway track.' Mrs Jones rested her arms on the table and stared across at the two girls. 'Look at home before you judge folk.'

'I don't know what you mean,' Violet said huffily. 'I'm a respectable girl and so is Hetty.'

'Well, for a start Hetty was an early baby, and we all know what that means, don't we?'

Violet stared at her, blinking rapidly. '*I* don't know what it means, Mrs Jones.'

'It means her mam and dad had a shotgun wedding. And you, Vi, your father ran off with Joe the Milk's daughter when you were a baby. Your mam calls herself a respectable widow and we all keep quiet about that.' She sank back in her chair. 'Don't forget that I've lived in Swansea all my life, worked in a dozen houses, some big some not so big, and I hear any gossip that goes around. I'd go so far as to say I hear the gossip before everybody else.'

Violet looked down at her hands and Hetty was biting her lip, her cheeks flushed bright red. Rhiannon felt almost sorry for the girls but they had only got what they deserved.

The next few hours flashed by in a whirl of activity. Supper was served, course by course, and it seemed as if the meal would go on all night. But at last the well-dressed guests had finished and slowly began to drift into the other rooms, leaving the table littered with napkins and empty plates.

Rhiannon sighed. There was a mountain of dishes to be washed—she'd be lucky to get to bed by midnight.

When she returned at last to the kitchen she saw that Mrs Jones's plump arms were folded over her ample bosom. 'Now then,' she said, 'you two girls can see to the dishes. Me and Rhiannon done most of the cooking and carrying.'

Hetty claimed her back was aching but Mrs Jones soon put her in her place. 'Don't you think we're all tired, girl?' She shook her head. 'I don't know what you think you get your wages for but it's not turning your nose up at doing dishes.'

'All right, then, don't go on about it.' Hetty glared at her but vanished into the back kitchen.

'Riddle out the fire, Rhiannon,' Mrs Jones said, 'and then you can go up to bed. You look fair

43

washed out.'

*   *   *

The next day, after luncheon, Mrs Buchan sent for Rhiannon.

'Good Lord!' Mrs Jones frowned. 'What can she want with you?'

'Only one way to find out.' Rhiannon undid her apron. 'I've got a funny feeling that Hetty has a hand in this.'

'Why's that? I know she's a cheeky little madam but I don't think she'd go running to Mrs Buchan with tittle-tattle.'

'We'll see.' Rhiannon made her way up the stone steps towards the hallway, her mind racing. What was she going to do if she was dismissed? Where would she go? She would never find a decent job again if folk were reminded she was one of the shanty-town women.

Mrs Buchan was alone in her room and for that Rhiannon was grateful. If she was to be humiliated at least it would be in private. She bobbed a curtsy. 'I hope I haven't done anything wrong, Mrs Buchan?'

'It's come to my attention that you are of questionable reputation.' Jayne Buchan stared at her in open curiosity. 'Is it true that you were once . . . how shall I put it? . . . a loose woman?'

There was little point in lying. 'It's true, Mrs Buchan, but I gave up that life a long time ago. I worked as a respectable housekeeper for Mr Cookson the engineer for almost a year.'

Mrs Buchan stared at her. 'And you were not averse to sleeping in his bed, I understand?'

44

Rhiannon sighed in resignation. 'That's right. It seemed fair exchange for a life of comfort with only one man to please instead of many.'

'Well, I don't see how I can keep you on here.'

'That's all right, Mrs Buchan, I understand. I'll pack my things at once.'

'What made you do it, Rhiannon? Surely working in service—indeed, anything—must be preferable to being a whore.'

Rhiannon was stung by Mrs Buchan's tone. She drew a deep breath, willing herself to be calm. She longed to ask if Hetty had been the bearer of ill tidings but what was the point? She decided to be truthful, and if it shocked Mrs Buchan out of her smugness so much the better.

'I lost my innocence while I was still only a child,' she said flatly. 'The lodger in the house where I lived thought he would teach me a lesson about life and he kept on teaching me until I was old enough to protest.' She shrugged. 'After that it seemed easy to fall into another man's arms in return for food and a place to sleep.'

'How dreadful.' Mrs Buchan stared at her in wide-eyed horror. 'Was this man ever punished?'

Rhiannon shook her head. 'Why punish a man for deflowering a girl from the slums? It probably happened every day where I lived. I lost my self-respect. I thought I was worthless, fit only for the company of drunkards who would use me for a night then pass me on to the next man. I'm sorry for it now and if I could go back I'd change my life.' She sighed heavily. 'I don't expect you to understand, Mrs Buchan. I'll go and pack and get out of your way as soon as I can manage it.'

'No, wait,' Mrs Buchan said. 'I'm impressed by

what you say and, what's more, I'm going to keep you. I think you deserve a chance in life, a chance you never had as a child. I can see you've repented of your old life and tried to reform.' She paused. 'Another thing, Cook speaks highly of you and I have a lot of respect for her opinion. If you keep out of trouble while you're here I'll have no reason to dismiss you.'

Rhiannon looked at her in surprise. 'Will you really keep me on?'

'I never say anything I don't mean.' Mrs Buchan smiled. 'I've got a feeling you and I are going to get on very well indeed. You may go now, Rhiannon.'

'Thank you, Mrs Buchan.' At the door Rhiannon paused. 'Was it Hetty who told you about my past, Mrs Buchan?'

'Hetty? Why, no. It was that dreadful Miss Cookson. She was at a rather inferior gathering I attended at the assembly rooms and she forced her card on me. When I refused to take it she became quite sharp and told me I was employing a whore of Babylon. Silly woman.'

'Well, don't worry, Mrs Buchan, I won't let you down. You have my word on that.'

'I know you won't, Rhiannon, because if you do, you'll be out on the streets before you can look round.' She smiled. 'But remember what I told you before. My bark is worse than my bite.'

Rhiannon nodded. 'I'll remember, Mrs Buchan, and thank you very much indeed.'

Mrs Jones was waiting for her anxiously. 'What did her ladyship have to say?'

'She's heard about my past life but she's keeping me on anyway.'

'Wait till I get hold of Hetty—I'll flay her alive.'

46

'It was nothing to do with Hetty. It was that dried-up old spinster Miss Cookson who told Mrs Buchan about me.'

'Nasty woman! Never mind—put the kettle on, Rhiannon. I'm that thirsty I could drink the well dry.'

'Oh, one other thing, Mrs Jones,' Rhiannon said. 'Mrs Buchan thinks very highly of you. She told me your good opinion of me was one reason she was keeping me on.'

'Well I never!' Mrs Jones sank into a chair, her face wreathed in smiles. 'And there was I talking of leaving.' She glanced over her shoulder, but the younger maids were in the scullery. 'Not that I'd be likely to get a position at my age, mind. I think Mrs Buchan only took me on because she was desperate.'

'Well, we're both in a good job and hopefully here we'll stay.'

The room fell silent—even Hetty and Violet were getting on quietly with their work. Rhiannon heaved a great sigh of relief. Tonight she would sleep easily in her bed, knowing her job was safe. Folk might talk about Mrs Buchan's temper but Rhiannon had seen another side of her today. Mrs Buchan had taken her on trust and Rhiannon vowed it was a trust she would never betray.

*   *   *

Sal Evans opened her still bruised eyes and looked across the room at the window: the slow, shadowy dawn was beginning to creep across the flagged floor and she felt reluctant to wake up. She heard the clock on the mantelpiece strike the hour and, sighing, sat up. The cold air struck her thin shoulders and she pulled the blanket quickly around her to sit cross-legged gazing sleepily around the none-too-clean kitchen.

The fire was almost out and reluctantly Sal crawled towards the hearth and threw a log on to the embers. The flames licked the log and sprang into life, giving off a comforting glow. She had been here in the bowels of the Paradise Park ever since the night of the beating, but how much longer would the caretaker allow her to stay? Even as the thought crossed her mind she heard steps outside in the passage and the door was pushed open. Quickly, Sal threw another log on to the fire and sparks flew across the hearth fading as she watched.

'I'm keeping the place warm for you, Mr Bundy,' she said. He grunted, and as he drew nearer the rancid smell of him almost turned her stomach. Still, he'd been kind to her. He'd found her lying in a pool of blood and had carried her down the back stairs to the kitchen where she'd been ever since.

'How you feelin' today, gel?'

'I'm much better, Mr Bundy,' Sal said, then added quickly, 'though my back still aches where that man kicked me, mind.' She was afraid that once she said she was better he would tell her to leave.

George Bundy scratched his backside. 'Strange folk, these rich gents, one minute all nice to you then kicking you to death jest because they slept with you.' He shuffled closer to the fire. 'They gets to feel guilty see, gel, 'shamed of themselves for sleeping with a whore and a young one at that. They take it out on folk like us to make themselves feel better, I suppose. My throat's fair parched—I drank a fair bit of beer last night and now I'm paying for it.'

Sal took the hint and scrambled to her feet. 'I'll make some tea, Mr Bundy.'

As she leaned closer to the fire the stale smell of her own sweat reached her nostrils. 'Are you working tonight, Mr Bundy?' she asked hopefully. With the old man out of the way she could boil up enough water to fill the enamel bowl and wash herself all over.

'Aye, always working, me. They don't care if they kill off us old ones with too much work. So long as they gets their pound of flesh the bosses are happy.'

Sal couldn't have agreed more but it was not her place to say so. 'The fire's going good now. Shall I fry you a bit of bacon and some eggs, Mr Bundy?'

'There's an idea, gel. I could eat a good breakfast this morning—I feels in the mood, like.'

Mr Bundy had eaten a good breakfast ever since Sal had been sleeping on the kitchen floor. Still, he didn't ask anything else of her, never tried to feel her breasts or push his hand up her skirt, and for that she was profoundly grateful. He treated her like a lost puppy and she was happy to wait on him till her bruises healed.

Whether her mind would heal was another matter. Sal was afraid now to go into the dark streets outside the Paradise Park. Ever since the beating she'd cowered in the kitchen, afraid of her own shadow.

The appetizing aroma of bacon sizzling in the pan filled the room and Sal grinned. Today she would eat, and tonight she would fall asleep on the floor in front of the fire. For now that was all she could want.

CHAPTER FIVE

Katie turned over in bed and opened her eyes. Bull was still asleep, his breathing soft and even. She admired his long eyelashes and resisted the urge to run her finger over the strong line of his jaw—it would be a pity to wake him.

She eased her heavy body into a more comfortable position and the baby inside her kicked a protest. Soon, her daughter would be born. Katie was sure it was a girl, and that Bull would adore her and be a wonderful father.

He opened his eyes and looked at her. 'Are you all right?' He propped himself on his elbow, the bedclothes slipping away from his broad shoulders. 'The baby's not coming, is it?'

Katie smiled and touched his cheek. 'No, silly!' She pulled his head down to hers and kissed him. A cramp caught her side and she fell back against the pillows. 'You'll know when the baby's coming—I'll be screaming blue murder!'

He took her hand and they lay there silently as the sun began to poke inquisitive fingers through the curtains. Soon Bull would have to get up for work and the bed beside her would be empty. Katie savoured moments like this when she was with Bull in the warm bed.

'I thought Rhiannon was looking very well,' Bull said, and the spell was broken.

Katie felt a dart of fear. Did Bull still have feelings for Rhiannon? 'She's a beautiful girl, slim and lovely, not fat like me.'

'Ah, but you're all mine.' There was a note of laughter in Bull's voice. 'In any case, once you've had the baby you'll be like a willow wand again.' He squeezed her hand. 'But I'll always respect Rhiannon. She's made the best of a hard life. It takes guts to leave such a past behind her.'

Katie took a deep breath. 'I know you're right, Bull, but I worry in case you still have a lingering affection for her.'

He turned her face towards him. 'Yes, I still have an affection for Rhiannon, but it's you I love. Don't have a moment's doubt about me, *curiad*. I will never betray you with another woman because when I took my vows I meant every word I said.'

Katie snuggled as close to Bull as her swollen belly would allow. 'I know I look awful now, Bull, but I'll try my best to be lovely for you once the baby's born.'

'Don't talk like that! You make my heart ache with love for you, Katie. I'm so full of love that sometimes I don't think I can bear it.' He kissed her gently and his hand slid over the swell of her belly. 'Our baby was made in love and that love will never go away, my darling, so rest easy.' He kissed her cheek and then her mouth. 'Now I've got to get up for work. There's some trouble on the line above Swansea and I have to sort it out.'

He slid out of bed and Katie looked at his strong naked body. This fine, handsome, loving man was all hers. Surely she didn't begrudge Rhiannon just a little bit of his affection.

Bull kissed her again then left the room. When he had gone Katie felt as though the sunlight had faded. She prayed that God would keep her

51

husband safe. Sometimes Bull's work was dangerous: there were occasional landslides and once a tunnel had cracked sending a shower of stones on to the men servicing the line. She wished he could do some other work but the railways were in his blood: he had been a navvy and would always be a navvy in his heart.

There was a tap on the door and the maid popped her head in. 'Can I get you up now, Mrs Beynon?'

Katie wondered if she'd ever get used to having people wait on her. 'Yes, please, Bronnie.' Katie struggled to sit up. 'I feel like a cow and my legs hurt like toothache. I didn't realize having a baby was so wearying.'

'Oh, my mammy got five of us.' Bronnie put her arm around Katie's back and manoeuvred her towards the edge of the bed. 'Had us all like shelling peas, she did. Five girls, mind.' Bronnie laughed.

It seemed an age before she was washed and dressed but at last Katie was sitting in the kitchen enjoying the toast Bronnie put in front of her.

The door opened and Mrs Davies, the cook, came into the room. 'Anything else you want, Mrs Beynon? I got a nice bit of haddock on the cold slab, if you fancy it.'

'No, thank you, Mrs Davies. I feel full already.'

'I'm not surprised. You're carrying a big boy there, mark my words.'

'I hope not.' Katie smiled. 'I'd like a little girl to dress in pretty clothes.'

'You get what you're given,' the cook responded. 'By the look of it he won't be long popping out of there and then, my dear, you'll have a screaming baby to contend with.'

'I can't wait,' Katie said. 'I can't wait to hold my baby in my arms and I can't wait to be slim again.'

Mrs Davies put her head on one side. 'You'll be all right. Your sort don't run to fat.'

'I hope you're right.' Katie drank her tea and gestured towards the pot. 'Have one yourself, Cook, you too, Bronnie.' She knew she was over-familiar with her servants but to Katie they were more like friends. She knew they would be loyal to her to the end.

'*Duw.*' Mrs Davies shook her head. 'Not many folk have treated me as kindly as you, Mrs Beynon.'

'I'll second that,' Bronnie said feelingly. 'I'm so happy here, Mrs Beynon, and my mam keeps telling me all the time how lucky I am.'

Katie was about to reply when a sharp pain caught her. 'Oh dear!' She sucked in her breath and held her stomach. The pain intensified, and she felt a moment of panic. 'What's happening? Do you think the baby's coming, Cook?'

Mrs Davies put down the tea cup. 'Wouldn't surprise me. Begging your pardon, Mrs Beynon, let me just feel your belly for contractions. Aye, you're as tight as a drum. I'd say the boy *bach* is on his way into the world.' She began to roll up her sleeves. 'Bronnie, put the kettle on, girl, let's have plenty of hot water. Get some clean cloths as well, and a sheet of brown paper to keep the bed fresh and dry.'

'Had you better go for the midwife, Cook?' Katie's voice held a touch of hysteria.

'All in good time. It will be many hours yet before you hold your little one in your arms. Come on, let's get you up to bed.'

53

'I've only just got up!' Katie forced a smile. 'It's not really going to take hours, is it, Cook?'

'Always does,' Mrs Davies said. She helped Katie back upstairs and sat her on the bed. 'I'll get your shoes off and then I'll get you into a clean nightgown. Now, don't you fret, you're a fine strong girl and the birth won't be too bad, you'll see.'

Katie felt as if she was a child again as the cook undressed her and carefully pulled a nightgown over her head.

'I can see how your belly's getting tighter and that's what's supposed to happen. I know it hurts but it means the baby's trying to come out into the world.' She went to the door and called down the stairs. 'Bronnie, hurry with that brown paper, there's a good girl.'

Bronnie clattered up the stairs and rushed into the bedroom with clean cloths over her shoulder and the brown paper fluttering like a flag between her fingers.

'Stand up for a minute, *merchi*, let's get the bed ready before your waters break.' Mrs Davies prepared it deftly, then lowered Katie gently on to it. 'There, you'll be all right now. All we got to do is wait for the midwife. Bronnie, go and fetch her now. I'll get a couple of bowls of nice warm water.'

Katie felt her heart flutter in fear as Mrs Davies left the room. She didn't want to be alone: the pains were really bad now—they seemed to ebb and flow like the sea, each contraction stronger than the last.

'Bull, why aren't you here with me?' Katie felt tears well in her eyes but brushed them away impatiently: it was stupid to cry when women had babies every day of the week—there was nothing to

54

be frightened about. She moaned as another pain gripped her and then, thankfully, Mrs Davies was back in the room.

'I'm sorry, Mrs Beynon.' She looked pale and worried. 'Bronnie went down the road to call the midwife but she was out on another delivery and no one knows how long she'll be. Still, Bronnie left a note on her door and I'm sure she'll come in plenty of time. Anyway, first babies are always slow.'

Katie tried to relax but the pains had intensified. 'Cook, I'm frightened, can Bronnie go to find Mr Beynon?'

'Aye, I'll send her right away, but you keep calm. You've a while to go yet.'

The cook left the room and Katie could hear her giving instructions to the maid. 'Mr Beynon will be up beyond high-street station I expect, girl. Tell him his wife's time has come and he's wanted here.'

Mrs Davies was soon back and she sat on the bed holding Katie's hand. 'That little brew of herbs I made up for you yesterday, I've put it to simmer on the fire. It's not very nice to taste but it might help you sleep a bit.'

Katie knew that nothing would make her sleep: the pains were getting faster and more intense by the minute. But she was wrong, the brew Mrs Davies gave her was vile but almost straight away she felt sleepy.

The time seemed to pass in a haze and Katie wondered if the baby would ever be born. Questions crept through her mind: where could the midwife be and why wasn't Bull here?

It was after midday when a fierce urge to bear down took Katie's breath away. She closed her eyes tightly with the effort, grunting low in her throat as

55

she struggled to give birth. She was wide awake now, and when the pain subsided she looked up at Mrs Davies. 'You'd better help me. My baby is coming and it looks like you're going to be the one to deliver it.'

Mrs Davies came to the bed and looked down at Katie's straining body. 'I think you're right, *merchi*. Here, let me hitch up your nightgown—it's no time for modesty. Let's get this little 'un of yours into the world.'

*   *   *

Bull Beynon was thinking of Katie as he walked along the track beside one of the navvies. Her time was near and he wished he could have stayed with her this morning. The man walking beside him coughed, jarring Bull out of his thoughts.

'Good thing you spotted that cracked bit of track, Seth,' Bull said, 'or we could all have been in deep trouble.' He tapped the toe of his boot against it. 'This piece of line will have to be replaced.'

'Aye, sir, this broad-gauge track, it's no good, yer know. Before long all railways will be using the narrow gauge—I'll wager my week's pay on it.'

'Maybe you're right,' Bull said, 'but for now this line needs maintenance. Get the men on to it right away and remember to tell the signalman to switch tracks from here to Swansea.'

Bull left the trackside and made his way towards the high street: he was meeting several of the Great Western Railway shareholders. He was getting used to lunching at the Mackworth in the company of the town's élite. It surprised him even now to

56

realize how far he'd come from his old life as a navvy. Yet he'd enjoyed those days—days of challenges when he'd thought the line from Chepstow to Swansea would never be finished. His thoughts turned to Rhiannon: she was a lovely girl who had made the best of her life in spite of the bad start she'd had. After old Cookson died she'd found a place with Mrs Jayne Buchan and was doing well, he'd heard.

'Hello, Bull.' He looked up and blinked.

'Why so startled? I'm not a ghost. It's me, Rhiannon—you know, the girl you used to live with.'

He smiled at the irony in her words. 'I was surprised to see you, that's all. I was just thinking about you.'

She was fresh and lovely, her dark hair, free of her bonnet, lifting in the wind. He remembered how intimate they'd been, but he had no regrets: now he had his Katie, his beautiful wife, and he would never want any other woman.

'You look well, Bull, and how is Katie?'

'She's getting rather big now,' he smiled, 'and she can't wait for the baby to be born. She's set her heart on having a girl so I hope she's not disappointed.'

'Once it comes she'll love it whatever it is. That's the way we women are.'

Bull looked at Rhiannon with fresh eyes. Had she ever borne a baby? How little he knew of her in spite of the months they'd spent together.

'I hear you're working for Mrs Buchan now, Rhiannon. Are you happy?' He watched her shrug her shoulders and frown. She had often told him that happiness was an elusive goal that she would never reach, but she seemed content with her life.

Her next words confirmed what he'd been thinking. 'I'm secure there, well fed and clothed, and with a nice warm bedroom all to myself.' She flashed him a smile. 'There was one tricky moment, though. When Mrs Buchan found out about my past she was going to dismiss me.'

'What stopped her?'

'It's almost as if she admired me for getting out of that old way of life.'

'She's not alone in that. I admire you too, Rhiannon.'

Her colour rose. 'Do you, Bull?'

He took a deep breath. 'If I wasn't in love with Katie I'd be proud to have you on my arm, Rhiannon. Any man who wins your heart will be a lucky fellow.'

'My heart is already taken.' He knew she wasn't being coy, that she was just telling him the truth. 'But I know you well enough by now not to expect anything. You're an honourable man, Bull, perhaps the only honourable man I've ever met.'

'You just haven't moved in the right circles, Rhiannon. There are plenty of good men about, if you look in the right places.'

'Where am I likely to meet any?' Rhiannon asked. 'I'm tied to the house except for my days off and then there seems nowhere to go.'

Bull was about to speak when he saw the familiar figure of the maid running up the high street, bonnet flying.

'Mr Beynon, sir, I've been looking for you for ages! You have to come home right away.' Bronnie paused to take a breath. 'Mrs Beynon's time has come and she wants you to be there with her.'

Bull looked at his watch. He should be at the meeting in fifteen minutes but that would have to wait. 'Go along to the Mackworth, Bronnie,' he said. 'Tell Mr Morton-Edwards I've been delayed.'

Bronnie nodded, 'Yes, Mr Beynon.'

Bull turned to Rhiannon. 'I have to go.'

'Of course you do. Go on, then, I can see you want to be with Katie—and quite right too.'

Bull saw her longing for him in her eyes and pity tugged at him. 'You'll meet a nice fellow one day, Rhiannon, someone you can love and trust, but in the meantime, if ever you're in trouble come to me.'

'Thank you.'

Bull hurried away.

*   *   *

'Just one more push should do it, missus.' Mrs Davies was red in the face and sweating copiously.

Katie looked up at her and felt a warm glow of gratitude. 'Thank you for being so good to me, Cook. I won't forget it, I promise you.' She sucked in her breath as the uncontrollable urge to bear down swamped her. All she could do was strain and push and pray that her ordeal would be soon over.

'The head is crowning!' Mrs Davies said excitedly. 'Come on now, Mrs Beynon, you're nearly there.'

Katie hardly heard her, so intense was the need to push her child from her body. She growled low in her throat, as she concentrated on the birth of her baby.

Dimly she heard Bull's voice in the doorway and then the need to bear down again overcame her. It

59

was as if the whole world was holding its breath. She screamed then strained until she thought she would faint from the effort. Her body seemed to be on fire and then the pain was over. Her child was born. Katie opened her eyes cautiously. 'My baby, is she all right?'

'You have a fine healthy child, Mrs Beynon,' Mrs Davies said, 'but it's not a girl. You have a strong, beautiful son.'

She handed the baby to Bronnie, who was red from running. 'I'll see to Mrs Beynon now and when she's comfortable she can hold her baby.' She sniffed, and a tear ran down her face.

'Thank you, Cook, you've been wonderful,' Katie said shakily. She waited patiently as Mrs Davies took away the signs of the birthing and brought a bowl of clean scented water to wash her, then helped her into a fresh nightgown and propped her up against the pillows. She held out her arms as Bull came into the room. 'Let me have him, my lovely, let me see my boy *bach*, my own little boy.'

Bull put the baby gently into her arms. He felt heavy against her breasts. 'Are you pleased, Bull?' she asked quietly. 'You're not disappointed it's a boy, are you?'

Bull coughed and looked away, but not before she had seen the glisten of tears in his eyes. 'I'm so proud of you both, so very proud.' Bull's voice was gruff with emotion. 'I have what every man wants, a son to carry on my name.'

'A name,' Katie said, swallowing a lump in her throat. 'We've got to think of a name for him.' She turned to Mrs Davies, who had on a fresh apron now, her hair hidden by a gleaming white cap.

'Cook, what's your full name?'

'Dorothy Jessica Joan Davies, but I'm usually called Dot.'

'Well, we can't call a boy Dot but what about John? It's as near to Joan as we can get. How does that sound to you, Bull?'

'I think John is a splendid name.' Bull put his hands on Mrs Davies's shoulders. 'I can't thank you enough for what you've done for us today.'

'Don't be silly, sir, I'm glad I've had a bit of experience so I could help Mrs Beynon when she needed it.' She moved to the door. 'I'm going to make us a nice cup of tea—we could all do with it, I'm sure.'

'Good idea.' Bull closed the door after her departing figure and returned to the bedside. 'I'm so proud and happy, Katie, that words can't express what I feel for you and our little boy.'

It was then that Katie began to cry: huge tears formed on her lashes, ran down her cheeks and into her mouth.

'What's the matter, my love? Are you in any pain?' Bull asked anxiously.

Katie gulped. 'No, Bull, I'm just so happy, that's all.' She turned her face towards her husband and he wiped away the tears with his thumbs. Katie relaxed against the pillows and sighed with contentment. 'All I ever wanted out of life is here in this room, Bull, my darling. Come,' she said, 'give the mother of your son a kiss.'

As his lips touched hers, Katie knew that this was the happiest moment of her life.

CHAPTER SIX

The Paradise Park stood solidly against the sky. It was built of old stone that looked mellow in the sunlight, but closer inspection revealed cracks in the walls, and the peeling paint on the ornate doors gave the hotel a run-down appearance.

In the kitchen, Sal was sitting near the fire trying to dry her clothes. She had had a bath and had used the last of the water to soak her skirt and her turnover but now she realized that they would not be dry for several hours.

Shivering, she wrapped the blanket around her and crept to the door. It opened on to a long passageway that led to the back stairs. Up there, in one of the rooms, she would find clothes belonging to the maids. Sal knew she had no alternative but to help herself to a skirt, a turnover and one or two undergarments. The flagged floor under her feet was cold and she wished she had shoes. But she must count her blessings: she was lucky that Mr Bundy was still letting her sleep in the kitchen. The wooden treads on the stairs to the servants' quarters had lost most of their varnish, testifying to the frequent comings and goings of many feet. At the top, puffing with the effort of running up, Sal opened a door. The room contained only one bed and Sal guessed that it was the housekeeper's. The wardrobe door creaked ominously as she opened it. She saw at once that the clothes inside it were several sizes too large for her.

She searched all the rooms on the servants' floor, but found only one of each garment hanging in the cupboards. She knew she couldn't steal from girls as poor as herself. She crept back downstairs and paused on a lower landing. Several guest rooms led off a broad passage. These rooms were occupied by men who stayed one night then left before dawn. Cautiously Sal opened a door and peered inside. The room was empty and she saw a chemise, a skirt and a turnover lying on the bed. The turnover was knitted in a cheerful red and fitted nicely on her shoulders.

She dressed quickly, folded up her blanket and made for the door. As she stepped into the passage she cannoned into a man, a gentleman by the look of him. He had a gold watch hanging from the pocket of his well-made suit and his shirt was of the finest linen. He caught her arm to steady her. 'Careful, child.'

'Sorry, sir, I'll get out of your way, will I?' Sal recognized him at once: he was Mr Morton-Edwards, a rich man and generous, if what she had heard of him was correct. She heard voices on the stairs and looked round in panic. 'I've got to hide, sir, or I'll be thrown out.' But it was too late: a plump, balding man came on to the landing and Sal recognized him as Mr May, the owner of the building. With him was an old lady, clutching a bag close to her side.

'What are you doing here, girl?' Mr May looked down at her. 'Go and see to your customers at once. It doesn't do to keep the gentlemen waiting.' It was clear he had no idea that she'd been sleeping in the kitchen.

Sal stood still, not knowing which direction to take. Fear made her throat so dry she couldn't speak.

'Are you deaf and stupid, girl? Get out of our way before I throw you out.'

'Hold on,' Mr Morton-Edwards said abruptly. 'Don't talk to her like that. She's only a child.' He turned to Sal. 'How old are you?'

Sal thought about telling him she was older than she looked but after a moment she thought better of it. 'I'm twelve, sir, and if it pleases you, sir, my name is Sal.'

'Where are your parents, child? Do they know you do this sort of thing?'

'I 'aven't any mam or dad, sir, I'm on my own.' Her hopes rose. If he was a customer perhaps he would just give her money and send her away. She didn't want to lie with him—by her standards he was an old man—but she didn't want him to think she wasn't up to the job either. 'I'm very experienced, sir,' she said. 'I don't think you'll be disappointed in me.' She bit her lip, forcing tears to well in her eyes.

Mr Morton-Edwards thrust his hands into his pockets and she heard the jingle of coins—sovereigns, she hoped. But he didn't bring out any money. Instead he looked at her closely. 'Do you like this work, then, child?'

Oh dear, he was going to try to reform her. She shook her head. 'Not much, sir, but I got to do something to keep alive, haven't I?'

'Have you ever tried to get out of it, Sal? Have you looked for work elsewhere?'

'Oh, aye, sir, I worked for a nice family for a while but the master . . . well, he wasn't so nice.'

'Didn't you ever have the chance to try to find another decent job?'

'I did, sir, once. I met a lady, Rhiannon Beynon

she called herself. She wanted to save me from this life but that didn't work out because she had no money or job herself.'

'Rhiannon Beynon, eh?' He smiled down at her. 'Well, she did find a position. She's working for my daughter.' He hesitated. 'My daughter might be able to take you on too.'

'I'd like that but I'm not like Rhiannon—she had experience in a good home, sir.' She sighed. 'This life is all I know.'

'Well, you wouldn't be able to work here for very long anyway. I'm considering buying this hotel, and so is Mrs Paisley.' He gestured towards the old lady. 'Whoever buys the hotel plans to turn it into a decent, respectable place.'

That meant her easy life in the kitchen would soon be over, Sal thought. This time real tears welled in her eyes.

'Why don't you work for my daughter? I'm sure she'd take you on, and Rhiannon would help you settle in.' Mr Morton-Edwards turned to the owner of the hotel. 'Mr May, I've had second thoughts about buying the place. It isn't what I expected. I want an establishment that would serve as a railway hotel and this place needs too much work. Still, perhaps you and Mrs Paisley here can come to an amicable agreement.' He caught Sal's arm. 'Come along, I'm taking you with me now.'

To Sal's surprise, Mr Morton-Edwards took her down the front stairs and dropped some money on the table in the hall. 'Send for my carriage to be brought round, there's a good chap,' he said affably to the man at the door. The porter looked at him, eyebrows raised, and Sal nearly laughed. He obviously thought Mr Morton-Edwards was one of the customers, and men about unsavoury business did not usually flaunt it in the faces of the lower orders.

On the drive through town, Sal wondered if she was wise to go with this man, who was a stranger to her. For all she knew he might beat her or, worse, murder her and leave her in a ditch somewhere. But, then, if he'd meant her harm, he would hardly be seen with her in full view of the people at the Paradise Park.

Mr Morton-Edwards was silent as they drew up outside the door of a magnificent house. He stepped down from the carriage and gave her his hand to help her. Then Sal knew he was a real gentleman, not like the ones who came to the hotel.

He rapped on the door with his cane. It was opened at once by a neatly dressed maid, wearing a spotless apron and a starched cap, who bobbed a curtsy then stood back to allow him inside the elegant hall. 'I'll tell Mrs Buchan you're here, sir.' She looked doubtfully at Sal, then disappeared across the hall and into one of the rooms. Mr Morton-Edwards didn't wait for the girl to reappear. 'Stay here, there's a good girl,' he said, and then he, too, vanished.

Sal hopped from one foot to the other, wishing again that she had shoes. She envied the maid her beautiful house slippers in soft satin. They were plain but expensive, if Sal was any judge.

'I'll see the girl, of course, Father.' The voice came from one of the rooms. 'I don't promise to take her on, but I'll talk to her.'

Mr Morton-Edwards came into the hall with a woman Sal guessed was his daughter. She was pretty in a delicate way with soft pale gold hair, just like her father's. Her eyes rested on Sal and studied her.

'This is Sal,' Mr Morton-Edwards said. 'I believe she knows Rhiannon. Now, don't jump to conclusions, Rhiannon was trying to get the girl off the streets.' He smiled. 'It seems Rhiannon has the same impulse as you to save unfortunate women.' He glanced at Sal. 'Though in this case she's more of a child than anything else, which is why I thought you might take her in out of the goodness of your heart.'

'Why don't you?' Mrs Buchan asked. 'I'm not setting up a home for poverty-stricken harlots, Father.'

'Well, I brought her here because I've more servants than I can cope with.'

'That's true.' Mrs Buchan smiled. 'There was a time when you ran your house with as few servants as you could manage. Now you seem to have a multitude.' She looked at Sal again. 'Are you willing to work, girl, and to stay away from the menfolk of my household?'

'Oh, I am, Mrs Buchan. I'll work my fingers to the bone. As for men I've had a gutful of them,' Sal said.

'All right, then. Go down to the kitchen and Cook will take care of you. Tell Rhiannon that you are to share her room. Now come along, Father, and tell me just how you came to meet this girl you're trying so hard to rescue.'

They went into one of the rooms and the door was closed firmly behind them. Sal looked around her, wondering how to find the kitchen. She saw a darkened passage that led, she guessed, to the back of the house. From there a flight of stairs took her downwards. Sal paused, her feet cold on the bare steps, and listened to the sound of voices coming from below. This was where her new life would begin.

*   *   *

Rhiannon was putting a joint of beef into the oven when the door opened and a small, vaguely familiar figure came slowly into the kitchen. The girl was wearing odd clothing that hung on her slight form like washing pegged to a line. Then she recognized the tip-tilted nose and the bright blue eyes. 'Sal!' she said in astonishment. 'What in the name of all the angels are you doing here?'

Mrs Jones looked up from rolling out the pastry for a meat pie and raised her eyebrows. From the scullery, Violet and Hetty came into the kitchen and all of them stared at Sal in open curiosity.

'I got a job here.' Sal stumbled over the words, overwhelmed by the attention she was receiving. 'Mr Morton-Edwards was out on business and, well, he saw me and brought me here.'

'Why did he bring you here instead of taking you to his own house, girl? The cook looked at her suspiciously.

'I think I know the answer to that, Mrs Jones,' Rhiannon said quickly. 'Did you tell the master we'd met before, Sal?'

Sal nodded. 'That's right, and it's because of you I'm here. I'm so pleased to be off the streets that I'll work hard and do anything that's asked of me.'

'Well, you can start with the dishes,' Hetty said spitefully. 'I'm fed up of doing them. Just look at my poor hands, red and chapped and splitting with the cold, they are.'

'I'll decide what the girl does.' Mrs Jones glowered at Hetty. 'Now, first of all I want you, Vi, and Hetty and you too, Rhiannon, to fetch your spare shoes down here for the girl to try on. Can't have her walking on the cold flags with bare feet, can I?'

'I can't spare any of my shoes,' Violet said. 'I'm nearly through these as it is. What about you, Cook? You got more shoes than any of us.'

'Don't talk daft, Vi. My feet are like canal barges and my shoes would never fit this child. Now, no more arguing, do as you're told.'

When the girls had gone, Mrs Jones ushered Sal into one of the chairs. 'Now, then, tell me exactly how you came to meet Mr Morton-Edwards 'cos your story about Mr Morton-Edwards picking you up from the street don't fool me for one minute.'

Sal glanced around nervously. 'I told you, Mr Morton-Edwards was out on business.'

'What you tell me will go no further. Come on, girl, before the rest of them come back. That Hetty couldn't keep her mouth shut if she tried.'

'Well, it's none of my business but Mr Morton-Edwards was at the Paradise Park. Not as a customer,' she added quickly, 'he was thinking of buying the hotel but he changed his mind.'

'Quite right too! A decent man like Mr Morton-Edwards should have no truck with a place like the Paradise Park.' The cook looked closely at Sal. 'So what were you doing there? Working, was it?'

Sal nodded miserably. 'I don't want to shock a nice lady like you, but it's true I have worked at the hotel. Going with men was the only way I could

69

earn a living, see?'

'All right, I'm not blaming you,' Mrs Jones made a wry face, 'but I'm surprised Mrs Buchan took you on.'

Violet and Hetty could be heard arguing as they clattered down the stairs and Mrs Jones winked at Sal. 'Right, we'll say no more about all that. You just keep your mouth shut about Mr Morton-Edwards's business.'

Rhiannon came into the kitchen behind Violet and Hetty, and an array of shoes was laid out before Sal. She looked down at them, scarcely believing she was really going to have a pair for herself.

The only ones that were anywhere close to fitting her belonged to Rhiannon. 'Have them and welcome, Sal,' Rhiannon said. 'I'm good on shoes, a pair lasts me ages.'

'Oh! They're lovely.' Sal admired her feet in the neat boots. 'I can't believe you're all being so kind to me.'

'Don't think anything of it,' Mrs Jones said. 'Soon we'll get you some slippers as well, to wear when you're above stairs.' She clapped her hands together briskly. 'Now, let's get to work, shall we? Otherwise the food will never be cooked and the kitchen will stay looking like a pig-sty.' She pushed the kettle on to the fire. 'Vi, you and Hetty can do the vegetables and don't cut the potato skins too thick. We're trying to keep the bills down so as Mr Buchan's happy.' The two girls went into the scullery grumbling to themselves and the cook smiled. 'Right then, Rhiannon, little Sal here looks half starved so fetch out the bread and a nice fresh bit of cheese, will you?'

Sal looked down at her boots and twisted her ankle admiringly. Mrs Jones tapped her arm. 'Sit down by the table, Sal, and get your fill of good food. I don't suppose you've eaten anything today, have you?'

Sal shook her head. 'I could eat a scabby horse between two cart shafts I'm so hungry!'

Rhiannon laughed and even Mrs Jones smiled. Sal looked down at the bread and cheese. *'Duw!* This is a lovely bit of grub.'

'We don't want any more of those coarse sayings round here, miss.' Mrs Jones's tone was brisk, but a smile tugged at the corners of her mouth. 'You learn to speak properly by here or I'll put you out in the scullery with Vi and Hetty and those two will work you to death.'

Sal looked suitably abashed but she tucked into the food with relish while Mrs Jones went on making a meat pie, and Rhiannon whisked a dozen eggs in a bowl ready for a custard tart. Sal could see that everyone ate well here, including the servants. Although her place in the household was probably the lowest, she knew that she would be better fed than the upstairs maids who thought themselves superior to kitchen staff.

It was early evening when Mrs Buchan summoned Rhiannon and Sal to the drawing room. 'She's not going to chuck us out after all, is she, Rhiannon?' Sal's voice held a tremor.

'I doubt it,' Rhiannon said. 'She's not the sort of lady to take you on in the afternoon and change her mind by the evening.'

Mrs Buchan was seated in an easy chair, her skirts spread out like the petals of a flower around her dainty feet and her soft hair like spun gold in

71

the lamplight. Sal had never been so much in awe of anyone.

'I've come to a decision,' Mrs Buchan said. 'I hope you're both going to be pleased with what I've planned.'

Sal swallowed a sigh of relief: it didn't sound as though she was going to be dismissed on her first day at work.

'I want to train you up to a better station in life,' Mrs Buchan said. 'My house steward has marched out in high dudgeon—I never did get on well with menservants, they tend to be too arrogant for their own good. Anyway, I want you, Rhiannon, to take over eventually as housekeeper. What I propose is that you learn the correct way to set out cutlery and china for an ordinary meal and also for a banquet. You were housekeeper to Mr Cookson for quite a long time, I know. Do you think you could cope with the responsibility of a large establishment like mine?'

Sal saw that Rhiannon's face was flushed with pleasure.

'Oh, yes, Mrs Buchan, it would be an honour,' Rhiannon said, 'and I'm sure I could manage. As you say, I have had some experience and I'm willing to learn as much as I can.'

Mrs Buchan nodded. 'For the time being I will be in charge of the housekeeping records but I will want you to learn to balance the books. You can read and write, can't you?'

'Oh, yes, Mrs Buchan,' Rhiannon said quickly, 'and Mr Cookson made sure I knew about the finances of the household.'

'Good. And you, Sal, can learn to serve food to my guests in a gracious manner, I'm sure.'

'Yes, Mrs Buchan, it'll be an honour, Mrs Buchan.' Sal felt it safe to repeat Rhiannon's words, but she was not quite sure she wanted to leave the kitchen: it was so cosy there and the food was plentiful and always at hand. Still, if Rhiannon thought that what Mrs Buchan was offering was a step up, she would go along with it. Mrs Buchan's next words confirmed that she had done the right thing. 'I'll have the seamstress make you both some suitable clothes. I can't have my servants letting me down, can I?' She waved her hand. 'Right, you may go.'

Rhiannon ushered Sal out of the room and towards the kitchen. At the top of the steps she hugged Sal and kissed her cheek. 'We're going to be proper servants, Sal. We'll have good dresses and cloaks, and the milliner will make us bonnets for outdoors, and the cobbler will make us new shoes. Best of all, we'll have more wages. Are you happy, Sal?'

Sal knew now why Rhiannon was so excited. 'I think that bit of luck you was talking about when we first met has rubbed off on me. If it wasn't for you, Rhiannon, I don't suppose I'd have got where I am.'

She followed Rhiannon down the steps towards the kitchen, her heart full of happiness. There would be no more men doing dreadful things to her, no more waiting outside coaching inns and public bars and, best of all, she would have her own shoes made to measure. This was the start of a new life, and Sal would make sure that she lived it to the full.

CHAPTER SEVEN

'You know I love being with you, Eynon,' Llinos looked at her friend, 'but I don't think either of us is ready for marriage just now.'

'I am.' Eynon took her hand, oblivious to the other people in the tearooms of the Mackworth Hotel. 'You know I've always loved you, Llinos, and now that we're both alone I thought we could live out the remainder of our years together. Your boys are away leading their own lives and it must be very lonely for you in that big house. I'm rattling around in mine too, so surely we'd be better off living together?'

'I'll have to think about it, Eynon.' Llinos touched his cheek. 'You're very dear to me, you know that, but marriage is such a big commitment. Now tell me about Jayne and her good works.' She had changed the subject deliberately: she did not want to hurt her old friend but she wasn't sure she wanted to be tied in matrimony ever again.

Eynon smiled. 'News travels fast in Swansea. Well, all Jayne's done is take on two girls who've had a bad start in life. She wants to give them a chance to better themselves.'

'I never thought Jayne would be so understanding about those less fortunate.'

Eynon smiled. 'Marriage has changed her. She's not the selfish little girl she used to be.' He sighed. 'But that was my fault. I pampered her.' He shrugged. 'Love sometimes makes fools of us all.'

Llinos knew what he meant and she had loved her husband to distraction. She and Joe had been so happy together. He was handsome, kind and perceptive, all that she could have wanted in a life partner. That was until they had both strayed.

'What are you thinking?' Eynon's voice interrupted her thoughts. 'I hope you're considering my proposal.'

She sighed heavily: he was determined not to let the subject drop. 'I was just thinking that fate has dealt us both a strange hand. Because I took a lover I'm a fallen woman in the eyes of the townsfolk, every bit as bad as the girls Jayne has taken on, yet you, a pillar of respectability, want me to marry you. How would the gossips take that, I wonder.'

'I don't give a fig for the gossips, you know that, Llinos. I've loved you from the moment I first saw you all those years ago, when you were struggling to make ends meet at the pottery.'

Llinos nodded. 'I know, Eynon, but our lives have gone in such different directions since then. You are eminently respectable while I have an illegitimate child. It just wouldn't work, my love.'

'I've told you, none of that matters to me. In any case, I'm no saint—I've had two wives and more mistresses than I can count but it was always you I wanted, Llinos. Stop putting obstacles in the way and please say you'll marry me.'

'Just let me think it over, Eynon. Getting married is such a momentous decision, particularly at our age.'

'Nonsense. Our age is just right. We've gone through the trials and tribulations of life and come out the other side a little wiser.'

Llinos wondered what it would be like to live with Eynon. They got on well as friends, they

75

laughed together and sometimes, in the past, they had cried together. They were closer than many married couples—but would everything change if they were tied to each other?

She was wise enough to know that he would not be content with a marriage that offered only companionship: he would want passion as well as affection. Was she too old to give him that? She was past fifty now, and although she still had her figure and there was little grey in her hair, she might no longer be capable of passion.

'I can see you're giving my proposal some thought.' Eynon smiled at her. 'I think I can read your mind too.'

'I don't know what you mean.' To her chagrin she was blushing.

Eynon rubbed his thumb over her wrist. 'I still have a lot of passion in me, Llinos, and we would be husband and wife in the full sense.'

'But am *I* capable of passionate love now, Eynon?' Llinos said. 'I'm quite an old lady, you know.'

'You're still a beautiful, desirable woman, and many men lust after you.'

Llinos smiled to herself. Eynon still saw her as an eager young girl. Her heart lifted a little. Perhaps, after all, she was not too old to enjoy a man's embraces.

She could see he was about to speak again and held up her hand. 'No more, not now, Eynon. I'll think about it.' She sat back in her chair and picked up her gloves. 'At this rate we're never going to get over to see Jayne, are we?'

'Come along, then.' Eynon rose to his feet and held Llinos's chair for her while she shook the creases out of her full skirts. 'Don't worry about seeing Buchan. He's away, supposedly on business, for a few days.' Eynon gave a short laugh. 'Dallying with some woman more like.'

Llinos examined her feelings. Once she would have been cut to the quick by such a remark but now she didn't care where Dafydd was or what he was doing. 'What's going on there, Eynon?' she asked. 'Jayne hardly ever sees Dafydd and they live more like strangers than husband and wife.'

'I don't meddle,' Eynon replied. 'I know they never share a bed but beyond that I don't ask.'

Llinos looked up at Eynon and sighed. He would never have grandchildren while Jayne was married to Dafydd. She knew all about Dafydd's affairs— Eynon discussed the subject openly with her—but most married men had their mistresses while still preserving some sort of relationship with their wives.

Outside, the street was thronged with people. It was market day and bakers' vans vied with vegetable carts, but when Eynon lifted his hand, his carriage appeared as if by magic. Eynon was well thought of in Swansea, but if she married him would his reputation be ruined too?

Well, for now she would put the idea of marriage out of her head: she needed to compose herself for her visit to Jayne. Eynon's daughter had never liked her, just tolerated her as one of Eynon's friends. Llinos suppressed a sigh. Taking tea with Jayne was not going to be pleasurable.

*   *   *

'So, Rhiannon, you seem to be coping well with the

77

job of housekeeper,' Jayne said, 'but I must learn to call you by your surname and add Mrs to it. I know you're not married but you lived with your man for quite a time and I understand you are known as Mrs Beynon. I think that sounds much more impressive than Rhiannon, don't you?'

Rhiannon felt a thrill of pleasure. 'I've always been happy to be called Mrs Beynon,' she said. 'I can't thank you enough for entrusting me with this position, Mrs Buchan, and I will do my best to live up to your expectations.'

'You'll live up to them,' Jayne said, 'because if you don't you'll be out of a job. Now, you know we're having visitors for tea, don't you?' She didn't wait for a reply. 'I want you to tell Cook we'll have some rich cake and a variety of pastries and biscuits. My father also likes thinly cut bread with salt butter. Is that clear, Mrs Beynon?' Jayne allowed a smile to turn up the corners of her mouth.

'I'll do that right away, Mrs Buchan.'

'Oh, before you go I must tell you that you look very smart today. The seamstress has done an excellent job. And your hair tied back in a bun gives you an air of respectability. I don't expect anyone would recognize you for the . . . well, you know what I mean.'

'For the harlot I used to be, Mrs Buchan? I'm not afraid to hear it because it's the truth, but you've given me the opportunity to leave that behind and I'll always be grateful.'

Jayne had noticed Rhiannon had a certain dignity about her, with a broad streak of common sense. Soon she would be able to trust her to handle the accounts. She had the feeling that

Rhiannon would be good with figures and that she would find ways to cut the household bills.

'How is Sal doing? Can I trust her to serve tea today?'

'I'm sure you can.' Rhiannon smiled, and Jayne saw how pretty the girl was. It was a good thing that Dafydd had his retinue of whores and did not feel the need to turn his attentions to the servants.

'Right, Rhiannon, you may go, but remember, anything you hear discussed at my tea-table is not to be repeated below stairs.'

When the girl had left the room Jayne stood on tiptoe to look at herself in the mirror. Her hair gleamed and her skin was flawless. It wasn't her father or Llinos she wanted to impress but Guy Fairchild: he was also coming to tea and his presence would brighten the gloomiest occasion.

The doorbell chimed and Jayne held her breath, praying he had arrived early: then she would have him to herself, if only for a few minutes. She realized she was behaving like a foolish girl. She was a married woman and shouldn't even think of another man in a romantic way. But Guy was so charming and Jayne knew that he enjoyed her company.

She felt her colour rise as the door opened and Guy was shown in. He came towards her and took her hands. 'My dear Mrs Buchan, how delighted I am to be invited once again into your lovely home.'

'Please don't be so formal. My name is Jayne.' She smiled up at him. 'After all, we are friends now, aren't we?'

'I sincerely hope so. I would dearly like our relationship to be more than that but, alas, you are married.'

Alas, indeed, Jayne thought. Why hadn't she listened to her father when he warned her not to marry Dafydd Buchan? 'Come,' she said, 'sit beside me, here on the sofa.'

He took his seat eagerly, his thigh so close to hers that Jayne could feel the warmth of him through her gown. She made no attempt to move away—surely it was not improper for friends to sit close together, especially when other guests were expected.

'How is business, Mrs . . . Jayne? I hear shares in the Great Western are climbing steadily.'

'It gives me a great deal of satisfaction to know I was wise in buying them in the first place.' She hesitated. 'But perhaps you think it's not very ladylike to involve myself in such things.'

'On the contrary, I think it's clever of you to have had such foresight. It shows you are level-headed as well as beautiful.'

Jayne blushed. 'Oh, Guy, do you really think I'm beautiful, or are you just being polite to the wife of a friend?'

He looked into her eyes and moved a fraction closer to her. 'Jayne, if only you were free I would—' He stopped abruptly as the door opened and Eynon Morton-Edwards came into the room, followed by Llinos Mainwaring.

Jayne watched as Guy rose politely and exchanged greetings with her father. She paid especial attention when he took Llinos's hand: would he, too, be bowled over by her charm as other men were? But his greeting was perfunctory and as soon as he could, he resumed his seat beside Jayne.

'We were just discussing the rise in Great

Western shares, Father,' she said warmly. 'The railway has certainly brought prosperity to the town and because of our forethought we are enjoying some of the benefits ourselves.'

'Do you own shares then, Mr . . . ?' Eynon asked.

'Please, sir, call me Guy, everyone else does, and the answer to your question is no. My arrival in Swansea was a little too late. By the time I moved here the shares had been taken by knowledgeable people like yourselves.'

Jayne could see that her father was not impressed by Guy's charm. On the contrary, Eynon was looking at him with suspicion. But, then, any newcomer to the area was suspect in her father's eyes. 'Shall we take tea in the conservatory?' she asked. 'The sun is shining and we might as well enjoy it while it lasts.' Jayne had an ulterior motive in wanting to sit in the convervatory: once tea was over she could show Guy the plants she'd had brought in from abroad. Her father would be happy to talk alone with his beloved Llinos.

Sal and two of the other maids served the tea, and Jayne, watching the girl, saw that she had learned quickly and well. She looked so different now from the barefoot, bedraggled child she had been when Jayne had first set eyes on her. She had gained a little weight and her hair, clean and glossy, was pinned up, no longer in a tangle around her shoulders.

'So, Jayne,' Eynon said, once the maids had left the room, 'how are your lame ducks?'

'If you mean Rhiannon and Sal, they are serving me better than anyone I've employed before.'

'Got them hidden in the bowels of the kitchen, have you, *cariad*?' her father asked indulgently.

'No, indeed I have not!' Jayne said. 'Sal served the tea, and I'm quite amused that you didn't recognize her. As for Rhiannon, she has taken over as housekeeper and I don't have to check her honesty as I did with my previous servants.'

'What's this, then?' Guy asked, his eyes on Jayne. 'Are you a benefactor for poor women as well as being clever and lovely to look at?'

'That is exactly what she is,' Eynon answered. 'These girls were once street-walkers but Jayne is trying to make respectable women of them.'

'And doing very well, too, from what I've seen,' Llinos broke in. 'I think you are to be applauded for what you've done, Jayne.'

For once Jayne was grateful to Llinos. 'You see, Llinos agrees with me. And, Father, you've done your fair share of looking after those less fortunate. Forgive me for reminding you that it was you who brought Sal to me in the first place.'

'I'm only teasing, Jayne. I congratulate you on your efforts with these girls. They both need a bit of good fortune and I'm proud that you are providing it.' He smiled wickedly. 'You don't usually keep your servants for long—perhaps this time will be different.' He looked around. 'Where is Buchan? Has he gone away again? He seems to spend more time travelling than he does at home.'

'He's got a lot of business in London these days, you know that, Father, and I'll thank you to keep your opinions to yourself.'

'Oh, Jayne,' Llinos said quickly, 'have you seen the new gallery that's opened in the Mumbles? It's full of the most beautiful paintings and some exquisite sculptures. Perhaps we could drive down there together some time?'

Jayne smiled and nodded but did not commit herself: the last thing she wanted was a day out with Llinos Mainwaring. Still, it was good of her to change what had been a tricky subject.

'These pastries are delicious,' Llinos said. 'You must give my compliments to your cook.'

'And mine.' Guy looked into her eyes as if he could read her thoughts. 'Would you be kind enough to show me your plants, Jayne?'

'I would love to.' Jayne put down her plate, and stood up. 'Father, please pour yourself and Llinos more tea while I show Guy around.'

Side by side, they walked into the centre of the conservatory where the rare plants grew in an exotic mix of foliage. 'Don't take too much notice of my father,' she said quietly. 'He likes to tease. The way he talks, you'd think I was the most ill-tempered woman in the country.'

Emboldened by the fact that they were hidden from view, Guy took her hand and smoothed her palm with his thumb. 'You must be a delight to all who come in contact with you, Jayne. Forgive me if I seem forward but the more I'm in your company the more I want to be with you.' He hesitated. 'I know I shouldn't say this but I'm very attracted to you.'

Jayne's heart pounded. She glanced into Guy's face and saw that he meant every word he said. She knew she should take her hand away, rebuke him for his impertinence, but she was longing to draw his head down to hers, feel his lips on her own. 'Guy!' She was breathless with emotion. 'Oh, Guy, I feel the same.' He bent so swiftly that she had no time to move away, even if she'd wanted to. He kissed her, a gentle butterfly kiss, then drew her to him. For as long as she dared, she remained in his arms. The blood was racing in her veins and her heart felt as though it would burst.

Then, he drew away. 'I can't apologize for kissing you, Jayne. I've wanted to do that ever since I met you.' He was close to her, looking intently into her eyes, and Jayne felt as if she would drown in the joy he roused in her.

She put her hand over his lips. 'Don't say any more, Guy. Let's go back to the others before they grow suspicious.' They walked around the central area of plants and by the time her father and Llinos were in view Jayne had composed herself.

The rest of the afternoon passed in a haze of happiness for Jayne. Now and again she caught Llinos looking at her curiously for a sudden silence had fallen on the gathering. Jayne searched her mind for something to say. 'I hear you were thinking of buying the Paradise Park, Father,' she said.

'I wanted to make it into a good railway hotel, a decent place for people to stay when they have to break their journey.'

'Well,' Jayne said, 'the last thing you'd call the Paradise Park is decent!'

'People's perceptions can change, Jayne, as you've proved, and the hotel could be turned into a fine establishment if someone was prepared to put in the work.'

'Why didn't you take it on, then?'

Eynon shrugged. 'I just felt it wasn't for me. It needs someone young, someone like you, Jayne, with lots of time and energy.'

There was a knock on the door and Sal bobbed a curtsy as she came into the room. 'Shall I clear away the tea-things, Mrs Buchan?'

'See, Father? This is Sal. Doesn't she look lovely?' Jayne patted Sal's arm. 'And don't you think I've taken on enough with two fallen women without taking on a hotel full of them?'

'I suppose you're right,' Eynon agreed.

At last it was time for her guests to leave. Jayne stood at the window and watched as Guy swung easily on to his horse. He was a fine figure of a man, anyone could see that, and she was thrilled that he'd held her in his arms and kissed her.

She waved goodbye to her father as he climbed into his carriage, and then she returned to her seat in the conservatory to dream about the most wonderful afternoon of her life.

CHAPTER EIGHT

'Rhiannon, there's lovely it is to see you!' The room was filled with sunlight and Katie was holding her baby close to her breast, looking the picture of domestic bliss.

Rhiannon swallowed hard. In other circumstances this might have been her home and her baby, with Bull coming home to her at the end of the working day. 'Aye, I've got time off at last. Mrs Buchan is good to me but she sometimes forgets I need a couple of hours to myself.'

'Well, now you're here sit down and talk to me. I'm going off my head, talking to myself all day.'

'I don't believe you,' Rhiannon said. 'You look like the happiest girl alive, and quite right too.'

'I am happy, Rhiannon,' Katie said softly. 'Bull is

85

a wonderful husband and we are so much in love, and sometimes I can't believe that all this happiness will last.' She paused to kiss the baby. 'Now I'll put him down for a nap and we can have a nice cup of tea.' Katie giggled. 'I'm still not used to being waited on. I feel guilty that I sit around like a lady of leisure while other people clean, cook and do the washing.'

'You and Bull have done well, and you both deserve everything you've got.'

'I won't be a minute.' Katie got to her feet. 'I want to hear all your news.'

Listening to the sound of Katie's light footsteps on the stairs, Rhiannon felt the peace of her surroundings seep into her. Occasionally, a horse and carriage drove past, the clip-clop of hoofs echoing pleasantly in the silence of the day. But for the most part there was only the singing of the birds and the shifting of coal in the grate to distract her from her thoughts of Bull, how he had come home to her each night ready for a meal and to make love to her. The difference between Bull and all the other men she'd slept with was that he had treated her like a lady.

'There.' Katie returned just as the maid brought in a tray of tea and some slices of lardy cake. She sat down opposite Rhiannon. 'I want to hear about the high life you're leading in that big house up on the hill.'

'Well, I've been made up to housekeeper now,' Rhiannon said. She was on safe ground, talking about her new life: there was no possibility of hurting Katie. 'I wear sensible but well-made dresses, and when I'm working I have a bundle of keys hanging from my belt.'

'I noticed your clothes were made of fine material,' Katie said. 'Mrs Buchan must think highly of you.'

Rhiannon leaned forward and spoke earnestly. 'I've come a long way from the street-girl I used to be, and it's all because of you, Katie. If you hadn't suggested going to Mrs Buchan's house I'd still be on the streets. I owe you a lot.'

'You don't owe me anything,' Katie protested.

'I'm second-in-command to Mrs Buchan herself,' Rhiannon said, unaware of the pride in her voice. 'I'm learning to keep the household accounts and to make sure everyone from the cook to the scullerymaids does their work properly.'

'What about the menservants?'

Rhiannon smiled. 'Mrs Buchan doesn't get on with menservants. She has to have some, of course—any big house is judged on the number of men who work in it—but now that I've taken over as housekeeper I try to keep the peace.'

'And they don't try to take liberties?' Katie put her hand over her mouth. 'I'm sorry!'

'All the staff know of my past life but none of them would risk their jobs by treating me with disrespect.' Rhiannon smiled. 'In any case, most of them would rather deal with me than with Mrs Buchan. She's got a temper on her that would make anyone run for cover.'

'So you're happy, then?' Katie asked anxiously. 'I hope so, because I won't feel so guilty then about taking Bull away from you.'

'You didn't take him away, Katie. He has a mind of his own and no one on this earth would make him do anything he didn't want to. I've got a good job, it's fulfilling and rewarding, and I've been able to take in Sal, a little friend of mine from the streets. Of course I'm happy. I think Mrs Buchan's happy too because she's helping us fallen women.'

'Oh, I've heard all about Mrs Buchan and her ways.' Katie chuckled. 'Gossip of that kind runs through the gentry and their servants like a dose of the plague.'

'What do people think of it all?' Rhiannon asked curiously.

'Some think it very good of Mrs Buchan, others say she's only doing it to keep her mind off Mr Buchan's mistresses. What do you think, Rhiannon?'

Rhiannon stroked her cheek thoughtfully. She knew Mrs Buchan did not love her husband but his indiscretions hurt her. Still, her duty was to her mistress; a housekeeper's watchword must be loyalty. 'I think Mrs Buchan's a fine, honest lady, and as for her husband's affairs, I don't know anything about them and I don't want to.'

It wasn't true. Many a night Rhiannon had heard Mrs Buchan ordering her husband to be more discreet. He always replied that if a wife did not know her place in the bedchamber a man was entitled to do what he wished with other women.

'I'm sorry, I shouldn't be prying.' Katie's apologetic voice broke into her thoughts. 'I know it's not right to gossip, especially about those who pay your wages. It was silly of me to ask any questions at all.'

'No harm done. Let's change the subject.' They talked then of mundane things, of the baby's funny little ways, of the price of food and clothing, and Bull wasn't mentioned once. At last Rhiannon looked at the clock. 'I'd better be off, then. I'll see you again soon, I expect.' But Rhiannon doubted she would visit Katie again: to be in the house of the man she loved was far too painful. 'I just wanted to make sure you were all right and to tell you how well I'm getting along.'

'So that I don't feel guilty about having all this happiness?'

'To tell you that you needn't feel guilty about anything,' Rhiannon said firmly. She kissed Katie's cheek. 'I'll say goodbye for now, then. Take care of yourself and that lovely baby.'

Outside, the sun was still shining through the trees, dappling the roadway with light and shade. Rhiannon turned once to wave to Katie then walked briskly towards town.

It was quite a long way and it would take her an hour or more to reach the Buchan household, but it was good to be out of doors, to enjoy the peace of the day, to be free for a time of the busy duties of housekeeper.

As she passed the notorious Paradise Park Rhiannon's pace slowed. It was here that the women of the streets conducted most of their business. It was here that poor little Sal had plied her trade. She stared up at the façade and wondered why Mr Morton-Edwards had even considered buying it. True, it was near the railway station, but other than that it had nothing to recommend it. Or did it?

Looking at the building dispassionately, Rhiannon noticed its good square lines and the large windows with ornate mouldings around them, and saw that it must once have been beautiful. With a bit of work it could be so again. Surely, as a respectable hotel, it would bring in more money than it did as a bawdy-house? If only she had the money she would buy the Paradise Park and make it a thriving business. Well, there was no harm in dreaming. Rhiannon drew her cape around her shoulders and continued the long walk home.

*   *   *

'How dare you come home smelling of cheap perfume!' Jayne was furious.

Dafydd was usually more careful: he knew his wife was aware of his womanizing but until now he had never rubbed her nose in it. 'What? Complaining about the company I keep? That's rich coming from you, my dear wife,' Dafydd said coldly.

'I don't know what you mean,' Jayne said. 'What are you insinuating?'

'I have no need to insinuate anything. I'm telling you that I do not approve of your servants Rhiannon and Sal, whores the pair of them.'

'But they are trying to better themselves and I'm helping them. That doesn't mean I condone the way they lived before they came to me.'

'Well, you're such a shrew that I suppose we're lucky to have any servants at all.'

Dafydd had a way of picking on her weak points: he was stating the truth but in a way that put her in the wrong. Jayne sighed but she said nothing. He was right, after all: her temper had cost her several good servants.

Dafydd sank into a chair and stared at her. His direct gaze was unnerving and Jayne forced herself to stay calm. 'If you have something to say then say it,' she said evenly. 'Don't look at me as though I was less than dirt beneath your feet.'

'I was just wondering what Guy sees in you,' he remarked.

Jayne's heart began to pound.

'He certainly admires you. He's always talking about your beauty and your business acumen.'

'Well, isn't it nice to be admired by someone?' She tried to sound offhand but Dafydd had wrongfooted her again. 'I certainly don't get any admiration from my husband.'

Dafydd laughed. 'Husband! That's a fine word to use for a man you don't sleep with and don't even like.'

Jayne turned away from him, tired of the argument and of going over the same ground again and again. Their quarrels always followed the same pattern: he would goad her until she was almost incoherent with rage, then tear into her.

'You should be ashamed to call yourself a married woman,' he went on relentlessly. 'You're nothing more than a glorified housekeeper, except that some lucky men sleep with the housekeeper.' He laughed. 'And our Rhiannon is very beautiful and very experienced. Do you think I should take advantage of that?'

Jayne looked at him with disgust. 'Whatever I say you'll twist it to your own advantage so I'll keep quiet.'

'So you're not going to defend your little whore's honour?'

Jayne shook her head. 'Do your worst but for what it's worth I don't think you'll get very far with her. She has changed. She's more of a lady than half the women you go out with.'

'Fighting talk, eh? Well, I might just take up

your challenge.'

'It wasn't a challenge, Dafydd. I was just stating the facts. Now, do you mind if we drop this? I have more important things to do than to listen to your vile talk.'

She got to her feet and left the room to the sound of Dafydd's laughter. Sometimes she felt she could kill him. She walked for a time in the garden, trying to cool her temper. She hoped from the bottom of her heart that Rhiannon *had* changed, but she wasn't sure how able the girl would be to resist the wiles of her master. Well, she would doubtless find out if Dafydd had meant what he said about seducing her.

At least Guy liked and admired her: he thought her beautiful and clever. What a pity she hadn't met him before she married Dafydd. Everything might have been so different.

*   *   *

Dafydd poured himself some more port, and stared into the glass. Damn Jayne and damn her self-righteousness! She always left him feeling he'd been bested. Still he'd rattled her when he'd mentioned Rhiannon's good looks; he'd been half joking when he said he'd like to seduce her but the more he thought about it, the more he realized that it would be an ideal way to get back at his wife. Not only would he be bedding a desirable woman but he would blow a hole right through Jayne's attempt to rescue a fallen woman.

Rhiannon would present a challenge. These days, the girl went about her business quietly and with dignity. No one would ever guess she had once been a shanty-town woman living with any navvy who gave her bed and board in exchange for her favours.

He rang the bell for the maid and Sal came into the room, bobbing a curtsy. She was neatly dressed with a crisp white apron over her black dress. She had light golden hair and would be a beauty one day. He could not help feeling sorry for the child. If Jayne had achieved anything worthwhile it was in rescuing this little girl. 'How are you getting on here, Sal?' he asked. 'Are you settling in?'

She seemed taken aback by his question and moved from one foot to the other nervously. 'I like it very much, sir,' she said, in a small voice.

'And are you learning about the ways of a respectable household?' he asked.

She looked around as though seeking escape.

'It's all right, Sal, I'm not going to harm you. I'm just interested in hearing your views. Do you get on with Mrs Buchan?'

Sal seemed to warm to him. Her eyes shone and she clasped her hands together. 'Mrs Buchan's that good to me, sir.' Her voice had lost its nervousness. 'She's learned me so many things.'

'Taught you, Sal, she's taught you. Anyway, what sort of things?'

'How to tell good linen from bad, how to lay a table properly, and she's even got me learning to read a bit.'

'Excellent. And what about Rhiannon, is she happy here too?'

'Oh, yes, sir. She's really clever, is Rhiannon, she can do anything Mrs Buchan asks her to do, even the household accounts. These days, we never run out of necessities.'

'Good. Now, Sal, I want you to send Rhiannon to me. I'd like to make sure she's doing everything properly.'

'Oh, she is, sir, really she is.'

'That will be all, Sal, and keep up the good work with the reading and writing. A bit of education will stand you in good stead in the future.'

He watched as the girl went towards the door. For a moment he felt nothing but admiration for Jayne and for what she was trying to achieve.

When Rhiannon came into the room she wore an expression of surprise. It was not often that she was called on to have dealings with the master of the house. 'Yes, sir?' She dipped in a graceful curtsy. 'Sal said you wanted to see me.'

'That's right, Rhiannon.' He studied her: she looked ladylike in her good clothes, with the keys of the house hanging at her waist. The silky material of her gown did little to conceal the generous thrust of her breasts. She put up her hand to her throat, evidently noting his scrutiny. He smiled. 'I've had a chat with little Sal and she seems happy here. How about you, Rhiannon? Any complaints?'

'None, sir,' Rhiannon said gravely. 'I'm very happy with the job Mrs Buchan has seen fit to trust me with.'

'I can see that a rise from whoredom to housekeeper is quite a leap, but don't you miss your old way of life sometimes?'

'I don't even like to think about it now, sir,' Rhiannon said, and there was a sharpness in her tone that he did not miss. 'It was a dreadful way of life, and I'm glad it's all in my past now.'

Dafydd knew he was being rebuked, and

deservedly so. 'And your mistress, Mrs Buchan, does she treat you well?'

He saw her face soften a little and realized she was fond of Jayne too. It was going to be more difficult than he had thought to seduce her.

'Oh, yes, sir. Mrs Buchan treats me very well—I can never repay her for what she's done for me.'

'And what is that, exactly? A good bed to sleep in, food to put in your stomach and clothes to put on your back, is that worth giving up your life of variety and enjoyment for?'

'Most emphatically so, sir. What I appreciate more than anything is that Mrs Buchan has given me back my self-respect.'

He could see she would need careful handling: this girl was intelligent as well as beautiful.

'May I go now, sir?' She stood still, her large eyes assessing him with age-old wisdom.

'Yes, of course you may. I don't want to keep you from your duties.' He watched as she walked gracefully to the door, her head high. In spite of his attempts to humble her she had kept her dignity.

'One more thing, Rhiannon,' he said easily. 'Mr Fairchild and Mrs Buchan are good friends, are they not?'

She gave him a bleak look. 'I wouldn't know anything about that, Mr Buchan. I suggest you ask Madam yourself.'

Dafydd smiled. She had guts all right. She was also loyal to Jayne, and that would be the biggest hurdle to overcome if he wanted the girl in his bed. Still, Dafydd Buchan had never been frightened of taking up a challenge and this was one to which he was positively looking forward.

CHAPTER NINE

Llinos shivered, feeling the cold even though all the fires in the house were blazing. The chill of autumn was in the air, and before she knew it Christmas would be upon her. She would be spending it alone.

She picked up the letter from Sion, her younger son, who was away at school. He wanted to stay with a friend over the holidays and Llinos could not blame him. The pottery house was quiet these days, and even though the kilns outside sent waves of heat into the leaden sky and apprentices called cheerily to each other in the yard there was an emptiness in the old house that Llinos could not fill. It was at times like this that she missed Joe most: her husband had been loving, full of arcane wisdom learned during his childhood with the American Indians and she had loved him deeply.

She stood at the window and looked out at the gathering gloom. On an impulse, she rang for the maid. She would have her carriage brought round and visit Eynon—he never minded her arriving unannounced.

As she left the house, a chill wind whipped around her ankles. She climbed into the carriage and hugged her collar close to her face. She hoped that Eynon would be at home: she needed warmth and company, and in that moment she knew that if he asked her again to marry him she might be tempted to say yes.

As she'd expected, Eynon welcomed her warmly. 'Come in, Llinos. Father Martin's here and he'll be glad to see you too.' He hugged her and she clung to him. 'But not half as glad as I am,' he added softly.

'Thank you for putting up with me, Eynon. I know it's not polite to arrive on your doorstep like this.'

'Nonsense! You are my dearest friend and my house is open to you at any time of the day or night.'

Father Martin was seated before the fire, his legs spread apart, his lap full of apple peelings. He looked up at her apologetically. 'Forgive me if I don't get up, Llinos, but I don't want to make a mess on Eynon's good carpet.'

Llinos kissed his round cheek.

Eynon led her to the armchair at the other side of the huge fireplace and held her hand as she sat down. The room was cheerful and comfortable; the marble mantelpiece gleamed and the logs burning in the grate sent out a pleasant aroma. 'I'll get you a hot toddy, Llinos,' Eynon said. 'You look frozen.'

A silver jug of hot water and a bowl of sugar stood on the table. Eynon mixed brandy, sugar and water in a glass and stirred it vigorously. Llinos felt cosseted as he handed it to her then kissed her hair. She was warmed by Eynon's love for her but could she marry him? Her life would be changed dramatically and for ever: she would have to move from her home for a start, and she'd lived there as a child and as a woman. The house had seen the birth of her two sons, Lloyd and Sion. It was there that her dear Joe had breathed his last. The house held a thousand memories, some good, some less so. Perhaps it would be no bad thing to leave it all behind, and there was always her dear friend and partner Watt Bevan to look after the china factory. He had been with her for many years and knew the business as well as she did.

'Have you heard any gossip about Jayne, Llinos?' Eynon's voice broke into her thoughts.

'Gossip?'

'Well, there's been talk because she's employed girls of dubious character but now people are saying she's seeing too much of this London chap, Guy Fairchild. I'm worried it will get out of hand.'

'I've heard nothing untoward. Surely you don't think there's anything to worry about? Jayne is such a stickler for convention.'

'I'm worried about her. I know she's not happy with Buchan. It was the biggest mistake of her life when she married the man. I did warn her but she wouldn't listen to a word I said.'

'Eynon, I'm the wrong one to talk to about this.' Llinos stared at him, her brow furrowed. 'I bore Dafydd a son so I can hardly say a word against him.'

'Will you at least concede that he has changed?' Eynon was determined to pursue the subject. 'He has become tight-fisted and grasping, and all he thinks of is getting his hands on Great Western shares.'

'Do you think that Dafydd is treating Jayne badly, then?' Llinos asked. 'If so, she is more than a match for him, believe me.'

Eynon nodded. 'I know you're right, but the marriage is a sham. They don't sleep together so they will never have children and I will never be a grandfather.' He paused. 'Now there's a story going around that Jayne and this London man are lovers.'

'Oh, I don't believe that for a minute,' Llinos

said, 'and you know what the townsfolk are like. Soon they will get tired of picking on Jayne and find another poor soul to gossip about.'

'Well, I hope you're right. I don't like to see Jayne so unhappy with Buchan, but for all that I can't see her allowing herself to be taken in by this man, who might be after her fortune for all we know.'

Father Martin coughed, reminding them of his presence. 'For goodness' sake, stop fussing about what Jayne might or might not do. She's her own woman, and she'll please herself whatever you say or do.'

'Quite right,' Eynon said. 'Now, who's for another drink?'

*　　　*　　　*

Jayne sat in the tearooms of the Mackworth Hotel and smiled across the table at Guy. As she was concerned about appearances she'd brought Rhiannon with her. The girl was sitting with her hands folded in her lap and her head high as if she was used to grand company. She would fit into any society, Jayne thought. She was beautiful too—so beautiful that she had hesitated to bring her along as chaperone, but she needn't have worried: Guy's attention was firmly fixed on herself.

'So, Jayne,' Guy let his hand brush hers as he reached for the sugar, 'are your shares still rising?'

Jayne knew that this inconsequential talk was for Rhiannon's benefit: had they been alone, Guy would have been telling her how much he admired her, and how she was wasted on Dafydd Buchan.

'Will you excuse me for just a moment?'

99

Rhiannon said quietly. 'I need to go to the ladies' room.'

Rhiannon spoke very well, Jayne realized, with some surprise—she was not like a girl from the streets.

'That's all right, Rhiannon. Take your time,' Jayne said, lifting her eyebrow meaningfully. She could count on Rhiannon to be tactful enough to leave them alone for a little while. Rhiannon saw more than anyone gave her credit for.

'Jayne,' Guy said urgently when Rhiannon had gone, 'I wish I could take you away from here.'

Jayne felt as if the room was suddenly full of flowers, of birds singing sweetly and angel harps playing golden music. She shouldn't listen to Guy's words, wonderful though they made her feel: she was a married woman and nothing would ever change that. 'Guy, I feel the same about you but it's impossible, you know it is.' She felt his hand reach for hers beneath the table and as her fingers curled in his a warmth ran through her. 'What a pity I didn't meet you before I married Dafydd,' she murmured.

'Say you'll meet me alone, Jayne. I can't bear to sit so near you and not take you into my arms.'

'But, Guy, how could we arrange that? It would be impossible.'

'Maybe not,' Guy said. 'Dafydd is going away for a few days on business, isn't he?'

'That's the first I've heard of it,' Jayne said tersely, 'but, then, Dafydd and I stopped talking to each other a long time ago.'

'You could take a trip—into the country, perhaps, to see a sick aunt. Make any excuse and I will book us into a coaching inn as man and wife.'

'I wouldn't dare,' Jayne said. 'I'm not brave enough to flout convention like that.'

'No one need ever know,' Guy coaxed. 'Please, Jayne, how can I live my life if I'm never to possess you?'

'But it's so dangerous, Guy. What if I did come away with you and I conceived a child? Dafydd would know right away it wasn't his—and so would half of Swansea.'

'That would never happen, Jayne. I can't have children.' Guy squeezed her hand. 'I have had three mistresses and one wife, whom I lost to the cholera, and none of them conceived my child. Please, Jayne, I have never felt like this about any of the other women in my life. By day you are in my thoughts, and by night you torment my dreams. I'll die if I can't have you.'

'But would a few days together be enough for us, Guy?' Jayne asked. 'It would be like offering a child a sweet then snatching it away. No, I can't do it, it's impossible.'

'Don't say that. Just tell me you'll think about it—please, Jayne, I'm begging you.'

Jayne saw Rhiannon threading her way back through the tables towards her. 'I'll think about it. Now, change the subject, please.'

Rhiannon seated herself at the table and Jayne looked at Guy. 'We were talking about the shares, Guy, do you wish to acquire some for yourself?'

'I wouldn't mind a few, just for the fun of seeing them rise.' He shrugged. 'I don't need to bother with them, though. I've enough irons in the fire in London.'

'I could give you a few of my shares if you were really keen.' Jayne felt she'd give him the world, if

101

it would please him.

'Don't even think about it. You have a good investment there and you should keep it.'

'No, really, Guy, I would like you to have some. We'd be able to compare notes on how they performed.'

'We'll see.' Guy smiled. 'Now, I hope you ladies will forgive me but I must go. I have a meeting to attend.'

Jayne got to her feet at once. 'It's time I was getting back too. The nights are so cold and dark at this time of year.' She felt a great sense of disappointment: she could have stayed and talked with Guy all night but he was a businessman and had work to do. She was lucky that he had spared as much time for her as he had.

As she sat in the carriage on the way home Jayne's thoughts were on Guy; if he took some of her shares she would have a good excuse to meet him and they would have an interest in common.

'What do you make of him, Rhiannon? Mr Fairchild, I mean.' Somehow Jayne wanted to know what Rhiannon thought—the girl must be a good judge of men.

'I think he's a very clever man,' Rhiannon said. 'He's handsome, too. He's keen on business and ruthless where his finances are concerned.'

'Are you saying you don't trust him?' Jayne forced herself to speak calmly: she mustn't let anyone know how she felt about Guy.

'I'm not saying that,' Rhiannon said quickly, 'and to be fair to him he is very taken with you.'

Jayne felt a thrill at Rhiannon's words. 'Do you really think so?'

'I know it's not my place to say so but I think

he's falling in love with you. Take that business about your shares.'

'What about them?'

'I realize that these railway shares are very much in demand, yet when you offered to let him have some he advised you to keep them for yourself.'

'Yes, he did, didn't he?' Jayne subsided in her seat and closed her eyes. She wanted to be alone with her thoughts, to consider the possibility that Guy might be in love with her. Surely a woman like Rhiannon, who had known so many men, would see through a mere flatterer?

Guy—in love with her! It was a wonderful dream. She sighed happily, and made plans to see him again soon.

* * *

'You're doing well, girl.' Mrs Jones was seated at the table, her plump hands idle for once. 'I never thought when you came here that you'd go up in the world quite so soon but *chwarae teg*, fair play, we've never run out of anything since you took over as housekeeper.'

Rhiannon smiled. 'Nice of you to say so, Mrs Jones. I take my duties very seriously. You never know where all this training will lead.'

'And what about me?' Sal was perched on a chair, her bare feet swinging inches above the slate floor. Now that she had shoes, she couldn't wait to get them off her feet. 'I'm doing well, too!'

'You are, *cariad*,' Mrs Jones said indulgently, 'and you should be glad the mistress don't care much for men-servants or you wouldn't be allowed anywhere near the dining-table.'

Sal glowed. 'I like being here. It beats walking the streets and waiting for a customer to come along, especially on these cold dark nights.'

Mrs Jones tutted. 'Don't speak of that, Sal. You're a respectable girl now and you should behave like one.'

'Well, I do,' Sal said quickly, 'but I can't forget what happened to me in the past, can I?'

'You must forget it if you mean to get on, girl.' The cook tapped Sal's arm. 'Now, pour us some of that tea before it gets cold—and get your shoes on. You look like a street urchin.'

Reluctantly, Sal slipped them on. 'All right, Cook, I'll keep my shoes on just to please you.' She reached for the teapot and filled the cups.

'So, Rhiannon,' the cook said, 'what went on this afternoon with Madam? Why did she take you to town with her? Buying new clothes, was she?'

'She had some business to attend to and then she took me for tea in the Mackworth Hotel. Really posh it was.'

Mrs Jones, as Rhiannon had expected, was distracted by the idea of her sitting in an elegant hotel drinking tea like the gentry.

'What was it like? Come on, tell us everything about it.' Mrs Jones put her plump elbows on the table and supported her several chins in her hands.

'Well, the carpet was so thick you couldn't hear your footsteps at all,' Rhiannon said. 'And the china, well, it was almost as good as the china the mistress has us bring out for her guests.'

'And who else was there?' Mrs Jones asked. 'Did you see anybody important?'

'I wouldn't know who *was* important,' Rhiannon said. 'I just sat still and let the others talk.' As soon as the words were out she knew she'd made a mistake.

'Others? What others?' Mrs Jones asked, a frown furrowing her brow. 'You didn't mention there were other people with Madam.'

'Oh, that gentleman, Mr Fairchild,' she said vaguely. 'He only stopped to pay his respects and then the mistress and I came home.'

'I knew he was sweet on her,' Mrs Jones said. 'I can't understand why Mr Buchan doesn't say something. You'd almost think he was throwing the pair of them together. He must be cooking something up or he would be playing merry hell at his wife being seen in public with another man.'

'But it was only for a few minutes and I was there,' Rhiannon said. 'No one could talk about a public meeting like that, could they?'

The cook shook her head. 'I don't know about that. The Mackworth was where Mr Buchan used to take Mrs Mainwaring and we all know how *that* turned out.'

'I don't,' Sal said. 'What happened?'

Mrs Jones glanced over her shoulder but the other maids were in the scullery out of earshot. 'Well, she had a child by him, a by-blow.'

'Oh, so the gentry aren't much better than the likes of me, are they?' Sal said. 'What did her husband think about it?'

Mrs Jones shrugged. 'Well, seems he'd been straying after another woman so I suppose it was tit for tat. Anyway, he put up with it and was good to the boy into the bargain.'

'Where's the kid now?' Sal asked.

'At some posh school, so I heard.' The cook struggled to her feet. 'Right, let's get things ready

105

for the morning and then we can all go to bed. Vi and Hetty can damp down the fires and set them ready for tomorrow.'

It was an hour later when Rhiannon climbed into her bed. Sal scrambled into hers and snuggled down under the blankets, head and all, trying to get warm. A moment or two later she peeped out. 'Is Mrs Buchan going to take this Guy character for a lover, do you think?'

'I don't know, Sal. And now we'd best get some sleep. It's going to be another long day of hard work tomorrow.'

Rhiannon snuffed the candle and pulled the bedclothes up to her chin. A thin sliver of moonlight cut a pathway through the dark and she sighed, thinking of the nights she'd spent in the old ramshackle hut with Bull. Folk might think she was doing well for herself, housekeeper in a large establishment, but Rhiannon would have given it all up for a night alone with Bull Beynon.

CHAPTER TEN

'How far have you got with my dear wife, Guy?' Dafydd Buchan took a sip of the fine brandy served at Carrington's gentlemen's club and gazed at the other man. His friend had managed to charm Jayne, that much was obvious, but he seemed increasingly reluctant to talk about it. 'Come on, man, has she said she'll part with any of the shares?'

'She offered me some the other day when I met her at the tea-rooms,' Guy told him flatly.

'And?' Dafydd felt like hitting him: he was procrastinating deliberately. Was it possible he wanted the shares for himself? 'Did you agree to take them?'

'I thought it best to wait until she knew me better.' Guy held up his glass and the waiter hurried to refill it.

'Why wait at all?' Dafydd asked. 'Look, Guy, I hope you're not playing me false.'

A strange expression crossed Guy's face. 'I'm sure I don't know what you mean. All the time I was with your wife Mrs Beynon was there to chaperone her. Does your wife always take her housekeeper out to tea? I would have thought one of the lesser maids would do just as well.'

'Don't change the subject.' Dafydd was impatient. 'I don't mean to suggest you have designs on my wife but I'm wondering if you've an urge to buy into the Great Western yourself.'

Guy relaxed visibly. 'Good Lord, no!' he said. 'I haven't the least interest in the Great Western. And if you're worried about your wife's reputation there is no need—we are never seen alone together in public.' He paused. 'I must say you have a very beautiful housekeeper, Dafydd. It's a wonder your roving eye hasn't lighted on her.'

Dafydd smiled. So Guy, too, had noticed Rhiannon's looks—but who could miss such sensuality and the knowledge of men that lurked in her eyes? 'Oh, don't worry, I have plans for sweet Rhiannon.' Dafydd leaned back in his chair. 'I thought I might amuse myself by taking her to my bed. She'd be a damned sight more satisfying than my dear wife ever was.'

'You don't *really* want to make a mistress of a

107

mere servant?' Guy asked. 'In any case, you'd ruin the poor girl's chance of making a good marriage.'

Dafydd frowned. Guy didn't know what Rhiannon had been before she came to work for Jayne. Perhaps he would keep the truth to himself for now. He wanted the first chance with Rhiannon: she'd be desperate for carnal love by now—she'd not been with a man for many a month. The thought excited him. 'So, tell me, then, Guy, why is this plan taking so long to bear fruit? I thought you'd have the shares by now. Don't tell me your powers of persuasion are waning?'

'Be patient. I thought I'd play a waiting game to make sure of Jayne's trust. If I seem too eager she'll smell a rat. She's an intelligent young woman.'

'Maybe you're right, but I wish you'd get on with it. I'm getting tired of waiting.'

'Impatience is the way to failure. You hook your fish first and then you reel her in. Take things slowly, and you might well get what you want.'

'That's easy for you to say but those shares are going up day by day. It galls me to think of Jayne and her precious father crowing over me because they're in on it and I'm not.'

'I'm doing my best,' Guy said. 'I know she likes me, but how much? Enough to trust me to do the best for her?'

Dafydd held up his glass and a waiter appeared and refilled it with brandy. He scarcely acknowledged the man before he returned to his questioning. 'How long do you think it will be before you have something to offer me? For heaven's sake, man, move yourself!'

Guy leaned back in his chair. 'Hold on, Dafydd.

Have you forgotten that I'm not getting anything out of this?'

Dafydd was taken aback. He thought about it for a moment and came to a decison. 'Look, I promised I'd buy the shares from you with a five per cent commission. Well, what if I make it ten?'

He watched Guy's expression become thoughtful. 'Wouldn't you be losing out on the deal then?'

'Initially perhaps,' Dafydd said, 'but I have a gut feeling those shares will continue to rise in value.' As soon as he spoke Dafydd wondered at the wisdom of revealing his thoughts to Guy. What if he bought all the shares from Jayne then went back to London?

'Look,' Guy leaned forward in his chair, 'why don't you send Jayne away somewhere, to a spa or something?'

'What good would that do?' Dafydd asked sharply. 'You can hardly work on her if she's away, can you?'

'I could turn up at the same hotel. It would be a tremendous coincidence, of course, but these things happen—especially if the location is fashionable, say Brighton or Bath.'

'What do you think that would achieve?'

'I would have the time and the excuse to be with her a great deal. Tell her to take the delicious Rhiannon with her and then I could charm them both.'

Dafydd digested the plan. It might just work. Of course, he would make sure Rhiannon didn't go with Jayne: she could take young Sal. Apart from anything else, he needed Rhiannon to run the house for him. 'You may have something there,' he conceded. 'I'll suggest it, but I can't guarantee that Jayne will go. She never does anything to please me.'

'You have to be cunning,' Guy said. 'Tell her you want the house redecorated perhaps.'

Dafydd didn't like to think that Guy understood women better than he did. As far as he was concerned he had pleased all of his mistresses. 'All right,' he said at last. 'We'll play it your way, but if you don't succeed soon, we might as well give up on the plan and think of something else. Now, how about another brandy?'

*   *   *

Bath was a beautiful place to be even now, with the trees bare of leaves and leaden clouds hanging low over the rooftops.

'Oh, isn't this lovely, Mrs Buchan?' Sal said happily. 'I'm so excited—I've never been away from Swansea before, not in all my life, and I've never stayed in a posh hotel like this one with silk sheets on the bed. I'm so glad you brought me and not Rhiannon.'

Jayne looked out of the hotel window at the lovely sweep of houses across the road; Bath was a gracious place but also lonely. Yet this morning, when she had woken in the unfamiliar room, Jayne realized that all she was missing from home was Guy. She could do without Dafydd's ill-humour and the tiresome visitors for whom she had to make a show of being happily married.

'Shall I put out your clothes ready for supper, Mrs Buchan?'

'I suppose so.' Jayne felt a little impatient with

110

the girl: she was so young in many ways. She would have preferred Rhiannon to come with her but, as Dafydd had pointed out, the household would fall apart without Rhiannon in charge.

There was a discreet knock on the door and Sal hurried to answer it. 'It's a letter, Mrs Buchan.'

'I can see that,' Jayne said. She took the envelope and opened it. Her heart missed a beat as she saw the signature. She sank on to the bed. Guy was downstairs in the foyer of the hotel and he wanted to see her.

She folded the letter, resisting the urge to kiss the name penned at the bottom. 'Help me tidy my hair, Sal,' she said. 'I've a visitor.'

In the foyer Jayne paused. Would Guy be as anxious to see her as she was to see him?

'Jayne, my dear.' He was standing in front of her, smiling. He took her hand and kissed it, and Jayne felt the urge to run her fingers through his soft dark hair.

'Guy, dear Guy, I've been longing to see you.' She held on to his hands, not wanting to break the moment of intimacy between them.

'Come and sit down.' He led her to a shadowy area of the huge foyer. 'Sit next to me, let me be as close to you as I dare.' He took her hands again and kissed them, his lips warm.

Jayne's heart was beating swiftly as she looked into his face. She felt like a girl again, in love for the first time. An ornate oil lamp cast a glow over the two of them and Jayne felt as if they were locked in a secret world together. She felt the heat of his thigh against hers and a thrill such as she had never experienced with Dafydd shot through her. She felt dizzy with desire for Guy, even though she knew they could never be man and wife.

'Say something, Jayne. Are you pleased to see me?'

'Of course I am—but, Guy, we have to be careful. We can never be more than friends in the eyes of the world, you know that.'

'None of that matters. I never meant to fall in love with you but my heart sings whenever you come near me. I can't go about my daily business without thoughts of you constantly in my mind.'

She looked at him, at the earnest expression on his face, and in that moment she knew she couldn't lie to him. 'I love you, too, Guy,' she whispered. She glanced round, as if fearful she might be overheard. Her face was flushed and her heart was fluttering like a frightened bird. She was sixteen again. The waiter hovered into sight and the dream faded.

Guy ordered a brandy for himself and a cordial for Jayne. She leaned against him. Why hadn't she met Guy first? She had been headstrong, rebelling against her father in marrying Dafydd. Now she was regretting it, and it was too late to do anything about it. 'How long are you staying in Bath?' she asked shakily. Guy shook his hair away from his brow and Jayne watched him, mesmerized by his charm and fine looks. Guy was all she could ever want in a man, thoughtful, caring and willing to laugh at himself, which Dafydd was incapable of doing.

'I'm staying just as long as you are,' Guy said. 'I have no ties, Jayne, no wife, no family to answer to. I am my own man.' He smiled. 'Or I was before I met you.'

'This is madness,' Jayne said. 'I should tell you to

go away and leave me alone but I can't. Surely it won't do any harm for us to spend a little time together?'

'Of course not, and I promise I will behave like a perfect gentleman, if that's what you want.'

'And what about Dafydd? Does he suspect you've come after me? It must seem strange, both of us being away at the same time.'

Guy looked thoughtful and for a long moment he did not speak. Then he sighed and shook his head. 'Jayne, I should tell you the truth.' Then he stopped: the waiter was back with glasses and bottles on a tray. He took an interminably long time to pour the drinks, then dusted the table with the napkin he had over his arm. Jayne couldn't wait for him to go away.

At last they were alone again and she looked at Guy questioningly. 'What were you going to say, Guy?'

He shrugged. 'Dafydd is too intent on his business interests to give much thought to the woman he is supposed to love and cherish.'

Jayne knew instinctively that whatever Guy had been going to say he had changed his mind. Still, he was right: all Dafydd cared about was business and right now that meant getting his hands on shares in the Great Western Railway. Would he go so far as to ask Guy to try to persuade her to sell her shares? It was an awful thought, but Jayne was suddenly suspicious. 'I know what Dafydd wants more than anything in the world,' she said. 'My shares in the railway. Should I give them to him, Guy?'

Guy brushed a curl off her forehead. 'Let's forget about business and Dafydd. As for the shares, I have no interest in them but I've heard

113

they're a good investment so you should hold on to them. Now, let's talk about something more interesting—you.'

'I don't know.' Jayne held back, still not sure of Guy's motives. 'I wouldn't mind getting them off my hands. They're more trouble than they're worth. Why don't you have them, Guy? I'll sell at a fair price.'

'I don't want anything to do with any shares, Jayne, believe me. Can we forget the Great Western and think about ourselves? Let's talk about tomorrow. Where would you like me to take you?'

'I'll let you decide.' She tried to read his expression but he appeared honest and open. Was she being fooled? He was either being very clever or he genuinely had no interest in the shares.

'We'll have to take Sal along with us, of course,' she said. 'We must give no one the chance to gossip about us.'

'As long as I'm with you I don't care if a whole retinue of servants comes with us.'

'That's all right, then.' She smiled. 'I think I'm going to be happy while I'm in Bath.' That was an understatement.

'I'll drink to that,' Guy said quietly, and his eyes were full of admiration.

*   *   *

Sal glanced out of the window of the carriage and marvelled at how she'd come up from being a street-walker to hold the position of lady's maid to one of the richest women in Swansea. She glanced down at her good boots and the long hem of her

114

fine dress, and preened with delight. Here she was, Sal the orphan, riding in a warm carriage around Bath like a lady.

Mrs Buchan was seated opposite her with the gentleman at her side. At first, Sal wondered if her mistress had taken a lover but there appeared to be nothing improper between them: Mrs Buchan went to her bed alone and Sal was witness to that. But they did care about each other, that was plain. Mrs Buchan was like a little girl with her head full of dreams. She was very pretty, Sal thought, and not the dragon she was rumoured to be. Mind, her husband was no better than he ought to be, but weren't all men the same under the skin? Sal had lain with gentlemen and with navvies from the railway, and once they took their clothes off there was nothing to tell them apart. All of them had used her, grunting and groaning like pigs, none of them giving a damn about her feelings.

She had vowed she would never marry because then she'd be the plaything of one man instead of many. Also, she would have to raise children and look after the house with no payment at the end of it. Sal did not believe in love—well, she hadn't until now. Mrs Buchan's cheeks were flushed and her eyes alight. She never looked like that when she was with her husband but Mr Buchan often raised his voice to her and chased other women shamelessly, even flirting in front of Mrs Buchan. How was it that women were supposed to be 'respectable' while men could be like dogs in the street, chasing after whoever took their fancy?

'This is heaven, Jayne,' Sal heard the gentleman whisper, as he leaned towards her mistress—so close that his lips were almost on hers. 'I wish we could be together for ever.'

Instead of being flattered by the attention Mrs Buchan took out a lace handkerchief and dabbed her eyes with it. 'I wish that, too, but let's just enjoy these few days together. They will have to last us for the rest of our lives.'

Sal swallowed hard. Poor Mrs Buchan, she would be faithful to the end. Her awful husband did not deserve her. Sal plucked up her courage to speak, risking Mrs Buchan's anger. 'Know what my mam used to say, Mrs Buchan?' Sal did not wait for a reply. 'She used to say life is ours for a very short time so we mustn't waste a precious minute of it. She said we must grasp life with both hands and not miss our chances when they are put under our noses.'

It was the gentleman who responded. 'Well said, little girl,' he smiled at her, 'I think your mother was a wise woman. Don't you agree, Jayne?'

Jayne leaned across to pat Sal's hand. 'My life has already passed me by and it's too late to change it.'

There were tears in her eyes and Sal felt so sorry for her. 'No, Mrs Buchan, while you have life and breath it's never too late.' She leaned back in her seat feeling that she had said enough, any more would be regarded as familiar, but she hoped Mrs Buchan would snatch at any little bit of happiness that came her way. If that meant going to bed with a man not her husband then good luck to her.

CHAPTER ELEVEN

Rhiannon counted the damask napkins, checked they were clean, and put them in the dining-room drawer ready for when dinner was served. It was a lovely, peaceful day of winter sunlight with the promise of spring in the air.

The door opened and Mr Buchan came into the room. As usual, he was frowning. 'I want everything to be in order for tonight,' he said. 'I'm expecting a special guest.'

Rhiannon inclined her head. She'd heard of this 'special guest' from the maids' gossip in the kitchen: it was Mrs Dunaway, a fast woman by all accounts who would sleep with any man she could get her hands on.

'I can see by your face that you disapprove.' Mr Buchan came closer and put his hands on her shoulders. 'I'm surprised at you, Rhiannon. After the life you've led I would expect a more liberal approach to the sins of the flesh.'

'It's not my place to approve or disapprove, sir.' Rhiannon felt the master was too close for comfort but when she tried to move away he held her fast.

'Would you deny me a little bit of comfort when I have a wife who doesn't even share my bed when I request it?'

'I've found that men will please themselves, sir, whatever the wife does or does not do.'

'Ah, yes. I know your experience of men is endless.' He pushed his leg between hers. 'How about sharing a little bit of that passion with me, Rhiannon? I could be very good to you.'

Rhiannon eased herself away from him. 'I've given up that life, sir. I never liked being a whore and now I don't have to be one.'

'I could insist,' Mr Buchan said, 'but I would prefer it if you came to me of your own free will.'

'That will never happen, Mr Buchan,' Rhiannon said flatly. 'Would you like me to do anything else to make your guest welcome, sir?' She changed the subject adroitly, reminding him of the busy evening ahead, and Mr Buchan moved away from her.

'You can make sure the coal scuttle is well stocked. I don't want maids prying when I'm entertaining my guest.'

Rhiannon couldn't resist a jibe. 'You will be entertaining her in your bedroom, sir?'

Mr Buchan's eyes glinted. 'No, Rhiannon, *she* will be entertaining *me* in my bedroom.' He walked to the door and stopped to look back at her. 'I want you, Rhiannon, and I always get what I want in the end. Bear that in mind.'

'Yes, Mr Buchan, I will.'

When the door closed behind him Rhiannon stuck out her tongue, a childish gesture but it made her feel better. Men were all the same, thinking a woman should lie down for them whenever they wanted and no questions asked. Well, Mr Buchan could whistle. He would never have his way with her.

In the kitchen, Mrs Jones, as usual, was up to her elbows in flour. 'Well, then, who's this jade coming here alone tonight?'

'Her name is Mrs Dunaway,' Rhiannon said. 'I don't know much about her except what Vi and Hetty told me, but she can't be up to much good.' Rhiannon was happy to impart a snippet of gossip

118

that would be all around the house later anyway. 'After supper the master will be entertaining his guest in his bedroom.' She laughed. 'Or, as he put it, *she* will be entertaining *him*.'

'That's brazen, that is.' The cook rubbed her hands on her apron. 'What sort of man brings a loose woman into his own home? There was a time when Mr Buchan was a hero, working for the ordinary folk.'

Rhiannon looked at her in surprise. 'What did he do for the likes of us?'

'He fought against the toll rises—one of the Rebecca rioters, he was. Although he was rich he could see the tolls were ruining folks' livelihood.'

'How did they do that?' Rhiannon found it hard to see Mr Buchan as a rebel. These days, he was out for himself.

'Well, farmers and the like had to pay to go through the gates and that put up the price of grain.'

'Well, the master has certainly changed since then. He's not the sort of man you'd think of now as a hero.'

'I don't know about that.' Mrs Jones dropped the cake mixture into the patty tins. 'Put those in the oven for us, Rhiannon, there's a good girl.' She sank into a chair, wiping the sweat from her brow. 'Mind, the master is still handsome and if he wasn't so wrapped up in himself he'd be a good person.'

Rhiannon found it hard to think of Mr Buchan as a good person. The way he'd tried to force her to sleep with him was more the act of a self-centred man. She had met enough of his sort in her early days on the streets. Such men took what they wanted then spat on you when they were finished.

119

Still, it was pointless telling Mrs Jones about the incident: she would probably say that, given Rhiannon's past, it was not surprising that the master thought he could have a bit of fun with her. But Rhiannon would never allow herself to be used like that again.

*   *   *

Bea Dunaway was young and rich; she had been the wife of an old man who had died obligingly and left her his fortune. She was not beautiful, Dafydd thought, but she was warm and passionate and had the knack of making a man feel ten foot tall. If only women could learn early in life how to please a man there wouldn't be room for so many mistresses. Women brought trouble on themselves by rebuffing a man's overtures. Just look at Rhiannon! The girl had been a street-walker, a floosie, a shilling stand-up—heaven knows what sort of men she'd had between her legs—yet she had rejected him, her master. The girl was a fool! He could have given her so much, had she been willing. And how galling it would be for Jayne to have her servant sleeping with him. He had never before taken a woman below his social standing, but with Rhiannon living under the same roof it would be the final humiliation. Yet he had a grudging respect for the girl: she was loyal to her mistress *and* she had given up her old way of life. He would be a cad to take away the self-respect the girl had gained.

'Hello!' Bea's voice broke into his reverie. 'You were far away then. What were you thinking about, Dafydd?'

'You, of course,' he lied glibly. 'I was wondering what it would be like to take you to bed and make passionate love to you.'

She lowered her eyelashes, like the coquette she was, and smiled. 'You are very forward, sir.'

'Am I, Bea?' He took her hand and looked earnestly into her eyes. 'I want you so much, my darling girl, and I must have you tonight or I'll die.' He was in danger of going too far, but Bea Dunaway was vain enough to swallow his lies.

'Oh, Dafydd, you are so impetuous, really. You must learn some patience. A lady likes to be wooed you know.'

It seemed that more flattery was what she wanted so, cynically, Dafydd gave it to her. 'We shall have supper and I'll not taste a morsel of it for want of you, Bea. Don't you know the torture you put a man through? If this is a test of my patience, I'll understand. I don't want to move too swiftly for you—I'd wait for you for ever.'

But Bea's full bosom was rising and falling, and she was breathless with pleasure. 'You are a naughty boy,' she said, 'but because you are so eager for me perhaps we should postpone supper until we have, how shall I put it? Satisfied your most urgent need?'

They went upstairs hand in hand and Dafydd smiled to himself, wishing Jayne were here to witness his indiscretion. This was the first time he had brought a woman into his home. The thought gave him pleasure. Was he becoming as hard and callous as Rhiannon seemed to think?

For a moment it was as if he stood outside himself and watched a stranger as he took Bea Dunaway to bed and made love to her—with little satisfaction other than a sense of physical release. He did not value the woman: she was a whore because it gave her pleasure to be so. Rhiannon had been a whore out of necessity. What's more, she never pretended to be a lady while Bea hid behind a smokescreen of respectability.

As soon as he'd finished he rose from the bed and went into the dressing room, glad to be away from Bea's vacuous chatter. He wanted a challenge. He was tired of women who pretended a chastity they did not possess. Give him an honest whore like Rhiannon Beynon any day.

Over supper, Bea chatted incessantly and Dafydd wondered how quickly he could get rid of her. This was the first and last time he would bring a woman home with him: it was not easy to get rid of them once his needs had been satisfied.

At last, weary of her company, he sent Bea home in his carriage with the promise of a gift to thank her for her 'beauty and charm'. He might just as well have put his hand into his pocket and handed her some sovereigns, but if he had she would have been mortally offended.

When she had gone, he rang the bell for Rhiannon. She came at once and stood in the doorway, as though worried he might pounce on her and ravish her. You'd think she'd be honoured at the prospect. Would he ever understand women?

'Have the bed in my room made up with clean linen,' he said, his voice sharp. 'I can't sleep with the smell of that woman in it.'

'Then perhaps you shouldn't have allowed her there in the first place . . . sir.' Rhiannon spoke equally sharply. 'I shall see that the work is done at once.'

'Wait,' he said. 'Come back in here and shut the door, Rhiannon. I won't bite.'

Reluctantly she came into the room and stood looking at him anxiously. 'Was there something else, sir?'

'You think me a cad, don't you, Rhiannon?'

'It's not my place to think anything of the sort, sir,' she replied, her eyes downcast.

'For heaven's sake, can't I find a woman who will speak her mind without beating around the bush?' He looked at her more kindly: she was a servant in his employ and he was putting her in an invidious position. 'Look, Rhiannon, I know you think I'm all sorts of a villain to bring another woman into the house but it was a mistake and I won't be repeating it.'

'Right you are, sir,' Rhiannon said flatly.

'So what are you thinking about me? That I am as hateful as all those men who paid you for your services? Right now that's the way I feel about myself.'

Her expression softened. 'I know men have needs, sir,' she said at last, 'and I know they have little control over them.' She glanced at him. 'But a man who demeans a woman demeans himself.'

Dafydd took a sharp breath. He had asked for the truth and he had certainly got it. 'You're quite the philosopher, aren't you, Rhiannon? I didn't expect it from a girl of your background.'

'Because you see me as a woman without morals, sir, doesn't mean I lack intelligence.'

'No, I'm beginning to understand that. Will you pour me a brandy, Rhiannon? I feel in need of one.'

She obeyed at once and handed him the glass.

When he took it, she stepped back a pace.

'I'm not the heartless man I appear to be, Rhiannon,' he said. 'I'm sometimes very lonely and unhappy.' Why on earth was he unburdening himself to a servant? 'My wife no longer loves me, I have no heirs and no likelihood of heirs because my wife refuses to have me in her bed.'

Rhiannon remained silent, though her large eyes seemed to hold a certain sympathy.

'I can't blame her. I married Jayne while I was still in love with another woman and it didn't take her long to realize that.' He drank his brandy and looked straight at her. 'Rhiannon, I'm not the unfeeling monster you believe me to be.'

'No, sir.'

He watched as she moved to the door and his heart sank. He hadn't touched her with his words; she was still wary of him, and in truth he couldn't blame her.

'That will be all.' He waved his hand dismissively. Why couldn't he do without women? They were more trouble than they were worth.

*   *   *

Rhiannon was glad to escape to the kitchen. 'Is there a cup of tea going, Mrs Jones?' she asked, flopping into a chair.

'Aye, just freshly made, too. Hetty and Vi are still in the scullery. Now, come on, Rhiannon, tell us all about this woman the master brought home.'

'I don't think he'll see her again,' Rhiannon said. 'He wasn't overly pleased with her. Oh, he wants his bed stripped and remade. Vi,' she called, 'come in here, I've got a job for you.'

Violet came into the kitchen, a hangdog expression on her face. 'More jobs? My poor feet are killing me as it is.'

'It's just that the master wants his sheets changed. Go on, it won't take you long.'

'Can't Hetty do it?'

'No, she can't, so get a move on, girl,' Mrs Jones said impatiently. 'I don't want the master complaining about us to Mrs Buchan when she gets home.' Violet left the room, dragging her feet.

Rhiannon gratefully took the cup of tea the cook handed her. She envied Mrs Jones who could rest whenever she had a spare minute. Being a housekeeper was more tiring than she had imagined—much more so than lying on her back all day, but at least now she had some dignity.

'What you smirking about, Rhiannon?' Mrs Jones rested her plump arms on the table. 'You looked like you was thinking about a lover then.'

Rhiannon laughed. 'All of them? I'd have to spend the rest of my life remembering all the men I've slept with.'

Mrs Jones clicked her tongue in disapproval. 'Really, Rhiannon, I don't think you should remind everyone what your trade used to be.'

'What's the point in hiding it? So long as Mrs Buchan knows the truth and is satisfied with my work there's nothing to worry about.'

'I suppose not.' Mrs Jones shifted her feet. 'What was it like being a woman of the town?' She glanced over her shoulder in case anyone was eavesdropping.

'It wasn't any fun,' Rhiannon said. 'At least, not until I met Bull Beynon. He made everyone respect me and life was different then. But he married a good woman, and who can blame him? Perhaps one day I'll meet someone else who will love me in spite of my past.'

'Bull Beynon, now there's a man to pine for.' Mrs Jones winked. 'I've seen him about town and if I was twenty years younger I'd give him a run for his money.'

'Mrs Jones!' Rhiannon pretended to be shocked. 'I thought you were long past thoughts like that.'

'Aye, maybe I am, but a body's got to have dreams. Well, this won't get the work done—I'll be glad to finish and get to my bed.'

'You go on up, Mrs Jones, I'll see to what's left.'

'There's good you are. The breakfast table has to be set for the morning and the fire in the kitchen needs damping down, but Hetty can do that. Go get her, Rhiannon. She and Vi have been hanging around that new young footman too much.'

She heaved herself to her feet and in the flickering light of the candle Rhiannon could see the weariness on her face. What a fate to work until you drop! Was that to be the pattern for her own life?

CHAPTER TWELVE

Llinos sat in the sun-filled conservatory and closed her eyes, enjoying the warmth. Eynon was busy watering the plants, even though Llinos had asked him to leave it to her gardener. He was getting stubborn in his old age.

She opened her eyes and looked at him: he was absorbed in examining an orchid. He was so dear to her and so much a part of her life that she couldn't imagine being without him. He looked up and met her gaze. The sun glinted on his pale gold hair and his grey eyes appeared incredibly blue in the bright light. 'What are you looking at me like that for, Llinos?' There was a wry smile on his face. 'Were you wondering when I grew so old?'

'I was just thinking what a handsome man you are,' Llinos replied. 'And you aren't old because if you are then I am too, and I refuse to be old.'

He put down the watering-can and came to sit beside her. The sun shone in through the glass and it was hot in the conservatory. The curve of the orchid bed threw a shadow on the marble floor and Llinos felt she might have been in some exotic land rather than here in her own house. Eynon seemed to read her thoughts. 'It was a good move to have this glasshouse built.' He smiled. 'I never like conservatories usually because they seem to imprison the plants, which should be free to breathe the fresh air,' he said, taking her hand, 'but you have brought such exotic plants and flowers here that I can only applaud your ingenuity and imagination, Llinos.'

'Flatterer.' Llinos squeezed his hand. She glanced covertly at him: he was smiling, happy as always to be close to her.

'Why don't you marry me, Llinos?' he asked. 'I will never grow tired of asking you, so you might as well say yes.'

'Let me think about it a little longer, Eynon,' Llinos said gently. She had got through the worst of the winter alone and yet, as the months went by, she was increasingly lonely. 'How is Jayne and why has she gone off on yet another trip all alone?'

127

'She's not alone. She has Sal with her.'

'I know, but Jayne is hardly likely to talk much to a servant, is she?' Llinos looked at Eynon thoughtfully. 'She isn't meeting a lover, is she?'

'I doubt it,' Eynon said. 'Buchan says she's frigid.'

'All the same, she seems quite taken with that London man.'

'Guy Fairchild,' Eynon said. 'She certainly enjoys his company but you know how strait-laced she is.'

Llinos, too, had been strait-laced until she met Dafydd Buchan. But her fall from grace had come after Joe had been unfaithful to her and hurt her so badly that she no longer believed in her marriage vows. Did Jayne feel the same about Dafydd? 'Jayne must feel she owes no loyalty to Dafydd,' Llinos said. 'After all, he's had many lovers, too many to count.'

'And does that still trouble you, Llinos?' Eynon's tone was anxious.

Llinos shook her head. 'I got over Dafydd Buchan a long time ago. He means nothing to me now and I can say that with my hand on my heart. I don't know why he fascinated me so much in the first place.' She paused. 'I looked on him as a hero, a man who helped those less fortunate than himself.'

'I'm sure that was part of Jayne's infatuation for him but the lustre soon wore off their marriage. Still, I don't think she is the type of woman who would take her revenge by sleeping with another man.'

Llinos was not so sure: Jayne was a sensible, mature woman, and if she wanted a liaison she would plan it carefully, like a military manoeuvre.

'Well, we can't live our lives through our children,' she said. 'Look at me, two sons and I hardly ever see them.'

'Well, marry me, and we can keep each other company by the fire when the nights are cold.'

Llinos laughed. 'Don't you ever give up, Eynon?'

He took her hand. 'I'll never give up on you, Llinos, you can be sure of that.' He bent over suddenly and kissed her full on the lips, and it was then that Llinos felt the first stirrings of passion for the man she'd looked on all her life as a friend.

*   *   *

Rhiannon sank back in her chair and closed the account book with a sigh of relief. These days, with Mrs Buchan away, she was handling almost everything to do with the running of the house. It was a lot of hard work and sometimes she felt she needed the mistress's guidance. What's more, she missed Sal too, especially at night.

Some nights, tucked up in the warmth of their beds, they talked about what sort of day they'd had and usually ended up thanking the Almighty for their new way of life. Occasionally they talked about the old days when neither of them had known where the next meal was coming from. Sal was the only one, apart from herself, in the household who understood what being on the street meant.

Rhiannon looked round the small office Mrs Buchan had provided for her. It was warm and cheerful, with plenty of oil lamps and a good fire roaring in the grate. She was lucky to be in such a position. She closed the cover of the inkwell and wiped the nib of her pen.

Rhiannon felt a warm glow as she thought about her work. Now she could order food in large quantities, she could take stock of linen and cutlery and, best of all, she was entrusted with the accounts. Rhiannon had always been good at reading and writing. Naturally quick as a child, she had been well educated by the lodger. What a pity his teaching hadn't stopped there. She shuddered as she thought of his hands touching her, holding her, while he did unmentionable things to her.

Rhiannon rose from her chair and stood close to the fire, staring into the flames. Where would she go from here? Would she always be a servant at someone's beck and call, or could she aspire to higher things?

A coal shifted in the grate, the tick of the clock seemed suddenly loud in the silence, and all at once Rhiannon felt terribly alone. All her skills at housekeeping, all her cleverness with figures did nothing to assuage the loneliness she felt when she thought of Bull and of the lowly home she'd shared with him on the trackside of the Great Western Railway.

She picked up the account books and slid them into the shelf above the desk. It was time she joined Mrs Jones and the maids in the kitchen for a chat before bed.

In the hall, she came face to face with Mr Buchan. Rhiannon nodded respectfully and would have passed him by but he held out his hand and stopped her. 'Rhiannon, I have had a letter from Mrs Buchan. She is coming home tomorrow. I want you to strip the bed in her room and cover the furnishings with dust sheets. From now on my wife will obey me and sleep in my room.'

Rhiannon hid her surprise. She didn't think Mrs Buchan would stand for such high-handedness. Still, as a servant it was her place to obey and not to ask questions. 'Shall I see to it in the morning, sir?' She was bone weary and her eyes were almost closing. When the master shook his head she suppressed a sigh.

'I want it done now.' His speech was a little slurred and it was clear he had drunk a great deal of brandy. 'I am wearied by women disobeying me, Rhiannon.'

'Yes, sir.' She kept her eyes averted. She knew he was referring to her own refusal to sleep with him as much as to his wife's. 'I'm sorry, sir.'

He caught her arm. 'Why won't you come to my bed, Rhiannon? Am I not as good as the navvies for whom you spread your legs so willingly?' Then he slumped against her and she realized he was almost unconscious. She propped him against the door lintel and rang the bell for the footman. He came at once, thinking the master had summoned him. The look of astonishment on his face when he saw the state of Mr Buchan was almost funny. 'Help me get him upstairs,' Rhiannon said sharply, and he obeyed at once. Together, they managed to get Mr Buchan into bed. She did not undress him, just pulled a blanket over him and snuffed out the candles. Then she went to carry out his orders. It would be interesting to see what Mrs Buchan made of the arrangement.

*　　*　　*

Jayne was waiting in the foyer of St Anne's Hotel

131

for Guy to join her. She saw him come in, watched his graceful stride as he crossed the floor towards her and felt a sense of pride: this man was in love with her.

He came close and held out his hands to her. She smiled up at him and then, disregarding the other people in the foyer, kissed him briefly on the lips. He held her close, and warmth flooded her at his touch. Perhaps it was wrong to feel this way, disloyal, a breaking of all her marriage vows, but at least she knew she was alive and that she was not frigid, as Dafydd claimed.

Reluctantly, she drew away from him. 'We're playing with fire, Guy.'

'Come away with me—for good. What does anything else matter if we're happy?'

'I couldn't do that, Guy. What about my father? He's getting older now, he needs me.'

'He would understand better than anyone how you feel. He's never liked Buchan, has he?'

'No, but he would be angry if I left my marriage to live as a mistress.'

'You would be like a wife to me, Jayne, I promise you. Just say you'll think about it.'

'I will. It would be hard to think of anything else.'

They ate a meal they hardly tasted, sitting at an elegant table beneath the flickering candles in the chandeliers, and Jayne felt as though she was in a world of magic, where reality had no place.

She drank some wine, and then some more, and soon running away with Guy seemed a reasonable thing to do. After the meal, Guy led her to their favourite sofa in the hotel's almost empty salon. She felt a rush of passion that frightened and surprised her.

'I want to take you to bed.' Guy's eyes were dreamy; his fingers traced a pattern along her jaw and came to rest on her lips. 'I want to be with you at every moment of the day, my sweetest Jayne. How can I live without you now that I've found you?'

'Please, don't torture me. I don't think I'm ready to give myself to you.' She rested her head against his shoulder and his arm encircled her. She felt safe, warm and protected.

'I never thought I'd talk like this to any woman, Jayne, but I wish I was a poet so that I could make up the words to tell you how much I feel for you. Instead I have to rely on plain speech to say that I love you enough to lay down my life for you.'

She looked into his eyes and knew that she wanted him with an urgency she could not deny. Why was she so reluctant to cross that final barrier? All her life she'd been taught that chastity was a virtue, but what did it give you except empty nights and an empty bed? 'I'm going upstairs now.' She took a deep breath. 'Wait for fifteen minutes then come to my room.'

He held her hands. 'Are you sure, Jayne? You know I wouldn't force you to do anything you didn't want to.'

'I was never more sure of anything in my life,' Jayne said, and meant it. Tonight might be her only chance to experience real passion. Her heart was thudding as she went to her room.

Sal was drawing back the bed covers. Jayne looked down at her silk nightgown with its lace edging and realized it would cover her from neck to feet—not the sort of nightgown to greet a lover in,

133

but it would have to do. 'Help me undress quickly, Sal, and then you can go to your room.'

Sal looked at her in surprise. 'Are you sure you won't need me for anything else, Mrs Buchan?'

'I'm sure.' Jayne smiled. 'You get an early night—I've been keeping you up far too late, and you're looking peaky.'

Soon, Jayne was in her nightgown, settled in a chair near the fire. Her mouth was dry with fear. Was she more afraid of Guy coming to her room or that he might change his mind and stay away?

Sal was putting clothes away slowly. 'Leave that, Sal.' Jayne was aware that her voice was sharp. 'I want a little peace before I go to bed.'

When Sal had gone Jayne smoothed down her nightgown and looked at her bare feet. What if she proved a disappointment to Guy? What if she felt the same indifference when he made love to her that she felt when Dafydd had come to her bed? Should she just lock her door and not answer when he knocked? She was so confused, so afraid, but excited too.

She heard the rattle of the door-handle and held her breath. He was here: this was the moment that might change her life for ever.

Guy came quietly into the room and knelt before her, resting his head on her knees. She ran her fingers through his hair, thick and springy to the touch. She tipped his face up to hers and looked at him for a long moment. And then he took her in his arms and kissed her deeply, passionately. A riot of sensations raced through her body. Jayne felt as if she was in a dream when Guy stood up, drew her to her feet, then lifted her in his arms and carried her to the bed.

She watched as he took off his clothes. His body was beautiful, strong and lean, and he stood for a moment looking down at her with such love in his eyes that Jayne wanted to cry. She held out her hand. 'Come to bed, Guy, please.'

He slid in beside her, his arms encircling her, holding her close. Neither of them spoke as Guy gently opened the buttons on her nightgown. He slipped his hand inside and cupped her breast. Jayne closed her eyes: she wanted this, it was so right, and nothing could ever rob her of the memory of this night. His touch on her nipples made her gasp with delight. His mouth was hot on hers, his tongue probing. Jayne clung to him. 'Now,' she said.

When he came to her, she was ready for him; her hands ran over him as she pressed herself against him. His breath mingled with hers and his mouth tasted sweet as he kissed her.

He made love to her gently at first and then with growing passion. Jayne heard her own voice cry out as sensation upon sensation encompassed her. And then, shuddering with pleasure, she became quiet in his arms, drowsing in a state of bliss. She had never known that being with a man could feel like this. It was as if Guy had given her a precious gift, one she would hold on to until the day she died.

*   *   *

'So, you've come home to me like a dutiful wife, Jayne,' Dafydd said, the sarcasm ringing in his voice. 'And from now on you'll sleep in my bed.'

'I haven't come home to *you*,' Jayne said. 'On the contrary, I'm leaving you, Dafydd. All I want is to pack some of my things and then I'm going.'

'I don't believe you,' Dafydd said. 'You haven't the courage to leave me.'

'Just watch me.' Jayne went upstairs with Sal trailing behind her. 'Fetch Rhiannon and then you can pack some clothes for me, Sal,' she said. 'I'll just collect my papers.' She went into her room and stopped suddenly. Everything was covered in dust sheets. How dare Dafydd do this to her? Well, it was one more nail in his coffin. 'Go on, Sal, fetch Rhiannon for me,' she said briskly.

Sal ran off as fast as she could. Jayne imagined the girl breaking the news to the rest of the servants. They and the whole of Swansea would have something to gossip about now, something that would be more than a seven-day wonder.

'Yes, Mrs Buchan, you wanted me?' Rhiannon, her eyes wide, came into the room and stood with her hands clasped in front of her.

'I want to know what's going on here. Why is my room closed up like this?'

'Mr Buchan's orders, ma'am. He made me move your things into his room.'

'Oh, did he? Well, it makes no difference because I'm leaving,' Jayne said. 'But I want you to look after things here for a while. You can continue to do the books and report to me at the end of the month. I'll give you an address before I leave and later you can join me if you want to.'

'I do want to, Mrs Buchan.' Rhiannon hesitated.

'What is it?'

'Are you sure about this? It's a big step to leave your husband.'

'It's what I want.' Jayne scribbled the address of the house Guy had rented for them that morning

136

and gave it to Rhiannon. 'No one else is to see that.'

'I understand, Mrs Buchan, and I'll do my best to see that everything runs smoothly here for the rest of the month.'

'I know you will. Now, bring my bags down into the hall, would you, please?' Jayne hurried downstairs and saw that Dafydd was standing in the hallway waiting for her.

'So you really mean to leave me, do you?' he said. 'Why now, after all this time?'

'I've had enough of you. What on earth made you think I'd share your bed again?' Jayne said. Dafydd grabbed her arm and Jayne twisted away from him. 'Would you bully me into staying, Dafydd?'

'Oh, go.' He flung her away from him. 'But you'll never meet another man who'll treat you as well as I have.'

'You think not?' Jayne smiled. 'Well, Dafydd, your opinion is of no interest to me. You've bored me ever since the day we were married. I don't know why I wanted you in the first place.'

Sal came into the hall with Jayne's reticule and stood shifting from one foot to the other. Jayne motioned her to open the door. The fresh breeze washed into the hall carrying with it the scent of apple blossom. 'Goodbye, Dafydd,' Jayne said. 'I hope you'll be happy. At least you'll have your mistresses to keep you busy.'

'Go back to your father like the spoiled child you are.'

His words stung. 'You are the one who is acting like a child. And I'm not going back to my father,' Jayne said. 'I'm a woman of independent means—

or have you forgotten?'

'Well, it's of no concern to me where you go.' Dafydd turned on his heel and walked towards the drawing room. 'You're not taking the servants, though. Rhiannon, put those bags down and you, girl,' he gestured towards Sal, 'you're not to lift a finger to help the mistress, is that understood?'

Jayne shrugged. It was Dafydd's last attempt to humiliate her. 'That's all right, Sal, you stay. I'll send for you when I need you.'

Jayne went outside and threw her bags into the carriage. The driver shook the reins, clucked at the horses and they moved forward along the drive. She sat back in her seat and sighed with relief as the distance between herself and her old life widened. Now she could look forward to a new life with the man she loved.

She was about a mile away from the house when she heard the thunder of hoofs behind her. She glanced over her shoulder to see Dafydd gaining on her effortlessly.

He caught the reins of the carriage horses and pulled them to a halt. Then he came round to the door and stuck his head through the window. 'Is it true you're going to Guy Fairchild?' he demanded.

Jayne lifted her head. 'You got it out of poor little Sal, did you?'

'Never mind that. Let me just tell you what a fool you are.' Dafydd was smiling, his hair ruffled by the wind, his cheeks red from riding. Even now, angry though he was, he was a handsome man. How strange that his looks failed to move her.

'I put Guy up to this, I told him to talk sweetly to you to get you to sell him the railway shares.'

'Liar!' Jayne said quickly. 'Guy wouldn't do

anything like that. You're just making it up because you can't believe I'm leaving you.'

'You stayed at the St Anne's Hotel and Guy joined you there at my request. Ask him, if you don't believe me.'

'I will. Now, let me pass, Dafydd, before I start to scream and bring the tenants running from their houses.'

'I'm telling you the truth, Jayne.' Dafydd spoke earnestly. 'Now Guy has played me false and taken you from me. I never wanted that.'

'What would Guy have to gain by taking me away from you?' Jayne asked desperately.

'Have you spoken about the shares?' Dafydd asked. 'No need to answer, I can see that you have. You offered them to him, didn't you?'

'What if I did?' Jayne lifted her chin. 'Guy is a rich and successful man. Why would he want a few railway shares?'

'Because I offered him a handsome reward for them and then it must have occurred to him that he could have you and the shares. He told me he had a fancy for you, not that he would be married to you for a king's ransom but he thought a dalliance might prove amusing.'

'You're lying!' Jayne said dully, but somehow his words rang true. She bit back the tears of humiliation. Then she told the driver to turn back and they headed for the home she loathed. Of one thing she was certain: she wouldn't be staying there with Dafydd, but neither would she be running off with Guy. All men were cheats and liars and from now on she wouldn't be dependent on any of them.

CHAPTER THIRTEEN

Dafydd was seething with rage as he stared at his wife across the long dining-table. Jayne looked pale and sick. She had spent the night in one of the servants' rooms, determined not to sleep with him at any cost. Well, that was going to change.

'So, I can assume that Guy Fairchild had his way with you?' Dafydd said, ignoring Sal who was pouring his tea. Jayne gestured to Sal to refill her cup. 'Go on, admit it, you've made me a cuckold.'

Jayne sparked into anger. 'All right, I admit it! And for the first time in my life I knew the happiness of being with a real man.'

Dafydd threw down his napkin and got up, his face red with anger. He grasped her arm and propelled her out of the room. How dare she make a whore of herself with Guy Fairchild? He pushed her into the bedroom and kicked the door shut with his foot.

'Tell me the truth, has he been in bed with you?'

'I've told you the truth. Are you too stupid to understand it?' She tried to extricate herself, but he tightened his grip. 'Dafydd, you're hurting me.' Her face was white and her eyes were dark with guilt. Dafydd knew then that she had been unfaithful to him, with a man he called a friend.

'You dirty whore!' He slapped her hard across the face and she tumbled back on to the bed. 'You have betrayed me and ruined a damned good friendship into the bargain. I see I'll have to teach you a lesson you'll never forget.'

He felt nothing but cold anger as he tore aside

her skirts. She tried to push him away but he easily overpowered her. 'You gave to another man what you have refused me, your legitimate husband. Well, I'll have no more of it!'

He thrust into her, wanting to hurt her, and he felt the burn of triumph as he heard her cries of distress. He felt no love, no joy, all he knew was that he would have his revenge on the woman who had made a fool of him.

As he pumped away at her, he was aware that she had become still and unprotesting beneath him. When he glanced at her white face he could see that she was crying. He felt no pity as he finished the act and rolled off her. 'From now on you'll do as I say.'

She put her hands over her face and he saw her shake with sobs. He felt glad that he had hurt her as she had hurt him. He left the room, turned the key in the lock, then went down to the sitting room. Suddenly his anger disappeared, like mist before the sun. He had acted like a beast—he had raped his own wife.

But how much could a man take? She denied him a normal marriage and, most importantly, children, yet she had allowed another man to be intimate with her. Well, he had dealt with Jayne. Now he must find Fairchild and thrash him to within an inch of his life.

He pushed himself out of his chair and went to teach Fairchild a lesson he would never forget. What Dafydd Buchan owned he kept, and that included his wife. He clenched his fists. He would not be satisfied until he had beaten the man senseless. Then, perhaps, he could begin to pick up the pieces of his life.

For some hours Jayne remained where Dafydd had left her, still and silent on the bed, her torn clothes in disarray around her. She felt like the whore he had called her, she felt dirty and used and, in that moment, she hated all men. At last, she roused herself and rang the bell for Rhiannon, wincing at the pain that burnt through her body. When Rhiannon came in, Jayne fell into her arms and cried bitter tears that stung her bruised face.

Rhiannon understood at once what had happened. She held her mistress gently, patting her back as though she was a child, and Jayne leaned against her, grateful for Rhiannon's comforting arms. After a while Rhiannon released her. 'Good thing I had the master key on my chain. I expect Mr Buchan forgot about that when he locked you in. Now, I'll get hot water fetched up and I'll soon have you feeling better.'

Jayne allowed Rhiannon to take over. She put rose petals into the bath and helped Jayne into the warm water, talking gently to her all the time. 'There, you'll soon feel better, let me help you wash.' Jayne relaxed as the warm water cleansed her body, washing away the odour of her husband. 'You've got some bad bruises coming up, ma'am,' Rhiannon said, 'but they'll soon fade. It's the memories that hurt most.'

'Did you feel like this when men used you, Rhiannon?' Jayne asked, in a small voice. 'Did you feel powerless to protect yourself against a man who would violate you?'

'Yes, I often felt like that, and the only thing I

wanted to do was to wash away the smell of the last man I'd been with. It was a terrible life, but you gave me and Sal the chance to escape it.'

'And you've repaid me a thousand times. What would I do without you, Rhiannon?' The water had cooled and, reluctantly, Jayne climbed out of the bath. 'I suppose I deserved it,' she said softly. 'I was unfaithful to my husband while I was away and he found out about it. No wonder he was angry with me.'

'No woman deserves to be raped,' Rhiannon said firmly. If she was surprised at Jayne's revelation she didn't show it. 'What will you do now?'

Jayne sat on the bed and held up her arms as Rhiannon pulled a clean shift over her head. 'I don't know.' Rhiannon untied her hair and began to brush out the tangles in smooth rhythmic strokes. 'Dafydd has made it plain that I'm to be an obedient wife in future and sleep in his bed, but I'll never do that,' she said. 'After what he did to me this morning I'll never forgive him.'

'Why don't you go home to your father?'

Jayne shook her head. 'My father is about to get something he's wanted all his life.' She sighed heavily. 'He's asked Llinos Mainwaring to marry him and I think she's going to accept. I can't spoil things for him by running to him for help now.'

'Well, you can't stay here, can you?' Rhiannon looked worried.

Jayne touched her hand. 'I'll survive but just now I'm too tired to think of anything.'

'What about the other man? Won't you go to him?' Rhiannon's eyes were full of sympathy. 'If this is a taste of what your husband is going to be like in future you won't be able to stand it—I know

143

that better than anyone.'

'No, I won't join Guy. According to my husband, Guy lied when he said he loved me.' She put her head in her hands. 'Men! Are they all cheats and liars?'

'Then set up your own home. You're a strong woman and you don't need a man. Look, Mrs Buchan, I know it will be hard for you to fend for yourself but in the end you'll have no choice. In any case, your husband would say anything to hurt you—he might be the one who's lying.'

'What Dafydd said made sense. It seemed they had made some sort of deal and Guy was to persuade me to let him have my railway shares. Then he would sell them to Dafydd at a profit.' She bit her lip and tasted blood. 'No doubt it was all a great joke—Guy Fairchild, the man who romanced a frigid wife and hoped to be paid handsomely into the bargain.'

'I thought Mr Fairchild was a real gentleman. And, what's more, I've learned not to take anything at face value. Speak to him, that's my advice. Give him a chance to put his side of the story.'

'You might be right. I'll think about it.' Jayne sat in her chair by the window, unable even to look at the bed where she'd been violated. She was exhausted and her head was pounding. 'I'll stay here while I think things out. Have Sal bring me a hot drink, Rhiannon, and something to soothe my headache.'

'Are you sure you'll be safe here, Mrs Buchan?' Rhiannon asked carefully.

Jayne forced a smile. 'Dafydd's done his worst. I'll sit quiet and think it all through before I do anything else.'

When Rhiannon had gone, Jayne looked out at the sun shimmering on the lily-pond in the garden. And then, abruptly, it went behind a cloud and the water looked dull and lifeless. Was life like that? A few minutes of brightness, then completely dark?

Sal came into the room and Jayne watched her put the tray on the table. The smell of the hot drink was enticing and Jayne took the cup between her cold hands.

'Shall I close the curtains, Mrs Buchan? The light won't bother your eyes then.' Sal spoke as though to an invalid, and it was obvious that she knew exactly what had happened to Jayne.

'No, open them wider—I'm tired of darkness.'

Sal fussed around her, plumping up the cushions. 'Here's a little rug to put over your knees, ma'am.' She looked at Jayne uncertainly. It was plain she had something more important to say.

'What is it, Sal?' Jayne sipped the strong-tasting drink and felt it run like fire down her throat.

'I heard the row, Mrs Buchan.' She spoke tentatively. 'I suppose the whole house heard it, but I was with you at the hotel and I think Mr Fairchild really loves you. He wouldn't do anything to hurt you.'

'Sal, you're still a child, what would you know?'

'Young I am, but I've known many men in my time and I can tell good from bad. See, it might be like this. Mr Fairchild thought it a lark at first to tempt those share things out of you but then he fell in love with you. It was as clear as daylight to me.'

A little shard of hope pierced Jayne's heart. Sal might be young but she was perceptive and, as she said, she knew men.

'Mr Guy didn't say much at all about money, did

145

he? He wasn't acting like a man wanting something from you. I could tell by the way he looked at you that he worshipped the ground you walked on. Let me take a letter to him, asking him to explain everything to you.'

'Thank you, Sal, I'll let you know later when I've had time to think.' Jayne finished her drink and put the cup on the tray. 'You can go now, and thank you for being so kind. I don't know what I'd have done without you and Rhiannon to take care of me.'

Jayne hardly heard Sal leave the room as she leaned back against the cushions. Her eyes were closing and her body felt weightless—the brew Sal had brought her must have been potent. She would sleep now, and when she had rested her head might be clearer. Then she could decide what to do about her future.

*   *   *

Dafydd rode swiftly through the streets, his whip in his hand, his head pounding. Guy would pay dearly for betraying him.

As he entered the town rain began to fall and thunder cracked overhead. Through the storm he could see the shimmer of lights from the windows of the tall houses along Henrietta Street. He stopped outside the one where Guy lodged.

The front door was locked but that didn't deter Dafydd. He put his shoulder to it and it gave easily. Rage gripped him as he made his way through the hall to Guy's rooms at the front of the house.

'What on earth are you doing?' Guy demanded. 'Why are you behaving like a thief, creeping

146

around the place?' Slowly, Guy put down the pen he was holding and got up. 'You know about me and Jayne.' It was not a question. 'I've fallen in love with her, Dafydd. I'm sorry, but I couldn't help myself.'

'*Sorry!* Is that all you've got to say, you bastard? Well, understand this, I don't take kindly to being cheated,' Dafydd roared. 'I certainly don't take kindly to any man sleeping with my wife, especially one who called himself a friend.' Guy's head dropped.

'Go on, deny it! Look me in the eye and tell me you never touched Jayne!' Dafydd bellowed.

'I can't.' Guy looked up then. 'I love her. I want to take her away from here—away from you.'

Dafydd moved swiftly and caught him by the throat. 'Not only that but you wanted the shares as well!'

'I don't care about the shares,' Guy retorted. 'It's you who's obsessed with them, not me.'

'Well, you won't have the shares and you won't have Jayne. I've taught her a lesson this morning, one she'll never forget.'

'What do you mean? What have you done to her, Dafydd?'

'I just took what was mine.' Dafydd shook him hard. 'Mine, not yours!'

'So you raped her,' Guy said coldly.

'She's my wife and I asserted my rights over her and, yes, if you like you can call it rape but my sweet wife enjoyed every moment of it.'

Before Dafydd had time to think Guy's clenched fist caught him on the temple. Dafydd reeled away from him but Guy struck him again, a tremendous blow to the stomach. 'You bastard!' Guy was almost spitting in fury. 'How could you hurt a woman like Jayne, you barbarian?' Then Guy's head came forward and Dafydd felt his nose crunch. Blood poured down his chin and dripped on to his shirt. This wasn't going as he'd planned. It was Guy who deserved the beating, not him.

He swung desperately and caught Guy squarely on the chin. Guy staggered for a moment then fell backwards on to the floor. Dafydd raised his whip and brought it down on Guy's shoulders, then began to thrash him in earnest, using the whip mercilessly, until at last his arm fell to his side. 'Keep away from me and my wife. If I see you again, it won't be a whip I'll bring but a pistol.'

As Guy attempted to rise Dafydd kicked him down again. Then he made his way out into the shadows behind the buildings. As he swung up into the saddle he was triumphant. Jayne would see no more of the scoundrel, he'd made sure of that.

When he arrived home, he looked for Jayne, anxious to tell her what he'd done to Guy. He found her sleeping in a chair in the bedroom. He shook her roughly and she sat up, staring at him in alarm. 'Dafydd, what have you done? Have you been fighting with Guy? Oh, God, is he all right?'

'I've given him the hiding he deserves.' Dafydd felt a great satisfaction as he saw the fear in Jayne's face. 'It's all right, I left him alive—just.'

Jayne stared up at him. 'I hate you, Dafydd. I hate you more than I thought it possible to hate anyone. I'm going to him! I'll kill you if you've hurt him.'

He caught her wrist. 'No, you won't. You'll stay here where you belong and I'll tell you exactly what I've done to your paramour.'

'Oh, Dafydd, what have you done? For God's sake, you haven't hurt him badly?'

'I don't think he'll come sniffing after you again.' Dafydd smiled, then winced at the pain in his split lips. 'Now, get some clean water and bathe my face as a wife should.'

He watched with satisfaction as Jayne fetched water and a clean towel and bathed his face, careful not to hurt him. She also brought him a cup of herbal tea and he drank it gratefully. At last he'd brought his wife to heel, which he should have done long ago.

Suddenly he felt weary and his bruised face ached. He climbed on to the bed and closed his eyes.

CHAPTER FOURTEEN

'The master's been fighting,' Sal gasped, as she rushed into the kitchen. 'I saw his face when I opened the door to him, all battered and bleeding he was.'

'Good,' Rhiannon said. 'I hope someone gave him the beating he deserved for the way he treated the mistress.'

'He didn't send for anyone to fetch water. Mrs Buchan must have cleaned him up herself.' Sal frowned. 'Horrible that is, a man making you do things when you can't even stand the smell of him.'

Mrs Jones wiped her hands on her apron. 'I never seen such carrying on in all my time as a cook to the gentry. Scandalous!'

'Well,' Sal said, 'I'm sorry for Mrs Buchan. She'll

have to get away from the master as soon as she can.' She sighed. 'Still, she's got everything, money, and most of all a mind of her own. She'll see her way through this, I'd bet my last shilling on it.'

Rhiannon felt as tired as if she'd been the one to suffer a vicious rape. She had washed Jayne, brushed her hair and dressed her in clean clothes, but she knew that it was inside that the woman would feel dirty. Suddenly she wanted Bull with an almost unendurable longing—he was the only one who had ever protected her from the horrors of Swansea's underworld. Then she was impatient with herself: why keep harking back to Bull and the time they had spent together? That part of her life was over and done with. She should put the past behind her. She was a new person now with a new life, and she must just get on with it.

*   *   *

That day was the longest Jayne had ever endured. She stayed in the bedroom and ignored Dafydd when he came in and glanced at her, uncertain how to speak to her. She believed he was shocked by his own behaviour and wanted to make things right between them. But things would never be right now: he had killed any last spark of respect she had had for him. She had spent the long day making plans in her head and they did not include living with Dafydd Buchan.

That night, she lay in bed beside her husband and watched his regular breathing, afraid to move a finger. She knew he was deeply asleep but she still waited, wanting to be sure he wouldn't wake and prevent her leaving.

150

At last, she edged out of bed and leaned against the bedside table for support. She hardly dared breathe in case she woke him. Carefully, she tiptoed across the room and cautiously opened the door. She paused to look back but Dafydd hadn't stirred.

Out on the landing, she waited for a long time, making sure that her husband was still asleep, then went upstairs to the maids' quarters and found some plain, workaday clothes that fitted her. She was almost ready to leave but she had one more task to do, and that meant going back into the bedroom where Dafydd was sleeping.

She stood outside the door, holding her breath, until she had plucked up the courage to go inside. Quickly she found a bag and put some clean clothes into it, then opened her jewel box and took out a few of her favourite gems, which she pushed into the bottom of the bag. The rest she wrapped in a chemise, then edged her way back on to the landing.

She went into the kitchen and hastily scribbled a note to Rhiannon, saying the jewels were hers to do with as she wished. The girl would probably need them when Dafydd found out his wife had gone: he'd be sure to think Rhiannon had had a part in it. She breathed in the clean smell of the room. The table, scrubbed white, seemed to glow in the soft light, attesting to the industry of her servants. She would miss them more than she would ever miss Dafydd.

Once she had believed she loved him. When they married, she was young and headstrong, and thought Dafydd was a hero. Now she was living to regret ever having known him.

151

She pulled her cloak close around her and crept along the back corridor, afraid even now that Dafydd would wake and drag her back to bed. She winced as the bolt ground back, but then she was out in the open and running across the gardens towards the gates and freedom.

*   *   *

'*Duw!* What's all this, then?' Mrs Jones asked, her brow furrowed, her eyes still half closed in sleep.

'It's a letter from the mistress.' Rhiannon sat down and wished Violet would get the fire going. She read the brief letter, then handed it to the cook. 'She's gone, run away,' she said quietly. 'There's going to be the devil to pay when the master finds out.'

Mrs Jones stared at the scrawled letter in bewilderment. 'Well, she says there's a gift for you, Rhiannon, for all your kindness to her.' She sank into a chair and rubbed her eyes. 'Get on with that fire, Vi, and stop pushing your nose into other folk's business. I could murder a cup of tea.'

'I only did what any human being would do,' Rhiannon protested. 'I washed her and dressed her after Mr Buchan . . . well, you know.'

'Aye, I know right enough. Our betters can be just as bad as the basest navvy working the tracks.' She pushed Rhiannon's arm. 'Go on, then, open the cloth, there's a good girl. Put us all out of our misery.'

Slowly, Rhiannon unwound the chemise. 'Dear heaven!' She looked down at the glittering gems in disbelief. 'What on earth has Mrs Buchan left me these for? Where am I going to wear such

152

baubles?'

'You don't wear 'em, girl,' the cook said. 'You take them one by one to Uncle Ben's pawn shop and make some money on them. You'll never go short again, and I suppose that's what Mrs Buchan intended.' She leaned over Violet as she knelt before the grate, coaxing the fire to burn. 'And you, miss, keep your mouth shut about all this. If word of it gets out to the other servants I'll know who to lay into with my stick.'

'All right, all right.' Violet glanced over her shoulder. 'I 'aven't seen nothing and I don't know nothing, right?'

'That's the way. Now, get the kettle on and let's have some tea. I'm parched. And as for you, Rhiannon, put those jewels away somewhere safe, and whatever you do, don't let on to the master that you've got them.'

Rhiannon folded up the chemise and hurried to her room. She tucked away the jewels and the note in her shabby bag and put it at the back of the cupboard. Mrs Jones was right: the gift Mrs Buchan had left her was as good as money in the bank.

*   *   *

Work in the kitchen was well under way when the bell rang loudly for Rhiannon to attend the master. 'Look out, he knows the missus is gone now,' Sal said warningly.

Rhiannon smoothed down her skirt. She was not looking forward to facing Mr Buchan's anger. She walked slowly up the stairs from the kitchen and paused for a moment in the hall. It was raining outside and she thought of Mrs Buchan outdoors in this awful weather all alone.

'Where is she?' Mr Buchan slammed the door of the sitting room behind Rhiannon. 'Where has my wife gone, Rhiannon?'

'I don't know, sir,' Rhiannon said truthfully. 'I haven't seen her at all this morning. Has she gone shopping, do you think?'

'Don't pretend to be more stupid than you are, girl. My wife has run off. Surely she confided in you?'

'But I haven't see Mrs Buchan since last night, sir, I give you my word of honour on it.'

'Honour? That's rich, coming from the mouth of a common prostitute.' He caught Rhiannon's wrist. 'I mean to find out where she is, so if you care about your future here in my house you'll show me the loyalty I deserve and tell me where my wife is.'

'I really don't know, sir,' Rhiannon said. 'I never saw her after she went to bed.'

'I don't believe you, Rhiannon. Give me one reason why I should.' He tightened his hold on her but she faced him fearlessly.

'If I had known she was leaving I'd have gone with her like a shot, sir,' she said firmly.

Mr Buchan looked at her searchingly then nodded. 'Yes, I believe you would.' He released her and sank into a chair, his head in his hands. Rhiannon felt a moment's pity for him, but his next words shattered it, like a stone breaking glass. 'I'm going to look such a fool! I, a respected businessman, can't control my wife! What are my colleagues going to think?'

'I wouldn't worry about that, sir,' Rhiannon said. 'I've heard some ladies talking about their husbands in a most disloyal manner, but not Mrs Buchan.'

'I don't care a fig about the ladies! I am concerned about the men of the town—I'm going to lose respect for this, don't you understand? But, then, why should you? You're just an ignorant girl who's been lifted above her station at my wife's foolish whim.'

'As you say, sir.' Rhiannon hung her head, hoping the tirade was over.

Then Mr Buchan stood up abruptly. 'If you didn't help her someone else did. Tell the servants to come to the hall and I'll speak to them one by one. I'll get to the truth if I have to dismiss the lot of you.'

It took the best part of a day for him to question all of the servants. Rhiannon was present at all times and she saw that the master wasted no time with Violet and Hetty, Sal and the other maids. It was the youngest groom who caught the full force of his temper.

'Now, Danny, did you drive Mrs Buchan to town in the early hours of this morning?'

'No, sir,' Danny stuttered. 'None of the horses have been out today because of the foul weather.'

'Well, you sleep over the stables, did you hear anything strange?'

'I thought I heard footsteps in the yard about four o'clock this morning, sir, but when I looked out through the window there was no one in sight so I never thought no more about it.'

'All right, you may go.' Mr Buchan stared at Rhiannon as the door closed behind the groom. 'Well, it looks like no one saw hide nor hair of my wife. Can you explain that, Rhiannon?'

'Well, sir, it's clear Mrs Buchan didn't want anyone to be involved with her disappearance. What she did she did alone.'

'I'm going down to the railway station to see if she boarded any trains today. You can go to the coaching inn and make enquiries there.' He stood up and stared at Rhiannon, his eyes narrowed. 'I can trust you to tell me the truth, can I?'

'I haven't lied to you in the past and I'm not going to start now, sir.' She prayed silently that the master wouldn't ask her if his wife had left a note because if he did she would have to lie through her teeth—anything to keep him away from Mrs Buchan.

It was late afternoon by the time Rhiannon was able to get into town. She alighted from the carriage and told the groom to wait. Danny was looking down at her from the driving seat as if he wanted to say something. 'What is it, Danny?'

'Well, miss, I did see something outside this morning but I was afraid to say anything to Mr Buchan.'

'What did you see?'

'Mrs Buchan was running like the wind across the yard. She was carrying a bag and I knew she was running away. Did I do right, do you think?'

'Yes, Danny, you did. Have you mentioned this to anyone else?' The boy shook his head.

'No, Miss Rhiannon, I been too afraid to speak otherwise I'd be blamed for not running straight to the master.'

'And why didn't you go to the master, Danny?' Rhiannon asked curiously.

'I was sorry for her, miss, and I wanted her to get away. I know things haven't been easy for her

156

lately.'

Rhiannon nodded. 'You did the right thing, Danny. Wait here, I won't be long.'

It was strange how the situation in the Buchan household had changed. At one time Jayne Buchan had frightened the wits out of the servants; now it was she who had gained their loyalty. Rhiannon remembered how she'd been warned about Jayne's temper and it was true that the mistress was irritable at times, but then who wouldn't be with a husband who slept with every woman he met?

Rhiannon sighed. Bull Beynon wouldn't ever be that sort of man; once he made his vows he'd be faithful unto death. She felt suddenly lost and alone. Life without Bull stretched endlessly before her and she knew she would never fall in love with any other man.

She called at the house Mr Guy Fairchild had rented but there was no sign of Mrs Buchan or anyone else. The windows were dark, giving the house a rather sinister appearance.

Her next port of call was the inn but Mrs Buchan was not there either. In all truth, Rhiannon hadn't expected her to be sitting there under the eyes of anyone who wandered in for a bite to eat or a mug of ale. She spoke to the landlord but he hadn't seen a lady travelling on her own.

Back in the street, Rhiannon looked up and down the length of the Strand, knowing her search was fruitless. Mrs Buchan was probably far away by now, ready to begin a new life as a woman alone.

Danny drove her to a few more inns along the roads of Swansea but at last Rhiannon admitted they were wasting their time. 'Come on, let's get back home,' she said.

Danny looked at her with big eyes. 'We'll be blamed for this. We'll all be dismissed and I can't afford to be out of work, not with my mother sick and my little sisters to keep.'

'Don't worry, Danny, you haven't done anything wrong. How can Mr Buchan blame you?'

Danny shrugged. 'I don't know but he will, mark my words.'

Rhiannon climbed back into the coach and settled her skirts around her legs. She adjusted her bonnet and retied the ribbons under her chin, wondering how long it would be before she was out on the street again. Danny was right: someone's head would roll because of Mrs Buchan's disappearance, and it would probably be hers.

When she returned to the house Rhiannon saw that the door to the sitting room was open. Mr Buchan came into the hall as she closed the front door. 'I'm sorry, sir,' she said, 'there was no sign of Mrs Buchan. No one at any of the inns had seen her.'

He took her arm and drew her into the drawing room, closing the door behind him. 'She's gone to that bastard Fairchild,' he stormed. 'Curse the man! I should never have brought him into my home or introduced him to my wife.' He was still holding Rhiannon's arm. 'You knew something was going on between them, didn't you, Rhiannon?'

'I knew nothing of the sort, sir.' Rhiannon pulled away her arm. 'I don't think Mrs Buchan is the kind of lady to discuss her affairs with the servants.'

'Ah, but you weren't an ordinary servant, were you, Rhiannon? For some unknown reason my wife favoured you above the others. I'm surprised you have stayed so long—she must have turned over a

158

new leaf and become less irritable.'

'You could be right, Mr Buchan.' Rhiannon's tone was guarded. She didn't know what the master required of her. Was it sympathy, or was his temper about to erupt? You could never tell with Mr Buchan.

'I still can't believe it,' he said bitterly. 'How could she do this to me? Her reputation is ruined and she's dragged my good name into the dust along with her own.'

Rhiannon knew that the mistress had been provoked: any man who took his wife by force wasn't worthy of respect but she kept her thoughts to herself.

Suddenly he spun round to face her. 'It's all your fault,' he said. 'You and that other whore you brought with you, your loose behaviour influenced my wife. Why else would she run away from a perfectly good marriage?'

'I don't think you can blame me or Sal,' Rhiannon said. 'Mrs Buchan is a determined lady, she didn't need to be influenced by the likes of us.'

He didn't answer, just rang the bell and ordered that Sal be brought to the sitting room. The girl came in, her head hanging, her shoulders slumped, as if she knew she was going to be chastised.

'You were with your mistress when she spent a few days away at the hotel. What did she get up to? Tell me, or it'll be the worse for you.'

'I don't know what you mean, sir,' Sal answered, her voice trembling.

'Look at me, girl!' Mr Buchan lifted her chin none too gently. 'Did she let that man into her bed when she was away?'

'I don't know, Mr Buchan, I didn't see any man.'

'Don't lie!' He slapped her face, and Sal stumbled, catching hold of a table to steady herself.

Rhiannon stepped forward but Mr Buchan pushed her aside. 'Come on, you little bitch, tell me everything that happened in that hotel or I'll take a horse-whip to you.'

Sal was white to her lips and Rhiannon could bear it no more. 'Leave her alone,' she said loudly. 'Does it make you feel big to terrorize a child like Sal? And before blaming the rest of us why don't you listen to your own conscience?'

'How dare you talk to me like that, whore!' He caught her chin in his hand, his fingers digging painfully into her skin. 'Who do you think you are, talking back to your betters? I've a good mind to flog both of you.'

'Wouldn't you rather rape us as you did your poor wife?' Rhiannon slapped his hands aside. 'I had to clean her up after you'd finished with her. The poor lady was beside herself with fear and pain. If you wanted to humiliate her you succeeded beyond your wildest dreams.'

'That's enough!' Dafydd Buchan thundered. 'Get out of my house right now, both of you, before I do something I'll regret.'

Rhiannon caught Sal's hand and pulled her out of the room. 'Come on, let's go upstairs and get our things. Quickly, Sal.'

'What'll we do? Where will we sleep? I don't want to be out on the road again.' Sal began to cry.

'Hush now,' Rhiannon said. 'We've got some good clothing and the gift Mrs Buchan gave me will pay our way for a long time yet.'

Once in her bedroom, Rhiannon began to stuff clothes into her bag. 'Make a bundle of your things,

160

Sal, and take some warm boots so we'll be all right in the winter.'

Suddenly the door burst open and Mr Buchan stormed into the room. 'Give me that!' He snatched the bag from Rhiannon's fingers and emptied the contents on to the bed. 'You will leave as you came, with nothing,' he said. He shook the bag and the soft chemise fell out, spilling jewels on to the floor. 'Oh, I see, you're a thief as well as a whore!' Mr Buchan snatched her wrist. 'You're not going anywhere until I've called a constable, and then, Miss High and Mighty, you can spend the rest of your life in gaol.'

He went out, leaving the tumbled clothes and jewellery where they had fallen. Rhiannon heard him turn the key in the lock and sank down on the bed, the fight gone out of her.

Sal burst into tears. 'I don't want to go to gaol, Rhiannon. I know what it'll be like—I'll be dragged out to serve any man who wants me and I won't even get a shilling for it to keep body and soul together.'

Rhiannon pulled her close and smoothed back her hair. 'Don't worry, Mrs Buchan left that note for me saying the jewels were mine, didn't she? He just didn't give me time to show it to him,' she said. 'We won't go to gaol, you'll see.'

CHAPTER FIFTEEN

Bull Beynon walked along the track inspecting the line minutely. There had been some trouble in the night: it seemed a coach had almost been derailed

161

and he needed to check there were no obstructions on this stretch.

'Everything looks fine, boss.' Seth Cullen was one of the navvies who had been left behind when the crew moved on to the up-country line. He was a local man with a good knowledge of the area and Bull had found him invaluable. Yet at one time Seth had been a troublemaker, fighting and drinking every night, chasing women and generally disturbing the peace. Seth had had a fancy for Katie, both of them coming from Irish stock, but she, a demure little miss, had brushed aside his advances in no uncertain terms.

Bull couldn't blame Seth: Katie was a beautiful woman and Bull had fallen in love with her the minute he'd set eyes on her. She was so sweet and innocent, her head full of hymns she'd learned at choir practice in the chapel. To Bull, used to the women of the shanty town, Katie was like an angel from another world. It never ceased to amaze him that she'd fallen in love with him too. And now they had a baby and Bull's heart swelled with pride: one day his son would have all the advantages Bull had never enjoyed.

He paused in his scrutiny of the line and looked out towards the bridge at the old Gorse Road without seeing the stone structure or the green fields that surrounded it. Here he was, Bull Beynon, family man, his goal to make his son as famous one day as the great Isambard Kingdom Brunel himself.

'Shall I go on ahead, sir?' Seth had drawn level with Bull and was waiting, hands thrust into his pockets, for directions from the boss.

'Aye, you go on, Seth.' Bull left the line and sat

on the grassy bank alongside it. He took out his pipe, lit it and drew on it with satisfaction. Seth watched him, rubbing his hands along his moleskin trousers. Bull smiled. 'All right, you can stop for a smoke as well if you like.'

Seth obeyed with alacrity. He perched himself lower down the bank, acknowledging Bull's superior position in the scale of things. He poked tobacco into the bowl of his pipe and sucked at it.

'I hear Rhiannon is doing well for herself,' he said, without looking at Bull. 'Housekeeper she is now, up at the Buchans' place. Not bad for a girl who was a camp-follower, eh?'

'Not bad at all,' Bull agreed. 'But, then, Rhiannon was always cut out for better things than being a navvy's woman.'

He thought of Rhiannon, waiting eagerly for his attentions as she lay beside him in the bed they had shared. She was a fiercely passionate woman, an intelligent resourceful woman. He had admired her when he lived with her, and he admired her still. How strange that the two women he cared about were so different. Rhiannon had been hurt by life while Katie had lived blamelessly. They were opposites in every way, yet somehow he had loved them both.

He examined his feelings: did Rhiannon still have the power to excite him with her dark, sultry beauty? No, he decided, he would always respect and admire her, but now there was only one woman in his life and that was his dear wife.

'I wouldn't wonder if Rhiannon don't get married to someone tidy, a footman or coachman or something like that,' Seth said. 'The girl deserves it, she's too good for the streets and you

163

must have known that when you took her in.'

'I did. Rhiannon will be a woman to be reckoned with, mark my words, and I wish her the greatest luck in the world,' Bull said quietly. 'She deserves it more than most.' Yet he felt a strange tug at his emotions to think of her with another man. He got to his feet abruptly. 'Right, we'd better get back to work otherwise we'll both be dismissed.'

Seth grinned. 'Can't see you getting the sack, Bull. Too valuable to the railway you are.'

Bull smiled without answering. Time, it seemed, had tamed the wildest wolf in the pack: Seth no longer brawled in the streets, or drank to excess; he was even renting a decent house. There was no doubt about it, the railway had brought prosperity not only to the rich of the town but to the ordinary working man as well.

Seth walked ahead a little further up the track and bent to examine the line that snaked towards Swansea. 'Look, something's here, Bull,' he called. 'A branch has come down from one of the trees and got wedged in the track. Could be dangerous.' He tugged at it but it wouldn't budge. 'Damn and blast!' He tried again, and a piece came away but the thick end was stuck fast. 'It won't beat me, boss. I'll get it out if it kills me.' He rubbed his hands on his trousers. He was still looking intently at the track when the whistle of an approaching train sounded faintly on the breeze.

'Get back from there, Seth,' Bull called urgently. 'Make it sharp—there's a train coming through the tunnel any minute now.'

'Plenty of time, Bull. One more pull and I'll get the bloody thing out.'

Bull began to run towards Seth. 'Leave it, Seth,

just get out of there! The train will be changing lines back here.'

Bull's warning came too late—he heard the sound of the train switching track and then Seth's agonized cry: 'God Almighty, I'm caught, Bull!'

Bull rushed towards Seth, fell on his knees and tried to prise apart the track with his bare hands. 'When I pull the line apart get your foot out of your boot, Seth.' His muscles screamed with the effort, but even Bull's great strength wasn't enough to move the rail.

He looked behind him and saw that the train was now in sight. He ran along the track pulling off his white scarf as he went. He began to call out and to wave the scarf above his head hoping to attract the attention of the driver.

The train seemed to be bearing down on him at great speed and still Bull stood in the middle of the line, calling and waving. He could smell the steam issuing from the tunnel and feel the heat of the cinders burning the grass at the side of the track. He ran back and grasped Seth round the waist. For a moment, the two men stood face to face each knowing what must happen.

'Go on, Bull, for God's sake do it.'

Bull used all his force to press Seth backwards on to the grass verge. He heard the crack as the man's leg snapped and Seth's cry, which was drowned by the rattle of steel upon steel as the train thundered towards them. He would never forget the startled look on the engine driver's face as he slammed on the brakes. The railway line seemed to scream in protest and still the train charged on. Bull lay across Seth as the man's body convulsed in pain and fear. And then it was upon them so close that Bull could feel the heat of the fire in the cab and see the sparks thrown up by the brakes.

The sound of Seth's scream as the train ran over his foot would remain with Bull until the day he died. The man struggled in his arms but Bull held him firm. The train came to a shuddering standstill a few hundred yards up the track.

Bull looked at Seth's mangled leg: the bone was protruding through the flesh, the foot severed. Bull wrapped his scarf around the exposed bone. He could not save Seth's leg but he might save his life.

CHAPTER SIXTEEN

Llinos was sitting in the conservatory reading a letter from Eynon. Yet again he was talking about marriage. Llinos loved Eynon, but could she make him a good wife?

She looked out of the window, not seeing the familiar bottle kilns that dominated the skyline, not even aware of the apprentices who shouted and laughed in the yard. Her life had been lived in the shadow of the potteries; she had been responsible for many of the designs on the quality wares but now perhaps she had no energy to keep the pottery fresh and alive? Watt Bevan would keep it flourishing and might bring in fresh ideas once she left him to make the decisions. He deserved to have a free hand, and it was about time she gave it to him.

She turned her back on the sight of her life's work, and in that one gesture, she knew Eynon had won. She would marry him and live out the remainder of her life in comfort, with the one man whose love for her had never wavered.

*   *   *

Rhiannon looked at the constable, knowing from the hard look in his eyes that he would spare her no sympathy.

'I didn't steal the jewels, you've got to believe me.' But even as the words left her lips, she knew they would make no impression on the man standing before her.

The young policeman with him was more sympathetic. 'You say that Mrs Buchan left you a letter, can you show it to us?'

Rhiannon rummaged once again through the spilled contents of her bag and shook her head. 'It's not here.' She looked up at Mr Buchan beseechingly. 'You must have seen it, sir, it was with the jewels.'

'I saw no such thing,' Dafydd Buchan said calmly, but his look told her that had she been more co-operative and gone to his bed she wouldn't be in this position now.

'Well, sir, we'll have to put her in the cells.' The hard-faced constable smiled thinly. 'And what about this young 'un here?' He gestured towards Sal. 'Is she guilty as well?'

'I've got no proof that the girl was in this with the so-called housekeeper,' Mr Buchan said, 'so you'd better take just the thief.'

'No!' Sal cried out. 'I saw the letter! I know Rhiannon didn't steal them things. Mrs Buchan wanted her to have them.'

Ignoring her, the constable caught Rhiannon by the arm. 'Come on, no nonsense now.'

Rhiannon nodded. 'Can I just say goodbye to Sal properly? I've looked after her for so long she seems like a little sister to me.'

'Aye, no harm in that.' It was the younger policeman who spoke. 'Go on, then, but don't make a meal of it.'

Rhiannon hugged Sal close and whispered in her ear, 'Find the letter, Sal, it's my only hope.'

'That's enough.' Her arm was grasped none too gently and Rhiannon allowed herself to be led from the house and into the waiting cab. She stared back at Sal, at the faces of Mrs Jones, Violet and Hetty, staring through the windows, and a lump rose in her throat. She was leaving behind the chance to be respectable. Now she was going to be a common gaolbird. She wanted to cry, but she wouldn't lower her dignity.

She was thrust into a carriage where she sat down and leaned back against the hard wooden seat. She closed her eyes, hearing the clip-clop of the horses' hoofs taking her to prison. She wished Mrs Buchan had never left her the jewels, then none of this would have happened.

The face of the prison was grim: it stared out across the Mumbles Road as if to challenge the sea itself as it rolled towards the shore. A sailing ship waited for the tide to take her out of the bay, the tall masts reminding Rhiannon of crosses in a graveyard. This was the last of the bay she would see for some time.

She was thrust unceremoniously into a room with no windows and bars over the door but at least she was on her own. She had expected to be pushed in with a crowd of cut-throats and thieves, all of whom would be flea-ridden and covered in sores.

'How long will I have to stay in here?' she asked, but the guard didn't bother to reply. He just slammed the door and walked away whistling.

The room was small, almost a cupboard. A wooden bench stood at one end and, even as she watched, a cockroach scuttled across its planks and began to climb up the wall. She had lived in some awful places but none had been as dark and desolate as this cell.

She stood near the door for a long time, hoping someone would come to fetch her, but at last she sank down on the bench knowing that she was inside the gaol at least for the night and perhaps for the rest of her life.

Tears burned her eyes but Rhiannon rubbed them away angrily. She would not cry—hadn't she learned yet that crying did no good? She lay down on the bench and curled her feet under her skirts for warmth. She must be prepared to wait. Sal would find the letter and, if necessary, steal it back from Mr Buchan. Then she would be set free.

*   *   *

Jayne sat up in bed and stared around her at the unfamiliar room. She'd come to St Anne's Hotel because she'd been there with Guy yet the empty room she occupied brought her no comfort.

A sliver of moonlight crept in through the open curtains. This was her second night away from home and Dafydd, but she still hadn't made up her mind what she was going to do. Should she go to Guy and ask him if he wanted her, or should she go home to her father?

She curled up, hugging the pillow to her, feeling lonely and wishing she'd brought Rhiannon with her or even Sal. She had hated leaving them at the mercy of her husband's anger. When he learned she'd run away the girls would be the first he would pick on. Still, they would be all right, even if Dafydd dismissed them both: the jewels she'd given Rhiannon would see them through, at least for a while.

It was a long time before Jayne fell asleep again. When she woke it was barely dawn, with a thin blue light and shadows stretching along the floor. The candles had burned out and the fire was mostly ashes, with a glowing ember here and there. Jayne sat up and looked ruefully at her crumpled dress. She hadn't even bothered to undress—all she'd done was kick off her leather boots.

She heard a light rap on the door and sighed with relief: one of the maids had come to see to the fire and to bring her breakfast.

'Come in,' she called, her voice still hoarse from sleep. The door opened and Jayne felt her breath catch in her throat. 'Guy!' He came into the room and closed the door behind him. He stood there for a long time just looking at her. 'Oh, Guy, your poor face!' She got up, went to him and touched the weals on his cheeks. 'My poor darling, you suffered all this for me!' Then she clung to him, and as his hands gently stroked her tangled hair, she realized she must look terrible, her eyes red and swollen with weeping.

'My little girl, thank God I've found you.' He held her close. 'I went up to the house when Buchan was out and questioned Sal, the little maid.

She told me what had happened. I hoped and prayed that I'd find you here.'

'Oh, Guy, have I done the right thing? Everyone in Swansea will know by now that I've run away from my husband. I won't be able to face anyone ever again, not even my father.'

'My darling, you've done the right thing—what does anyone or anything matter so long as we're together?'

'You're right.' Jayne rested her face against his neck, breathing in the scent of the man she loved. She knew she had to be with him, whatever it cost her. 'What are we going to do, Guy?' she asked. 'No one will want to speak to us, we'll be outcasts.'

'I don't care,' he said, 'just so long as I have you.' He hugged her close and kissed her eyelids, then her lips.

Jayne felt suddenly as though she had been roused from a long sleep. Dafydd had been the nightmare and now she was with her dream, the man she could love for all eternity—surely that couldn't be so wrong?

'We'll go back to Wales, perhaps to Cardiff,' Guy said. 'We can say we're married, no one will know any different.'

'Are you sure, Guy? Folk have a way of finding out every little secret and I wouldn't want to disgrace you.'

'No one will find out,' he said, 'and, Jayne, I wouldn't care if they did.' He kissed her again, then drew away from her. 'I'll book us seats on the mail coach for this afternoon.'

'Guy, you will come back, won't you?'

'Of course I'll come back. My life wouldn't be worth living without you.' He stood at the door for

171

a long time, simply looking at her. 'Jayne, I love you with every breath in my body. Just remember that, won't you?' And then he was gone.

Jayne rang the bell for the maid, rubbing the tears from her eyes and feeling lost and alone. For a brief moment she'd felt safe with Guy's arms around her.

The maid tapped on the door and opened it. 'I've come to build up the fire, miss, by your leave.' She bobbed a quick curtsy then bent down before the grate, poking sticks into the embers. Jayne guessed the girl had seen Guy come up to her room and doubtless had watched his departure too. Now her reputation would be in tatters: it just wasn't ladylike to entertain a man alone in her bedroom in the early hours of the morning.

Still, what did it matter? Whatever the maid thought would not change the situation. Jayne sighed. It was about time she washed and dressed in fresh clothing. By the time Guy returned she would be looking more like her old self.

Jayne was just tying up her hair when the door burst open. Startled, she looked round, her hand to her throat, as her husband stormed into the room. 'Dafydd, what are you doing here? How did you find me?'

He caught her arm roughly and dragged her to her feet. 'It wasn't difficult. Fairchild left a trail a mile wide.'

'What do you mean?'

'He was up at the house questioning the maids. Did he think I wouldn't learn about it?' He shook Jayne so hard that her hair fell down again. 'The fool didn't realize I was having him followed.'

He dragged her towards the door. 'Come along,

we're going home. I'm not going to be the laughing-stock of Swansea—the man whose wife ran off with his friend. You will play the faithful wife even if I have to kill you to do it.'

'No, Dafydd, I'm finished with you. I'll never live with you again and, whatever you say, you can't keep me prisoner for ever.'

'We'll see about that.' He pulled open the door and hustled her out on to the landing.

'Wait,' Jayne said desperately. 'I can't go without paying my bill.'

'It's already settled. Come on—and be quiet, or it will be the worse for you.' He smiled thinly. 'You won't get away from me, and I'll make sure that Guy Fairchild gets such a lesson in manners that he'll never come sniffing around you again. And it won't be a whip I'll use on him but a shotgun.'

'No, Dafydd, don't hurt him. It was all my fault, I asked Guy to take me away. If anyone's to blame I am.'

'Very touching, I'm sure. Now, do I have to carry you out of here?' He marched her down the stairs and Jayne bit her lip, trying to stop the tears flowing down her cheeks.

It seemed as if all of the hotel staff were in the foyer, as well as some of the guests. One of the porters sniggered as Dafydd dragged Jayne towards the door. 'That'll teach the flighty madam to play fast and loose,' he said gleefully.

Jayne's colour was high and her heart was thumping so loudly that she wondered if everyone could hear it. She prayed that Guy would not come back to the hotel until she and Dafydd were well out of sight. What might happen if the two men met didn't bear thinking about.

173

Dafydd took his horse's reins from the groom and pushed Jayne into the saddle. He swung up behind her and clicked his tongue, urging the animal into a gallop.

Jayne closed her eyes against the wind. She wanted to scream and cry that this was all wrong, that she belonged with Guy, that they were meant to be going away together but now Dafydd was ruining everything.

Several times, through the long, difficult journey, Jayne thought she would be unseated as Dafydd urged the horse faster. By now her eyes were streaming and she didn't know or care if it was the wind causing the tears or the terrible pain in her chest.

By the time they reached home Jayne was numb with cold and her clothes clung wetly against her legs as she slid down from the saddle. Dafydd dragged her into the house, pushed her upstairs and thrust her into one of the bedrooms. 'Undress,' he snapped, and when she stared at him, uncomprehending, he began to tear at her buttons.

'Are you going to rape me again, Dafydd?'

'Just shut up and get your clothes off!'

He tore at the fine material of her bodice but Jayne stood her ground. 'I am not getting undressed.'

'Yes, you are. Now either you undress yourself or I'll call the servants to hold you down while I take your clothes off for you.'

Jayne saw that there was no way out. Dafydd was more than capable of carrying out his threat. With shaking hands she took off her clothes until she stood in nothing but her chemise. She watched as Dafydd took the clothes to the door and threw them out on to the landing. He slammed the door, then came back to her and snatched her wrist.

'If you mean to force me then get on with it,' Jayne said.

'Don't flatter yourself,' Dafydd said. 'I don't need you, Jayne.'

'What about sons?' Jayne knew she was on dangerous ground but she couldn't resist the taunt.

'I have a son,' he said stiffly, 'or have you forgotten that?'

'If you mean the brat you fathered on Llinos Mainwaring then, no, I haven't forgotten, but the child is illegitimate or is that something *you*'ve forgotten?'

The slap came so abruptly that the shock forced Jayne back on to the bed. She put her hand to her chcek, blinking rapidly with the sudden pain of the blow.

'Are you not aware that I can make a will leaving everything to Sion Mainwaring?' Dafydd said, his face pale with anger.

'And will you recognize the boy publicly, then?' Jayne said, her voice rising.

'That is precisely what I intend to do. I'll proclaim it to the world, if need be.' He smiled maliciously. 'Though I'm sure most of the people in Swansea realized long ago that I am the boy's father.'

Jayne felt weary of it all. She wanted to lie down on the bed and close her eyes. 'I don't care a jot about you or your money,' she said quietly. 'You can go to hell, for all I care.'

Dafydd caught her wrists and closed his hands over them so tightly that she flinched. 'Now, madam, that's enough from you. Get this into your

175

head: you'll not see Fairchild ever again, do you understand?'

'And you understand this,' she said quietly. 'The time I shared with Guy was the best and happiest time of my life.'

Dafydd slapped her face again, harder this time, and she stared up at him, her eyes blazing. 'You hit me once more and I swear I'll do you harm, even if I have to wait until you're asleep to do it. And don't think I'll go to your bed again. Now that I've tasted real love I won't make do with second best.'

He pushed her away from him. 'You fool!' he said. 'I told you I put Guy up to it. He was supposed to get your shares out of you and he very nearly succeeded. You can't still believe the man loves you?'

'That is exactly what I do believe,' Jayne said coldly.

'Where is he now then?' Dafydd's voice seemed to penetrate her brain. 'Why has he not followed us? Because he saw you as a burden and a responsibility.' He paced about the room. 'Oh, a woman can be amusing for a while, just so long as she's another man's wife, but it's a different kettle of fish when she wants to be with you for ever. Suddenly the game isn't so enticing.'

He faced her. 'Guy wanted no more of you. He'd tasted the fruit and found it wanting. As for you coming to my bed, I wouldn't want you now. You're soiled goods, my lady.'

His words hurt her like stones. She tried to hang on to the thought that Guy loved her, but her confidence in him was shaken. Still, she wouldn't allow Dafydd to see how she felt.

'Perhaps you'll have the decency to leave me

alone now. I've had enough of you and your bullying ways, Dafydd, and I'll run away from here the minute I get the opportunity. You can't watch me all the time, can you?'

'No, but I can lock you in your room when I leave the house,' Dafydd said triumphantly. 'And without your friend Rhiannon to help you, you'll stay where I put you.'

'I thought you might blame Rhiannon but she had nothing to do with any of this.'

'Too bad, because she is behind bars, where she belongs. I've employed a steward to look after the affairs of the household and I'll make sure he watches your every move.'

'What do you mean Rhiannon's behind bars? What are you talking about?'

'You shouldn't have been so foolish and sentimental as to give her the jewels. I claimed she'd stolen them and the constable, of course, believed me.'

'How could you sink so low, Dafydd?' Jayne said. 'That girl never did you any harm.'

'Well, forget Rhiannon and think of yourself. You'll be just as much a prisoner as she is.'

'What about my father? Do you think he'll put up with you treating me so badly?'

'Your father will mind his own business.' Dafydd said, 'No one has the right to interfere between husband and wife.'

'You call yourself a husband? A man who has to imprison his wife to keep her is no man at all.'

Dafydd shook his head. 'I've had enough of this.' He strode towards the door and, with his hand on the latch, he turned to look at her. 'Why I ever married you I don't know. All you've brought me is misery.'

'Is that so?' Jayne said defiantly. 'Well, I could have made a much better match myself. All you are is a jumped-up potter from Carmarthen.'

He seemed about to speak again but then he let himself out of the room. Jayne heard the key turn in the lock and, wearily, she sank back on to the bed. She was shivering, so she slid between the sheets and pulled the covers over her but the cold had penetrated her bones.

She wanted to cry but the tears had formed a hard lump in her throat. 'Oh, Guy,' she whispered, 'please come and get me out of here.'

There was no response except for the shifting of the coals in the fire.

CHAPTER SEVENTEEN

'I'm sorry, Rhiannon, I've looked everywhere and I just can't find the letter.' Sal looked imploringly at her through the bars on the cell door.

Rhiannon did her best to smile. 'Don't worry, Sal, we'll think of a way out of this, you'll see.' She spoke bravely but her heart was sinking: without the letter she might be locked in this stinking prison for ever.

'It must be terrible in here for you, Rhiannon,' Sal said, 'with women screaming and men cursing and swearing. We'll have to get you out somehow.' She paused for a moment, biting her lip. 'I don't know how, mind, because I've done my best to talk to Mrs Buchan but the master keeps her locked in her room. He's making sure she don't run away again.'

'How can he treat his wife like that?' Rhiannon said, forgetting her own predicament for a moment. 'Why doesn't he let her go and find happiness where she can? It's obvious she doesn't want him.'

'He's afraid he'd look a fool if his wife went off with another man, and he's determined not to let that happen. He's even got a steward in to watch us all, a Mr Sanderson. He's horrible.'

Rhiannon sighed. Her position seemed hopeless. 'Well, I'm sorry for Mrs Buchan, the poor lady deserves better, but you'll have to talk to her, Sal, she's my only hope.'

'Don't you go feeling too sorry for Mrs Buchan. She's got water to wash in, nice clean sheets on her bed and food to eat. She's not living in a filthy prison like you.'

'Her room may not be dirty but it's a prison all the same,' Rhiannon said, 'and I know she'd help me if she could. Can you try to slip a note under her door or something, Sal?'

'Aye, I could try and I know she'd be down here in a flash to get you out.' Sal's face brightened. 'I could ask her to write another letter to say that she gave you the jewels—but it's going to be tricky, mind, none of us are allowed near her room.'

'Won't Vi or Hetty take a message to her?' Rhiannon asked hopefully. 'I know they'd do it if you asked them.'

'The master's got some other servants of his own besides Mr Sanderson. There's the new housekeeper, she's a hard-faced woman. I wouldn't like to come across her on a dark night.'

Rhiannon sighed. 'I don't know what I'm going

to do, then. It looks as if I'm stuck here for life.'

'Now, don't say that.' Sal pressed her face against the bars so that they made ridges down her cheeks. 'Mr Buchan's bound to let the mistress out some time, it stands to reason.'

'When have men like Mr Buchan ever acted reasonably? Like the rest of them, he thinks with what's in his breeches.'

Sal laughed out loud. 'Well, we knows better than most what men are like—we've had enough of them!'

'Keep your voice down, Sal!' Rhiannon cautioned. 'So far I've been left alone, but if anyone finds out what my trade used to be I'll have every man in the gaol after me.'

'Might not be a bad thing, mind,' Sal said. 'You might get out of here if you makes a friend of one of the guards.'

'Never again, Sal,' Rhiannon said. 'I'm never going to lie on my back for any man unless he's my husband.'

'Can't see you married somehow,' Sal said. 'You never going to have a bit of fun ever again, then?'

'If that's the way it's got to be.'

'Oh, look out, there's one of the guards coming now.' Sal glanced over her shoulder nervously.

Rhiannon, listening to the heavy footsteps getting nearer, felt sorry for the girl. 'Don't worry, Sal, no one can hurt you, not now.' She touched Sal's cold fingers as they curled round the bars. 'You're a respectable maid working for Mr Dafydd Buchan, businessman, and don't let anyone forget it.'

'You're right, but I'd better go anyway.' Sal's frightened blue eyes met Rhiannon's firm gaze. 'I'll try my best to do something for you.'

Sal sped away and Rhiannon rested her head against the bars on the door. If only she could get out of prison and set about clearing her name there would be hope for her. She might have lived the life of a whore but she had never stolen from any man, and there were a few who would testify to that.

After a moment, Rhiannon went to the back of her cell and sank on to the straw pallet. She closed her eyes and tried to rest, but the injustice of her situation burned within her and she knew it would be a long time before she found release in sleep.

*   *   *

'Mrs Buchan.' The voice at the door was little more than a whisper. 'Mrs Buchan, it's me, Sal. You got to help us—Rhiannon is in terrible trouble.'

Jayne went to the door and pressed herself against it. 'I know, Sal, but what can I do about it?'

'You can tell them the truth. You know Rhiannon didn't steal them jewels you gave her, and it's terrible to see her in gaol. She'll die there if we don't get her out. You should see how thin she's gone.'

'Now, listen, Sal,' Jayne said, in a low whisper, 'you must find me some clothes and then you must get the master key and unlock this door for me.'

'Oh, Mrs Buchan, I don't think I can do that,' Sal said. 'It's only because the steward's gone out with Mr Buchan and the new housekeeper's asleep that I've been able to get up here at all.'

Jayne's heart sank. 'Oh, Sal, I have to get out of here or I'll go mad. Can't you do anything to help

181

me?'

'Well, I did a bit of lock-picking when I was . . . well, you know . . . so I could try and get your door open, I suppose.'

'Go on, then, Sal, try your best—you'll be well rewarded, I'll see to it.' Jayne heard Sal's light footsteps running away across the landing and then as she waited, hardly daring to breathe, she heard the girl return. There was a grating sound in the lock and Jayne looked round the room, wondering what she could cover herself with. Dafydd knew how to humiliate her.

The door opened and, cautiously, Sal came in. 'Here, mistress, put this on.' She held out a shawl.

Jayne took it gratefully. 'Good girl, Sal!' She looked ruefully at her bare feet. Sal immediately took off her own shoes. 'Have these, Mrs Buchan. I'm used to going barefoot and you're not.'

Jayne peeped out of the door but there was no sign of anyone on the landing or the stairs. Sal came out behind her, closed the door and locked it again with the bent pin she had used to open it.

'No one will realize you're gone until supper-time.' She led the way down the back stairs. 'We'll have to steal one of the horses,' she whispered. 'We'll go to your father's house—you'll be safe there.'

Jayne was amazed at Sal's common sense: the girl had never struck her as being very bright. On an impulse she caught Sal's arm. 'Thank you, Sal. I'll never forget what you've done for me today.'

Outside she breathed in the fresh air of the gardens and stood for a moment looking up at the sky. She was free.

Sal tapped her arm and led her round the corner

of the building towards the stables. 'You wait here, Mrs Buchan, I'll get a horse out of there if it kills me!' She smiled. 'The groom might take a bit of persuading, mind, but I'm used to that.'

Jayne frowned as she watched Sal disappear into the stables. She pressed herself close to the wall, afraid of being caught: she couldn't bear to be shut in her room again—she would rather die.

She heard giggles coming from inside the stables and closed her eyes as she realized what Sal was doing with the stable boy in exchange for a horse.

When Sal came out a short time later she was leading Foxglove, one of the oldest, slowest animals.

'Sal, I'm sorry,' Jayne caught her arm. 'I didn't mean you to . . .'

'It was nothing I haven't done before.' She smiled cheekily. 'And a ride for a ride isn't a bad bargain. Come on, we got no saddle but we'll manage.'

Out of sight of the stables, Sal helped Jayne to mount then swung herself up on to the horse's back and clicked her tongue, urging the animal into a trot. 'How far is it to your father's house, Mrs Buchan?' she asked breathlessly.

'Only about three miles,' Jayne said. 'We'll keep off the roadways—I know a short-cut over the fields and we're less likely to be seen then.'

'Three miles,' Sal said. 'Well, we'll have sore backsides by the time we get there, I'll bet a shilling.'

Jayne smiled as she guided the horse through the back gates and out towards the woodlands beyond. 'Don't worry, Sal.' She turned her face so that Sal could hear her. 'A sore backside is a small

183

price to pay for freedom.'

*   *   *

Dafydd Buchan stood inside his wife's bedchamber, hardly able to believe his eyes. 'Someone will pay for this!' he shouted at the frightened steward. 'How could anyone help her to escape? The keys were all kept by you, Sanderson!'

'Someone must have found another key, sir,' Sanderson said. 'I've been with you all afternoon and I had the master keys with me.'

'Assemble all the servants in the hall.' Dafydd clenched his fists. 'Someone must have helped my wife. She couldn't have done this on her own.'

He stormed down the stairs and strode into the drawing room, leaned on the mantelpiece and looked down into the fire. She had bested him. She had somehow got away and she would probably go straight to her father. Jayne would never come back to him now, unless he could trick her into it.

Sanderson knocked on the door. 'The servants are all waiting for you, Mr Buchan.'

Dafydd straightened and went out into the hall. He stared at the assembled servants, trying to read the truth in the faces gazing back at him.

'That young one, Sal, she's missing, sir,' Sanderson said. 'No one has seen her since early this afternoon.'

'Where are the grooms? I said all the servants, Sanderson—are you a complete fool?' Dafydd barked.

Sanderson moved rapidly, sending a footman to fetch them.

'Did anyone see Mrs Buchan leave the house?'

184

Dafydd asked. No one spoke. Dafydd took up his whip from the hall stand and cracked it in the air. 'I said, did anyone see anything? Have you all lost your senses? What about you, Cook?'

'Last I seen of Mrs Buchan was when I took Madam's breakfast up to her, sir,' Mrs Jones said quietly. 'Mr Sanderson let me in and out and locked the door behind us. Mrs Buchan refused to eat anything. Gone to skin and bone she is, always refusing her food.'

'When I want a report on my wife's health I'll ask a doctor,' Dafydd said. 'So Mrs Buchan was in her room then and you didn't let her out?'

'No, sir, it was more than my life was worth, though I can't say I wasn't tempted. Pathetic, it was, Mrs Buchan like a caged bird.'

'That's enough!' Dafydd cracked the whip again. 'Has anyone else got anything to say?'

There were murmured sounds of dissent. 'So, Sal did it all herself, did she?' Dafydd said. 'A slip of a girl achieved what no one else could and got my wife out of here?'

Sanderson returned with the grooms; the old one was breathing heavily from the exertion of hurrying to the house and the young lad looked as though he'd seen a ghost.

'Which of the horses is missing?' Dafydd asked. 'Come on, it's not too difficult a question, is it?'

'Foxglove, Mr Buchan,' the young groom said quickly. 'There's no tack been touched but, then, there wouldn't be. I was in the tack room cleaning up.'

Dafydd walked closer to the boy. 'What did you say, Danny?'

'Well,' the boy stuttered uncertainly, 'I was in the

185

tack room most of the afternoon, cleaning all the saddles.'

'So you know my wife took her leave some time in the afternoon, do you? How did you come to that conclusion?'

The boy looked confused. 'I suppose I must have heard Foxglove crossing the yard, sir.'

Dafydd took the boy's shirt between his fists and tightened his grip. 'Tell me the truth. You helped Mrs Buchan to get away, didn't you?'

'No, sir, I didn't see her, I swear to God I didn't. It was Sal, she came to me offering me all sorts if she could have a ride on Foxglove. I didn't have the heart to say no.'

Dafydd pushed the boy outside on to the drive, raised his whip and brought it down across his shoulders. 'Tell me the truth! Did you see my wife go off with this girl Sal?' He cracked the whip again, and the boy screamed.

'Stop, sir!' Mrs Jones pushed her way through the crowd of gawping servants. 'The boy is telling the truth. I saw Sal go to the stables and she was on her own. She led out Foxglove and her and Mrs Buchan rode away on the main stretch towards town.'

Dafydd looked at her, his eyes narrowed. 'You dare to stand there and tell me my wife's gone? Why didn't you come to me as soon as I returned?'

'Because I thought Mrs Buchan would pine away and die if she stayed in that room any longer.' She stared up at him, her old face creased in a frown. 'Are you going to give me a whipping, too, sir? It shouldn't be too hard to finish me off—my old bones won't take much punishment.'

'Get out of my house right now!' Dafydd ground

186

out the words between his teeth. 'As from this instant you are dismissed.'

'Right you are, then, sir,' Mrs Jones said. 'I'll pack my bags right away.' She walked away slowly, her shoulders bent.

In spite of his anger, Dafydd felt almost sorry for the old woman. 'The rest of you get back to work,' he said sharply. He watched for a moment as the servants dispersed, then he, too, returned to the house. He stood in the window of the sitting room for a long time, thinking about Jayne: she had more courage and determination than he'd given her credit for. He thought he'd broken her spirit but he'd been wrong.

He wondered where she had gone. Perhaps to find Fairchild but more likely to her father's house. If that was the case Dafydd knew he had a chance of getting her back: Eynon couldn't be with his daughter all the time.

He sank into a chair. Why did he want her back? She didn't love him, had never loved him. And with his cruelty, he had lost any hope of repairing their marriage. He realized now that he had lost Jayne for good and, strangely, that he would miss her. His anger at her betrayal with Guy had stemmed from more than damaged pride: too late, he knew that he loved his wife.

He got up, poured himself a drink and took it with him to sit before the fire. He felt old and jaded. He had taken many women but the diamond among them had slipped through his fingers. Perhaps it was only what he deserved. And then, taking him by surprise, hot tears flowed from his eyes and rolled down his cheeks.

CHAPTER EIGHTEEN

Llinos looked at Eynon, her face alight with laughter. 'I said yes, Eynon, I've ridden over today to tell you that I will marry you.'

'Llinos, my lovely girl, come here, let me hold you, and then I might believe you mean it.'

Llinos felt comfortable in his embrace: she did not experience the deep love she'd felt for Joe or the quickening of the pulse she had known with Dafydd but somehow she felt safe and cherished.

Gently Eynon tipped her face up and kissed her. It was their first real kiss, and she felt wonderfully happy with his lips on hers. They had been friends for so long that she had not imagined they could ever be lovers but now she knew she had been wrong.

He sighed. 'I've waited so long for this, my lovely Llinos. Say you'll marry me very soon.'

She touched his cheek. 'I will, Eynon. I'll marry you as soon as you and Father Martin can arrange it.'

He bent to kiss her again, but a commotion in the hallway made them stare at each other in bewilderment. The door of the sitting room opened and two bedraggled figures staggered into the room.

For a moment Llinos failed to recognize the mud-spattered woman who stood dripping rainwater on to the carpet, then she realized she was staring at Eynon's daughter.

Eynon moved abruptly away from her. 'Jayne! My God! What's happened to you?'

Jayne's hair fell in wet strands over her face. She held the soaking shawl closely around herself.

'I've come home, Father, and I've brought Sal with me.' She gestured to the barefoot girl shivering at her side. 'If it wasn't for her I'd still be a prisoner, locked in my room like a caged animal.'

Eynon took his daughter in his arms. 'My dear child, what in heaven's name has been going on? Come, sit down by the fire, let me pour you some brandy. You're as white as a ghost.'

Jayne clung to him. 'Oh, Father!'

Llinos touched Eynon's arm. 'Perhaps I should go. I'm sure Jayne would like to talk to you in private.'

'No,' Jayne said, 'you might as well hear the truth from me because the scandal of it will be all over Swansea in a few hours.'

'Don't go, Llinos, I need you here,' Eynon said. 'Perhaps you'll bring Jayne a drink from the table over there.' Llinos poured some brandy and held out the glass to him.

He took it. 'Jayne, drink this and then we'll get you some clean, dry clothes and you can tell me the whole story. I can't bear to see you sitting there wearing just that dirty shawl.'

'No, just listen, Father. This won't take long,' Jayne said. 'I left Dafydd for another man, for Guy Fairchild.' She lifted her chin defiantly. 'Be careful what you say because I intend to spend the rest of my life with Guy.'

'Jayne, my love, what are you saying? If you left Dafydd, how is it you were held prisoner by him?'

'When I ran away, he came after me and forced me to go back to the house. He took all my clothes and locked me in my room. I've been a prisoner for

189

days and it's only thanks to Sal that I managed to escape.'

Eynon was about to speak again but Llinos caught his eye and shook her head silently. He nodded almost imperceptibly, and Jayne went on talking.

'Dafydd found Guy and took a whip to him and, oh, Father, it's all such a mess.' Big tears rolled unchecked down Jayne's mud-stained cheeks. 'Dafydd's gone mad! He's abused me in the worst sort of way—he's even had poor Rhiannon put in prison and I just can't live with him any more so I've come home to you, Father.'

'How did he abuse you?' Eynon's voice was ice cold. 'Did he beat you?'

'He *forced* me, Father, and it was then I knew my marriage was dead. Don't let him take me back because I swear I'll kill myself rather than live with him.'

'I'll kill *him*!' Eynon's face was white.

'Now, Eynon, keep calm,' Llinos said gently. 'Nothing can be gained with further violence. Jayne is safe now. She's done the right thing by coming home. No woman deserves to be treated roughly, even by her husband, but you going off in a temper won't achieve anything.'

Jayne looked at her gratefully, 'Llinos is right, Father.' She pushed her wet hair off her face. 'I knew you of all people would understand, Llinos, though I've no right to expect you to stand up for me, not after the way I've treated you.'

'That's all in the past now.' Llinos took Jayne's arm. 'Come along, let's get you into some dry clothes and then we can all calm down and talk things over sensibly.' She turned to Eynon. 'Ask

190

some of the maids to take hot water upstairs for Jayne to bathe.' Her eyes beseeched him to understand: Jayne needed comfort and support now.

'Come on.' Jayne gestured to Sal. 'You must have a hot bath too or you'll catch your death.'

As Llinos went upstairs with Jayne, and one of the maids took Sal to the kitchen, she heard Eynon giving instructions to the maids, his voice edged with anger. She prayed that Dafydd would have the sense to keep away from him, at least for the time being.

Soon the maids were climbing the stairs with jugs of hot water to fill the bath and Llinos picked up the rough shawl Jayne had been wearing.

'I would never have thought it of him,' Llinos said, without thinking. 'I can't imagine Dafydd behaving violently to any woman, let alone his wife. No woman deserves that sort of treatment from any man.'

Jayne glanced at her with world-weary eyes. 'But, then, your Joe never beat you or imprisoned you when you took a lover, did he? It takes a very special man to behave like that and Dafydd is not a special man.'

'I realize that now,' Llinos said. 'He's just an ordinary man who reacted badly when he found his wife no longer wanted him. He must care for you a lot, don't you think?'

'Don't be fooled, Llinos. He told me point-blank that he intended to make your son his heir.' She stepped into the bath. 'He said he would recognize Sion publicly as his son.'

'He can keep his hands off my son,' Llinos said hotly. 'That boy is fiercely loyal to Joe's memory. I

191

won't have Dafydd bandying my name around so that everyone can start gossiping about me again.'

'Oh, I wouldn't worry about that,' Jayne said drily. 'Everyone will be so interested in me, aghast that I've left Dafydd for Guy, that they won't bother with stale news any more.'

She was probably right, Llinos thought. Mrs Jayne Buchan was a woman of note: the daughter of a rich man and the wife of an even richer man. The scandal would rock the town from end to end.

When Jayne had got into the bath, Llinos left her and returned to the drawing room to be with Eynon. He was sitting in his chair with his head in his hands and Llinos put her arms around him. He spoke without looking at her. 'I thought tonight was going to be the happiest time of my life, with you agreeing to marry me at last. Now this happens. What am I going to do about it, Llinos?'

'Jayne's happiness and well-being are what's important now. Our wedding can wait a little longer.'

'No.' He sat up straight then, his arms closing around her waist. 'No, Llinos, I don't want to wait. Our plans will go ahead as soon as possible, have no doubt about that. But what am I going to do about Buchan? I feel I want to kill the man with my own hands.'

'I think Dafydd is already being punished.' She spoke softly. 'His pride is hurt, of course, but in his heart he loves Jayne, I'm sure of it. The fates will take care of Dafydd's punishment. There's no need for you to lift a finger.'

Eynon smiled. 'That sounds like Joe's philosophy.'

'I suppose it does but I believe it. What does it

say in the Good Book? "What you sow you will reap"?'

'I suppose you're right. You're a wise old owl, aren't you, Llinos? And I love you for it.'

'I'm glad to hear it.' She kissed his cheek. 'But you must understand that Jayne is a woman now, not a child. She'll organize her life the way she wants it to be, not to satisfy convention, and I admire her for it.'

'Well, you've always been a bit of a rebel yourself, haven't you, Llinos? And I suppose that's why I love you so much.' Eynon stood up and wrapped his arms around her. She clung to him, happy that she could bring him some comfort, however small.

*   *   *

'Well, Rhiannon, it looks like you're going to get out of here.' The guard opened the door of the cell and stood smiling at her as if she was his best friend.

Carefully, as if fearing even now that this was a hoax, Rhiannon stepped out into the corridor. 'Why am I to be let out? What's happened?' She blinked a little in the sudden light from the lamp the gaoler held aloft.

He gestured to a shadowy figure at his side and Rhiannon frowned. 'This is Mrs Paisley. She is in charge of the Paradise Park Hotel and she has honest work for you.'

Rhiannon stepped back a pace. 'I'm not going there—it's a whore-house.'

'It's not like that any more.' The woman stepped forward and Rhiannon saw that she was dressed in

193

respectable clothes with a good cloak over her shoulders. 'I know the Paradise Park has had a bad reputation in the past but now I've bought it. I intend to run it as a proper hotel.'

'Am I being let out of prison just to work for you, then? You must have a lot of influence in Swansea.'

It was the guard who replied. 'You've been in prison, girl. It wouldn't be easy for you to find decent work. Now Mrs Paisley's offered you a position you should be grateful for it.'

'Look, my dear,' Mrs Paisley put her hand on Rhiannon's arm, 'I've been talking to Mr Morton-Edwards. He came forward and cleared your name, but you know as well as I do that mud sticks.' She shrugged. 'What you do now is up to you.'

Rhiannon nodded. 'I see. Thank you, I'll take the position, of course.' She collected her small bag of possessions and followed Mrs Paisley to the door of the prison. When she stepped outside, she breathed in the salt air that blew in from the sea and knew that, for whatever reason, she was free.

'I have to thank you, Mrs Paisley,' Rhiannon said. 'But why would you pay me good money to work for you when plenty of respectable girls are looking for a job?'

'Well, you've had excellent experience as a housekeeper to Mrs Jayne Buchan, and if Mr Morton-Edwards is willing to put his trust in you that is enough of a recommendation for me.'

'How did Mr Morton-Edwards know I was innocent?'

'It's a long story, child, but the bare facts are these. Mr Morton-Edwards' daughter has gone home to him and I expect she told him the truth about what happened. He had an interest in the hotel himself but thought that too much work was involved in renovating it so I took it on. Now, are you sure you're up to the job I've offered you?'

'Well, I've had experience looking after a household, keeping accounts and such, and I know how to lay out the silver for a banquet. Mrs Buchan has trained me well.'

'There we are, then.' Mrs Paisley began to walk slowly along the road and Rhiannon fell into step beside her, matching her footsteps to those of the older woman. She sighed heavily. Such a lot had happened since she was taken into prison.

Mrs Paisley glanced at her. 'Why the sigh? Surely you're happy to be free, and you've got a good position waiting for you.'

'I can't help but think you don't really need me. You must have found out about my regrettable past.'

Mrs Paisley glanced at Rhiannon. 'My dear, when you're as old as I am you'll realize that today's matrons are yesterday's harlots.' She smiled. 'But I will be relying on you to sort out the respectable couple from a man taking a loose woman to one of the bedrooms for the night.' She paused for breath and stopped walking, her hand on her heart. '*Duw*, the old lungs are not what they used to be.'

Rhiannon looked at her in concern. 'Are you all right, Mrs Paisley?'

'Aye, just getting old, my dear. Come on, it's not far now.'

In spite of her shortness of breath Mrs Paisley was determined to talk. 'I'll pay you fair wages, though it won't be much, not right away. When things improve at the hotel we can review the

195

situation.'

Rhiannon said nothing but took a deep breath of the fresh air. It was so good to be free.

She walked slowly along Potato Street and through Calvert Square, and as she turned the corner into Wind Street there in front of her was the Paradise Park. Her heart lurched. She had rarely done business there: most of her customers had been navvies, and too grudging to spend money on a night in a hotel, but the place still gave her a feeling of shame.

However, the Paradise Park had once been a splendid place and Rhiannon remembered that she had admired it once before. She could imagine how it must have been in the past, fitted with fine furniture and wonderful chandeliers. But that was before it had become a place where men took their doxies. Now it was run down and badly in need of attention. Rhiannon hesitated outside the doors. She felt as though she was about to slip back into her past. But she had a future here and a sudden surge of optimism made her smile. She would make the Paradise Park a good place to be, however hard she had to work.

Inside the hotel it was clear that Mrs Paisley had already begun to improve the look of the building. Gone were the cheap red curtains that had once hung over the windows: they had been replaced with new ones made from good material in sensible colours. The lighting, too, was different: instead of low lamplight kept on at all times, the sun was allowed in through scrupulously clean windows. With a few chairs and tables the foyer would make a good place to meet and take tea.

'I'll show you to your room,' Mrs Paisley said,

'and when you've settled in we'll talk.'

'Talk about what?'

'Well, for one thing we'll have to get you some clean clothes.' Mrs Paisley wrinkled up her nose. 'I suggest you get washed, and by then there will be a fresh outfit on your bed. And, for goodness' sake, do something with that wild hair, will you?'

The furniture in Rhiannon's room was plain but good; the curtains were made from the same fine material as those in the foyer, the same pattern too. Rhiannon smiled: Mrs Paisley had clearly bought an end-of-line cloth cheaply. Still, that was good: it showed the lady had money sense and that was something Rhiannon could appreciate. But it was clear, too, that Mrs Paisley needed lessons in running a hotel profitably. As yet no guests inhabited the rooms and the foyer remained empty and unused. Rhiannon hugged herself. Here was a new beginning and she meant to make the most of it.

The next day Rhiannon started work on the books. Mrs Paisley, she found, had a good head for figures but was haphazard in recording her outgoings. So far nothing was coming in and Rhiannon wondered how well off Mrs Paisley was.

At lunch, which they took at the bare kitchen table, Rhiannon brought up the subject of money. 'All your funds are outgoing, Mrs Paisley. Now, if we were to let the top floor to travelling businessmen there would be money flowing in instead of just out.'

'Have you looked at the top floor?' Mrs Paisley asked. 'The entire place needs cleaning out and we'd need workmen to hang wallpaper. Then there's furniture, beds and the like; we can't let empty rooms.'

'There should be plenty of beds here. If I can get new sheets and blankets somehow, we'd be in business.' Suddenly Rhiannon felt alive for the first time since she'd been accused of theft and flung into gaol. 'I'll get you men who'll work for the price of a night out, and wallpaper too. Just trust me.'

'All right, then,' Mrs Paisley said. 'But, Rhiannon,' she continued, meeting her eyes, 'please don't let me down.'

'I won't let you down, you can count on that.' Rhiannon beamed. 'I'll make a start right away, shall I?'

'Good heavens, you're like a whirlwind, girl—go on, then, if you're set on it. Here, you'd better have some money to start with.'

Rhiannon took the purse Mrs Paisley gave her and tucked it inside the waist of her skirt. 'Give me an hour or two and I'll have it all sorted out.' She went to the door. 'And, Mrs Paisley, your trust in me will be well rewarded, I promise.'

It was good to be walking in the fresh air, and Rhiannon sighed with contentment. She had a good job, a roof over her head, and she was free as a bird. When she had helped Mrs Paisley to knock the Paradise Park into shape she could move on, if the mood took her.

'Rhiannon!'

The voice came from behind her but Rhiannon recognized it at once. 'Bull Beynon, you gave me the fright of my life, creeping up behind me like that.'

He looked down at her and took her hands. 'I heard you were sent to prison and I meant to come to visit you, but Katie wasn't too well and then the baby had croup and . . . well, I'm sorry, Rhiannon.'

'You don't have to apologize to me, Bull, there was nothing you could have done.'

'Well, it's a good thing Mr Morton-Edwards put the authorities straight, isn't it?'

'I know he cleared my name but that's all.'

'I meet with him sometimes and he told me his daughter has been sending letters to everyone concerned in the case, stating that there was no theft of jewels, that they were a gift to you from her.'

'I see,' Rhiannon said. 'That was good of her.'

'It's only what you deserve. What are you doing now you're out of prison?' he asked, releasing her hands suddenly as if he had become aware that he was being over-familiar.

'I've taken a position at the Paradise Park. It's going to be a respectable hotel and I want it to be the best in Swansea. I need men to clear the rooms and cart the rubbish away.'

'I can help you with that,' Bull said. 'A few navvies are left in town and they've been laid off because there's no work for them. I'll rally them and send them round, shall I?'

'Oh, Bull, that's very kind of you. I'd thought of the navvies already but I'd rather you approach them than me.'

'If you'd have a place for Seth Cullen I know he'd be grateful. The poor man lost his leg in an accident but he's healing well and keen to work again.'

'If you recommend him that's good enough for me.'

Bull smiled down at her. 'I wish you all the luck in the world. If anyone deserves to succeed you do.'

Rhiannon flushed with pleasure. Bull's good wishes meant a great deal to her.

She watched him walk away from her and resisted the temptation to run after him. She pulled her jacket around her waist and felt the money pouch in her skirt, which reminded her that she still had a job to do.

Rhiannon made her way to the back of the Mackworth Hotel and slipped inside. There was a hum from the kitchens, the clatter of pans, the clink of china and the sound of voices. One day, she thought hopefully, the Paradise Park would be as busy and as thriving as the Mackworth.

She found the caretaker in a small room tucked away in a corner of the lower floor of the hotel. He looked up from his desk with surprise. 'Yes?' he asked, his eyes appraising her. 'Have you lost your way?'

'No.' She smiled in what she hoped was a charming manner. 'I might be able to put a bit of money your way, though, if you can help me.'

He got to his feet at once. 'What do you want? Not after gentlemen residents, are you?'

'No!' Rhiannon spoke hastily. 'I'm looking for some end-of-roll wallpaper, stuff that's been left over—you know the sort of thing.'

He frowned. 'Aye, I might be able to help you there—for the right price—but I'll have to have a root round in the cellars.'

'Perhaps I can wait here for you?' Rhiannon took the purse out of her skirt and shook it so that the coins jingled pleasantly.

'I won't be long.'

While Rhiannon waited for him to return she looked round the corridors and peered into a few rooms to see how they were decorated. Mostly the paper was of a silky appearance in discreet colours that blended with the furnishings. It would do well for the Paradise Park.

It was almost half an hour later that the caretaker returned. He had dust on his cheek and some rolls of paper under his arm. 'There's quite a lot down there, too much to carry,' he said. 'In any case, I'd have to move it in the dark.'

Rhiannon nodded. 'What if I give you some money now, as a gesture of good faith, and the rest when you bring it over to the Paradise Park?'

'Aye, can't see anything wrong with that.'

Rhiannon tipped some coins on to the desk then held out her hand. 'We'll shake hands on the deal, shall we?'

'Aye.' He took her hand briefly, then stepped back as if fearing she might attack him.

'I'll see you later on tonight, then,' she said. 'Meet me at the back door of the hotel and if I like the goods I'll give you the rest of the money.'

'No, you give me the rest of the money whether you like the paper or not. I'll have gone to a lot of trouble, mind.'

Rhiannon nodded. 'All right. See you later on.'

She felt triumphant as she left the hotel. At least she'd set the ball rolling. A smile curved her lips. And she had seen Bull, he had held her hands and promised to help her. That showed he still cared. Didn't it?

*   *   *

Sal stood in the darkened back hallway, staring up at the steward in alarm. 'What do you want, Mr

Glover, sir? I got duties to attend to.'

'Never mind that. Now, you know what I can do for you here in Mr Morton-Edwards's house, don't you, girl?'

Glover moved closer, trapping Sal against the cold, whitewashed wall.

'I'm sorry, sir, I don't know what you mean.' Sal began to tremble.

'Don't play the innocent with me, girl! I know what you used to be—a common trollop peddling yourself to anyone who had the price of a bed for the night.' He pinched her breast and she yelped.

'Now, come on, I can be nasty to you or I can be really good—I can get you all the easy jobs.' He took her hand and looked at the red, roughened skin and the broken nails. 'You could have hands like a lady, girl, wouldn't that be nice?'

'I've stopped doing all that, sir.' Sal looked up at the man's red face and cruel mouth. She didn't mind a bit of fun but she knew in her bones that lying with Glover would be anything but that.

'Don't that appeal to you, girl? A nice soft job here with me looking after you?'

'Not if it meant putting up with your pestering.' Sal tried to push him away but Glover held her fast.

'Don't be silly! What's another man after all those you've had?' He was crushing her against the wall, his hand between her legs.

Sal realized she would have to be cunning to get away from him. 'All right, but not here where we might get caught.'

He fumbled in her bodice, his thumb and finger twisting her nipple. 'Where, then?'

'I'll finish my chores and come to your room after, sir. Would that be all right?'

There was a sound from the kitchen and Glover moved away from her. 'Do that, girl. I'll leave my door open for you.' He touched her cheek but his fingers were hard. 'And don't think you can play me fast and loose because if I don't get what I want from you tonight you'll be out in the streets tomorrow.'

'Mrs Buchan wouldn't let you throw me out,' Sal said quickly.

'Oh, but Mrs Buchan wouldn't know anything about it until it was too late. In any case, she'll be running off to her lover before long, the whore! Now, come to my room later, or first thing in the morning before anyone else is up I'll throw you out myself.' He forced his mouth down on hers and Sal resisted the urge to gag. At last he released her. 'Do you understand?' he asked.

'Yes, sir,' Sal said, and Glover eased himself away from her. 'I'll see you later, sir,' she said softly.

Once Glover had disappeared Sal rushed up the back staircase to her room and wrapped her few possessions into a bundle. She would have to leave. Happy as she was working for Mrs Buchan, she knew that Glover could make her life hell, and if Mrs Buchan left, as he had said she would, what would become of her then? Better to run away than service Glover whenever he demanded it.

Sal crept down the stairs, pushed back the bolts on the huge door and then she was running free, towards the only place she knew: the streets of Swansea Town.

CHAPTER NINETEEN

As Bull left the railway station and began to walk home his thoughts were on Rhiannon. He remembered the feel of her hands in his, the dark lustre of her hair, and the look in her beautiful eyes as she gazed up at him. He had to admit that he felt desire for her—but, then, any man would when confronted with such loveliness. So why did he feel guilty? In admiring her and offering to help he was just being a friend, wasn't he?

He'd proved his friendship by finding a few navvies willing to work for her at the hotel and Seth Cullen, in particular, had jumped at the chance to be earning money again. He might be handicapped but he was still a fit young man and, somehow, since the day of the accident Bull had felt responsible for him.

As he turned into the gateway of his house, his spirits lifted at the thought of his wife and his child. He opened the door and the scene that greeted him almost brought tears to his eyes. Katie was kneeling on the floor with the baby, who was gurgling away happily as he stared at the flickering fire.

'Hello, love.' Katie turned her face up for his kiss. 'You're early, not that I'm complaining.'

Bull took his son in his arms and kissed the top of his head. The baby snuggled into his neck and love filled Bull's heart.

'Had a good day, Bull?' Katie scrambled to her feet and put her arms around him, resting her head on his chest. They were so close, a little threesome, all that Bull wanted in the world.

'Aye, good enough,' he said. 'I saw Seth Cullen in town and he's so grateful that I found him a job he wanted to take me to the Cornish Mount and buy me a drink.'

'Oh, you didn't tell me you'd got the poor man a job, Bull. No wonder he's pleased, what with his bad leg and all. How did that come about?'

Bull released her and looked away. 'Rhiannon asked me to find men to work at the hotel for her.'

Katie sat in her chair, her hands folded in her lap. 'What hotel is this?'

Bull sat opposite her. 'I'm sorry, I forgot to tell you. I saw Rhiannon the other day, she's got herself a place working at the Paradise Park.'

'Good for her. Is she getting over being locked up in gaol?'

'She seems well enough, but Rhiannon is a strong woman. It would take more than a few setbacks to break her spirit.' He fell silent. Rhiannon . . . why did her name always come into his mind? He must be careful or she would come between him and the wife he loved.

'What are you thinking about, Bull?' Katie said softly. 'You've gone far away from me to somewhere I can't reach you.'

'Just work, love. Why do you ask?'

She looked away from him. 'You seem to be thinking a lot about Rhiannon these days, that's all. Not that I'm jealous, mind, I know you love me and the baby and you wouldn't let anyone come between us.'

'Look at me, Katie,' he said. 'You are my wife and I do love you. No one is going to come between us, so don't you ever think that.'

205

'I couldn't blame you for thinking about Rhiannon, Bull, she was part of your life before I came along.' She paused. 'And I have to admit she's beautiful—she could turn any man's head.'

Bull got up and took her in his arms. 'But not mine. I chose to marry you, didn't I, Katie?'

'Yes, Bull, and I'll always be grateful for that.' She put her soft arms around his neck. 'Now I'd better get my working man a good meal before he beats me for being a bad wife.'

Bull watched as she moved towards the fire and heaved the big pot of stew on to the flames. The appetizing aroma of lamb *cawl* filled the kitchen and Bull took a deep breath: he was the luckiest man in the world, he had a fine wife, a strong, healthy son, and a good career ahead of him. So why when he closed his eyes did he see the face of the woman who had once been his lover?

*   *   *

Rhiannon let herself in through the back door of the Paradise Park and put her hand over her mouth as she tried not to cough. The workmen were moving out the worn furniture that had once stood in the foyer and there was dust everywhere. She spotted Seth Cullen, who was directing the rest of the navvies, and raised her hand to him in greeting. She stepped over a pile of gaudy paper that had been stripped from the walls and made for the back stairs.

'Thank goodness you've come home, girl.' Mrs Paisley was seated in her favourite chair near the window that looked over the busy street. 'The navvies are asking for more money. They didn't think that work in a hotel was going to be so hard—well, that's what they're saying.'

'They're trying it on. I'll have a word with them—they'll listen to me,' Rhiannon said.

'See?' Mrs Paisley's face brightened. 'I knew you'd be invaluable, didn't I?' She patted Rhiannon's hand. 'You know, I've realized how lucky I am to have you working with me. You have beauty and intelligence, and that's a rare combination.'

Rhiannon smiled. 'My past has made me wise to a lot of things, Mrs Paisley, especially when handling men. I'll make the navvies so glad to have a job that they'll work with a will, you'll see.'

Mrs Paisley began to cough, a harsh sound that worried Rhiannon. 'Shall I get your medicine?' She went to the cupboard and picked up the brown bottle, but it was empty. 'I'll nip out and get some more. You can't go all night without it—you'll never sleep.'

Mrs Paisley nodded gratefully. 'All right, but don't be long.' The sentence ended in another fit of coughing and Rhiannon brought her a glass of water. 'Sip this slowly and I'll be back before you know it.'

Rhiannon retraced her steps down the stairs and stood for a moment looking at the navvies, who suddenly seemed very busy. 'Listen, boys,' Rhiannon said, 'I want to talk to you when I get back so I'll thank you all to be here.'

'You're not going to sack us, are you, Rhiannon?' Seth Cullen looked at her anxiously.

'That's something I'll have to think about. If you're not content with the fair wages you're getting I might have to find other workers.'

She let herself out of the building, chuckling to herself at the startled look on the men's faces. When she came back she would give them a good talking-to, and they would listen to her with respect.

She waited in the shop as the medicine for Mrs Paisley was made up and, as always when she had a spare moment, she thought of Bull. She forced herself to look at the shelves in the shop, concentrating on the bottles of strange-sounding mixtures. She didn't want to think of Bull—she could never have him in her arms again.

As she went back to the hotel she practised what she was going to say to the workmen. She was determined they would do a fair day's work for the money they earned.

She turned the corner into Potato Street and collided with a woman laden with two heavy bags. 'Sorry!' She took a step back and then she looked more closely at the woman. 'Mrs Jones, what on earth are you doing out and about?'

'Oh, Rhiannon, it's you. My heart almost stopped when you bumped into me—I thought I was going to be robbed.'

'But why aren't you working?'

'I've been dismissed. I told Mr Buchan a few home truths and he didn't like it. Sent me packing, he did. I've spent a few weeks at Dai Evans's lodging-house but I've run out of money now so I'm on the street.'

'Oh, Mrs Jones, I'm so lucky to have met you when I need a cook for the hotel.'

'What you talking about, girl? What hotel is this?'

'I'm working at the Paradise Park. It's going to

be respectable, a fine hotel again, and I need good staff to make the place a success.'

'Do you mean it, Rhiannon? Have you really got a job for me? I'm a bit old to be wandering the streets.'

'Well, you can come back to the hotel with me right now, if you like.'

'If I like? You're an angel from heaven, girl. I was going to spend the night under the viaduct and I wasn't looking forward to it, I can tell you.'

Rhiannon took one of the bags from Mrs Jones and began to walk slowly towards the hotel. 'What about Sal? Is she all right?'

'I don't know what happened to Sal, girl. She might be back on the streets by now, for all I know.'

'I'll look for her later on,' Rhiannon said. 'I think I know the sort of places she might go to.' Places where she herself had looked for trade.

Rhiannon took Mrs Jones in through the front door of the hotel and led her to a back room that had been cleared of rubbish. It was small and bare but clean, and the bed was made up with fresh sheets. 'Will you be all right here, Mrs Jones? There are candles in the drawer and I'll light a fire for you later on.'

The old woman sank on to the bed and Rhiannon felt sad that she should have been discarded after years of service as though she was an old mop. Well, Rhiannon would make sure she didn't end her days the same way. She meant to carve out a career for herself; to be respectable and well placed, and the Paradise Park was the key to her future.

*   *   *

209

Later, when the men working on the hotel had been dealt with, Rhiannon went out looking for Sal. She made her way through the town, pausing where the light spilled out of the open doorways of inns and men would be looking for the company of a woman to while away the dark hours of the night. She eventually made her way to the Strand, where the Fountain Inn stood squat and rambling, but there was no sign of Sal and no one had seen a young girl roaming the streets looking for trade.

At last, tired and sad, Rhiannon turned back. She felt bone weary, and there was little chance of finding Sal now.

*   *   *

Sal sat in the shabby room at the back of the Salubrious Inn and stared at the stranger, who was in a great haste to take off his clothes. She shifted uneasily in her chair, feeling cold in her chemise, which was none too clean. It was as if she was living in a nightmare that had taken her back in time to the bad days when she was a whore for any man who would pay her.

'Come on, then, gel, what you doing just sitting there? Get your things off, let the dog see the bone.'

He stood over her and Sal could smell the beer on his breath. Her stomach heaved, as she slid the strap of her chemise off her shoulder. 'No need to rush, mister, we got all night.'

'You might have, but I got to get home to my missus so hurry yourself up, will you?'

'But I thought I was getting a bed for the night

out of this,' Sal said dismally. 'You promised we'd stay here till morning.'

'Never mind that, gel, I'm not made of money. It's a quick tumble for me and then I'm off home.'

Sal gathered her clothes together. 'You said a night's bed and board.'

The man grabbed her thin arm. 'I'm not letting you off that easily, my girl. I was expecting a good time and you're going to give it me.'

Sal remembered the humiliation she'd suffered, as well as the beatings, and at the hands of a man just like this. Well, she wasn't going to be a soft fool any longer. Her foot shot out and caught the man between the legs.

'You whoring bitch!' He fell to the floor, his hands between his legs. 'I'll kill you for this, you just watch me.'

Sal rushed down the stairs and out of the back door into the darkness, pulling on her clothes as she went. She ran blindly along the streets, not knowing where she was going but determined to put as much distance between the Salubrious Inn and herself as she could manage.

She headed into Potato Street and pulled up sharply as the tall figure of a man came towards her. She shrank back against the wall but he stopped close by and peered at her through the darkness. 'Are you all right?' he said quietly. 'Don't be afraid. I'm Seth Cullen and I've been working at the Paradise Park.'

Sal didn't move; she was frozen to the spot with fear. She swallowed hard and tried to talk but her voice wouldn't come.

'I won't hurt you—it's just that you look like you need help.' He stepped closer. 'Poor little thing, you're not much more than a child. What are you doing out here on your own?'

Sal forced herself to speak. 'I'm looking for somewhere to stay the night. My dad's thrown me out and I got nowhere to go.' It was an outright lie but she could hardly tell the truth and land herself in more hot water.

'Look, let me take you to the Paradise Park. It's gone all respectable now, with Bull Beynon's woman in charge. You must know Rhiannon. Everyone in Swansea's heard of her, a bad girl made good an' all that.'

'Rhiannon's in the hotel?' Sal felt her heart lift with hope. 'You are telling me the truth aren't you?'

'I said you'd know her. Let me take you in and get her for you, I promise I'm not out to hurt you. I'll walk,' he smiled, and she saw the shine of his teeth, 'or rather I'll *limp* in front of you.' He patted his leg. 'It's false, see, accident on the railway.'

His words reassured Sal and, slowly, she followed him up the steps of the hotel and into the dimly lit foyer. 'Rhiannon!' he shouted, at the top of his voice.

Abruptly a door opened, and Rhiannon was looking at Sal in disbelief.

'Oh, Rhiannon, thank God I've found you!' Sal ran into her arms. 'I can't do it any more—I can't give myself to any drunk for a few pence just to be thrown to one side like a stray animal. I'd rather starve to death!'

'There's no need to starve, Sal.' Rhiannon held her close. 'I've been looking for you all evening. I've got work for you here, honest work like we did up at Mrs Buchan's house. Mrs Jones is here too

212

and it'll be like old times with the three of us together, you'll see.'

With Rhiannon's arms around her, Sal felt a deep sense of calm: she was going to be with her old friends and have a respectable job again. But for now the promise of a good meal and warm bed was enough happiness for anyone in one day.

CHAPTER TWENTY

Llinos opened her eyes and stared at the long dress hanging on the wardrobe door. She admired how the light fell on the silk folds of the old-gold skirt and told herself that soon, the day after tomorrow, she would be wearing that dress and promising to be Mrs Eynon Morton-Edwards.

Her features softened. Dear Eynon, he was so excited, just like a child waiting for a birthday gift. She fell back against the pillows and stared at the ceiling, wondering how it would feel to leave the pottery house. She would no longer look out of the windows and see the bottle kilns shimmering in the morning mists, or hear the apprentices calling to each other as they carried the pots to be fired. And, worst of all, she wouldn't have the close companionship of her dear partner Watt, who had always been like a brother to her. She would miss it all, there was no doubt of that, but she needed to start again, to live in a house where every corner did not resonate with the shadow of her husband, Joe. In Eynon's fine house overlooking the sea, she could make new memories in place of the old ones.

Llinos ate a leisurely breakfast of toast and

honey, and later did her rounds of the pottery sheds, telling herself that she could come back here any time if she missed the old place. Eynon had suggested putting the pottery up for sale but Llinos balked at the idea: she preferred to leave Watt in charge of everything. He would manage without her: since Joe had died she had left most of the business to him anyway.

Llinos sighed. Marriage to Eynon meant giving up more than the pottery: it meant giving up her personal freedom too, and now, with the wedding day drawing near, she wasn't sure she was ready for it.

She made her way into the painting shed and watched as one of the decorators worked on a transfer pattern, filling in the colours by hand with great delicacy.

'Morning, Llinos, you're looking happy. Thinking about your husband-to-be, are you?'

Llinos turned to see Watt standing over her. His hands were streaked with paint and there was a dab of colour on his cheek. She drew him towards the door. 'I think I'm getting cold feet,' she said, her voice low. 'Will I like being a wife again, after all this time?'

'Wedding nerves,' Watt said. 'Everyone gets them, Llinos, or was your first wedding so long ago you've forgotten that?'

'Hey, cheeky!' Llinos slapped his arm playfully. 'I'm not that ancient!' She sobered. 'Oh, Watt, am I doing the right thing?'

'Of course you are, Llinos. You've known Eynon since you were both children.' He smiled. 'You know you love him and it's obvious to everyone, even me, and I'm pretty dense when it comes to feelings—or I was once.'

'You've always given me the right advice when I needed it.'

'And I'm giving you good advice now, Llinos. Marry Eynon, put all your doubts to one side. I think this marriage will be the making of you.'

'All right. I'll pretend I'm a young girl again, marrying my first love. It's a bit of a stretch for an old lady but if I try hard enough I might just succeed.'

'Rubbish! Anyway, you're as beautiful now as you were when I first set eyes on you.' Watt smiled down at her. 'I was nine and you were about sixteen. I thought you were beauty, spirit and intelligence rolled into one. Had I been born in more privileged circumstances I'd have wanted you for my own.'

'Oh, Watt, you've never said anything like that before.'

'Well, I'm older and I know that in Rosie I've got the best wife any man could want, but now I can express my appreciation of you as I never did when I was young. I suppose I understand the world a little better. That's what getting on in years does for you.'

'Oh, Watt,' Llinos kissed his cheek, 'I don't know what I'd have done without you all these years. You've been my right-hand man always.'

Watt laughed. 'Except when I was off on my travels, but I was always glad to come home.'

'And I was always glad to see you. Now, enough of that, I'd better get indoors and sort out some more patterns. After today it will be your job to make up fresh designs. We need to be a bit more modern now to keep up with other potteries.'

'I hear you, boss.' Watt smiled.

Llinos gave him a playful slap and left him to get on with his work. As she walked slowly back to the house she was feeling more at ease with herself: as Watt had pointed out, it was natural to feel nervous at the thought of being married again, especially at her age. Still, she would make Eynon a good wife and they would share their last years together and be happy.

*   *   *

Bull Beynon walked into the shed where one of the engines of the Great Western Railway stood idle. The inspection was to be carried out by Mr Steel, an engineer who was more experienced than himself.

'Morning, Beynon. You've kept the rolling-stock in good condition, I'm glad to say, although in this weather it's difficult to inspect anything properly. Your reputation precedes you—we all know you treat this railway of yours as if it was your own child.'

'Morning to you, Mr Steel. I'm glad we meet with your approval.' Bull spoke easily: he was always at home with other men who loved the railway. 'What's this talk about bringing in the narrow gauge, though? Is there any substance in the rumour?'

Mr Steel scratched his beard. 'Aye, there's talk, but that's all it is right now. I can't see the broad gauge being replaced for years yet.'

'So, you think it will come one day?' Bull thrust his hands in his pockets. 'It would be a mistake. The wheels of an engine running on a narrow-gauge track won't be as stable as they are on the broad gauge.'

Mr Steel sighed heavily. 'We know that, Beynon, but the powers-that-be have different ideas. Anyway, my job's done for now. Let's go and have a beer in one of your excellent taverns, shall we?'

Bull led the way out of the shed and indicated the Terminus Inn, a short distance from the yard. The men fell into step and Bull mused on what Steel had told him. Why, he wondered, did folk have to interfere with something that was working perfectly well? Brunel had invented the broad gauge and he was a man who knew what he was doing.

The public bar was almost empty, though a haze of smoke drifted in the air and the smell of stale tobacco permeated the room. 'I'll sit by the fire, Beynon, and you call the landlord over. We'll have a good draught of ale to oil our wheels.' He laughed at his own joke, and as soon as he sat down he refilled his pipe, pushing the tobacco into the bowl with practised fingers.

Bull called the landlord, then sat on the old wooden settle beside Steel. 'It's a filthy day and the rain's getting worse.' Bull frowned. Katie had gone into town this morning with the baby. He hoped she would cut short her shopping trip and take a cab home.

'Well, at least we're in by the fire, Beynon. No need for us to prolong the inspection, not with a man like you in charge.'

The landlord brought the drinks, which saved Bull making a reply; praise always embarrassed him. The beer was dark and bitter, just as he liked it, and he drank with relish.

'I've been asked to speak to you this morning, Beynon,' Steel said, wiping the white froth of the beer from his moustache.

Bull looked at him, trying to read his expression, but the man's head was lowered and it was difficult to guess what he was thinking. 'Speak to me about what?' he prompted.

'How would you like to be a magistrate at the Sessions, Beynon? Swansea needs men of character like you to sit on the bench.'

Bull was taken by surprise. This was not what he had expected. He rubbed his chin, giving himself time to think. 'What would it entail?' He didn't want to be involved in anything that took him away from his work on the railway.

'Well, you'd be expected to make decisions that are fair and just. It's no easy thing to commit a man to prison. It wouldn't take up all your time—you would still have your job on the railway. As you get older, though, you might find it easier to be a judge than a railwayman.'

Bull couldn't see that time ever coming, but he needed to give the matter serious consideration. He would speak to Katie and see what she thought of the idea of her husband sitting in judgement on those less fortunate than himself. 'I'm very flattered but I'd like time to think about it,' Bull said slowly. 'I love my work on the railway and I never did see myself ever going for something like this.'

'It would be a great step up for you and, as I said, we need men of your sort.'

The two men drank in silence. After a time Steel put down his tankard. 'I'd better be going. I've got a report to write and that's a job I hate.' He stood

218

up and laid his hand on Bull's shoulder. 'Don't move, you just sit here and finish your drink, then go home and talk to your wife. Bull,' he lowered his voice, 'I want you to take the job—it's an honour you deserve.'

Bull sat for a long time staring into the fire. He knew that Steel was right: being elected a magistrate was a mark of honour the town bestowed on a man who was seen to be honest and true. Usually men of education and high birth formed the judiciary, and Bull had come from the working people of the town. Still, he would wait to see what Katie had to say about it. She was a fount of common sense and would tell him exactly what she thought. He finished his beer and got to his feet.

At the door of the inn, he collided with a woman. He held her away from him in embarrassment. 'I'm so sorry,' he said.

'Bull! Watch where you're going—you nearly knocked me off my feet. I'm quite shaken up.'

'Rhiannon, it's you.' He looked down into her flushed, rain-damp face with strange feelings running through him. Her eyes gleamed like dark gems and her hair curled in tendrils from under her bonnet. She had never looked more beautiful. 'Come on,' he said, 'I'll take you back inside and we can shelter from the rain for a while.'

He moved towards the fire, but his place had already been taken by an old man with a dog so Bull led the way to a corner seat. He lifted his hand to the landlord and asked for two hot toddies. When the drinks were put on the table, he risked a look in Rhiannon's direction. 'What are you doing out in this weather, anyway?' he asked. Suddenly he felt the urge to kiss her moist lips. 'You women will brave any weather to do a bit of shopping, won't you? My Katie was coming to town this morning but I hope she's stayed indoors.'

'How is Katie? Is she keeping well?' Rhiannon asked. 'I haven't been up to see her lately.'

'She's loving every minute of being a mother, and I'd say she's very well indeed.' Bull spoke lightly. 'But what are you doing in town?'

'I just came to order some provisions for the hotel.' She was talking fast, and Bull knew that she was as affected as he was by their chance meeting. The mention of Katie's name had not eased the tension between them: rather, it had heightened it. 'You've got a good position in the hotel, I understand, so why don't you send one of the servants to run the errands?' he said. 'If you're in charge you should make other people do some of the hard work.'

Rhiannon smiled, and he thought again how beautiful she was.

They finished their drinks in silence and Bull put down his glass. 'Well, I'd better be getting back home,' he said uneasily. 'Which way are you going?'

'To the Paradise Park.' Rhiannon was looking up at him through thick, dark lashes. 'I suppose, as we're going in the same direction, we might as well walk along together—that's if you're not ashamed to be seen with me.'

Bull drew her to her feet and put his hands on her shoulders. 'Never say that to me again, Rhiannon.' His voice was stern. 'I wasn't ashamed when I lived with you and I'm not ashamed now.'

'I'm sorry,' Rhiannon said quickly. 'It was wrong

of me even to suggest it. You've never been a man to put on airs and graces and I'm sure married life and a grand job are not enough to change the real Bull Beynon.'

They walked in silence for a while, and Bull couldn't help but remember the days and nights they had spent together in the small hut at the side of the railway track. They had been happy times . . .

'You're quiet, Bull,' Rhiannon said. 'If you want to go on ahead, please don't feel you have to wait for me.'

'I like walking with you.' He felt he owed her an explanation. He and Rhiannon had always been honest with each other. 'It's just that I feel a bit guilty, a bit disloyal to Katie, because I still enjoy being with you.' He felt it was a clumsy explanation.

Rhiannon smiled up at him, with a sparkle in her dark eyes. 'We still care a little for each other, Bull, because we were close, weren't we?'

He didn't know what to say. She was right, of course, but he didn't want her to look on his words as encouragement.

'It's all right, Bull.' She had read him well. 'We're friends and we'll always be friends. I know there's nothing else for me where you're concerned, and I don't hope for anything other than your liking and respect.'

He was relieved: he felt that he had cleared the air with Rhiannon and now he could afford to enjoy her company. 'You always were a woman with a great deal of common sense,' he said, and touched her arm lightly.

'Bull!' The soft, unmistakable voice of his wife drifted across the road towards him and Bull

221

looked up, startled.

He saw Katie's happy face as she held their baby, wrapped in the Welsh shawl, firmly to her breast. Bull's face suffused with colour, and he felt guilt like a heavy weight on his shoulders.

Suddenly the road was filled with traffic, horses drawing vans, hansom cabs and, drawing ever nearer, the midday mail coach to London. He saw Seth Cullen hovering behind Katie. He seemed to be holding her back but then she stepped into the road, her eyes fixed on him. 'Katie, watch out!' he called. It was too late. She stumbled and fell on to her knees, her face a blur as she stared at him. He met her eyes, then rushed towards her through the traffic.

The four horses drawing the mail coach were hurtling along the road. Bull cried out his wife's name, as if the power of his voice could hold the coach at bay. The horses, frightened by the noise, reared and their hoofs lashed the air.

'Dear God, no!' Bull was unaware of hands holding him back, and watched in horror as Katie was struck down by flying hoofs. For a few seconds the coach jerked forward as the driver struggled to bring the animals under control and then the air seemed still as Bull stared at the limp body of his wife.

As he closed the distance between them, his legs felt as if lead weights were dragging him down. It seemed an eternity before he reached her, fell on his knees and took her in his arms. The baby was still and silent, wrapped against her lifeless body.

'Katie, my love.' He looked down into her face and saw a trickle of blood run from between her lips and make a trail along her jaw. 'Katie, speak to me.' He touched her lips with his, as if to breathe life into her, and then he became aware that hands were reaching out to him trying to draw him away. He shook them off.

'Move aside, everyone, let the doctor in, for pity's sake.' It was Rhiannon's voice, but Bull only dimly recognized it. The doctor, young, fresh-faced, a man Bull had never seen before, knelt beside him.

'I'm Dr Frost,' he said. 'Let me see if I can help. Is this your wife, sir?' he asked Bull, who nodded. He couldn't speak.

The doctor lifted Katie's limp wrist, then tried to listen to her heart. After a moment he shook his head. He turned his attention to the baby, then rested his hand on Bull's shoulder. 'I'm sorry, but there's nothing I can do for them. They are beyond human help.'

'What do you mean?' Bull said dully. He knew what the doctor meant but he couldn't bring himself to believe it.

'Your wife and child are both dead. Let these good people help you take them to the mortuary. There's nothing else you can do.'

'No!' Bull said. 'I'm taking them home. My wife and baby are not going to lie alone in a house of death.'

'But you can't carry both corpses.'

'Corpses?' Bull winced. He turned to look over his shoulder. 'Rhiannon, carry my son to my house.'

She came at once, white-faced, with tears on her cheeks. She took the limp infant without a word and hugged him close to her breast. Bull picked up Katie in his arms to take her to their home, where

223

she belonged.

As he walked away he did not see the crowds of onlookers or hear the excited talk about who had been at fault. No one had been at fault except him: he should have been with her, he should have kept her safe. He closed his eyes for a moment and then tears, salt and bitter, began to run down his cheeks splashing on to the face of his dead wife, his tears mingling with her blood. His love, his reason for living, was gone and it was all his fault.

CHAPTER TWENTY-ONE

Seth stood at the edge of the cemetery, watching as Katie Beynon and her baby were laid to rest side by side in the ground. 'I tried to stop her running into the road,' Seth muttered. 'I did, I tried my best.'

At his side, his cap in his hand, was his uncle Tom, his grey beard trembling in the cold wind blowing across the gravestones.

'Poor little thing,' Seth said. 'The poor child didn't deserve to die like that.' He leaned against a tree. 'Damn this leg of mine! Sure the Blessed Virgin knows the pain I'm in from my poor stump but I deserve it for not saving Bull's wife and child. If it wasn't for him I wouldn't be alive today.'

'It wasn't your fault,' Tom said. 'And haven't I tried to tell you that more times than I can count?' He clicked his tongue against his teeth in exasperation.

'It don't help none telling me that. I was so close to her I should have been able to stop her. Well, it's too late now.' Seth took a last lingering look at the small group of people around Katie's grave. As he turned away there were tears on his cheeks.

*　　　*　　　*

Rhiannon stood a little distance from the grave. The mourners had gone and she was a solitary figure in the gloom of the cemetery. She saw the flowers at the foot of the wooden cross. 'Poor Katie.' She bit her lip, knowing how Bull must be suffering at the loss of his wife and child.

She took one more look at the fresh grave, then left the cemetery. She must put Bull Beynon and his tragedy out of her mind, think of other things. But the scene haunted her. She felt again the heaviness of the dead baby against her breast, saw the haunted look in Bull's eyes as he carried Katie back to her home. 'Stop it!' she said softly. 'Just think of something else.' She focused her mind on the hotel: it was shaping up well, with the ground-floor work almost finished. But it was hard to get the tradesmen and their apprentices to move quickly.

She had kept on one of the navvies to do the labouring—Seth Cullen, with his bad leg, needed the work more than any of them, and he seemed to get along well with Sal; she often saw them talking together.

She was pleased that Mrs Paisley had let her take on both Sal and Mrs Jones: it was good to know she would have friends around her when the hotel opened for business.

'*Duw!*' Mrs Paisley looked at Rhiannon as she came into the kitchen. 'Where have you been till this time? I was getting a bit worried about you.'

'I stopped to watch the funeral.' Rhiannon sank into a chair and unlaced her boots. 'Lord, my feet are killing me.'

'What funeral was that?'

'Katie Beynon and her baby. You should have seen the little coffin, Mrs Paisley, tiny it was, made with good shiny wood and gleaming handles, just like the one Katie had, but so pitifully small. It's frightening to see how quickly two lives can be snuffed out.'

'I never knew Bull Beynon or his wife,' Mrs Paisley said, 'but, then, I've always kept myself to myself.'

Rhiannon kicked off her boots. 'Aye, it was awfully sad—the funeral, I mean, and I was so sorry for Bull. Still, he's got his work. He's very well thought-of in railway circles. He even met the great Mr Brunel himself at the grand opening of the Swansea station.'

Mrs Paisley sniffed. 'Noisy, smelly things, trains. I don't know why we can't manage with horse and carriage as we always did.'

'But just think, Mrs Paisley,' Rhiannon said, 'the trains will bring in more business to Swansea. Travelling men will need accommodation and we will be providing it for them.'

'Aye, I suppose you're right. You got a good head on your shoulders, Rhiannon, I'll give you that.'

'Well, I hope you'll be pleased when I tell you I've put an advertisement in the Cardiff and Bristol newspapers offering rooms on the middle floor. We should be getting bookings any day now.'

'But we're not ready for customers yet! The place is in an awful mess!'

'Well, I've offered a special price for now until

226

the alterations are complete. I'm sure the men will put up with a bit of dust to get a good night's lodging with a hearty supper for less than other hotels are charging.'

'But the rooms are not ready!'

'They are. We've been working on them, me and Sal, and Mrs Jones has helped a bit too. The pair of them have chosen their rooms already. They've cleaned and painted until their fingers were raw. As for the letting rooms, the carpets are swept, there's freshly laundered sheets on the beds and, thank goodness, the kitchen is practically ready so Mrs Jones can do the cooking.'

Mrs Paisley sank into a chair and pushed her small glasses on to the bridge of her nose. 'Well I never!' She looked at Rhiannon as though she'd grown two heads. 'You're moving too fast for an old girl like me. And who, dare I ask, is paying for these advertisements?'

'You are, Mrs Paisley,' Rhiannon said, 'but I expect you to be well rewarded by all the trade they'll bring.'

'Well, we'll see.' Mrs Paisley fanned her face. 'I don't know about this advertising business. Word-of-mouth was always good enough for folk around here.'

'That was when the Paradise Park was little more than a bawdy-house,' Rhiannon said gently. 'We need to look beyond Swansea, at least for the time being. Once we're known to give good value for money the recommendations will see our rooms filled.'

'You young people today seem to know a lot more than us old folk.'

Rhiannon looked at Mrs Paisley—really looked

at her, perhaps for the first time. She saw an old lady, stoop-shouldered and walking with a slight limp. Yet when she talked about converting the Paradise Park into a first-class hotel her face lit up, giving her an aura of youth and enthusiasm that was undeniably charming.

'Come on now, Mrs Paisley, stop talking as though you're in your dotage. There's a lot of ideas and enough hard work left in you to last quite a few years.' She smiled. 'There'd better be—I can't manage this hotel on my own.'

Mrs Paisley looked at her shrewdly. 'You could manage more than a hotel, if you ask me, girl, but if the good Lord spares me you won't have to.'

The front-door bell rang out stridently. 'I wonder if we've got a customer already,' Rhiannon said hopefully.

She hurried to answer it, then stared in surprise at the man standing before her.

'Bull!' He was ashen, his eyes were dull and his big shoulders were slumped. 'Oh, Bull, my love, come in, you look awful.'

He stepped into the foyer. 'Rhiannon, I need someone to talk to. I can't stand being on my own in that house a moment longer.'

'You know you're always welcome here,' she said quickly.

'You're the only true friend I've got, Rhiannon. All the others are workmates or casual acquaintances. I can't talk to them about my grief—they'd tell me to act like a man.'

'Go upstairs to my room,' Rhiannon said. 'It's the first door on the right when you reach the second landing. I'll tell Mrs Paisley I've got a visitor.'

228

She opened the door to the kitchen. 'It's a friend, Mrs Paisley,' she said. 'He was Katie's husband and he's in sore need of company.'

Mrs Paisley looked doubtful for a minute then nodded. 'I think I can trust you to be discreet with your friends, Rhiannon, but I don't want any unseemly goings-on. We mustn't give folk the wrong impression of the Paradise Park.'

'You can trust me,' Rhiannon said. 'Bull is only after company, someone he can talk to about his wife.'

'Go on, you. I'll fetch you a drink up in a minute or two, perhaps a drop of brandy. Then I can meet this Bull Beynon for myself.'

Rhiannon nodded then went to her room. Bull was sitting with his head in his hands, oblivious of where he was. She glanced around her, at the good curtains beside the windows and the candle-holders on the table. It was a fine big room, facing the front of the hotel, and at first Mrs Paisley had demurred about Rhiannon occupying it. 'We could make this a double room with a sitting area for gentlemen guests and their wives.'

'But it could be my office as well as my bedroom. I can keep the books, write the notices and all sorts of things here. It will save me finding another room for an office.'

In the end Mrs Paisley had given in. 'Well, mind you look after the place. It's one of the best rooms in the hotel.'

'And the one in most need of refurbishment,' Rhiannon had added drily.

Now she studied Bull. From the colour of his face she knew he was in a bad way. 'Bull, I know you're sick with grief, but are you coming down with something too? You don't look well.'

'All I know is that I feel like death itself.'

Rhiannon laid her hand on his forehead. 'You're real clammy, Bull. You must be sickening for something.' She let her hand rest on his brow a moment longer. 'There's a lot of illness around just now, and a child's just died of the whooping cough. Are you feeling poorly, Bull?'

He shook his head. 'No, just sick at heart. I've just put my wife and child into their graves and I can't bear it.'

'Oh, Bull, my lovely!' Rhiannon put her arms around him and he laid his head wearily against her breast. 'That's right,' she whispered, as he began to sob. 'Let it all out.'

Bull clung to her crying like a baby and Rhiannon felt tears burn her own eyes: she'd never seen Bull like this before, so vulnerable, so helpless. She held him close and brushed back his hair as if he was a child. After a time, his sobs ceased and he lifted his face to look at her. 'I'm sorry to put you through this, Rhiannon.' He looked like a small boy, lost and bewildered. 'I've been trying to act like a man, to take the blows life has dealt me as a man should, but, oh, Rhiannon, I can't believe I've lost Katie for good.'

'There, there, who said a man can't be allowed to cry?' She brushed away his tears with her fingers. 'You're the bravest man I know, Bull Beynon, and if you can't bring your sorrows to me who else can you bring them to?'

He caught her hand. 'Thank you, Rhiannon, I needed to shed some tears. They've been making my throat ache ever since I put my sweet wife and baby in the ground.'

230

'I know, Bull, I know.' Rhiannon wondered where Mrs Paisley was with the drinks. 'I'll fetch you some brandy. It'll make you feel better. I won't be a minute.'

As she opened the door, Mrs Paisley was just reaching the top of the stairs with a tray. 'Oh, there, take this off me. I'm fair winded, coming up them stairs. I'm not as young as I was and my legs are letting me know it.'

Rhiannon turned back to the room. 'Bull, this is Mrs Paisley. She's saved me a trip and brought some brandy up for us.'

Bull got to his feet and Rhiannon, looking up at him, realized she'd forgotten just how big he was. His presence seemed to fill the room as he moved forward to shake Mrs Paisley's hand. 'You've got a good girl here, Mrs Paisley,' he said. 'Rhiannon is one of the truest and best, you won't go far wrong with her helping you.'

'Don't be daft, man! I've worked that out for myself.' She looked at him sagely. 'You come to Rhiannon for a bit of comforting, then, have you? I heard you lost your wife and child. There's sorry I am for any man bereaved like that.'

Bull swallowed hard. 'It's all right other folk feeling sad for me, but I can't go on feeling sorry for myself, can I?' He smiled suddenly, and Rhiannon's heart lifted with love for him: she knew he was being brave to put the old lady at ease. 'I'll have a drop of that good brandy now that you've been so kind as to bring it up for me. Will you do me the honour of joining us, Mrs Paisley?'

'Oh, aye, a right charmer, this one.' Mrs Paisley looked almost coquettish as she allowed Bull to pour her a glass. 'I'll sit here in the window and

231

watch the world go by for a few minutes.'

Rhiannon listened as Bull talked to Mrs Paisley about the business of the hotel. 'I can see this place will be a goldmine,' Bull said. 'The improvements you've made already give the place a bit of style.'

'I'm glad you approve. Don't want to put money into it, do you, Mr Beynon?'

'I'm no speculator,' Bull said gently. 'I'm a plain man working on the railway, grafting for a living.'

'More than that, if I'm to believe what Rhiannon says. It seems you're very clever with plans and things. Perhaps you could advise us on a few ways to make the building more comfortable.'

Rhiannon sat back in her chair, her untouched drink in her hand, and watched with pride as Bull discussed the design of the new bathrooms being built along each landing. She could almost believe she was Bull's woman again, happy and safe with him to take care of her. The dream evaporated as Bull put down his glass and took Mrs Paisley's hand.

'I'd better get home now. I've a dozen jobs to do around the place.' His face was shadowed.

Rhiannon could read him like a book—hadn't she lived with him long enough to know his thoughts almost before they were formed? 'If you want any help packing up clothes and that sort of thing, don't be afraid to ask, mind.' She touched his arm. 'But I'd leave it for a bit, if I were you.'

'I would be grateful,' Bull said at once. 'I don't relish the thought of seeing to Katie's things or of packing away the baby's clothes. Perhaps you could give them to someone needy?'

Rhiannon felt his grief as if it was her own. 'It will get easier,' she said softly. 'You can't believe it now but pain does fade, given time.'

'Maybe.' Bull moved towards the door. 'Thank you, ladies, for your company and for sharing that fine brandy with me.'

'Come to visit us any time. A good man is always welcome under my roof.' Mrs Paisley's voice was unusually gentle. 'Go on, Rhiannon, see your visitor out, then come down to the kitchen. It's time we had our supper.'

At the door Rhiannon paused and looked up at Bull. 'Any time you want to talk, come to see me. I'm always here.'

She wished she could reach up and kiss him, hold him in her arms as she used to when they were lovers.

'You're a good girl, Rhiannon.' Bull took her hands. 'I'll never forget your kindness to me.' He straightened his big shoulders. 'Now, go back indoors to Mrs Paisley. Good luck to both of you. I'm sure between you the hotel will flourish. Good night, Rhiannon.'

As Rhiannon watched Bull stride swiftly away she felt tears run down her face. She loved Bull as much as ever and to know he was alone with his terrible pain and grief was like having the heart cut out of her.

'Good night, Bull, I love you,' she said, but her words were carried away on the soft night air.

CHAPTER TWENTY-TWO

The wedding, which Llinos had thought would be a quiet affair, turned out to be the highlight of the year for the inhabitants of Swansea. It was as if, by marrying Eynon, Llinos had become an honoured and honourable member of the community once more. People crowded around the lychgate of St Paul's, waving and cheering, and as she looked round her at the happy, smiling faces, Llinos held back her tears with difficulty.

She clung tightly to Eynon's arm as they left the church and when, at the carriage steps, he bent to kiss her lips, the crowd went wild, throwing flower petals and rice over them.

Llinos felt like a young bride as she smiled up at her new husband. 'I love you, Eynon Morton-Edwards, do you know that?' She felt the tears brim over and hurriedly climbed into her seat before they flowed down her cheeks.

'Crying on your wedding day, my darling? We can't have that.' Eynon took out a spotless handkerchief and dabbed at her face. 'There, now, let's see you smile. All brides should be smiling on their wedding day.'

'Oh, Eynon.' She buried her face in his shoulder. She was as nervous as a virgin and that was absurd: she was with Eynon, her dear friend, he would take care of her and love her and she would never be alone again.

*   *   *

Jayne watched from a distance as the carriage rolled away along the road. So he had done it. Father had married the woman he had always loved, and by the look on both their faces they were going to be very happy. Well, now it was time to think of herself. With her father happily settled,

234

she could begin to plan her future with Guy.

Her face softened as she thought of him. Guy Fairchild, her lover. It might be shameless to revel in her faithlessness but Jayne no longer cared: she and Guy had met secretly ever since she'd returned to her father's house. She realized now how stupid she'd been even to listen to Dafydd's claim that Guy only wanted her for her shares. Guy had proved over and over again that he loved her. But for now she wanted to keep him and their love to herself.

Guy brought her gifts, diamonds and rubies and emeralds as big as pigeons' eggs, but the one gift she treasured above all was the plain wedding band he had slipped on her finger in place of the one Dafydd had put there.

It was good to feel so alive, so much in love. Tonight she would see Guy again—he would come to the woods to find her, and they would lie in the grass beneath a canopy of trees and make love.

'Lovely day for a wedding, isn't it?' The voice startled her out of her thoughts.

Jayne spun round to see Dafydd standing uncomfortably close to her. 'Go away, Dafydd, I don't want anything to do with you.' She moved away from him but he kept pace with her. 'What are you doing here anyway?' she demanded.

'I have every right to see the mother of my son get married, don't you think?'

'I think you should go away and leave me alone.'

'You are still my legal wife, or have you forgotten that?'

'I've forgotten nothing about you, or about the long unhappy years I spent with you. I'm glad it's all over between us and that there's nothing more

235

you can do to hurt me, Dafydd.'

'We'll see about that.' He caught her elbow and propelled her along the path. Two men appeared as if from nowhere, flanking Jayne and cutting her off from prying eyes.

'Dafydd, this is madness! Stop it or I'll start screaming!'

He clamped his hand over her mouth and pushed her towards his waiting carriage. He thrust her up the steps so violently that she fell in on her knees. Then he climbed in after her and the two men seated themselves at either side of her so she could hardly move. Jayne began to panic as Dafydd called to the driver to move on.

Jayne struggled to sit upright, pushing aside Dafydd's hand. 'How dare you treat me like this?' she said. 'You know I don't love you, Dafydd. However many times you make a prisoner of me you'll never have me.'

'But whatever you do, whoever you run to, you are my wife in the eyes of the law. Any judge would uphold my rights over you.'

Jayne stared at him, hating him. 'You will never keep me, Dafydd. The minute you turn your back I'll be gone. And once my father realizes what's happened he'll send his men to fetch me home.'

'The way he did before?' His voice was heavy with sarcasm. 'I don't think he'll get very far, not if I call the constables and tell them I'm being threatened.'

Jayne stared out of the window, wondering if it was safe to jump clear but the road was rolling past at a remarkable speed. Still, anything was better than allowing Dafydd to imprison her again.

She made to open the door of the carriage but

Dafydd caught her in his arms and pressed her back into the seat. 'You don't escape that easily, my dear wife.' He pressed his mouth to hers in a cruel kiss, which held no passion and certainly no love. Jayne tried to struggle but he was too strong, so she became passive, neither reacting to nor repelling his advances.

When he moved away from her she looked into his eyes. 'You will never possess me again, Dafydd. I'd rather kill myself than stay with you for the rest of my life.'

'As for possessing you, I don't want to,' Dafydd said easily. 'You're a cold woman and once Fairchild has had enough of you he'll toss you aside, as if you were one of the common whores with whom he usually finds his pleasure.'

One of Dafydd's men laughed crudely, and Jayne felt the colour rush into her face. But she remained silent. She knew that Dafydd was trying to rile her. Well, it would take more than a few lies to turn her away from Guy this time. Now she knew that Guy loved her for herself, not for anything she could give him.

She took a deep breath. 'Look, Dafydd, if I gave you my railway shares, would you let me go?'

'I might, but then again I might not.' He smiled without warmth. 'I don't quite know what I'm going to do with you yet. I might send you to a convent or have you certified insane.'

Jayne drew a ragged breath, knowing he was capable of anything. If a husband swore that a faithless wife had lost her senses his word would be respected.

'Ah, I see the truth is dawning on you. If I have you certified I shall have all your money as well as the railway shares. It's a tempting prospect, Jayne.'

'Dafydd, you couldn't do that—my father wouldn't allow it.'

'Your father carries some weight in Swansea, I'll grant you that, but what if I take you to my home town, have you declared insane and committed to an institution in Carmarthen or Llanelli?'

'You don't think my father would stand by meekly while you did all that, do you? You underestimate the scope of his influence and I'd advise you to think carefully before you do anything so drastic.'

'Oh, I have thought carefully, Jayne, my dear.' Dafydd stared at her for a long moment in silence. 'However, if you give me a legitimate heir perhaps then I'll let you run away with your lover.'

'Never!' Jayne said fiercely. 'I'll never go to your bed again, Dafydd, not willingly. Of course, you could force me again but I would bide my time until I could find a way to be rid of you permanently.'

'So you would stoop to murder, would you?'

Jayne studied this man who was her husband. Would she be able to kill him in cold blood? She doubted it, but who knew what would happen if she were forced to share Dafydd's bed again?

'Are you going to answer me?'

'Dafydd, I don't know what I'd do if you pushed me too far. All I do know is that everything is over between you and me. I don't love you, it's probable that I never loved you, and I would rather die than be subject to you.'

Jayne fell silent and stared through the carriage window. As the streets of Swansea sped by she saw that Dafydd was not taking her to his Swansea

238

home, he was heading west towards Carmarthen. It was there that he had fought a battle against the rise in the toll charges; there that her father's wife Isabella had been killed beneath the hoofs of a horse. And in Carmarthen there was a big building that housed the insane, the House of Bedlam, people called it. Jayne shivered. Dafydd might just be prepared to carry out his threats.

She looked at this man, a stranger, her husband. His eyes were closed as if he was sleeping, but she knew that if she moved he would be wide awake in an instant. She must keep calm, think carefully and plan her escape. Dafydd would not stay at home all day every day: he had a business to run.

It seemed an eternity before the carriage jolted to a halt outside a tall grey stone building that was unfamiliar to Jayne. Dafydd opened his eyes and sat up. 'Welcome to my latest acquisition, my dear wife,' he said. 'I bought this place especially for you, Jayne. Did you think my appearance at your father's wedding was a coincidence? Well, if you did you were wrong. I knew your father would be occupied with the beautiful Llinos—indeed, he would be so eager to get his wife home that he would forget the existence of his daughter or anyone else for that matter.'

Dafydd alighted from the carriage and grasped Jayne's arm as she came down the steps. He gestured to the two men and they bundled her unceremoniously into the house. 'You can go now,' Dafydd said, and the men disappeared.

The room Dafydd had chosen for her was at the top of the house. It was so spartan that Jayne knew it must be among the servants' quarters.

'I'm to sleep here?' she asked, her eyebrows

239

raised. 'Well, even sleeping in servants' quarters is preferable to sleeping with you.'

'For heaven's sake, do think of something different to say.'

'If I tell you enough times that I will not be intimate with you perhaps it will sink into your head.'

'That's enough!' he said sternly. 'I have no intention of being insulted by you.' He looked at her disdainfully. 'You're no better than a whore, no better than the servant Rhiannon, or that poor child Sal. Indeed, you are worse because those girls chose to shake off their sordid past and became decent citizens.'

'Well, if I'm such a bad lot why bring me here? What on earth do you hope to gain from all this?'

'I might not gain anything but the satisfaction of parting you from your lover,' Dafydd said harshly. 'But at least I know you'll not be lying with him tonight or any other night, if I have my way.'

He moved to the door. 'I'll say goodbye for now, Jayne, and I do hope you'll soon settle into your new surroundings.'

'Am I not even allowed food or to wash and change my clothes?' Jayne demanded.

'You'll stay in your wedding finery for now. It will be a bitter reminder of all you have left behind.'

He left the room, closed the door, and she heard the key turn in the lock. She sank on to the bed and put her hands over her eyes. She was a prisoner, and what could she do about it? She had no friendly servants to help her now. Would she be condemned to spend the rest of her life in this room in this ugly house, far away from all that she loved?

Jayne longed to cry but the tears seemed stuck in her throat. She tried to think calmly, reasonably. Surely Dafydd must let her out of the room some time, if only to allow her the benefit of some fresh air. But, then, Dafydd had no intention of being kind to her in any way—he had made that abundantly clear.

Jayne kicked off her shoes and stretched out on the bed, conscious that outside the small window of the room was the big wide world filled with love and laughter, and she was no longer allowed to have any part in it.

She closed her eyes as, at last, the tears came. She felt so helpless. 'Oh, Guy, will I ever see you again?' she whispered, but there was only the silence of the empty room to answer her.

* * *

'Well, my lovely bride, we've had a wonderful day and our honeymoon is just beginning but I think it's high time we retired to our beds, don't you?' Eynon smiled at her and Llinos, absurdly, felt her colour rise.

'What—blushing, Llinos?' Eynon put his finger under her chin and tilted her face upwards. After a moment, he kissed her and Llinos put her arms around him. They stood locked in an embrace for some time before she moved away.

'Right, then, husband, bed it is.' She held his hand, as he led the way up the curving staircase towards the huge suite of rooms he'd booked for them in the hotel on the beach. Outside the window, she could see the intermittent glow from

241

the lighthouse stretching fingers of gold across the sea.

Eynon stood behind her and drew her back towards him. 'It's a beautiful night, my love.' He kissed the top of her head. 'Llinos, I've dreamed of this so many times, you coming here as my bride. I can hardly believe that this is real.'

'It's real,' Llinos said softly. 'We're man and wife, Eynon. You might even be sorry you married me when you see how ill-humoured I am in the mornings.'

'I'll never be sorry, Llinos. The only thing that makes me sorry is that this didn't happen years ago when we were young.'

She turned to face him and cupped his cheeks in her hands. 'Let's not wait any longer, Eynon. Make me your wife in every way, and then we shall sleep and wake up in the morning wrapped in each other's arms.'

'I should call the maid to help you undress but I think that tonight I shall take charge of that myself.'

He began to open the hooks and eyes at the back of her dress and as his warm hands brushed her neck Llinos felt a great sense of tenderness towards him.

She helped him to undress her and, shy of her nakedness, slipped between the cool sheets on the large bed. Eynon cast aside his own clothes and then he was in bed beside her. His arms reached towards her and she prayed she would not disappoint him.

Gently, he lifted her hair and kissed her neck. His mouth was warm and he was breathing hard, so aroused he could hardly contain himself, yet he took his time, careful not to hurt her. 'You are so beautiful, Llinos.' He leaned on his elbow and looked down at her, and the lamplight was kind, bathing her in a rosy glow that took away any signs where age had left its mark.

At last, he drew her to him. 'I'm going to make us one flesh, my darling,' he whispered, his breath hot against her cheek. And then he came to her and she gasped with happiness as he moved her to his rhythm. Their passion united them, they were together locked in each other's arms, possessing each other with a joy that Llinos had thought was gone for ever. And when it was over she kissed him and whispered, 'At last I have come home.'

* * *

Dafydd stood before her, his arms folded across his chest, a set look on his face. 'Guy has the temerity to come here after you,' he said sharply. 'He won't believe you don't want him unless you tell him yourself, Jayne.'

Jayne stared at her husband in bewilderment. 'What makes you think I'll do that? I love Guy and I want to be with him.'

Dafydd reached in his pocket and took out a small pistol. 'You'd better persuade him that you want to give your marriage a second chance or I will have to shoot him—in self-defence, of course.'

Jayne felt the colour leave her face. 'Dafydd, you wouldn't.'

'Believe me, Jayne, I would, and Guy Fairchild wouldn't be the first man I've killed.'

Jayne stared at this man who was her husband. 'I never knew you at all, did I, Dafydd?'

'Don't be so melodramatic! Do you think I went through the riots, burning down gates, storming the workhouse, without killing anyone?'

Jayne realized he meant every word he said. She stared up at him fearfully. 'When is Guy coming?'

Dafydd looked at his watch. 'Any moment now. That's why I've brought you new clothing and that's why I've allowed you into the sitting room so that you can say goodbye to him for ever.'

The doorbell rang through the house and Jayne swallowed hard. She would have to make Guy believe her. She would have to convince him that she wanted to stay with Dafydd—or watch him die.

When he came into the room and stood before her, his eyes warm and loving as they rested on her, Jayne felt as though she was going to plunge a dagger into his heart. She looked away from him, afraid that her courage would fail her.

'I think my wife has something to say to you, Fairchild.' Dafydd's voice had a hard edge to it and his hand was in his pocket—with the pistol, no doubt.

'Guy, I'm sorry but I've decided to stay with Dafydd, to give my marriage a second chance.'

'I don't believe you,' Guy said at once. 'He's making you say this, isn't he, Jayne?'

She licked her dry lips and forced a note of determination into her voice. 'I mean it, Guy. I can't break my father's heart by running away with you and leaving him to face the shame of it.'

He came and stood close to her. 'Jayne, would you be saying these things if your husband wasn't standing there looking like the Day of Judgement?'

Jayne wanted to throw herself into his arms, to beg him to take her away with him but, from the corner of her eye, she saw Dafydd inch the gun out of his pocket.

'Guy,' she said, 'I don't want you. I intend to stay here with my husband. Now, will you please leave me in peace?'

Guy turned on his heel and marched to the door without saying another word. She heard the front door slam behind him and then she collapsed into a chair. 'I'll never forgive you for this, Dafydd. I'll hate you all the days of my life. Is that what you wanted?'

'I wanted you to turn that man away so that you can live your life under my roof as a wife should. Now, get back upstairs before I lose my temper with you.'

Jayne walked slowly away from her husband and climbed the stairs as though her feet were cased in lead. She felt as though there was nothing to live for any more. She went into her room and closed the door. It no longer mattered that she was to be locked in her room. There was no life for her any more, not without Guy, because anywhere she lived would be a prison now that Guy believed she no longer loved him. *Dafydd Buchan, I hate you!*

She sank on to the bed and sat there, staring ahead of her, seeing nothing but the pain in Guy's face.

CHAPTER TWENTY-THREE

'I can't get anywhere with Buchan.' Eynon was rubbing his eyes tiredly. 'He has refused to see me.' He threw down a letter he was holding. 'And this, from Jayne, claims she is living with Buchan willingly. It just doesn't ring true.' He thumped his fist on the table. 'He's forced her to write this, I know he has.'

Llinos took him in her arms. 'Don't be so angry, Eynon. We'll find a way to bring Jayne home, you'll see. Dafydd can't be so heartless as to keep her imprisoned in that awful house for long.' Even as she said the words she knew that Dafydd had become selfish and arrogant, and was quite capable of keeping Jayne a prisoner for as long as it suited him.

'Well, I can't just sit and wait for him to let her go. I must do something to help.'

'What if I went to see him?' Llinos kissed Eynon's cheek. 'He might talk to me.'

'I don't want you going anywhere near that man,' Eynon said fiercely. 'I don't trust him as far as I could throw him.'

'But, Eynon, if it would help Jayne surely it's worth a try? And don't worry about me—I'm well over my infatuation with him now.'

'I know that, but I don't like to think of you going anywhere near that scoundrel.'

'He'll see me, I'm sure, and at least I can find out if Jayne's all right.'

'Maybe you're right—but you would need to take someone with you. I can't have you going there alone.'

'That's something we can arrange,' Llinos said thoughtfully, 'and I can try to make Dafydd see sense.'

'All right, but don't make it a long visit. Ask to see Jayne so that you can confirm she is well.' He shrugged. 'As to her frame of mind, I can only guess at how unhappy she must be.'

'I'll go tomorrow. I won't warn him that I'm coming—I think it's best to take him by surprise.'

Eynon touched her cheek. 'You're sure it won't be too upsetting for you?'

'Believe me, anything I once felt for Dafydd died a long time ago. Now all I see when I look at him is a man who must have his own way whatever anyone feels or thinks.'

Llinos sat in a chair near the window and stared out at the pewter grey sea below her. White water lashed up against the rocks. It was a gloomy day, full of wind and rain, and reflected Llinos's feelings. The prospect of trying to persuade Dafydd to let Jayne go was not one she relished. But it had to be done and, in all truth, she was the best person to do it.

*   *   *

The first guest to inhabit a room at the Paradise Park was a Mr Summers. He was young and vigorous, with dark hair and flashing eyes, the type some women might find attractive. To Rhiannon, though, he was simply a sign that the enterprise was going to succeed, that the Paradise Park was on its way to being a thriving business.

'I think Mr Summers intends to stay here every time he visits Swansea.' Mrs Paisley was sitting in Rhiannon's room, toasting her feet beside the fire. 'More of his kind is what we need.'

'Well, this is where your famous word-of-mouth will come in handy,' Rhiannon said, 'and where my idea of advertising is reaping rewards.' She held up a letter. 'This is from a Mr Clements. He's a

247

chemist thinking of setting up a practice in the area and he's bringing his family with him this afternoon. As he has four children, that's several more rooms to be occupied. Soon we'll be looking at a full hotel. You'll see, Mrs Paisley, before long we'll be making a good living for ourselves.'

'Just as well there'll be some money coming in because there's a devil of a lot going out,' Mrs Paisley said drily.

'We needed to advertise our hotel, though, you can see that now, can't you?' Rhiannon asked anxiously, and was relieved when Mrs Paisley nodded.

'Aye, it had to be done, girl. You go on now and see to the paperwork because I'm going to have a nap.' She smiled wickedly. 'All this making a go of things has tired me.'

When Mrs Paisley had left the room Rhiannon stood at the window, looking at the busy street outside, where traders cried their wares in raucous tones. This was the town she had become used to: in her days as a whore she had walked the length of it, the back-streets as well as the main streets where elegant shops opened their doors to the rich and influential. Well, perhaps soon she would be rich herself, although she could never be influential. The gentry would never allow a whore into their closed circle.

She glanced along the street and her heartbeat quickened: Bull was walking past the Paradise Park, his head bent as he listened to his companion, a man several inches shorter than he was. Rhiannon watched him hungrily, drinking in the dark crispness of his hair beneath his hat and remembering how many times she had run her fingers through it as they made love.

Bull glanced up in her direction and their eyes met. After a moment, he raised his hat to her, and then he was gone from her sight, lost in the mêlée of the busy roadway.

Mentally, Rhiannon shook herself. There was work to be done: she needed to bring the books up to date, send out letters to people enquiring about rooms. 'Standing here staring into the street won't get the work done,' she said aloud.

A knock on the door startled her. 'Come in.'

'Oh, Rhiannon, *cariad*, I don't want to disturb you but I've got to know how many folk want dinner tonight.'

'Mrs Jones, come in and sit down. Now, let me see, there'll be Mr Clements and his family, Mr Summers and, of course, Mrs Paisley. I'll eat with you and Sal in the kitchen.' Mrs Jones frowned, and Rhiannon hid a smile. 'I'll dine with the guests when I'm more used to things, but for now Mrs Paisley will do the honours. Tell me what sort of menu you're planning for tonight.'

'We'll have soup to start and a nice bit of poached salmon to follow.' Mrs Jones crossed her meaty arms over her chest. 'Sal fetched us a fine bit of beef for the main course and I'm going to stuff that with oysters.'

Rhiannon nodded, grateful that the cook was experienced enough to make a meal fit for the gentry, let alone travelling businessmen and their families. 'And to follow?'

'Apples stuffed with cream, and chopped peaches served with a good thick custard. How does that sound?'

'Wonderful. You're a treasure, Mrs Jones.'

'It's easy to be a treasure when there's plenty of money to go round, but I'm proud to say this dinner is economical to make. I bought a cheap cut of beef and I'll cook it real slow. As for the fish, I got it for nothing.'

'How did that happen?'

Mrs Jones laughed. 'Not because of my charm, *cariad*, I'm too old for that sort of caper. No, I did a favour for the fishmonger's wife, cooked four chickens for her in that lovely big oven we got in the kitchen.' She paused. 'I know we have to go careful for a while so I'm looking for any way I can find to cut costs.' She squared her shoulders. 'But I can't stand here gossiping all day, I've got work to do.'

On an impulse Rhiannon hugged her. 'I don't know what I'd do without you.'

Mrs Jones brushed a hand over her eyes. 'Don't talk daft. If it wasn't for you I'd be on the streets.'

As the door closed behind Mrs Jones, Rhiannon went to stand in the window again. She hardly saw the traffic, or heard the calls of the street vendors. She was hoping for another glimpse of Bull Beynon.

* * *

'So he's sent you now, has he?' Dafydd Buchan stood looking at Llinos, the woman he had loved so dearly, lost to him now because of Morton-Edwards—curse him! Why did the women in his life turn to other men?

'No one sent me!' Llinos said, her eyes alight with anger. 'You should know me better than that. I came of my own accord.'

250

'All right, but for heaven's sake, sit down. Don't stand there glowering as if you want to stick a knife in my heart.'

Llinos sat down. 'I don't want to quarrel with you, Dafydd, I just want to be sure that Jayne is all right.'

'Of course she is. How is my son?' Dafydd saw Llinos frown. 'There's nothing wrong, is there? Sion is well, isn't he?'

'He is well and happy.' She looked up at him and her beautiful eyes were filled with tears. 'But he would rather be with his friends than with his mother.' She shrugged. 'I suppose that's natural.'

Dafydd sat beside her, taking her hands in his. 'What the boy needs is a fatherly hand to guide him.' He felt a flicker of anger as Llinos took her hands away.

'The only father Sion knew is dead and buried. Don't try to have a part in his life now, it's far too late for that.' She sat up straight. 'I would very much like to see Jayne.'

Dafydd sighed. He could never refuse Llinos anything—not when she looked up at him so earnestly with those wonderful eyes.

'You can go up to her room,' he stood up reluctantly, 'but I'll have to lock you in. You can ring the bell when you want to leave.'

Llinos looked at him and he could read the scorn in her eyes. 'Is that the only way you can keep a woman these days, Dafydd?'

'Don't interfere in my business, Llinos. No one is allowed to do that, not even you.' He felt ashamed but he would never let Llinos know that. 'This is a favour I'm doing you, and please don't get any foolish ideas about helping Jayne escape because

251

you'll both be closely watched.'

He walked up the stairs ahead of her but on the landing he paused. 'I was cuckolded by my dear wife. Do you think any man could take such betrayal and not be bitter?'

Llinos didn't reply and Dafydd unlocked the door and let her in to the room that had been his wife's prison for more than a week. He locked it again, went back downstairs and stood, hands thrust into his pockets, wondering to what depths he had sunk in imprisoning a woman who despised him.

He took a deep breath. Jayne had brought it all upon herself. It was only right that she suffered for what she had done. It made his blood boil to think of her in Guy Fairchild's arms. Fairchild would marry someone else now and then Jayne would learn what loneliness and betrayal meant.

*   *   *

Dinner was turning out to be a jolly occasion and Rhiannon, her dark hair tied up in a knot, helped to serve it. She was able to observe the guests seated around the long table and knew they were enjoying a hearty meal in pleasant company.

Mrs Paisley came into her own when guests were present and kept them amused with stories about the days when she was young. Her easy manner encouraged laughter and even Mr Summers, who at first kept his distance, was drawn to speak about his travels.

Once back in the kitchen, Rhiannon sank into a chair. Mrs Jones looked at her and smiled. 'Worn out, are you, love?'

'Yes, but I'm contented too. You're to be congratulated on providing a dinner fit for a king, Mrs Jones.'

'Well, there's praise indeed!' The cook was flushed with pleasure. 'It's nice to have a pat on the back now and again. That's something the gentry don't realize.' She looked up as Sal came into the kitchen with a tray full of dishes. 'You can leave those until later, Sal. Come and sit down and we'll all have a nip of the sherry, shall we?'

Rhiannon smiled her approval. 'That sounds like a very good idea. I think we've worked our fingers to the bone tonight. Soon we'll need more staff, we can't go on doing everything ourselves.'

'Vi and Hetty are out of a job.' Sal placed the dishes on the side of the sink and sank into a chair. 'Seems they were dismissed soon after us.'

'I wouldn't want that Hetty round here,' Mrs Jones said. 'Tongue like a viper that girl's got.'

'Oh, go on, she's not that bad,' Sal protested.

Rhiannon poured the sherry into three glasses and handed them round. The dishes could wait. Most of the upstairs work was done and the guests would be retiring to their rooms before long. She supposed the beds should be turned down but even that could wait while she drank some of the amber liquid. It was warm and comfortable in the kitchen and everyone deserved a respite before getting back to work again.

Perhaps it would be a good idea to employ Hetty and Violet, she thought. They knew the way Mrs Jones liked to organize her cooking, they had both shopped for the best cuts of meat, they were bright girls and, most of the time, good workers.

'You're quiet, Rhiannon.' Sal held her small feet

close to the fire, her thin legs protruding from under her skirts, and Rhiannon felt a wave of pity for the girl. The last few weeks had been hard on her. Still, now that she was in a good job and had good food to put in her belly, Sal would soon blossom again.

'It's not a bad idea of yours to bring in Hetty and Vi. I'm sure they'll both work harder than ever now that they know what being out of work feels like. Do you think they'd like a job in a hotel, Sal?'

'They'd jump at the chance!' Sal smiled. 'So long as the pair of them keeps their eyes off my Seth we'll get on just fine.'

'Oh, he's your Seth now, is he?' Rhiannon said teasingly.

Sal blushed. 'Well, he seems to like me and he doesn't care anything about my past.'

'Well, good luck to the pair of you.' Mrs Jones heaved herself out of her chair. 'He'll be getting a good one if he gets you, my girl. Now, come on, Sal, me and you will do the dishes, let Rhiannon rest a bit.'

'Why should I be allowed to rest?' Rhiannon asked.

'Well, you got to do more paperwork and you're running the hotel. I don't see it fair you should be a kitchenmaid as well.'

'All right. I'll go and turn down the beds.' Rhiannon got to her feet and stood at the door for a moment watching Sal pile dishes into the sink. The aroma in the kitchen was a mingling of sweet and savoury smells, the fire crackled cheerfully in the big hearth and all was peace and harmony.

Rhiannon crossed her fingers for luck and, for good measure, sent up a silent prayer that all the good things would continue. She'd seen enough bad things to last her a lifetime.

CHAPTER TWENTY-FOUR

Jayne sat quietly in her room, a feeling of resignation washing over her. She had tried to get away from Dafydd, she had pleaded with him, threatened him and even attempted to bribe him, but he wouldn't budge an inch. It seemed she was doomed to spend the rest of her life in captivity. Not even a visit from Llinos had changed his mind.

Her father had called—more than once she had heard his angry voice in the hall—but Dafydd had always denied him entrance. He was not even allowed to see Jayne, let alone speak to her. 'Please, Father, bring some men and get me out of here,' Jayne whispered, under her breath.

Now the ringing of the doorbell vibrated through the house and Jayne lifted her head, wondering if her prayers were about to be answered. She hurried to the door and pressed her ear against the keyhole. Had her father arrived with a band of men to demand her release? Perhaps she might even dare to hope that Guy had come back for her. But, then, Guy thought she no longer loved him: he had gone away thinking she wanted to be with Dafydd.

She backed across the room as she heard footsteps coming up the stairs. The key turned in the lock and the door swung open. Jayne tried to hide her disappointment as Llinos came into the room.

'Jayne, Dafydd's given me permission to visit you

again.'

Jayne held out her arms. 'It's good to see a friendly face.' She kissed Llinos's cheek. 'Is he letting me out of here?'

Llinos smoothed back Jayne's tangled hair. 'I don't know.' She looked troubled. 'He wasn't easily persuaded to let me in.'

'Oh, I see.' Jayne sank on to the bed and gestured for Llinos to take the plush armchair near the fire. 'But, then, Dafydd would never refuse you anything.'

'He's a stubborn man, though.' Llinos looked down at her hands, and twisted her bright new wedding ring. 'He's angry, but his pride has been hurt more than anything.' She looked up and Jayne met her eyes. 'His intention was for Guy Fairchild to get your shares from you. He never thought you two would fall in love.'

'Well, it just serves him right!' Jayne knew she sounded childish. 'He's a fool! I offered him the shares and he wouldn't take them!' Jayne tried hard to keep her voice level. 'I think all Dafydd wants now is to punish me for loving Guy and not him.'

Llinos stared out of the window and Jayne knew that she had no ready solution to her problem. But perhaps, just perhaps, there was something Llinos could do for her.

'Llinos, will you find Guy and give him a message? Please tell him I was forced to lie to him and I love him. I need him to come for me or I'll die in this room.'

'Mr Fairchild has left the area,' Llinos said gently. 'I think you and Dafydd convinced him you were giving the marriage a second chance.'

It seemed that all her struggles to be free had been pointless. If Guy had gone away, if he believed she would rather be with Dafydd than with him, there was no point in fighting any more. She might just as well resign herself to living alone in this one room for ever.

'Jayne,' Llinos leaned towards her, 'what did you mean when you said Dafydd forced you to lie? How could he force you to do something you didn't want to?'

'He had a pistol,' Jayne said, 'and he would have used it if I hadn't done what he said.' She sighed heavily. 'Don't be shocked. There's a darker side to Dafydd, a side you've never seen.'

'I can believe that,' Llinos said. 'I knew he was capable of violence when he ran with the rioters, but I never thought he'd bring that side of him into his home.'

'You know my husband better than I ever did,' Jayne said, 'and now I no longer care. I just wish to God he still wanted you.' She put her head in her hands.

'Don't be downhearted, Jayne,' Llinos said softly. 'If it will help I'll try to find Mr Fairchild, tell him what really happened.'

A glimmer of hope crept into Jayne's heart. 'Would you do that for me, Llinos?'

'I could try,' Llinos said. 'With your father's help I'm sure I'll manage to track him down.'

'Where do you think he's gone?' Jayne asked. 'The world is a big place, he could be anywhere.'

Llinos pushed a curl away from her face. 'I did hear he'd gone to Cornwall. Watt Bevan was down there on business and he saw Mr Fairchild. It seems he was investing money in some china-clay business.'

'Are you sure it was Guy he saw? Putting money into china clay doesn't sound like Guy,' Jayne said doubtfully. 'He doesn't know anything about the pottery business and never showed any interest in it.'

'Well, I don't think Watt would be mistaken over something like that. He loves the china industry and he's every inch a businessman.'

'Oh, I'm not doubting Watt's word,' Jayne said, 'but I hardly dare hope that finding Guy would be so easy.'

'Strangely enough, Mr Fairchild was doing business with a man who used to work for me a long time ago. You wouldn't remember John. He's a man not over-blessed with scruples so I think Mr Fairchild would do well to watch his investments closely.'

Jayne was not the least concerned about Guy's ventures: he had money to invest and to spare and he was too clever to be duped in business matters.

'So, you know where to find him, then?' Jayne's voice shook with excitement. 'Oh, Llinos, please get a message to him as soon as you can.'

'I'll do my best,' Llinos said. 'But, Jayne, don't hope for too much. After all, what can Mr Fairchild do? You are married to Dafydd and have a responsibility to him, both in the eyes of the townspeople and the law.'

Jayne didn't give a fig for the townspeople or the law: she knew that Guy would stop at nothing to get her away from Dafydd and he was clever enough to use guile rather than knock on the front door again. 'Guy will get me away from here, I know he will. Just tell him the truth and that I'm being held against my will.'

'I'll do everything I can,' Llinos said, 'but he might have moved on, found himself other interests. After all, he's a single man—a rich and handsome man.'

Jayne shook her head in exasperation. Llinos, of all people, should know the power of love. Guy truly loved her, he wanted to be with her, and she hungered to be with him. 'Just get the message to him, that's all I ask.' Jayne went to where Llinos was sitting and knelt down beside her. 'I know I haven't always been kind to you and I wouldn't blame you if you turned me down, but I vow I'll never ask another thing from you if only you'll do this for me.'

Llinos hesitated, but then, after what seemed an eternity, she nodded. 'I'll do as you ask—but, Jayne, don't let anything slip in front of Dafydd.'

'I don't give Dafydd the time of day, let alone discuss my lover with him,' Jayne said firmly. She was filled with excitement, her mind racing, and it was hard to keep her voice low. 'I'm glad you came, you've given me new hope,' she said, her voice breaking with emotion. 'I know Guy loves me as much as I love him. Oh, Llinos, if only I could be with him again I'd be so happy.'

'Are you sure about that, Jayne?' Llinos asked. 'Do you want to spend your life as an outcast from society?'

'You've never worried about what people say, Llinos,' Jayne said. 'You had your son and everyone in Swansea knew that Dafydd was the father, so being an outcast never bothered you. In any case, Guy and I will go away, perhaps abroad to Paris or Italy. All I know is that I want to be with him.'

259

The door swung open and Dafydd stood on the threshold. 'I think you two ladies have had enough time to conspire against me,' he said, and Jayne could tell by the look in his eyes that he had heard Guy's name mentioned. She remained silent as Dafydd moved further into the room.

'So, you've been discussing your lover with Llinos, have you, Jayne?' he said, in a hard voice. 'Well, you'll never see him again so don't fool yourself into thinking Llinos can help you.' He moved closer to Jayne. There was a strange look in his eyes.

Llinos pushed him aside and hugged Jayne. 'I'll come back to see you again . . . if Dafydd will allow it,' she said.

'Come by all means, but don't try bringing Morton-Edwards and a gaggle of men with you. And, Llinos,' he caught her arm, 'don't meddle in something that is none of your business. I let you see Jayne to make sure she is well but if you overstep the mark you won't be allowed into my house again.'

'I understand,' Llinos said quickly. 'I don't want a war any more than you do, Dafydd.'

'Good. Now come along, it's time Jayne was having her afternoon rest. She's not as young as she used to be,' he said cruelly.

'Not as young as that harlot you bring into my house, you mean,' Jayne said flatly.

Llinos saw a glimmer of a smile cross Dafydd's face. 'Oh, so the servants have been talking to you, have they?'

'They haven't needed to. I could tell by the girlish laughter outside my door that you had a young woman in the house.'

Llinos stared at Dafydd, waiting for him to refute Jayne's words but he did not. 'Come along, Llinos, it's time you were going before my wife starts to spit like the cat she is.'

Jayne watched as Llinos was bundled out on to the landing. She pulled out of Dafydd's grasp. 'There's no need to treat me like that,' she said.

Dafydd apologized at once. 'Forgive me, Llinos, I sometimes forget myself after spending more than a few minutes in the company of my wife.'

Jayne watched Dafydd close the door and heard the key turn in the lock. She had hope now, and if Llinos kept her word, it would not be long before Guy came for her.

* * *

Llinos followed Dafydd down the graceful staircase, wondering what had happened to the young man with whom she had once been besotted. All she saw now was a man who lived life to excess in every way.

In the hall, Dafydd rested his hands on her shoulders. 'Don't judge me too harshly, Llinos.' He spoke gently, the anger gone from his face. 'Jayne has humiliated me, rebuffed me. What sort of wife will not sleep in her husband's bed?'

'The sort of wife who has grown tired of being bullied and ridiculed. You can't claim you've been a good husband to Jayne, not even in the early days of your marriage.'

'Oh, but you're wrong there. I fell in love with Jayne—some time after I married her, I'll grant you—but love her I did.'

'Well, none of this is my concern,' Llinos said. 'I

came here because Eynon asked me to and because I feel sorry for Jayne. What sort of life is she leading, locked up like an animal? Can't you let her go, Dafydd?'

'I might release her some time but not just yet. Jayne needs punishing for what she's done to me.'

Llinos moved towards the door, 'I'd better go, there's nothing more I can do here.'

'Wait.' Dafydd caught her hand and held it tightly. 'Don't look at me with such disgust, Llinos. What would any man do who learned his wife had been unfaithful?'

'You're asking the wrong person, Dafydd, or have you forgotten that I betrayed my husband with you? Joe forgave me, but he was a better man than you could ever be.'

Dafydd drew her to him. 'You loved me once, Llinos, and you were eager for my embrace. I remember how you cried out in joy when we made love.' He touched her cheek. 'And you are still beautiful, Llinos. You're the sort of woman who never loses her looks. There's a magnetism about you that no man could resist. I still care about you, Llinos. You're the mother of my son, after all.'

Llinos sighed. 'I'll never play the unfaithful wife again, Dafydd,' she said. 'I don't feel anything for you now, except perhaps anger that you could treat Jayne the way you do.'

With an abrupt movement Dafydd's grip tightened and then his mouth was on hers. Llinos remained still in his arms. She neither responded nor rebuffed him and at last Dafydd released her.

'Do you really feel nothing for me now?' He was like a small boy who had lost his favourite toy.

'I feel nothing for you, Dafydd. You will always

be Sion's father and I can never forget that, but as for caring for you or being bedazzled by you, that died long ago.'

Llinos hurried outside, welcoming the feel of the cool air on her cheeks. She climbed into her carriage and leaned back in the leather seat. How could one man cause so much havoc in the lives of the women with whom he became involved? Instead of going straight home, she told the driver to take her to Pottery Row: she would talk to Watt and find out more about Guy Fairchild's whereabouts.

Watt was in the painting shed demonstrating a new pattern to one of the workers. When he saw Llinos he put down his brush and wiped his hands on a cloth then came towards her. 'Llinos, why didn't you warn me you were coming? I would have had some tea or coffee waiting for you.'

'I just called in on a whim but some tea would be welcome.' She linked arms with him as they left the sheds and made their way across the yard towards the house.

It was strange to go in through the back door and smell the familiar scents of the house, knowing that she no longer lived there. Watt and his family were in residence now and they had made it their own. The designs Watt had created for the china were framed and hung on the walls and new curtains fluttered at the windows. The house held so many memories, most of them shared by Watt.

'Remember when my father came home from the war in France, Watt?' she asked quietly. 'He was so badly injured it was a wonder he survived.'

'I remember,' Watt replied. 'Joe was with him, looking after the captain so well you'd have thought he was his own father.'

'All a long time ago now, Watt, water under the bridge.' But she looked round at the familiar rooms and knew that part of her would always belong to the very fabric of the house.

When they were both seated in the drawing room Llinos looked up at Watt. 'How's Rosie?'

'Very well, thank you. She's gone shopping in town today,' he replied. 'But why are you really here, Llinos? Not thinking of taking up work at the pottery again, are you?'

Was there a hint of anxiety in Watt's voice? Llinos reassured him quickly: 'No, of course not. Eynon would be furious if I even thought of such a move. No, I've come to ask you about Guy Fairchild. Jayne asked me to find out what I could about him.'

'I didn't see much of him, but I was surprised when I discovered he was associated with a man like John Pendennis.'

'I know what you mean.' Llinos frowned. 'When John worked for me he was never trustworthy—he even thought he could take the pottery away from me once, do you remember?'

Watt nodded. 'How could I forget?' He rubbed his beard, which was streaked now with white. 'It did occur to me to warn Fairchild but it didn't seem to be any of my business.'

'On the other hand, it might be that John has changed. He's an older and perhaps wiser man now.'

'I don't think so, Llinos,' Watt said. 'According to gossip, John had his revenge on a local man who offended him. It seems he ruined the man, took his business from him. No, I don't think he's changed.'

'Well, anyway, this is not about John. I want to know if there is a way of contacting Guy Fairchild.'

'I'll be going to Cornwall again next week so I could take a letter to him.'

'Fetch me some paper and a pen, Watt. I'll write to him at once and tell him what a state poor Jayne is in.'

'Llinos, you're a generous woman. The way Jayne has treated you in the past you'd have every right to hate her and yet you're helping her.'

'I'm married to her father, which makes me her stepmother. In any case, I can't bear to see her so unhappy. She's a prisoner in a horrible house that Dafydd bought with the sole intention of keeping her there.'

Watt smiled. 'You always were a champion of the underdog, Llinos, and I love you for it.'

While Watt went away to find pen and ink and some writing paper Llinos leaned back in her chair and stared up at the familiar ceiling of the drawing room. She had spent most of her life here, as a young girl alone struggling to survive, as a married woman, and as a widow. When Watt returned, Llinos scribbled a note and sealed it. She gave it to Watt. 'Keep it safe and promise me you'll hand it to Guy Fairchild in person.'

'I'll do that as soon as I arrive in Cornwall. Now that our business is concluded, perhaps you'd like to talk to Rosie. She's just come in and she's waiting in the sitting room, eager to see you.'

'I'd love to,' she said, and after a last glance around the room, she followed Watt out.

CHAPTER TWENTY-FIVE

Rhiannon followed Mrs Paisley around the hotel, admiring it in its newly refurbished glory, excitement bringing colour to her cheeks. The bookings were up on last month and satisfied customers were taking rooms every time their business brought them to Swansea.

'Well, what do you think of our little enterprise now?' she said, as she stepped into Mrs Paisley's small office on the ground floor.

Mrs Paisley didn't answer until she was seated at her desk. 'I'll tell you once I get my breath back.' She was puffing heavily and Rhiannon saw that the old lady had overtaxed herself. 'We've been up and down those stairs so many times I'm quite dizzy,' Mrs Paisley panted. 'Anyway, why don't you tell me what *you* think of it?' She redid her small greying bun and replaced her hat on her head, although she had no intention of venturing outdoors.

'I just knew in my heart that the Paradise Park was going to do well,' Rhiannon declared.

Mrs Paisley gave a little snort. 'I think you're understating the case, Rhiannon. This hotel of ours is flourishing, not just doing well. But it's early days, mind,' she added, a warning note in her voice. 'We still have to be cautious with the money.'

'You're right, of course,' Rhiannon replied. 'By the way, have you been to the bank yet?'

'Plenty of time for that. I've got the money hidden well, and no one will outsmart old Mrs Paisley in a hurry.'

Rhiannon bit her lip. The bank account was in

Mrs Paisley's name, and because of that the old lady had complete control of the finances. Her own name should be added to the account in case Mrs Paisley was too sick to go into town. Rhiannon was just about to put her thoughts into words when Mrs Paisley spoke again. It was as though she'd read Rhiannon's mind. 'We'll have to go down into town together and put your name on the account. It's not easy for me to get about with this arthritis bothering me.'

'That's a splendid idea.' Rhiannon moved to the door. 'Shall we go later today?'

Mrs Paisley mulled over the question, as though it was of great import. Then she nodded. 'Why not? I could do with a breath of fresh air in my poor old lungs.'

Rhiannon smiled to herself. Mrs Paisley took her time to make decisions and that pleased her: she was a steadying influence and would make sure that Rhiannon didn't get carried away with excitement and make rash decisions. Just then the tinkling of the doorbell sounded. 'I think our latest guest has arrived. I'll go and see to him.'

Rhiannon hurried into the hall, but Sal, dressed smartly in her maid's uniform, had already opened the front door and a tall gentleman dressed in black stepped inside. Sal moved back, making herself almost invisible, and Rhiannon smiled: Sal was learning fast.

'You are Mr Wellington?' She moved forward to greet the guest.

The gentleman removed his gloves before taking her extended hand in a firm grip. 'I am indeed, madam. I presume you are the proprietor of this hotel.'

'You presume correctly,' Rhiannon said. 'Would you like to inspect the room before you take it?'

Mr Wellington shook his head. 'No, dear lady, the recommendation I received from a colleague regarding your establishment is enough for me. Perhaps you have a boy to bring my boxes to my room?'

'I'll see to it, Mr Wellington. Sal, will you show the gentleman to suite three?' She watched as Sal, head bent demurely, led the way up the stairs. Sal had changed so much: these days, she was every inch a modest young woman following a respectable trade as a hotel servant.

Rhiannon looked at the boxes, of which there were at least six. It seemed her new guest intended his stay to be a lengthy one. She would have to employ a boy to do the heavy work. In the meantime it would be up to herself and the other servants to carry up the boxes.

It was a good thing she had taken on Vi and Hetty: after a spell of unemployment both girls had been eager to work. Still, a strong young man was needed, and Rhiannon made a mental note to discuss the matter with Mrs Paisley.

She lifted one of the boxes and balanced another on top of it, climbed the stairs with difficulty, hampered by her long skirts, and deposited them on the landing outside suite three. Another trip should deal with the smaller stuff, but she would need help with the two larger boxes. That would have to wait, however: now she had to discuss lunch with Mrs Jones.

In the kitchen the cook was kneading dough for the loaves she would bake for supper that evening.

'*Duw*, Rhiannon, don't creep about like that—

you nearly gave me a heart-attack!' Mrs Jones rubbed the flour from her hands. 'Still, I'll just put the dough to prove and then I'll be with you.'

Mrs Jones might have been getting on in years but she was still as agile as a woman half her age. She put the dough on a tray and covered it with a cloth then stood it in the hearth. 'Vi!' she called. 'Get some water for the kettle, there's a good girl, and be quick about it.' She sank into a chair, pushed back a strand of frizzy hair and kicked off her slippers. 'I expect you want to know what I've got for the main meal, do you, girl?'

'I do, but a cup of tea and a sit-down sounds good. My legs are aching from climbing up and down the stairs. We've got another guest and it looks as if he's planning to stay for some time, judging by the amount of luggage he's brought with him.'

'That's what we like to hear.' Mrs Jones rested her elbows on the table and looked at Rhiannon. 'I am grateful, mind, *cariad*.'

'What for?' Rhiannon said. 'It's me who should be grateful to you. Who else would work for nothing as you did until the money started coming in?'

Mrs Jones wiped her eyes with her apron. 'Aye, but I had bed and board and I can't forget that if it wasn't for you I'd be out on the streets.'

Violet came in with the kettle and set it on the side of the fire, then arranged the coals with the poker.

'Get on with it, Vi, or we won't be having this tea until supper-time.' Mrs Jones sighed. 'Got to keep on to them all the time, you have, or these girls won't do anything right.'

'I'm doing my best, Cook,' Violet said. 'I can't make the kettle boil any faster, can I?'

'No, but you can make it boil slower by fiddling around with the fire like that. The weight of the kettle will settle the coals, never mind you playing around with them.'

'Only trying to help, I was. There's no gratitude shown round here whatever a body does.'

'Gratitude!' Mrs Jones flushed. 'You gets your pay, girl, and you 'as a warm bed at night and good food. It's you who should be showing gratitude, no one else.'

Rhiannon switched her mind away from the wrangling between the cook and the maid: it was an everyday event—senior servants were privileged to rebuke the younger ones, and it was expected in the hierarchy of the kitchen. She settled back in her chair with a feeling of well-being. The business of the Paradise Park was growing and with that she was content.

*   *   *

Bull sank down on the grassy bank beside the railway track and shaded his eyes from the sun with his hand. The track gleamed like silver against the earth and in the distance he could see the smoke from the train coming into Swansea. He glanced at his watch: the train was on time and pride filled him. He watched as the engine drew nearer shooting sparks into the grass. Its sheer strength and majesty enthralled Bull. He felt the breeze as the carriages rolled past him and smiled. The railway was his life—more so since he'd lost Katie and the baby.

270

Suddenly the light seemed to vanish from the sky and instead of excitement he felt sorrow: he was alone in the world now, with no one to share his life. He'd enjoyed going home after work and telling Katie all about his day. She used to listen with rapt attention and even though she knew little about the running of a line she always showed an interest in what he had to tell her.

'Good day to you, Bull. Mind if I sit a bit with you?'

'No need to ask, Seth, this is a free country.' Bull felt a dart of pity as he watched Seth make his way cautiously along the bank, using the crutch he had made for himself.

'You look lonely, Bull. To be sure, I'm right sad you lost your little wife and babba and I wish I could have saved her for you.'

Bull sighed. Seth voiced the same words every time they met. Didn't he realize that the very mention of the accident sent Bull into a spiral of despair?

'See the two thirty roll past, then, Bull?' Seth changed the subject, as though sensing Bull's thoughts. 'Sure 'tis a wonderful thing, a railway engine.'

The two men fell silent. After a time Seth took out a flask and handed it to Bull, who took it and drank a mouthful of the gin then handed it back. He glanced at Seth: he was still a young man, but his injuries had left their mark in the lines of pain on his face. Yet the man was still drawn to the railway, still enchanted by the sight of the smoking beast rolling through the countryside like a dragon. It was in his blood just as it was in Bull's, and somehow that made a bond between them.

'I never thanked you proper, like,' Seth said. 'You saved my life, you did, and I'll never forget that.'

'You've thanked me already, Seth, and there's no need to thank me again. Any man would have done the same.'

Seth shook his head. 'No, they wouldn't. It took courage to pull me back.' He took another mouthful of gin. 'I hated you at first, mind, Bull, I wished you'd left me to die. Thought my life was over, I did, didn't believe any woman would want me like I am, but I was wrong.'

'Oh, you've found yourself a sweetheart, then, have you, Seth?'

'Aye, I have that.' He smiled, and Bull realized the man was quite handsome in a rough sort of way. 'Her name's Sal and she's a maid at the Paradise Park.' He glanced at Bull from the corner of his eye. 'Don't go getting any wrong notions, Bull. The Paradise Park is all respectable now, a place for gentlefolk to stay, businessmen from out of town.'

'I know,' Bull said, 'Rhiannon's running the place.'

'She's such a lady now, no one would think she had ever been . . .' he hesitated '. . . well, you know, a shanty-town woman.'

'Well, we all have things in our past that we're ashamed of, and Rhiannon had a tough life as a child. No one could blame her for taking the only way she knew to put food in her belly.'

'You were the making of that girl, Bull, turned her from a whore into a good woman, if you don't mind me saying so.'

Bull was strangely pleased by Seth's words. It

272

was comforting to think he might have helped Rhiannon make a better life for herself. He got to his feet. 'I'd better be off.' He stretched his arms above his head and looked up at the sky, a vast blue other world, far removed from unhappiness and pain.

Suddenly there seemed no point in going home to a house empty of love and laughter. Nevertheless, he walked away doggedly and climbed on to the road where he gazed at the busy streets. He felt small, a nonentity, a man alone.

*   *   *

'Well, I'm sorry we couldn't do all the business today.' Mrs Paisley clung to Rhiannon's arm. 'I suppose I was optimistic in thinking that the bank could sort everything out with one visit.'

'Never mind,' Rhiannon said. 'We've set things in motion. It won't take long for all the paperwork to be sorted out and then I can deal with the bank for you.'

'That will be a great relief,' Mrs Paisley said.

Rhiannon could see Mrs Paisley was very tired. 'I'll call us a cab—don't argue, my feet are aching and I can't face the walk back to the Paradise Park.' It was an excuse and both women knew it, but Mrs Paisley made no protest.

Once settled against the leather seat of the cab the old lady closed her eyes and even Rhiannon felt lulled by the sound of the horse's hoofs clip-clopping against the cobbles. She watched the crowds strolling past outside the shops as they drove along. It was a fine afternoon and it seemed the whole town was enjoying the sunshine. Then

273

she saw Bull, his tall, broad-shouldered frame unmistakable among the lesser mortals who thronged around him. She leaned as far out of the window as she dared, trying to see his face. When she did, her heart caught in her throat. There was a look of such utter sadness about him that tears came to her own eyes. She wanted to leap out of the cab, run to him, take him in her arms and kiss away the pain etched into his features. But she could do nothing except watch him, knowing that it was Katie he wanted in his arms.

She watched until Bull vanished from sight. Why was life so complicated? She had felt joyful, happy that her future was secure and now, with one glimpse of Bull's sad face, she was in the depths of despair.

The cab jerked to a halt outside the hotel and Mrs Paisley opened her eyes, coughing a little. 'Are we home already?'

Rhiannon nodded. She climbed down from the cab and held on to Mrs Paisley's arm, steadying the older woman as the horse jerked forward in the shafts.

'My head feels strange,' Mrs Paisley said, 'as though there's a heavy weight inside it.'

Rhiannon studied her carefully. She was rather pale and her hands trembled. 'Come on,' she swallowed her unhappiness, 'we'll have a nice cup of tea and you can put your feet up—we'll soon have you feeling as sprightly as a spring chicken.' She led the old lady towards the door of the hotel.

It was dim in the foyer as the lamps had not yet been lit for the evening. Rhiannon breathed in the scent of the place, the old leather, the beeswax polish and the roses in the bowl on the table, and felt comforted by it all. She might not have Bull by her side, she might never have a husband or children, but at least she had her pride in herself.

'That's strange.' Mrs Paisley pointed to the door of her office. 'I could swear I locked it before we went out.' She looked at Rhiannon, her face grey with fear. 'I left the money in there.'

In the office nothing seemed to have been disturbed. The desk was closed and the key was still in the small hidden drawer where Mrs Paisley kept it. All the same, Rhiannon thought it best to check everything. 'Look in the box, Mrs Paisley. Let's make sure the money is all there.'

Mrs Paisley unlocked the drawer and took out the tin box. Its key hung from her belt and the older woman glanced fearfully at Rhiannon before she turned it in the lock with trembling fingers. She flipped open the lid and gave a gasp of horror. 'The money's gone!'

'Now, keep calm, Mrs Paisley. Perhaps you put it somewhere else. Sit down and try to think clearly. Did you hide it in one of the other drawers?'

Mrs Paisley shook her head. 'I know I put the money in the box, but you have a good look, Rhiannon. I'm getting old and maybe forgetful.' There was an edge of hope in her voice, but as she sank into a chair she was ashen and her face was twisted in pain.

Rhiannon searched the desk slowly and methodically, knowing all the time that her efforts were in vain. The total takings gathered in the weeks the hotel had been open had disappeared.

'It's not here. The money is gone, Mrs Paisley,' she said softly. 'Try not to worry about it, we'll soon sort it out.' Her words rang hollow even in her own ears. The money was needed for supplies of food, for the staff to cook it, and for a million and one other things required to keep the hotel running smoothly.

Rhiannon became aware that Mrs Paisley was gasping for breath and clutching at her breast as though in pain.

'What is it, Mrs Paisley? What's wrong?'

'My chest—it's hurting as if the flames of hell were in there.'

'I'll get the doctor,' Rhiannon said. 'Now try to be calm, Mrs Paisley, everything is going to be all right.'

She rang the bell frantically, and soon Sal ran into the room. 'Fetch the doctor, Sal, and be as quick as you can.'

Sal needed no second bidding: she took one look at Mrs Paisley's grey face, twisted in pain, then turned and fled.

Rhiannon poured some water from the jug on the desk and held it to Mrs Paisley's lips. 'Have a sip of this.'

But Mrs Paisley shook her head, and as Rhiannon replaced the jug on the desk she turned in time to see Mrs Paisley slip to the floor.

Rhiannon bent over her, not knowing how to help.

'I can't breathe.' Mrs Paisley scrabbled at the neck of her gown.

Rhiannon loosened the collar with trembling fingers. 'The doctor will be here soon, don't try to talk.' She lifted the woman's head on to her lap but she could see that Mrs Paisley was very ill. She felt a sense of panic that the money was gone—and a drawer was full of bills to be paid. With Mrs Paisley so ill, it would be up to Rhiannon to sort out their financial problems. Could she do it alone?

'What a time for me to fall sick, girl.' It was as if Mrs Paisley had read her mind. 'I'm going to leave you with a lot of work, Rhiannon. Do you think you can manage on your own?' Her voice faded and Mrs Paisley closed her eyes. 'I'm that tired, girl, I think I could die of it.'

Rhiannon felt a stab of fear. 'Don't talk like that. You're not going to die—I won't let you.' She heard the front door slam and thanked God—Sal had returned with the doctor.

He was young, handsome and intelligent. He took in the problem at once. He knelt at Mrs Paisley's side and listened to her heart. After a moment he nodded. 'It's bed for you, my lady.' He smiled down at her. 'You're not to climb those stairs. Your heart is racing so hard you'd think you'd run ten miles. It's a bed downstairs for now, and that's an order.'

Rhiannon sent Sal to fetch the workmen who were still tidying up in the yard. The furniture was moved and a bed installed in the office. The men worked with a will, for all of them had learned that Miss Rhiannon was a fair employer and rewarded them for their efforts, not like the gentry who took everything for granted.

While Violet and Hetty undressed Mrs Paisley and made her comfortable in her bed Rhiannon went to the door with the doctor. 'Thank you for coming so quickly, Doctor . . . ?' Now she looked at him properly and realized that he was the doctor who had been present at Katie's death.

'Dr Frost, Richard, and I'm glad I was available. Don't worry about your mother now, she's had a nasty turn with that heart of hers, but with care she'll outlive a great many of us.'

He held out his hand and Rhiannon took it. 'Please send me your bill and I'll see to it.' How she was going to do that without any money she had no idea, but Rhiannon didn't want anyone, let alone the young doctor, to know that for the time being she was penniless.

He smiled warmly. 'Good day. I'll call in to see my patient tomorrow.'

The admiration in his eyes was unmistakable, but Rhiannon ignored it: she was in no mood for a flirtation. 'Thank you, Dr Frost.' She didn't wait to watch him walk away but closed the door and leaned against it with her eyes closed. How would she manage now? She had a sick old lady on her hands, guests to be cared for, and no money to speak of. She straightened her shoulders. She had been in worse situations than this and worked her way out of them. She would find a way out of this dilemma somehow. 'But how?' Her words echoed hollowly across the foyer. Right now she must see to Mrs Paisley and any other problems she would put out of her mind until the dear old lady was on the mend.

CHAPTER TWENTY-SIX

'We're nearly there.' Llinos leaned out of the carriage window and stared at the Cornish countryside rolling past, a green, lush land so like Wales that she immediately felt an affinity with it. She had visited Cornwall before some years ago, but had forgotten how lovely it was.

'Thank goodness for that!' Eynon said. 'The noise of the train is enough to give a man a headache—give me my own horse and carriage any time.'

The train drew to a halt at the station. It was decked with flowers, and the doors and windows of the station buildings were brightly painted and welcoming. As Llinos stepped on to the platform she felt the warmth of the sun on her face and she tilted her head to look up at Eynon. 'Now aren't you glad I coaxed you to come away on holiday?' She did not dare tell Eynon the real reason for their visit: if he knew she was looking for Jayne's lover he would be so angry. Watt had been unable to deliver her note to Guy—soon after she had seen him he had been taken ill and had cancelled his planned trip to Cornwall.

Eynon put his arm around her shoulders and squeezed her. 'I'm happy to be anywhere in the world, my love, so long as it's with you.'

The only transport available was a pony and trap and Llinos watched as Eynon negotiated the terms with the red-cheeked owner. The man nodded when he was handed a purse of money, beamed at Llinos then gave her a helping hand into the passenger seat.

She spread her skirts around her ankles aware of the cooling breeze coming off the sea. This was where Cornwall differed from Wales: the sea was rolling in from the English Channel with heavy waves pounding the rocky shores. At home the sheltering arms of the Bristol Channel cushioned the waves most of the time so that they licked the five-mile stretch of Swansea Bay like the tongue of

279

a kitten.

On the rare days that storms occurred, the wind and cloud over Mumbles Head gave a distant warning of the danger to shipping. Then the boats of the oyster-catchers dropped anchor as close to the shore as possible, knowing that the oyster beds would be impossible to fish when the tide was running fast and angry.

'We're here, Llinos.' Eynon's voice jolted her from her thoughts and she smiled up at him, blinking a little in the sunshine. 'You were far away then. What were you thinking?' he added.

'Just how lovely it all is.' She put her hand on his cheek. 'And being with you makes it all so much lovelier.'

Eynon smiled fondly and as he helped Llinos down the steps of the trap, he bent to plant a kiss on her cheek before he turned to the waiting groom. 'Give the animal a good brush down and stable him for me, there's a good lad.' He put his arm around Llinos's shoulder. 'What were you really thinking?'

Llinos waited as the groom touched his hat and led away the sweating horse, then waved her hand vaguely in the air. 'I was thinking about Swansea and the oyster-fishing. Beautiful as Cornwall is, I suppose I'm homesick.'

Eynon put his hand under her elbow and led her into the hotel. 'I've booked us in for a few days but if you want to go home just tell me.' Eynon nodded to the uniformed boy waiting to take his luggage and handed him some coins. 'The bags are on the step.'

The hotel was small but comfortable, furnished with homely sofas and colourful curtains. At the

280

desk a small moustached man inclined his head and consulted the pages of the book he held before him at an angle. Llinos hid a smile: anyone would think he was going to burst into song.

'Ah, yes, Mr and Mrs Morton-Edwards, you have the best rooms in the hotel.' He handed Eynon the key. 'I'll see to it that the lad brings your bags to your room right away, sir.'

The room was not over-large but it was bright and airy, with windows to the side and to the front overlooking the bay.

'I'm going to have a rest, Llinos, all that travelling has worn me out.' Eynon patted the bed. 'Are you going to keep me company, my love?'

His meaning was clear and Llinos laughed. 'Go on with you, Eynon! Anyone would think you were an eager young bridegroom, not an old married man!'

'Well, I'm certainly eager,' Eynon said, 'and less of the old, if you please.'

'I'm going for a walk,' Llinos said, 'I need some fresh air. Then perhaps I'll join you and have a rest before dinner.'

Eynon sighed, 'Just like a woman to keep a man waiting.' He stretched out on the bed. His hair, still pale gold, flopped over his brow giving him a boyish look.

Llinos smiled at him. 'You really are very handsome, you know.' She bent and kissed his lips. 'And just think, waiting will be good for you—it will make you all the more eager.'

She left the room just as the boy was bringing up the baggage and she held open the door for him to pass. She waited on the landing for him to emerge and when he'd closed the door behind him she motioned to him to wait.

'I'm looking for someone and you might be able to help me.' She took out the address Watt had given her and deliberately walked away from the door of the room, not wanting Eynon to hear what she was saying.

'I'm trying to find a Mr Guy Fairchild. He's down here on business, I believe.' She held out the paper. 'Can you tell me where Rose Mount House is situated?'

The boy looked down at his feet. 'Don't know, sorry, madam.' He scuffed the toe of one shoe with the other. 'Mr Hopkins on the desk might, though.'

'Thank you.' Llinos walked down the stairs, holding up the hem of her dress with one hand, the other on the highly polished banister. The man at the desk was no help at all. He shook his head vaguely when she mentioned the name of Guy Fairchild. Nor had he heard of Rose Mount House.

'What about Mr John Pendennis, then? Do you know of his whereabouts? I know he lives here in Charlestown.'

The man looked up at her sharply. 'Oh, yes, I know about Mr Pendennis, and so does everyone else in town. He lives a few streets away, just down the hill from here.'

'Mr Pendennis is not liked hereabouts?' Llinos asked.

'His methods of doing business are not liked and if your friend, this Mr Fairchild, is connected with him he won't have many friends in these parts either.' The man scribbled an address and handed it to Llinos. 'Be careful, Mrs Morton-Edwards, and whatever you do don't give business to Pendennis because you'll surely be cheated and robbed.'

Llinos stepped out of the hotel into the warmth of the early evening sunshine. It was all so beautiful that the sight took Llinos's breath away.

Outside the hotel a pony and trap was waiting to take visitors to the harbour. Llinos nodded to the driver and climbed aboard, seating herself with care for the ride down the hill might be a bumpy one. The driver clicked to the horse and the trap lurched into motion down the steep hill to the harbour where the china clay was loaded on to ships to sail to places like Swansea to serve as the raw material for making pots. The smell of it was enough to make her homesick and Llinos wondered why she involved herself in other people's business.

At the dockside, she stepped down from the trap and gazed around her. 'Will you wait for me, please?' she said to the driver. He touched his hat and took out his pipe. Llinos went up to one of the men attending to the loading of a ship. 'Excuse me, do you know where I can find Mr Pendennis, please?'

The man gave her a sour look and nodded to where a man in a well-cut coat, with greying hair, was standing at the quayside.

Llinos walked up to the man. 'Good evening, John,' she said. 'Don't you remember me?'

He frowned, not at all pleased to see her. 'Yes, I remember you, Mrs Mainwaring. What can I do for you?'

'It's Mrs Morton-Edwards now, John, and you can tell me where I can find Guy Fairchild. I want nothing else from you.' She saw the lines etched into the man's face and knew that, in spite of his prosperity, he was not happy. Her tone softened.

'How is life treating you, are you still with Lily?'

'Lily?' Pendennis looked as if he'd forgotten the woman with whom he had run away. 'Oh, she died some years ago.'

'I'm sorry.'

'Don't be sorry for me. I'm a rich man now and I don't want or need anyone's pity.'

'All right, John, but I need help. I have to find Guy Fairchild.'

He looked thoughtful. 'Why?'

'I can't discuss the reason with anyone but Mr Fairchild.' She moved a little away from Pendennis and leaned over the harbour wall, watching as a ship was loaded: chutes projected from the side of the dock enabling the thick, heavy clay to slide straight down into the hold.

'Anything in it for me?' Pendennis's voice broke into her thoughts, and she looked up at him quickly.

'All I want is to find Guy Fairchild. I'm not here to do business, I've left the pottery now, as you probably know.'

'Aye, I did hear something about it from Watt Bevan when he was down here, but he didn't say much. We never were the best of friends, were we?' He thrust his hands into his pockets. 'As for Fairchild, the last I saw of the man, and that was several weeks ago, he was staying at Rose Mount House. It's a small place on the other side of the bay.'

'Is it within walking distance?'

Pendennis looked at her with a spiteful smile. 'Not for someone your age. I'd take a pony and trap, if I were you.'

Llinos ignored the remark. 'I heard you were

doing business with Mr Fairchild. Surely you know if he's still in Cornwall?'

'Mr Fairchild and I didn't agree on certain matters and he might well have left Charlestown by now, for all I know or care.'

'Perhaps you would be so kind as to give my driver directions to Rose Mount House.'

'I told you, it's over there on the other side of the bay. Now, if you don't mind, I've business to attend to and you're wasting my valuable time.' He turned away from her and Llinos returned to where the trap was waiting. 'We'll drive round the bay,' she said. 'I'll have to ask directions to Rose Mount House when we get there.'

The task of finding Guy Fairchild was more difficult than she had thought. It might even be that she was here on a wild-goose chase. And even if she did find Mr Fairchild, would he welcome her or would he simply tell her to mind her own business? She settled back in her seat.

* * *

Rhiannon faced the servants, who had gathered in her office, and tried to think of encouraging phrases to cover the catastrophe but none came. She decided to settle for straight talking and hope they understood. She saw Mrs Jones ease one foot out of her shoe and hid a smile: the old cook would stick by her, she had no doubt of that. So would Sal, but Violet and Hetty might want to move on to more secure positions.

'We're in trouble,' Rhiannon said. 'As you know, Mrs Paisley's ill and has to take things easy until she's well on the road to recovery.'

There was a murmur of assent from the servants.

'I'm afraid there's more bad news,' she went on. 'Money has been stolen from Mrs Paisley's desk.' She held up her hand as Violet and Hetty looked at each other and began to talk at once. 'No one here is suspected, but at the moment I haven't got the money to pay you for your work.'

It was Mrs Jones who spoke up. 'We been in that pickle before, *cariad*, and we can manage again, I'm sure.' She paused. 'But who do you think took the money, Rhiannon?'

'Well, it's hard to tell, what with the workmen all over the place, but I do know it was none of you.' She looked around the group of servants and waited for them to speak.

'Well, I'm staying put,' Hetty said firmly. 'I've got a good bed and enough to eat and, what's more, I like working here in the hotel.' She glanced at Violet coaxingly. 'And we do get our time off regularly.'

Violet nodded. 'Aye, I might as well stay, I suppose.' She grinned. 'Who knows? I might meet a handsome guest who'll carry me off and treat me fine!'

Rhiannon raised her eyebrows but refrained from commenting. 'Good, we've got our main staff, then, but we can't get a boy in to help with the luggage. We'll have to manage that between us.'

'I've just thought of something,' Violet said quickly. 'I saw Seth hanging about the office the other day. Might not mean anything, mind.'

Sal spoke up for the first time. 'Don't go blaming Seth, he's honest as the day.'

Rhiannon held up her hand. 'We mustn't start quarrelling over this. I'm not pointing the finger at

286

anyone.' She moved away from her desk. 'Look, we've got a few minutes so let's all go down to the kitchen, have a cup of tea and work out how we're going to feed our guests until the end of the month.'

'I'll run down and put the kettle on,' Violet said, brightening up at the thought of a break in the middle of the afternoon, and disappeared with a swish of her skirts.

The others followed at a more leisurely pace, taking the lead from Mrs Jones, who was getting slower on her feet. 'It's my chilblains playing me up,' she explained.

'Well, you shouldn't sit with your feet up against the fire, should you?' Hetty snapped.

'Wait till you're my age, my girl,' Mrs Jones rounded on her, 'you might have bad feet by then.'

Hetty snorted and pushed back a tangle of golden hair that had escaped from her cap. 'I'll be an old married lady by then with a bunch of grandchildren round my feet.'

Sal gave her a little push. 'You'd better be quiet, Hetty, 'cos no man wants a shrew for a wife.'

Rhiannon listened with amusement. The news about the theft of money had made no lasting impression on the women: they were more concerned with mundane things like tea and chilblains. She felt more optimistic now: somehow they would get through to the end of the month when the guests paid their bills.

In the kitchen she sat for a while drinking tea and listening to the girls sparking off each other, until eventually she put down her cup and got to her feet. 'I'd better go and see Mrs Paisley. Hetty, will you make sandwiches and some tea and bring them up for me?'

'All right, it won't take a tick.'

Mrs Paisley was well enough now to sit in a chair, but it was thought wise to keep the bed in her office for the time being. When she saw Rhiannon she handed her a letter.

'What's that?' Rhiannon asked.

'It's from Dr Frost. Did I tell you he called when you were out and gave me a good checking over?'

Rhiannon's heart sank. 'It's probably his bill.' She unfolded the letter. She read it quickly and looked at Mrs Paisley in bewilderment. 'Why is he letting us off his fee?'

'Don't look a gift horse in the mouth, Rhiannon. Just be glad I told him about our misfortune.'

Rhiannon felt hot colour flood into her face and words of anger rose to her lips. She suppressed them: what good would it do to upset Mrs Paisley and perhaps make her sick again? Still, she couldn't let the bill go unpaid.

'Hetty is bringing you some tea in a minute.' Rhiannon tucked the note into her pocket. 'I'd better get on—there's lots to do.' Her first task was to see the doctor and put him straight on a few things.

Outside in the street, she took out the letter and looked at the address. Her heart missed a beat: the doctor lived almost next door to Bull Beynon. Perhaps she might catch a glimpse of him.

She walked swiftly, her skirts billowing around her ankles. She had no idea of how striking she looked, the autumn colours of her cloak setting off her dark hair to perfection. It did not take her long to reach the doctor's house but, to her disappointment, there was no sign of Bull. Even

288

though she lingered outside his house for longer than was necessary she could tell by the dark windows that no one was home.

A young maid opened Dr Frost's door and stared at Rhiannon with a puzzled frown. 'The doctor isn't seeing any more patients today, madam. I've had strict instructions not to let anyone else in. He's fair worn out.'

'I'm here to consult the doctor about a bill, not about my health,' Rhiannon said firmly.

The maid stepped back at once to let her into the hall. 'That's good, that is. The doctor don't often get his bills paid, too soft-hearted by far he is.'

Rhiannon was shown at once into the drawing room and Dr Frost was happy to see her. A fire burned in the grate and the easy chairs pulled up to it looked inviting.

'Miss Rhiannon, how nice of you to call, but I sorted out the business of the bill with Mrs Paisley. Didn't she tell you?' He gestured towards one of the chairs. 'Please sit down.'

Rhiannon's feet were aching and so was her back—she'd been at work on the accounts since early that morning, trying to stretch a few shillings. 'I'm not here to pay your bill, Doctor,' she said softly, 'well, not now anyway.'

'Please, call me Richard, and forget about the bill.'

'I can't do that, but I've a proposition to put to you.'

'I'm not a rich man but I do have a little money put aside. If it would help I'd gladly . . .' His voice trailed off as Rhiannon held up her hand.

'No!' she said quickly. 'Thank you very much . . .

289

but I'm not asking for money. What I have for you is a business proposition.'

'I'm listening.' He smiled and Rhiannon saw that he was a handsome man. He was also kind and honourable, the sort she had rarely come across.

'What if you become the hotel doctor? You would see to anyone taken ill at our hotel. Those patients would pay immediately for your services and the reputation of the hotel would be enhanced into the bargain.'

'Anything that enables me to work with you will be a pleasure. What you suggest is a splendid idea and I welcome it. As you have guessed, my patients are few because I'm new to the district.'

'Well, then, you agree?'

'I most certainly do. Now, may I offer you some refreshment? Tea, perhaps?'

Rhiannon got to her feet. 'It's very kind of you but I must get back to work.'

He walked with her to the door. 'I look forward to doing business with the Paradise Park in the near future.' He laughed, a pleasant sound. 'Not that I wish any of your guests ill but when away from home minor ailments do occur and I will be ready to treat them.'

Rhiannon said goodbye and retraced her steps to the hotel, where the appetizing smell of cooking welcomed her. She pushed open the door and handed her coat to Sal, who had obviously been waiting for her. 'Come down to the kitchen, Rhiannon,' she said, tugging at Rhiannon's arm.

'Oh, no, what's gone wrong now?'

'Nothing's wrong, far from it. Just wait until you see what we've managed to get while you were gadding about.'

'What do you mean?'

'I went down the market just before it was closing,' Sal said. 'Vi and Hetty came with me. You'll be so pleased when you see what we brought back.'

The kitchen table was full of vegetables, cabbage, beans and potatoes.

'How did you pay for these, Sal?' Rhiannon asked warily.

Sal burst out laughing. 'Just look at your face! It's all right, I didn't get up to my old tricks. I just offered to clear up the stalls, scrub down the carts, that sort of thing, and in exchange, I got the vegetables.'

Violet was practically hopping up and down on the spot. 'And me! Don't forget the 'orrible job I 'ad scrubbing down the fish carts. Ugh! Those scales sting like Old Nick, I can tell you, they stick in your fingers like needles.' She stood back to reveal the cold slab. 'But just look at the lovely fish I've got—and all for an hour or two's work.'

'Don't forget Hetty,' Mrs Jones said. For once her tone was approving. 'She got the best bargain of the lot. Brought home a lovely bit of topside of beef and another of silverside, she did. The topside's in the oven now and cooking just lovely it is too.'

Hetty glowed at the praise and Rhiannon realized the girl would have been a beauty if she hadn't always been in a bad mood. But perhaps she had never had anything to be happy about—she'd had to fend for herself from an early age.

'Thank you, girls, you've all been very clever, especially you, Hetty.'

Hetty glowed. 'Well, I know I aren't always easy

to get on with but this is the first time I've belonged anywhere. I look on you all as my family, the only real family I've ever known, and I'm not going to lose that willingly.'

Tears brimmed in Rhiannon's eyes. The loyalty and the kind-heartedness of the girls warmed her heart. Just when everything looked black, it seemed that the clouds really did have a silver lining.

'So we'll feed our guests well now and in the future, because the girls are planning to go and work every market day.' Mrs Jones sniffed. 'And I agree with Hetty. We're family now, your family, Rhiannon, and like every other family on earth we'll pull together, come what may.'

'All I can say is thank you, from the bottom of my heart.' Rhiannon swallowed the lump in her throat. 'I won't forget this ever, and so long as I have breath in my body I'll see that you all stay with me, whatever I'm doing and wherever I'm working.'

Violet chuckled. 'What about when you gets married? You won't want us with you then, will you?'

'I'll never get married,' Rhiannon said, and she meant it. The only man she would ever love was Bull Beynon and Katie's ghost would always be between them.

'Right then, supper's on the way but we want some roast potatoes done,' Mrs Jones said. 'I've boiled the stiffness out of them so, Vi, you just pop them in the oven for me, there's a good girl.'

Rhiannon stirred herself. 'And I've got to get the table set for our guests. Sal, will you come and help me?'

At the top of the kitchen steps Rhiannon put her arm around Sal. 'Thank you, Sal, I know you were the leader. The other girls wouldn't have thought of cleaning up at the market.'

'Aye, it takes us street girls to know how to feed ourselves, how to make a meal out of nothing, and how to keep clothes on our back.' She smiled slyly. 'And how to make a man happy.'

'Well, we've got guests to keep happy now, Sal,' Rhiannon said shortly, 'and we'd better get on with it or they will be having their supper at breakfast time.'

CHAPTER TWENTY-SEVEN

Jayne was lying on the bed, staring up at the ceiling and wondering how much longer she could stand being a prisoner. She had cried many tears, longed for Guy then cursed him for not coming to save her. But why would he, when he thought she no longer cared for him? She heard the rattle of the doorknob and sat up, swinging her feet to the floor.

Her husband entered the room and looked at her strangely. Then he held the door wide. 'Go on, you're free to go. I've had enough of you.'

Jayne wondered if this was some cruel trick. 'Do you mean it, Dafydd, or are you just playing with me?'

'I mean it. Go home to your precious father.'

Jayne slid off the bed. 'This wouldn't have anything to do with Llinos's visits, would it?' she asked.

'Just be glad I'm letting you go. If you want to ruin your life, that's up to you.' He followed her as she stepped out on to the landing and Jayne glanced at him over her shoulder. Perhaps even now when freedom seemed to be hers it would be snatched away from her.

'I've called a hansom cab and given the driver your father's address.' He put his hand on her shoulder and Jayne flinched.

'Don't worry,' his tone was bitter, 'I've no intention of ravishing you. I'll forgo that dubious pleasure. There are many women who would love me, so why should I hold on to one who cares nothing for me? And, yes, you're right, it was Llinos who helped me see the futility of keeping you here.' He smiled, but without humour. 'She always meant more to me than you. She's a real woman, a loving, passionate woman, while you are just a child.'

Jayne resisted the urge to give him the tongue-lashing he deserved: all she wanted now was to get out of this hateful place and away from her husband for good.

She waited in the gloomy hall while a silent serving girl brought her cloak. When Dafydd opened the door it was all she could do to stop herself rushing outside.

The sun warmed her and she realized how much she had missed the simple pleasure of being outdoors: the whole world looked bright and shining, the trees were swaying, dappling the forecourt with light and shade, and Jayne breathed in the sweet air, unable to believe her imprisonment was over.

The cab was waiting, the driver holding the reins loosely between his fingers. Dafydd helped her into the seat and Jayne leaned away from him, putting as much distance between him and herself as she could.

'Jayne,' Dafydd said, 'I won't apologize for my behaviour. You had your revenge by sleeping with my best friend. Since I found out about Guy I've been like a man possessed, wanting to punish you, but I've come to understand that I don't want you any more and perhaps I never did.' The words seemed hard for him to say, and somehow they didn't ring true. She looked into his eyes for the first time since she left the bedroom and what she saw there shocked her: Dafydd was in love with her.

The driver clicked his tongue at the horse and the cab jerked into motion. Jayne stared back at her husband as he stood on the steps of the gaunt, grey building where he'd made her a prisoner and all her anger evaporated: Dafydd was a man alone without love and at last he'd recognized that it was all his own doing.

She turned away from him and settled back in the seat, closing her eyes against the wave of joy that swept over her. She was going home to her father and perhaps, just perhaps, she might be able to find Guy and make all her dreams come true.

*   *   *

Rhiannon stood in the foyer of the hotel, her hands clasped together as she prepared to meet the flurry of new guests. They were not businessmen but holidaymakers, men with their wives and children who had come to Swansea to taste the delights of the five-mile stretch of golden sand and the mild air drifting in from the Bristol Channel.

Mrs Paisley, still pale and coughing, joined her

in the foyer. She was wearing her hat as she always did and held herself erect as the guests came into the hotel.

Mr and Mrs Powers from Yorkshire arrived first and suddenly the hotel seemed filled with light and laughter as their children chattered excitedly about the sand and the sea, and the bathing huts on the golden beach.

Rhiannon welcomed the guests and Mrs Paisley stood like royalty, accepting the tribute the visitors were paying her hotel and her town. They said Swansea was beautiful, its atmosphere so bracing.

'I hope you'll enjoy your stay here, Mr Powers,' Rhiannon said, then turned to his wife. 'Mrs Powers, if you need any help from my staff please don't hesitate to ask.'

She led the family of two adults and four children, with their nurse, up the stairs to a suite of the larger rooms. 'Once you're settled I'll send up a tray of tea and some cordial for the children.'

'Tea would be welcome,' Mrs Powers said, in a soft voice. Rhiannon recognized that her hotel was being patronized by real gentry and felt proud. She took leave of the family with a polite reminder that they should ask if they needed anything.

Mrs Paisley was waiting in the foyer and looked up expectantly as Rhiannon came towards her. 'Are they happy with their rooms?'

'Delighted.' Rhiannon sat alongside Mrs Paisley, noting how breathless the old lady was. 'But you should be resting. I'm quite capable of welcoming the guests on my own.'

Mrs Paisley put her thin hand over Rhiannon's. 'Let me enjoy a little bit of pleasure, my dear.' She sighed. 'I know I'm not much use in any practical

296

way, which is why I put you in charge of everything with the bank, but I'm not too old to welcome people into our hotel.'

Rhiannon smiled. 'It's kind of you to call it "our hotel" but, really, it's yours. You put in the money and all I've done is run it for you.'

Mrs Paisley looked at her steadily. 'You've done a great deal more than I can ever thank you for. If it wasn't for you, and the love the servants have for you, we would have had to close for lack of money almost as soon as we opened our doors.'

Rhiannon knew the old woman was right, but she patted her hand and got to her feet. 'Well, I'd better talk to Mrs Jones or we won't be having any dinner tonight.' She looked down at Mrs Paisley. 'Shall I help you to your room?'

Mrs Paisley shook her head. 'No, I'll just sit here for a while, enjoy the busy atmosphere of the Paradise Park.'

Rhiannon crossed the elegant foyer and made her way to the back of the hotel and the stairs leading down to the kitchens. By now Mrs Jones would have planned dinner, leaving Rhiannon to write out the menus.

*　　　*　　　*

It wasn't long before Rhiannon was obliged to call again on Dr Frost's services: one of the Powers children had fallen sick and though Rhiannon thought the child had enjoyed too many of Mrs Jones's sweets, and perhaps a little too much sun, she nevertheless felt the doctor should see him.

Richard Frost came at once and Rhiannon watched as he bent over the little boy and

297

examined him carefully, pulling down his lower eyelids, taking his pulse and listening to his heart. At last he straightened, a smile on his face. 'It's nothing that a little bed rest and abstinence from the sun won't cure.' He clicked his bag shut and smiled at the anxious Mrs Powers. 'May I suggest that he eats only plain food for a few days? No sweet stuff, nothing too rich.'

'Thank you, Doctor. Please send my husband your bill—and thank you once again for putting my mind at rest.'

Rhiannon led the way out of the room and Richard Frost followed her. On the landing she turned and held out her hand. 'Thank you for coming so promptly, Doctor, I'm very grateful. You handled that little boy so well, I was very impressed.'

He held her hand for a moment. He was quite a small-built man, standing only a few inches taller than her, but he had a presence that was difficult to ignore.

'You are very kind, Miss Rhiannon.' He hesitated. 'I hope you don't mind me calling you by your Christian name but it's the only one I know.'

'I'd be delighted for you to drop the Miss, and simply call me Rhiannon. As you've gathered, everyone calls me by my first name and I'm happy with that. And we know each other well enough now to be informal, don't we?'

He beamed down at her. 'I would like to know you a great deal better, if I might be so forward as to say so.'

'You're very kind, but I'm always so busy with hotel business. However, I imagine we'll see each other again before too long. I anticipate a flurry of

298

families arriving for the summer holidays and little ones are always falling sick, aren't they?'

Richard Frost looked disappointed. 'Well, then, I hope to see you before too long.'

He left the hotel, and as Rhiannon watched him walk away, she wished with all her heart that she could respond to his undoubted attraction to her. She sensed he would not be able to overlook her previous way of life. It would take an unusual man to do that, a man like Bull Beynon.

*   *   *

Llinos stood outside Rose Mount House and hesitated, wondering if she should go inside. It was a pretty place with good thatch on the roof, and the roses round the door provided a riot of colour that did the heart good. Hearing footsteps, she glanced over her shoulder and a smile of relief appeared on her face. 'Mr Fairchild, I've been looking for you,' she said quickly, worried that her courage might fail her. He was well dressed, in clean fresh linen and well-cut narrow trousers.

Now he smiled, and he was so charming that Llinos could see why Jayne had fallen in love with him. 'Mrs Morton-Edwards, what a coincidence meeting you here.' He took her hand and bowed over it politely.

'It's not really a coincidence,' she admitted. 'I came here with the sole intention of finding you.'

'Oh?' A wary expression crossed his face. 'And what could you want with me?'

She glanced round and gestured to a seat half hidden behind an overhang of trees. 'Can we sit down?'

'Very well.' He seemed reluctant to talk to her.

Llinos could understand his feelings of suspicion. He must have heard the gossip that she had once been Dafydd's mistress. Perhaps he believed she'd come here to warn him to keep away from Swansea. 'I've come on behalf of Jayne, my stepdaughter,' she said quickly, as she sat down and arranged her skirts. 'Please, Mr Fairchild, listen to what I have to say and then it's up to you which course of action you take.'

'I'm listening.' He spoke grimly, but he took a seat beside her and swivelled sideways to face her.

'It's about Jayne,' she began, and wondered how to go on.

'I gathered that much.' Guy Fairchild's voice held a touch of sarcasm.

Llinos decided to speak plainly. 'When Jayne told you she was going to give her marriage another chance, she lied. Dafydd had a pistol concealed in his pocket and he had threatened to shoot you if Jayne didn't succeed in sending you away.'

Guy Fairchild frowned. 'She sounded convincing enough to me. In any case, the idea of the man threatening to kill me sounds a bit far-fetched, doesn't it?'

'I suppose it does, if you don't know Dafydd well, but I'm telling you the truth. Since you went away Jayne's been kept locked in her room, unable to go out even into the garden.'

He digested this piece of information for a moment. 'I don't know what to think. Is Dafydd capable of such cruelty? I admit I find it hard to believe.'

Llinos looked at him in silence for a moment,

300

wondering how to convince him. 'Have you never seen Dafydd in a fit of rage, then?' She'd heard the story, as had everyone in Swansea, about Dafydd horse-whipping Guy to within an inch of his life.

'Yes, of course I have, but what a man does in anger is very different from what he does in cold blood.'

'Well, I assure you that since the day of my marriage to her father, Jayne has been kept prisoner in a house Dafydd bought especially for that purpose. Her father has been to see him more than once to urge him to be reasonable, but the law seems to be on Dafydd's side in this. Jayne is his wife and she should be obedient to him.'

Guy kicked at a stone lying on the pathway. 'Is this really the truth, Mrs Morton-Edwards?'

'It is.' She laid her hand on his arm. 'I even went to see Dafydd myself, to ask him to release Jayne, but I don't think my words carried any weight.'

'And are you here alone, or is your husband with you?' Guy looked up at her, his eyes steady as they met hers.

'I'm with my husband, but Eynon thinks this is a little break away from our worries. He doesn't know that I promised Jayne I would try to find you.'

At last Guy nodded. 'I believe you, Mrs Morton-Edwards, but what am I to do? If she's imprisoned as you say, how can I rescue her?'

'I should have thought that a man with your intelligence could work that out for himself.' Llinos knew her tone was impatient but she felt like shaking him into action. 'Wait until Dafydd is about his business—he travels the country sometimes, doesn't he? Then you can seize the opportunity to

301

get Jayne out of that terrible place and take her anywhere in the world you choose to go.'

He took her hand. 'Thank you, Mrs Morton-Edwards. I'll set off for Swansea this very day and I'll get Jayne away from Dafydd, don't you worry about that.'

He got to his feet and Llinos looked up at him. 'Good luck, Mr Fairchild,' she said. He gave a little bow, then walked across the grass and into Rose Mount House without glancing back.

Llinos sighed. Now she would have to go back to Eynon—he would be wondering where she'd gone.

He was sitting on the sea wall outside the hotel and in the evening sun his pale hair gleamed like gold. His face brightened as he saw her approaching.

'Where has my lovely wife been, then?' He rose to greet her. 'I was getting quite worried.'

'No need to worry about me,' Llinos said. 'I'm well able to take care of myself.'

He took her hands in his. 'Yes but you're a lovely woman and you shouldn't be out alone. It isn't proper.'

Llinos smiled. 'When have I ever done what's proper?' She stood on tiptoe and kissed his cheek. 'Come into the hotel and get us both a drink. I think we're going to need it.'

She slipped her arm through his. It was not going to be easy to tell Eynon her real purpose in coming to Cornwall.

Once inside the hotel, seated on one of the large, comfortable sofas with two glasses of brandy on the table before them, Llinos took his hand. 'I brought you here under false pretences,' she said. 'I came here to find Guy Fairchild and to tell him the truth about Jayne's decision to stay with Dafydd.'

Eynon frowned but said nothing. Llinos swallowed and looked down at her fingers, held in Eynon's warm hand. 'Guy is going back to Swansea straight away. He's going to do what we couldn't do and rescue Jayne from the prison where Dafydd's keeping her.'

'I think I guessed as much,' Eynon said, his voice low. 'And you never do anything without giving it a great deal of thought.'

'You're not angry with me?'

He bent and kissed her lips. 'I'm sad you didn't confide in me before, but I understand that you wanted to help Jayne get away from Buchan.'

Llinos leaned into his shoulder. 'You know something, Eynon?' She glanced up at him.

'What?'

'I love you very much indeed.'

'That's the nicest thing you've ever said to me, Llinos Morton-Edwards.' And then, regardless of the other people in the hotel foyer, he bent down and kissed her.

CHAPTER TWENTY-EIGHT

As the cab drew up outside her father's elegant home Jayne glanced behind her, worrying even now that Dafydd was following her and would take her back to her prison.

She pushed open the arched front door and stepped into the hall, breathing in the scent of beeswax, admiring the fine curve of the staircase. She had come home. She felt almost faint with

303

relief as she closed the door behind her.

A steward she didn't recognize came into the hall. 'Is Mr Morton-Edwards at home?' Jayne asked, pulling off her gloves finger by finger, impatient with the man for staring at her as though she was an intruder.

'Might I ask who is enquiring, madam?'

'I am Mr Morton-Edwards's daughter. What is your name?'

'I'm Saunders, madam, and forgive me for being forward but how do I know you are Mr Morton-Edwards's daughter? He left no instructions that we were to expect you.'

'My word is good enough! Now, ask someone to take my boxes upstairs and have the maids prepare a room for me. Any of them will confirm my identity. Where is my father? Why isn't he here?'

'He and Mrs Morton-Edwards are taking a short holiday.' The man divulged the information as though it was being dragged from him. 'I'm in charge of things here, madam, and I need proof of your identity.'

'All you need is my word,' Jayne said, in a dangerously quiet voice. The man stared at her for a long moment. 'I need my room *now*.'

'I'm sorry, madam, but I was instructed to take care of things while the master was away and I was not prepared for a visitor.'

'Well, I'm here now and you can take your orders from me. Otherwise you may pack your bags and leave. Is that understood, Saunders?'

'Very well, madam.'

'You may call me Mrs Buchan,' she said, 'and, Saunders, ask a maid to bring me a hot drink.'

The man bowed and departed, and Jayne went

304

across the hall and into the drawing room, feeling betrayed that her father was away. It was as if no one in the world cared about her—but that was absurd. Her father had been trying to bring her home ever since his wedding day. He had quarrelled with Dafydd, even threatened violence, but none of it had moved Dafydd to mercy.

Then a thought struck her. She rang the bell and Saunders appeared at once, as though he'd been waiting outside the door expecting her to run off with the family silver. 'Where has Mr Morton-Edwards gone?' she asked.

'I believe the master is holidaying in the West Country, Cornwall—that's it, Cornwall.' He spoke as if Cornwall was the back of beyond where all sorts of unmentionable things might happen.

Jayne bit her lip. Guy had gone to Cornwall. Was that a coincidence or was her father trying to find him for her? 'When is he coming back?'

'I believe he's expected this afternoon, madam.'

'Very well, you may go,' Jayne said shortly.

She looked around her at the familiar room. It was strange but wonderful, too, to be back in her father's house. The rooms seemed bright and sunny after the grim surroundings of the grey stone building where Dafydd had kept her prisoner.

She wandered to the window and stared out at the spacious gardens, not seeing the overhang of trees or the elegant statues lining the drive. She was imagining herself and Guy locked in a passionate embrace.

Their meetings had been so transient that perhaps she'd imagined he loved her. It might be that he had found another lady by now. Men were fickle: she'd learned that from her husband.

Bull sat in the high seat with two other magistrates overlooking the chamber where the court was in session and stared at the poor wretch standing before him. The man was accused of stealing a pig from a neighbour. It seemed he had killed it, cooked it and eaten the evidence. As he stared at the thin, ragged man Bull couldn't find it in him to condemn him. The only evidence presented to the court was a set of pig's trotters, and the word of the pig's owner. For Bull that was not enough to condemn a man to prison.

He listened to the drone of the accused man's voice: he was attempting to explain that he didn't like pork, and Bull could have laughed, if it hadn't been for the terrified look on the fellow's face.

Bull was getting accustomed to sitting in judgement at the petty sessions and most of the cases, like this one, were of a trivial nature. One man had been accused of selling his wife but the woman was such a shrew that Bull would have given her away if she'd been his wife.

Occasionally he witnessed real tragedy in the courthouse and found it hard to deal with. One such case involved a man accused of murdering his child for money, and Bull had spent days deliberating, trying to stem his anger when his gut instinct told him the man was guilty.

Another case that worried him was that Tom, Seth Cullen's uncle, had been accused of stealing money from the Paradise Park Hotel. The evidence was so trivial that, although he believed the man was guilty, Bull dismissed the case.

306

He became aware that the court had fallen silent now. The man before him hung his head waiting for Bull, the bench spokesman, to decide his fate.

'Because of the lack of witnesses in this case, but taking into consideration the loss of a pig to the farmer, I have decided that the accused work a week without payment on his neighbour's farm.' Bull stood up, indicating that the session was over, and went into his room at the back of the court. He took off his robes and hung them up, feeling he would rather do a good day's work on the railway than sit in judgement on poor folk who had little or nothing to live on.

Outside in the street he took a deep breath of fresh air and began to walk in the direction of the beach. He felt he needed to breathe the clean sea air and settle his mind before starting on the draft report he was writing for one of the railway engineers.

As he turned the corner he came face to face with Rhiannon. His heart lifted at the sight of her: she was neatly dressed, her hair pinned up under a fashionable hat, and the warm colour in her face told him she was happy to see him. 'Rhiannon, I'm glad to see you looking so well and prosperous—I hardly recognize you, these days.' He took her hand and gazed into her dark eyes. She was so beautiful, so breathtakingly lovely, that he wanted to take her in his arms and hold her close to him.

'And you, Bull, so posh I'm half afraid to speak to you.'

He looked down at his finely cut coat. 'I don't look like this when I'm working on the railway, as well you know.' He realized he was still holding her hand and released it reluctantly. 'I'm going to the

307

beach, will you walk with me a little way?'

Rhiannon hesitated, then nodded. 'I'd like that, Bull. I feel in need of a rest from the hotel and a little time off won't hurt.'

They walked in silence and Bull could imagine how they looked: a pair of well-dressed citizens out on a morning stroll as though there was nothing better to do. How different they looked from what they had once been.

'I know what you're thinking.' Rhiannon said softly.

He looked down at her. 'How?'

'I'm thinking the same thing as you. I'm remembering the old days when we didn't have much money and were so happy and content with our lives. I would love to go back to those days, if only for an hour.'

Bull was silent. He didn't want Rhiannon to entertain any false hopes about their relationship. What they'd once shared was gone: it had happened in a different lifetime, before he met Katie. At the thought of his beloved wife, a great sadness came over him; he could never replace her.

'Isn't that what you were thinking, Bull? What good times we enjoyed when we were together?'

Her soft voice held such entreaty that Bull relented. 'Yes, but we can't resurrect the past, can we?'

'I suppose you're right.'

If there was an edge of disappointment in her voice he chose to ignore it. 'Still, everything is going well for you now, isn't it?'

'Oh, yes, the hotel is doing well, we have families coming to stay, and I can see that the Paradise Park will be the best hotel in Swansea one day.'

He saw her glance up at him and resisted the urge to meet her eyes.

'I've even got a follower, a respectable man, a doctor. He's new in the area and needs to build up a practice. He and I have an arrangement. He treats the guests in the hotel should they fall sick, and that helps both of us.'

Bull digested her words in silence: it unsettled him to think of another man in Rhiannon's life. He swallowed his feelings and made an attempt to speak lightly. 'Well, that's good, then, isn't it?'

'Is it, Bull? Do you really want me to find another man?'

'I suppose it's inevitable. You're a beautiful woman and you're bound to marry one day. Naturally I'd like to see you settled and happy.'

'And what about you, Bull? Will you ever marry again?'

'No!' he said emphatically. 'I can never put another woman in Katie's place. It just wouldn't be right.'

'But, Bull, Katie would never have wanted you to be alone for the rest of your life. And although you can never put another woman in her place you can love again. It's not impossible.'

'It is for me.' Bull spoke quietly trying to stifle the wash of hot tears that rose to his eyes.

'Oh, Bull!' Rhiannon drew him into the shelter of the trees that fringed the beach. 'Bull, I hate to see you hurting.' She put her arms around him and held him close, patting his back as if he was a child. 'It's only natural to mourn Katie and the baby. You loved them very much and I know that better than anyone.' She looked into his eyes. 'But you have to think about the future. I know it's trite to say it, but

309

time heals everything. You'll never forget your love for Katie, no one would expect you to, but you must put aside your grief now. Mingle with the gentry—their doors are wide open to you. Go to the assembly rooms and enjoy the company of other respectable citizens. Attend the theatre, take one of the fine ladies you meet now to one of the posh balls. Start living again, Bull.'

He knew what it had cost her to say those words. She was letting him know that she was far below him socially and that she felt she had no place in the life he'd forged for himself. 'I'm sure everything you say is wise and right,' he said slowly, 'and perhaps I'll take your advice and try to be a bit more sociable.'

'I've got to go,' Rhiannon said. 'Will you be all right, Bull?'

'Yes, of course. Don't worry about me.' He watched her walk away, a slim, beautiful woman, and he experienced a tremendous urge to be with her, to lay her down on a soft bed and make passionate love to her. Immediately he was ashamed of the thought: he loved Katie, gentle, sweet Katie, his darling wife, how could he even think of giving his love to another woman?

He glanced along the beach, hoping for a last glimpse of Rhiannon, but the golden sands were empty of people; only the seagulls kept him company and their cry was mournful as they circled the air. Bull began to walk at a fast pace back to the town.

*　　　*　　　*

Jayne was sitting at the dining-table, having barely

310

touched her meal, when she heard the rattle of wheels on the forecourt outside. She threw down her napkin and hurried to the window, her heart pounding with fear. Had Dafydd changed his mind? Was he outside even now, determined to return her to the prison he'd made for her?

Relief flooded through her as she heard her father's voice then saw him alight from the cab and turn to give his hand to Llinos.

Jayne hurried into the hallway as the maid opened the door. 'Father, thank God you're home!' She buried her face in his shoulder and tears sprang to her eyes as he kissed the top of her head.

'Jayne, my dear little girl, what's happened?'

'He let me go.' Jayne looked up into her father's dear face.

He was tired from travelling but his eyes were shining as he met her gaze. 'So, Buchan came to his senses, did he? I wonder what made him change his mind.'

'I think I must thank Llinos for that.' Jayne, still clinging to her father, reached out a hand to Llinos. 'Thank you, I'll always be grateful to you for what you've done.'

The maid was waiting to take the coats and already the footman was carrying bags and boxes up the stairs.

'Come, my dear girl,' her father said, 'let's talk in private.'

Jayne allowed her father to lead her into the drawing room.

'Come now, no more tears, there's something else you can thank Llinos for.'

Jayne's heart lifted in hope. 'Llinos, you've found him for me, haven't you? Tell me, please,

311

you've found Guy.'

Llinos smiled. 'I did find Guy, and he's heard the full story of what's been happening. He's so angry that he fell for Dafydd's tricks and believed you wanted to stay with him.'

'Oh, Llinos, thank you!' Jayne hugged her stepmother and looked into her face. She saw, for the first time, why her father's love for her had never wavered. 'You are a generous-hearted woman and I'm a selfish pig!'

They sat together on the large sofa and Jayne kept hold of Llinos's hands. 'Tell me, how does he look? Is he well? Was he with another woman when you saw him?'

Llinos smiled. 'He was alone, and very shocked that Dafydd would sink so low to keep you apart.'

'When is he coming?'

'He thinks you're still being held prisoner by Dafydd so I'm not sure what his plans are.'

'Oh, Llinos, why didn't you ask him?' Jayne got to her feet, clasping her hands together. She wanted him here and now; she longed to be in Guy's arms, to know that what they had felt for each other had not changed.

'Guy is a grown man,' Llinos said. 'I could hardly question him about his intentions.'

'No, of course not. Forgive me, Llinos.' Jayne resumed her seat and smiled at her. 'I'm so ashamed now and sorry for the awful things I've said and done to you. I don't deserve you.' She looked up at her father. 'Or you, Father. I'll say now what I was too unkind to say at the wedding. I hope you will be happy together—your marriage is so right for both of you.' She hesitated, then kissed Llinos's cheek. 'Can you forget that I behaved like a spoilt brat and start again?'

'You were never a spoilt brat and I understood your unhappiness, Jayne. I saw how your marriage fell apart and I felt guilty about it.'

'You felt guilty?' Jayne was surprised. 'I never knew that.'

'Well, I had Dafydd's son and I know he taunted you about Sion.'

Jayne was saved from answering as her father came and encircled both her and Llinos in his arms. 'No more questions and answers now. My heart is overflowing with gladness that the two girls I love most in all the world are friends again.'

Jayne kissed his cheek and then Llinos's. It was good to be back with loved ones again, free from the awful house where Dafydd had held her for what had seemed an eternity. Tonight she would sleep happily knowing that soon, very soon, Guy would come for her.

CHAPTER TWENTY-NINE

Sal was astonished at the change in the garden at the back of the hotel. When she'd first arrived at the Paradise Park it had been overgrown with wild grass and weeds. Now, with Seth and another man working on it, the lawns were neat and even, interspersed with colourful flowerbeds. The hedges were trimmed in a uniform procession around the grounds and now, with the sun shining on it, the garden was as good as any found at the homes of rich folk.

Seth came into view around the side of the hotel

and Sal's heart skipped a beat. She was falling for Seth but she didn't know how he felt: he kept his thoughts to himself. He took her out on her days off work, he had even kissed her once or twice, but they never discussed her past and Sal wondered what he really felt about her.

'Morning, Sal.'

Seth limped towards her, but she hardly noticed the way he walked: she was intent on trying to read his expression, praying that there would be some sign of love in his eyes. 'Seth, can you help me?' Sal pointed to the small square herb patch. 'What's chives and what's parsley? Am I being silly not knowing the difference?'

'You're still speaking to me, then?'

Sal looked at him in surprise. 'Why wouldn't I?'

'Tom, my uncle, you know they think it might have been him who took the money from Mrs Paisley?'

'That's nothing to do with you, Seth. Now, come on, show me how clever you are at gardening and pick me some of these chives.'

'I'm not very clever, Sal. I wouldn't have known the difference between chives and parsley myself a few months ago.' In spite of his words, Seth sounded proud of himself. He took the scissors from her basket and bent over, wincing as though even now his leg still hurt. Sal wanted to rest her hand on his broad back, to ruffle the thick growth of hair that curved around his collar, but she was afraid to be too familiar in case he rebuffed her.

'Want a cup of tea, Seth?' she asked, as he put the herbs into her basket and brushed the dirt from his hands.

'Well, I wouldn't say no.' He smiled. 'I hope

314

you'll keep me company. A cup of tea's not the same without the company of a beautiful girl.'

'Cheeky!' Sal whirled away to hide the blush that had risen to her cheeks. How foolish she was, acting like a shy, innocent miss because a man paid her a compliment. Didn't all men tell you sweet things when they wanted something from you? 'I'll be back in a minute so don't go away.'

She hurried into the kitchen and the smell of fresh scones rose tantalizingly from the range. 'Cook,' she said hesitantly, 'do you think I could give Seth a scone to go with his cup of tea?'

Mrs Jones's glance was shrewd. 'Aye, don't see any harm in that, but you're not getting up your hopes in that direction, are you, girl?'

'I don't know what you mean.' Sal felt her colour rise again as she busied herself with the cups.

'You know what I mean, all right.' Cook cut through a scone and spread it with butter.

'No, I don't.' Sal felt as though her insides were trembling.

Mrs Jones pushed away her mixing bowl and leaned on the table. 'I don't mean to be unkind, Sal, but you know what you used to be and so does Seth. I suppose that's what I'm thinking. See, lovey, a man don't forget things like that. Oh, they'll be nice to you, take what they want and walk away. If that's all you want from Seth then go ahead, girl, but if you're hoping for marriage, forget it.'

It was a chastened Sal who took the tea and the scone into the garden. Seth was sitting on one of the wooden benches rubbing at his leg, and Sal felt a dart of pity for him. How she would like to comfort him, to rub a soothing balm into his poor stump, but then, as Mrs Jones had said, she was

315

just a whore not a proper sweetheart to Seth.

His face lit up when he saw her. 'Oh, Sal, you're a good girl! Honest to God, you are.' He took the tea, not realizing how ironic his words were, and beckoned her to sit down beside him. 'Come on, Sal, sit with me for a bit. I get lonely for a bit of company sometimes.'

So that was it. To Seth she was just 'a bit of company'. Well, what did she expect? Seth might not be rich, but he was a man who could offer respectability—so he was out of her reach.

'Can't stop, sorry,' she said, forcing a cheerful note into her voice. 'Cook's playing merry hell because I been out here so long.' She moved away from him, avoiding his eyes. 'Leave the cup and plate on the back step when you've finished.'

Mrs Jones looked up as Sal came back into the kitchen. 'Glad to see you're not hanging around out by there.' She was mixing flour with butter, eggs and sugar.

'No point, not after what you said to me.'

Mrs Jones stopped what she was doing. 'Look, Sal, perhaps I spoke out of turn. It could be that Seth is very fond of you but I just wanted to warn you.'

'No, you're right, Cook. Why would Seth want me when there are honest girls, like Vi and Hetty, working here right under his nose?' She shook the teapot. 'There's enough left in here for us to have a cup.'

Mrs Jones nodded. 'Aye. We'll have a little sit-down. A cuppa always seems to make things better.'

As Sal sipped her tea she felt a tear trickle down her face. After Mrs Jones's warning, no amount of

316

tea would make her feel better. She was a common harlot and no one was ever going to let her forget it.

*   *   *

Guy stepped down from the train and breathed in the familiar smells of Swansea. The copper works along the riverbank to the east of the town sent out low sultry clouds that sometimes hung low over the houses, and from the docks he could smell salt and fish, but Swansea was a good town.

He hailed a cab and handed his baggage to the driver. 'I'm going to a hotel, the Mackworth will do.'

'If you'll pardon me saying so, sir, I took a gent to the Mackworth a bit earlier and the place is full.' He took up the reins of the horse and glanced back at Guy. 'The Paradise Park is the place to go, these days. The food is good and the rooms are a treat to sleep in, so I've heard.' He smiled ruefully. 'Not 'ad the money to find out for myself, mind.'

'So be it.' Guy climbed up the steps into the cab. 'So long as it's clean and respectable, there's nothing more I want.' He settled back into his seat. All he wanted now was a change of clothing and then he would be ready to face Dafydd Buchan and ask—no, demand that Jayne be released at once. He couldn't see Buchan giving up easily but he would give way in the end, even if it came to blows.

An elderly lady greeted him in the foyer and had his luggage taken up to his room. She seemed frail and much too old to be running a large establishment like the Paradise Park. In his room, he took off his jacket and rang the bell for the maid

317

to bring up hot water. When she knocked and entered the room, Guy looked at her in surprise. 'Good heavens, it's you, Sal!'

'Oh, Mr Fairchild, how are you, sir? It's good to see you again.' She pushed the door shut and stepped closer. 'Begging your pardon for being forward, sir, but have you come for Mrs Buchan?'

'Least said on that subject the better, eh, Sal?'

'Yes, sir, but did you know Mr Buchan let her go? She's back at her father's house now.'

Guy took a deep breath. 'Are you sure of that, Sal?'

'I'm sure enough, sir. Seen her myself in town the other day, but she looked lonely.'

A warm wave of love engulfed Guy. Soon he would be with Jayne. He would take her away somewhere, make a fresh start as they'd planned.

'Thank you, Sal. I'd better get ready to go to her,' he smiled, 'and I promise you, she won't be lonely for long.'

*   *   *

Jayne stood in the window, staring out at the empty roadway leading from the house into the town. She kept telling herself that Guy would arrive any day now but so far there had been no sign of him. 'Oh, Guy, please come for me.' She whispered the words, which tore at her heart-strings. She would be nothing without Guy and life would not be worth living.

She was about to turn away when a movement caught her eye. She strained her eyes to see who was driving the horse and trap at full gallop towards the house. And then she knew. Guy had come to fetch her.

Throwing dignity to the winds she ran to the front door and pulled it open. 'Guy, my love, my dear love!'

He jumped down from the driving seat, hurried towards her and then she was in his arms. Guy rained kisses on her face and his tears mingled with hers.

He tried to speak but she shook her head. 'There'll be time for talking and making plans later. For now just hold me close and tell me you love me.'

His arms tightened around her and he looked earnestly into her face. 'I love you, Jayne. I want you to be with me for the rest of my life.'

She sighed happily. 'That's all I needed to know.'

*   *   *

Rhiannon was standing on the pavement outside Bull's house, staring up at the windows as if the force of her thoughts might bring him to her. She had no idea why she was here: she had meant only to walk along the sea-front, to clear her aching head, so that in the evening she could work on the accounts.

An idea struck her. What if she asked Bull to help her work out the figures? He was good at planning and business, and he could advise her on the possibility of adding a new tearoom to the hotel.

Rhiannon wanted the Paradise Park to be as good as the Mackworth, to have better facilities, if possible, than any other hotel in Swansea. But that would cost money and, right now, she had to be

319

careful. The takings were good but the outgoings were high.

Rhiannon stepped back in alarm as the door to Bull's house opened. He hesitated, then smiled at her. She felt as if her very bones were melting. 'Rhiannon, what on earth are you doing standing there? Come in, for goodness' sake. You know you're always welcome at my house.'

'I came to ask your advice. I wanted some help with the accounts. I don't know if I should spend some money or—' She stopped in mid-flow, knowing she was blabbering like a hysterical girl.

She found herself being led along the neat hallway and through into the impressive sitting room. Suddenly, she felt insignificant: Bull was far out of her reach, these days.

'What are you looking so unhappy about?' Bull pulled a chair round to face the fire. 'Why, you're shivering and it's a lovely warm day. Are you sick, Rhiannon?'

She shook her head vigorously. 'No, I just wanted to talk to you but now I'm here I feel I'm imposing.' Then she realized that, in spite of the shivering, her skin was burning.

Bull put the back of his hand on her forehead. 'You're ill. You foolish girl, you shouldn't be out and about when you've got a chill.'

'I'm all right,' Rhiannon insisted. 'I wanted to talk to you about the business but perhaps I should come back another day.' Now her teeth were chattering. Bull rang for the maid. 'I'm all right, really I am. I'll just call the doctor and he can give me a tonic. I won't trouble you any more, Bull.' She tried to get to her feet, but the room swung in an arc around her. Then she was slipping into a deep, dark abyss.

* * *

When Rhiannon opened her eyes, she saw the familiar face of Richard Frost staring down at her. He was holding her wrist and frowning. 'What is it, Richard, what's wrong with me?' Her voice came out thinly. She tried to sit up but her head pounded and she fell back against the pillows. Bull was standing behind the doctor, and Rhiannon realized how awkward this must be for him. 'I must get back to the hotel,' she said.

Richard bent close to her. 'Don't try to talk. You're far too sick to be moved. Mr Beynon is calling in a nurse and you will be well looked after here, I'm sure.' There was an edge of anger in his voice but Rhiannon was too tired to work out what it meant. 'You should never have been outdoors unattended anyway,' Richard continued. 'You are a foolish young lady to go visiting alone. Let this be a lesson to you.'

'We are old friends, Doctor,' Bull said. 'Rhiannon is quite safe with me, I assure you.'

'That is not the point, though, is it? It isn't proper for a young lady to visit a gentleman alone.'

Rhiannon closed her eyes. Clearly Richard knew nothing of her past: he imagined she was a well-brought-up young lady of gentle birth. If she hadn't felt so ill she would have tried to explain.

'So you think it's scarlet fever, Doctor?' Bull's voice echoed dimly in her mind before she drifted away again into a deep darkness.

Rhiannon was sailing over the town. She felt her wings lifting her higher than the Town Hill. She could see Poppets Hill and the stark shape of the gibbet outlined against the red earth. And then the sun was going down, she was drifting towards the sea, but she could no longer keep her eyes open. It was hot, so hot that it should have been the sun, not the moon, shining down on her. And then she was falling into a deep cavern where a bed of writhing snakes waited to claim her . . .

Rhiannon woke abruptly and gasped in fear. But the snakes had gone and all she could see now was the sunlight through the chink in the heavy curtains. For a moment she wondered where she was but then she realized she had been ill and remembered she was at Bull's house.

She heard the rustle of a starched apron and turned her head with difficulty. She saw a nurse coming towards her.

'Ah, Mrs Beynon, you're in the land of the living again. That's excellent!' She held Rhiannon's head and adjusted the pillows. 'You've been thrashing around like a crazy woman but that's the fever. It's broken now and you're going to be all right. I'll just go and give your husband the good news. He's been that worried he's hardly slept.'

Rhiannon wanted to tell the nurse she had no husband, but the woman disappeared through the door before she could frame the words.

Bull came into the room and sat on the bed. 'Thank God, Rhiannon, you've been so sick I feared for your life.'

'Oh, Bull, I'm sorry to be such a trouble to you.' She wanted to cling to his broad shoulders and beg him to let her stay with him for ever, but that was out of the question. 'I've got to get back to the hotel, they'll all be wondering where I am.' She was surprised at the weakness of her voice. She tried to take a deep breath but it hurt her chest.

'Don't worry about the hotel. I've sent a message to Mrs Paisley and she told me she'd manage on her own.'

'Oh dear, she's not well and here I am lying about the place like a sick cat.' Rhiannon wanted to find her clothes and shoes and ask Bull to call a cab to take her home, but she didn't have the strength.

'You're not to worry about anything. Just rest.'

The nurse bustled into the room just in time to hear Bull's last remark. 'There, didn't I tell you he'd been worried about you? You're a lucky girl, having such a good husband.' She tucked the bedclothes around Rhiannon's shoulders. 'Now, do as he tells you and get some rest. You're far from well and I won't have all my good work undone because you won't listen to my advice.'

'But, Nurse, I'm not—'

Bull laid his finger over her lips. 'Do as the nurse tells you, Rhiannon, and rest. There'll be time enough to talk later when you're feeling better.'

Rhiannon felt her eyes beginning to close. Bull was right, she must rest. As she snuggled down under the sheets, she felt a warmth around her heart. Bull was sitting close to her, taking care of her, just as he had in the old days long ago when they were lovers.

CHAPTER THIRTY

It was a crisp day and the leaves on the trees were turning to shades of red and gold. Now Bull had to be extra vigilant, looking for cracks in the line where the rail had expanded in the heat of summer and might now be contracting as the colder weather came in. He walked along the railway track, staring down at the iron rails gleaming in the mellow September sunlight. Uncharacteristically he wasn't thinking about work, he was thinking of Rhiannon, how sick she'd been, and how it had torn at his heart to see her laid low. Now that she was on the road to recovery she'd moved back to the hotel and Bull missed having her under his roof, close enough for him to touch her, hold her and kiss her full lips. Of course he had done nothing of the sort, he had treated Rhiannon as a dear friend, but he was beginning to see that she meant a great deal more to him than that.

He moved up the bank away from the railway. He might as well go home—he wasn't getting any work done today, not with his mind in confusion. He stepped on to the road and a pony and trap pulled up beside him. In it was Richard Frost. 'Morning, Mr Beynon. How is Rhiannon feeling now that she's back at work?'

'She's still a little pale and she needs to eat some hearty meals to build her up but when she makes up her mind to do anything there's no telling her to stop. She simply won't listen.'

The doctor stepped down from the trap on to the roadway. 'I wanted to talk to you, Mr Beynon.

Have you a minute to spare?'

Bull murmured his assent and the doctor moved closer. 'I must confess to being a little puzzled. Rhiannon is called Mrs Beynon yet I know she's not your wife.' He coughed, and it was clear to Bull that the man was more than a little embarrassed. 'What exactly is your relationship to her? This is not idle curiosity, you understand. I'm becoming fond of the lady and I want to know if it's proper for me to approach her.'

Bull was at a loss. He felt anger and, yes, a flare of jealousy, yet he could hardly tell the doctor the truth. He improvised quickly. 'Mrs Beynon is a courtesy title only. Rhiannon has never been married.' He was uncertain how to go on. 'Rhiannon is no relation, but she's a very dear friend. You do realize that Beynon is a common name in Wales.'

'Of course. Has she family or anyone I can speak to about my intentions?'

Bull shook his head. 'Not as far as I know. The best thing you can do is to talk to Rhiannon herself.'

The doctor smiled and suddenly Bull felt an urge to smack him on the nose. Instead he said, 'I'd better get on. I've got reports to write up and I'm sure you have patients to visit.'

'I have indeed. Well, good morning to you, Mr Beynon, and thank you for taking the time to talk to me.'

Bull strode away, fighting outrage that the doctor should question him about Rhiannon. What was he supposed to say, that she'd been a prostitute and had lived with him for many months? He knew he was being unreasonable but something about

Richard Frost set his teeth on edge.

The man was a good doctor yet Bull was wary of him. He seemed too good to be true but, then, perhaps he was being unreasonable. Perhaps he would think that way about any man who was interested in Rhiannon. He kicked at a stone, knowing he was behaving like a sulky child. Suddenly the day felt dark and dreary as Bull made his way back to his empty house.

*   *   *

Llinos was in the conservatory, tactfully keeping out of the way, and Jayne smiled. How she'd misjudged her all this time. Ah, well, she knew better now. Llinos would be on her side whatever she wanted to do.

'Llinos, I've had a letter from Guy.' Jayne felt like clutching the piece of paper to her heart. 'He's at the Paradise Park and he's going to come for me today. I have to be ready with my boxes packed. But first I have to talk to Father, try to explain to him how I feel.' She searched for the right words. 'I want him to understand that I know what I'm doing.'

'Eynon's been out since early morning, Jayne. He's in court today.' She smiled. 'But whether your father approves or not you'll be going away with Guy.'

'And you're not angry and disgusted with me?' Jayne watched Llinos's face but all she saw there was compassion and understanding.

'I've been in your position myself, Jayne, and love is heady stuff. But remember that I was shunned by polite society until your father married me, and even now I'm merely tolerated by the good ladies of the town. Think carefully before you do anything rash.'

'I want to be with Guy and no one is going to stop me. I don't care about my good name. In any case, don't you think the gossips have made free with my indiscretions already?' She moved away from Llinos and stood close to the door. 'I'm staying with Guy at the Paradise Park tonight, and first thing in the morning we're taking the train for London. Please tell Father that if he wants to say goodbye he will have to come up to the hotel.'

'I'll tell him—and, Jayne, for what it's worth, you go with all my good wishes and I hope you will be very happy.'

At the sound of hoofs and the rattle of wheels on the drive outside Jayne looked up sharply. Guy was here! She ran to the door, flung it open and then she was in his arms, her face turned up to his. 'Oh, Guy, I thought this day would never come.'

'So did I, but now we'll be together for ever, my darling,' Guy said. 'No one is going to come between us. I love you so much and I want to spend the rest of my life with you.' Then his lips came down on hers and suddenly the world seemed filled with light. Jayne knew in that moment that no sacrifice was too great as long as she could be with the man she loved.

*   *   *

Rhiannon looked down the guest list for tomorrow's Grand Opening of the Paradise Park. By now, most of the rooms were occupied, the good reputation of the hotel was growing, and the client list with it.

Sal came into the office and stood in front of Rhiannon with her hands on her hips. 'You're working too hard. You've been told by the doctor to take things easy for a while.'

Rhiannon smiled. 'I'm enjoying myself. In any case, there's so much to do before the official opening of the hotel.'

'Can't you leave some of the work to Mrs Paisley?'

'You know she's not up to it.' Mrs Paisley was becoming more and more confused, unable to remember even the smallest item. Rhiannon spent most of her time covering up the old lady's mistakes.

'Well, neither are you. You've been very ill, Rhiannon, we almost lost you.' Sal put her arm around Rhiannon's shoulders. 'I don't know what we'd all do without you to look after us.'

Rhiannon smiled. 'Well, I think *you*'ve got someone else who wants to look after you.'

Sal's colour rose. 'I don't know what you mean.'

'You know exactly what I mean. I've seen you with Seth in the garden when you were supposed to be picking herbs for the dinner.'

'Oh, Rhiannon!' Sal clasped her hands together. 'Do you think Seth could really care for me, after the way I've spent my life?'

'I think he cares for you very much. Remember, Sal, what you did was out of necessity. It was either go on the streets or starve.'

'I know you're right, but I can't believe I let myself fall into such a life. I could no more lie on my back for money now than fly to the moon.'

Rhiannon knew exactly how Sal felt. The days

328

when she had been any man's for the taking seemed part of another lifetime. She had lost all her self-respect, all her dignity, until she had met Bull. But thinking about Bull brought sadness to the day. She almost wished she was ill again, with Bull to take care of her. He had been so kind, so loving. She drew herself up sharply. Bull didn't love her, he loved the memory of his dear wife, Katie. She would be a fool if she read too much into his kindness to a sick friend.

There was a knock on the door and Violet peered into the room. 'The doctor's here to see you, Rhiannon. Shall I show him into the drawing room?'

Rhiannon frowned. What could he possibly want? She was well now, she didn't need Richard Frost to call on her.

'Tell him I'll see him in just a moment.' Rhiannon put aside the invitations to the opening of the hotel and lifted her hand to tidy her hair. 'I wonder what he wants, Sal.'

Sal smiled. 'You may be clever in some things but you're as daft as a brush when it comes to yourself, aren't you? Surely you've noticed he's smitten by you?'

'Don't be silly!'

'I'm not being silly. The man can't take his eyes off you. Whenever you're together he lights up like there was a dozen candles inside him.'

'Nonsense!' Rhiannon brushed down her skirts. 'Perhaps someone in the hotel needs his services.' She ushered Sal to the door. 'Now, go away and find something to do—and stop making up romantic stories in your head about me and Dr Frost.'

When she walked into the drawing room Richard Frost was standing near the fireplace and smiled at her. At that moment Rhiannon saw that Sal had been right: the doctor was taken with her. But he was smitten by the businesswoman she had become. He didn't know anything about her past.

'Rhiannon.' He moved uneasily from one foot to the other. 'I spoke to Bull Beynon earlier today and asked him about any family you might have.'

'I see.' Rhiannon felt a dart of unease. What had Bull said about her? He would never speak ill of her but he did not tell lies. 'Well, he probably told you I had no family.'

'Yes, and he told me that he and you were not related in spite of having the same name.'

'That's right. Please, Richard, do sit down, you're making me feel uncomfortable.'

'I feel at a loss, I should be speaking to a male relative about my feelings but as you have none I must, of necessity, speak directly to you.' He took her hand. 'Rhiannon, I have feelings for you, very deep feelings, and I want to ask you to do me the honour of walking out with me.'

Rhiannon's first impulse was to draw away her hand and tell the doctor the truth about her past life, but on reflection she thought that perhaps it would not be kind of her: perhaps he would feel foolish if he knew he was all but proposing to a harlot. 'You are very kind, Richard, but please, don't ask me to make up my mind to anything as important as that when I've so many other things to think about.'

'What things?' He seemed puzzled—he didn't know how much planning it had taken to organize the opening of the hotel.

330

'Well, there's Mrs Paisley, and you know that she's more of a hindrance than a help these days.' She sighed. 'Can we talk about this after the Grand Opening? Just give me time to think about it with all of my mind rather than half of it.'

'Very well.' He sounded disgruntled. 'You do understand what an honour I'm offering, don't you?'

'Of course I do, and I'm flattered, but my recent illness has made me weak and indecisive. Please, Richard, give me a few days and then we'll talk properly.'

'All right, then.' He moved to the door. 'We'll talk again when you're in a better frame of mind.'

As the door closed behind him, Rhiannon felt only a sense of relief. She must tell him the truth about her past and then, if he still wanted to walk out with her, she would make up her mind if that was what *she* wanted.

Sal was in the hall. She took one look at Rhiannon's face and smiled broadly. 'I told you, didn't I?' She caught Rhiannon's arm. 'He proposed, didn't he?'

'Oh, you and your questions! He didn't exactly propose but he wanted me to walk out with him, as he put it.'

'And you said yes?'

'I said I needed time to think about it.'

'You're mad! A fine upstanding doctor asks for your hand and you put him off! When are you going to get a better offer, Rhiannon?'

'I don't think I want any man, if the truth be told,' Rhiannon said quietly.

'And we know why, don't we?' Sal shook her head. 'Forget Bull Beynon, you're never going to get him. Do you want to end up an old maid?'

Rhiannon didn't reply. She was too busy wiping the tears from her eyes.

*　　　*　　　*

Richard Frost stood in the foyer of the hotel looking around him. It was a fine hotel, a thriving hotel, and if he married Rhiannon he would be part of it. He was surprised that she hadn't fallen into his arms right away but women were known to be coy. Keeping a man waiting was part of the game they played.

The large doors of the hotel swung open and he stepped back courteously as a well-dressed couple approached the reception area. He couldn't fail to hear what they were saying as they booked a room for the night. He was about to turn away when he realized the lady was Mrs Jayne Buchan, but the man she was clinging to, as if she would never let him go, was not her husband.

He watched, outraged, as they strolled hand in hand towards the ornate stairs. Their behaviour was beyond the bounds of decency. He must speak to Rhiannon at once, tell her exactly what was going on in the hotel. Perhaps there were other irregularities that should be drawn to her attention.

He decided he would like to look round the place, see what he could find out. He wasn't being inquisitive, he was merely protecting Rhiannon's reputation and the good name of the hotel.

In spite of his distaste at the scene he'd just witnessed, he felt a sense of pride in what she had achieved. He could see for himself how well she had done in turning the old building into a veritable palace. Rich curtains hung at the windows and fine carpet covered the floors. The walls were lined with silk paper and several paintings gave the hotel an air of solidity, as if it had been a grand hotel for many years. He wandered downstairs and found himself looking in on a busy kitchen; the cook was getting on in years but she ran her domain like a good captain would run a ship. The floors were spotless and the mouthwatering smell of roasting beef was enough to tempt any man's appetite.

He was backing out as the cook looked up at him. 'Sorry, I took a wrong turning,' he said. Another staircase led him towards the back entrance of the hotel and he decided to leave. As he made for the door he heard the sound of a woman's laughter. Curious, he opened the door and as it swung wide he stared at the two people before him. One of the maids was in the arms of a gardener, and her face was flushed.

'What is going on here?' His tone was stern. 'Does Mrs Beynon know that her servants cavort like heathens under her nose? Give me your name, man, so that I can advise Mrs Beynon whom she should dismiss.'

The pair sprang apart. 'I'm Seth, sir, and this is Sal. We're walking out.'

'That does not excuse unseemly behaviour. I'm leaving but later I intend to bring this matter to Mrs Beynon's attention.'

Seth indicated the back door. 'Quicker if you go this way rather than back through the hotel.'

The man was so brazen he was actually smiling. 'I don't know what you have to laugh about, man. I'm sure Mrs Beynon won't see the funny side of all

333

this. First I find people booking rooms who are not even man and wife, and now I find the servants acting as though such behaviour was the order of the day.'

'Lor' bless you, sir,' Seth opened the big back doors. 'Rhiannon wouldn't say a word about me and Sal getting together. She done it all herself, see?'

'What on earth do you mean?' Richard stared at the man. He was talking gibberish. Rhiannon would be as shocked as he was if she knew what was going on in her hotel.

'I mean, she was one of the girls herself,' Seth said easily. 'She don't try to hide it neither. Rhiannon was a shanty-town woman and now she's bettered herself and I take my hat off to her.'

Richard felt a rush of horror, quickly followed by incandescent rage. 'Mrs Beynon a whore? I don't believe you—I should knock your head off for even thinking such a thing.'

Seth looked puzzled. 'Didn't you know about her past, then, sir? She was all right when she lived with Bull Beynon, see, got respectable then, no more walking the streets, like.'

'Oh, my good Lord!' Richard said, as the blood rushed to his head. He'd been a fool—he'd offered for the hand of a woman no better than she should be.

Seth put his hand over his mouth. 'Sorry, sir, I thought everyone knew about Rhiannon. And then there's Sal, same thing, she was a street girl but I don't mind that. I love Sal and I mean to marry her one day when she's older, never mind what she used to be.'

Richard pushed the man aside and stepped out

on to the quiet back-street, feeling as though the whole world was tumbling around him. He had practically proposed to a whore!

Well, he would never forgive Rhiannon Beynon for this. He would make her pay dearly for humiliating him in such a way and what better time to do it than at the Grand Opening of which she was so proud? He began to walk more swiftly, not seeing the street pedlars or the sun-dappled roadway: his mind was on something much more important. He was plotting his revenge.

CHAPTER THIRTY-ONE

Rhiannon woke early and sat up to gaze at the mellow sun streaking into the room. She ran her fingers through her long hair, unaware of how the cloud of dark tresses accentuated her fine-boned face. Excitement gripped her. Her hotel, the Paradise Park, had become one of the best in Swansea and she had played an important part in its success.

Violet came into the room with a tray of tea and biscuits, and set it on the table beside the bed. 'Tomorrow's the big day, in't it exciting?'

Rhiannon smiled. 'It is exciting, Vi, and whoever thought we'd come this far?' She picked up the cup and sipped the hot tea with a sense of pleasure. She was now looked on as a respectable businesswoman and the shame of her past was gone, lost in the mist of time.

It was not surprising really, though: the men she slept with had been from the ordinary working

335

classes, navvies mainly, and most of them had moved on with the railway. A few of the ladies of the town might remember Mrs Buchan taking her in, training her to be a housekeeper, but none of them had ever set eyes on her. No, her past was not going to interfere with her life as she lived it now.

She put down her cup and picked up the list of guests who would be attending the opening. Most of the town dignitaries, including the mayor, had accepted the invitation and quite a few of the more respected families of the town too.

Rhiannon had left invitations in all of the bedrooms for the guests so the ceremony was going to be well attended, there was no doubt about that.

She must run over her speech of welcome, make sure it was dignified, yet with a touch of humour; the servants would have handed round liberal amounts of good wine by the time she got up to speak and, hopefully, the atmosphere in the ballroom would be genial. Rhiannon had butterflies in her stomach as she thought of standing before a roomful of strangers. It was a pity Mrs Paisley didn't feel up to conducting the opening ceremony—she was much more used to public occasions.

The old woman was still lying in her bed when, a little while later, Rhiannon went to talk to her. She was looking careworn and her eyes, usually bright as a bird's, were dull.

'Good morning, Rhiannon.' Mrs Paisley sat up with difficulty and did her best to smile. 'Are you all ready for the big day, then?'

'I will be when you promise to be at the ceremony. It's not until tomorrow and perhaps you'll have more strength by then.' Rhiannon took the old lady's hand. 'How are you feeling today?'

'I'm all right, Rhiannon. Don't forget you've been ill yourself and you're still looking peaky—you should think of yourself more.'

'I'm much better now.' Rhiannon felt a tug at her heart-strings. 'Bull nursed me like a mother and I can't tell you how kind he was to me.'

'You still love him, don't you?'

Rhiannon was taken aback at Mrs Paisley's forthright question but she decided she might as well be honest. 'I'll always love him.'

'But you've got the doctor paying court to you now and you'd be a fool to turn him down.'

'Aye, Richard might be keen now but if he knew of my past he'd run a mile.'

'How do you know that?'

'You forget, I've known many men. I know what makes them happy and it's not marrying a whore.' She shook her head. 'Whores will do things for money that a wife would not countenance.'

'It's not like you to be so blunt,' Mrs Paisley said gently. 'Look, girl, you know I'm very fond of you, don't you? Well, I've made a will leaving my share of the business to you.'

'Don't talk like that, please!' Rhiannon said. 'You're strong, you'll outlive me, don't you worry!'

Mrs Paisley pursed her lips. 'That's nonsense, and we both know it. But when I go, you'll be all right. You've made this hotel what it is. All I did was to put down the deposit on the building but you furnished the place and decorated it, then kept it running with your friends when we had little or no money.' She smiled, and Rhiannon saw how beautiful Mrs Paisley must have been when she was young. 'It's because of you that our venture paid off.' Mrs Paisley finished the sentence on a huge yawn.

Rhiannon tucked the blankets around her. 'Rest now so you'll be bright and breezy to face tomorrow.'

'Very well, I'll do as you say. But, Rhiannon, whatever happens, the opening ceremony must go on, promise me.'

Her words made Rhiannon feel uneasy. 'Of course the ceremony will go on. What on earth could happen to stop it?'

'Quite right.' Mrs Paisley snuggled down under the blankets. 'Now, go away and stop pestering me. I want to sleep.'

Rhiannon left the room, closing the door quietly behind her. In the passageway the sun was still shining but, all at once, the day seemed dark.

*   *   *

'She's gone away with that fellow and she didn't even say goodbye to me. I can't understand it.' Eynon slumped in his chair.

'Jayne had to follow her heart, my love. She didn't mean to hurt you, I can promise you that.'

'Well, she has hurt me,' Eynon said.

Llinos hid a smile. He sounded just like a sulky child. She put her arms round him and held him close. 'Jayne has her own life to lead now, and though we might not be easy with the path she's chosen we have to accept it's what she wants. She loves Guy, really loves him, and would you want her to live most of her life without love?'

He looked up into her face. 'That's what I did.'

Llinos kissed him and his lips tasted sweet. Her

338

heart ached with love for him. She had always loved him, even though she might not have known it. It didn't diminish her love for Joe: her husband had been as close to her as her own heartbeat. Yet Eynon had always been there deep inside her. 'And did it make you happy, my love, pining for what you couldn't have?'

Eynon shook his head. 'You know it didn't. I never knew what real happiness was until the day you married me.'

'Well, then, let your daughter find happiness while she's young. Now, let's change the subject, shall we? How about this invitation to the opening ceremony of the Paradise Park Hotel? I'm sure you'd like to go. Weren't you interested in buying the place at one time?'

'I was, but I'm not sure I want to go to the opening. Everyone will be gawping at us, talking behind their hands about my daughter running off with another man. I'm not sure I could put up with that.'

Llinos took his hand in hers. 'You put up with it when I was disgraced, or have you forgotten that?'

'That was different,' Eynon said.

'How was it different? You loved me then, so you say, and you were still my friend. Gossip didn't turn you against me, did it?'

Eynon smiled. 'All right, then, we'll go to the blasted ceremony, if that's what you really want.'

'In that case,' Llinos said playfully, 'you'd better take me to town to pick up my new hat and gown.'

Eynon stood up and took her into his arms. 'You wicked woman, you know how to get round a man when it comes to spending his money.'

Llinos disengaged herself from his embrace.

'Well, my secret's out, I married you for your money.'

Eynon picked up a cushion and made a pretence of throwing it at her. 'Get out, woman, before I give you the good hiding you deserve.'

Llinos closed the door behind her and sighed. She'd persuaded Eynon to mingle with the Swansea gentry at the hotel ceremony but she knew it would be an ordeal for both of them. As Eynon had pointed out, folk would be pointing them out as the odd couple.

She could imagine what they would be saying: that she was no better than she should be and now her stepdaughter was going down the same road. Still, the gossips would have to be faced at some time, and tomorrow was as good a day as any.

*   *   *

As the day wore on, Rhiannon's concern for Mrs Paisley grew and by tea-time she knew the old lady was really ill. She sent Violet to fetch Dr Frost and was amazed when the girl came back almost at once, tears trembling on her lashes.

'What on earth's wrong, Vi?' Rhiannon caught her arm. 'Why isn't the doctor with you?'

'He was so strange. He told me he had better things to do than run up to the Paradise Park every five minutes.'

Rhiannon frowned. 'That doesn't sound like Dr Frost. Are you sure he wasn't sick himself?'

'His face was like a thunder cloud when I told him he was needed here.'

Rhiannon wondered what on earth had come over him. Why was he acting so strangely?

'All right, go and fetch another doctor, Vi, there's a good girl, and be quick about it.'

Rhiannon didn't have time to worry about Richard's strange behaviour because Mrs Paisley suddenly took a turn for the worse. Her breathing was laboured and her face was like parchment.

Rhiannon sat at her side, a bowl of cool rosewater on a table nearby. Every few minutes she dipped the cloth in the bowl and bathed Mrs Paisley's burning forehead. By the time Violet returned with the doctor, an old man with a white beard and a kindly look in his eyes, Mrs Paisley was asleep.

'Her breathing's bad, Doctor,' Rhiannon said, 'and she hasn't opened her eyes for over an hour.'

The doctor listened to the old woman's heart for what seemed a long time, then shook his head. Rhiannon knew what that meant and a great dread filled her. Mrs Paisley couldn't die, not now when they were so near their moment of triumph.

'How long?' Rhiannon whispered.

The doctor snapped his bag shut. 'There's no telling. It might be hours, might be days.'

Rhiannon made an effort to think straight. She must see that the doctor was paid for his services. She followed him from the room. 'Your bill, Doctor, do you think you could send it up to me? I don't want to leave Mrs Paisley alone for too long.'

The old doctor nodded, and Rhiannon watched him go downstairs and through the door with a feeling of dread. She wanted to drag him back although she knew there was nothing he could do.

When Rhiannon returned to the room Mrs Paisley's eyes were open. The old woman held up her hand and Rhiannon took it. 'You must promise me you'll go on with the Grand Opening, or I'll not rest easy.' It was an effort for her to talk: each word came out as a gasp.

'I promise,' Rhiannon said, her voice full of tears.

Mrs Paisley patted her hand. 'You're a good girl, the finest I've ever met.' She closed her eyes wearily. 'You've been like the daughter I never had and I'm proud of you, girl, so proud.'

Rhiannon fought the tears that burnt in her eyes. 'And you've been better than a mother to me. Don't leave me, please, don't leave me.'

Mrs Paisley gave a big sigh and then, as Rhiannon watched, the breath left her body.

Rhiannon didn't know how long she sat there holding the cold hand, refusing to believe Mrs Paisley was gone from her for ever. It was only when Mrs Jones came into the room and took Rhiannon in her arms that she began to cry great gulping sobs that hurt her chest.

'There, there,' Mrs Jones said gently, 'you did all you could, girl, no one could have done more. Come downstairs and let me make you a nice hot cup of tea. That will make you feel better.'

Rhiannon allowed herself to be led downstairs and into the warm kitchen, which was full of the smell of bread baking. The fire was blazing in the hearth but suddenly Rhiannon began to shiver. She knew in that moment that her life, without Mrs Paisley, was never going to be the same again.

CHAPTER THIRTY-TWO

Bull stared at the invitation to the Grand Opening of the Paradise Park, not sure that it was wise for him to attend. It was Rhiannon's moment of triumph, setting the seal on her efforts to put her past behind her and be a respectable citizen of Swansea. She wouldn't want him there as a reminder of what she'd once been.

He sank into his chair, looked around the elegant room and pondered on his own rise from navvy to inspector and manager; his comfortable home had been made his by the goodwill of the engineers on the Swansea line, men who respected his knowledge of the Great Western Railway. It was a lovely home, yet without a loving wife to share it with him it seemed empty.

When he heard a knock on the front door he looked up in surprise. It was seldom that he had visitors: his only callers were the tradesmen selling bread or milk. After a few moments, the maid showed Seth Cullen into the room and he stood there, his hat in his hand, looking anxiously at Bull.

'Good to see you, Seth, sit down.' Bull could hardly fail to see how Seth had changed over the years. He was no longer the wild-drinking, fast-living navvy he'd once been: now he was smartly dressed, his hair neatly combed and his one boot polished so that you could see your face in it.

'I have to talk to you, Bull.' Seth rubbed his hands together. 'It's about Rhiannon.'

Bull felt a dart of anxiety. 'She isn't sick again, is she?'

Seth shook his head. 'No, nothing like that. She's upset, though. Did you hear that old Mrs Paisley died yesterday?'

'I didn't know, and I'm very sorry. She was a grand old lady and very fond of Rhiannon. Is that why you're here? Does Rhiannon want me to see to the burial arrangements for her?'

'No, Rhiannon will do all that herself. No, I'm worried about the hotel's Grand Opening tonight. That's what I've come about.'

Bull was finding it hard to follow Seth's line of conversation. 'Want a drink, Seth?'

'Aye, a drop of whisky would go down well.'

Bull poured the drinks and handed a glass to Seth. 'Now, what's this all about? Tell mc slowly and clearly.'

'Well, when the old lady was taken sick, Dr Frost wouldn't come and see to her, right nasty he was to one of the maids. I'm afraid he might cause trouble tonight just to shame Rhiannon.'

Bull was more confused than ever. 'Why on earth would he do that? The man admires Rhiannon.'

'Aye, well, that's just the trouble.' Seth looked uneasily into his glass. 'I think I let the cat out of the bag—you know, about Rhiannon's past.'

Bull was beginning to see what Seth was getting at. 'You told him Rhiannon was once a shanty-town woman?'

'Aye, I did. Didn't mean no harm, mind, I thought everybody knew. I don't care about such things but the doctor is cut of a different cloth from you and me. He went as purple as a ripe plum when I told him and I thought he was going to burst.'

344

'Well, that was silly of you, Seth, you should have kept your mouth shut—but perhaps it's just as well the truth came out sooner rather than later.'

'It won't end there, though, Bull. I think the doctor is going to make a nuisance of himself. I heard him going on about it to some old geezer in the Beaufort Inn. He's a bitter man and he didn't like being made a fool of. Right peeved, he was, I can tell you.'

'All right, Seth, leave it with me.' Bull got up from his chair. 'You did the right thing coming to me, but keep quiet about it.'

'Oh, don't you worry, I've learned my lesson and I won't say nothing to no one else.'

Bull followed him to the front door. 'How are you and Sal getting on? I gather you're sweet on her.'

'Aye, I mean to marry her one day. I don't care nothing about her past, that's dead and gone. I love the Sal she is now.' He looked up at Bull. 'I'm not like that Dr Frost, no, sir.'

When Seth had gone Bull picked up the invitation. He would go to the hotel tonight, if only to see that there was no trouble. Carefully, he tucked the invitation into his pocket. He'd be damned if he'd let Frost ruin everything Rhiannon had worked for.

*   *   *

Rhiannon watched the preparations for the evening's event with a heavy heart. Mrs Paisley was lying in the chapel of rest and she should be here enjoying the moment for which they'd both worked so hard. Nevertheless she had promised to go

345

ahead with the Grand Opening and she meant to keep her word.

In the kitchen, Mrs Jones was organizing everyone with the ease of long practice. The other cooks hired for the occasion were happy to take direction from her and even Violet and Hetty were working with a will.

'Rhiannon, come and see what we've done so far.' Mrs Jones took her arm. 'The ballroom looks a treat and I think you'll be pleased with it.'

Lining the walls of the large room were tables covered in pristine damask cloths, groaning under the weight of the feast. Great hams rested cheek by jowl with platters of venison and beef. A salmon with its head intact but the skin removed to reveal its pink flesh made a colourful display, and huge cheeses stood at each end of the tables.

Rhiannon walked around the room, admiring the dishes of pickled beetroot, thick chutney and a variety of sauces. 'You've done us proud, Mrs Jones,' she said. 'I'm only sorry that Mrs Paisley can't share it all with us.'

Mrs Jones gave her a hug. 'Don't you fret. She's here in spirit, I'd stake my life on it.' She dabbed at her eyes with a large handkerchief. 'Well, I can't stay here grizzling, I've got puddings to steam and custard to make.' She looked critically at Rhiannon. 'Hadn't you better go and get ready? You look a sight, if you don't mind me saying so.'

Rhiannon looked at her crumpled skirt and touched her hair, which was hanging loose on her shoulders, and smiled. 'You're right. I must look more like a shanty-town girl than a businesswoman.' She glanced up at the clock on the wall. 'I'll go up to my room.'

'Just one more thing,' Cook said. 'I know tonight's going to be hard for you without Mrs Paisley here, but you have to put that out of your mind and try to smile.'

Rhiannon swallowed the lump in her throat, and made her way slowly from the ballroom and up the gracious stairs.

*   *   *

The lamps were lit in the foyer and candles shimmered in silver holders along the window-sills. Rhiannon looked around her approvingly, as she stood near the door prepared to welcome her guests.

The servants were ready with trays full of glasses of fine wine, and Rhiannon acknowledged that she had Mrs Jayne Buchan to thank for teaching her how to make a social evening a success. Jayne would not be attending the opening: she had caused a scandal by leaving her husband and running away with another man. But her father, Mr Morton-Edwards, was among the first to arrive with his new wife, and Rhiannon smiled in gratitude. 'Thank you for coming, Mr and Mrs Morton-Edwards.' She resisted the urge to bob a curtsy, reminding herself she was no longer a servant but the proprietor of the Paradise Park Hotel. 'I hope you both enjoy the evening.'

'I'm sure we will, and may I say how splendid everything looks? You've worked wonders here, and I'm half sorry I didn't buy the place myself now.' He rested his hand on her shoulder. 'Well done, Rhiannon, you should be proud of yourself.'

As the couple moved on to mingle with the other

guests Rhiannon caught sight of Richard Frost who, strangely, seemed to be avoiding her eyes. She forgot about him then as she welcomed more guests.

When almost everyone had arrived Rhiannon stood near the door feeling alone and vulnerable. None of these people were her friends: her friends were the maids and Mrs Jones, all of whom had worked until they dropped to make the opening the success it was. She knew the people here were merely curious: all they wanted was a good night out with plenty of food and wine. If only Bull would come then perhaps she would feel better.

When she judged that most of the guests had arrived Rhiannon made her way to the dais at one end of the room and held up her hand. 'I'm not going to make a long speech,' she said, 'and I'm sure that will be a relief to you all.' Her words raised a few smiles and she began to relax. 'I just want to welcome you all to the Paradise Park. This evening is just a sample of what guests here can expect.' She paused. 'Good wine, superb food and warm, welcoming surroundings. Please pass the news on to your friends that the Paradise Park is now officially open for business.'

A scattering of applause greeted her words, and Rhiannon was about to step down when a voice called her name from the back of the room. Rhiannon looked up in surprise to see Richard Frost waving his arms for silence.

'I don't think you good people here know what sort of woman she is.' He gestured towards Rhiannon. 'She might be dressed in fine clothes but she's nothing more than a street girl, a shanty-town woman who lived off ignorant navvies. Go on,

348

woman, deny it if you can.'

A hush fell and curious eyes turned in Rhiannon's direction. She felt her colour rise but she lifted her head proudly. 'What I used to be is nothing to do with what I am now. At least I've learned the error of my ways and tried to make a success of a respectable trade.'

'Hear, hear!' Eynon Morton-Edwards stepped forward. 'This young lady worked for me, and I know that her honesty and integrity are beyond question. Give her a chance to carry on with her respectable business and don't condemn her. Rather, congratulate her for putting her past behind her.'

Richard wouldn't be silenced and his voice rose. 'As well as being a harlot this woman is a gaolbird. How can anyone patronize such a woman and such an establishment? I'm sure you must all be aware that this hotel was once a bawdy-house. Who's to say it won't be one again?'

Rhiannon bit her lip. Richard Frost had certainly done his homework. She looked round at the sea of accusing faces, wishing she was anywhere but on the dais in full view of everyone. She just wanted to crawl away into a hole and hide. There seemed nothing she could say in her defence.

Richard Frost hadn't finished with her yet. 'She's a whore and a thief. She has no right to be mingling with respectable folk. She should be drummed out of the town. What sane person could trust her now?'

'I could.' Bull's voice rang out with conviction.

Rhiannon jumped: she hadn't seen him come into the room.

The crowd parted as he made his way towards

349

her and then he was taking her hand, smiling down at her in the way she loved. Suddenly she felt strong, as though she could face anything with Bull at her side.

He held up his hand for silence. 'I think most of you here know me for an honest man.' There were murmurs of assent. 'I am a magistrate, and I can tell you that Rhiannon was falsely accused of theft. She was, unfortunately, caught up in the quarrel between a certain married couple. She was subsequently released because she was cleared of all charges.'

Bull looked directly at Richard Frost. 'As for you, Doctor, isn't it true that Rhiannon gave you work at the hotel, providing you with the sort of living you would not have otherwise enjoyed?' He didn't wait for a reply. 'And that your intention was to ask her to marry you?'

'You don't know what you're talking about, man,' Richard Frost blustered. 'I'm a good doctor and I came to help out at the hotel because I don't like to see people sick and suffering.'

'You had no qualms about it once being a bawdy-house then, did you? It was only when Rhiannon rebuffed your advances that you became angry. You were a man rejected, made to look the fool you are.'

'I—I—' Richard Frost was suddenly white, his face pinched, as he stared around the room, sensing the crowd's hostility now. Then he turned and rushed out of the hotel into the night.

'Now,' Bull said, 'before you good people go on to enjoy the rest of the evening I'd like you to give me your attention for a little longer.'

Rhiannon looked up at him as he took her hand

and held it to his lips. 'Rhiannon, over the past weeks I've come to realize how much you mean to me. I know I can't be happy without you so will you do me the honour of consenting to be my wife?'

Suddenly it was as if the room was full of rainbows, and stars seemed to burst inside her head. She looked into Bull's eyes, saw the love there, and her breath caught in her throat. Then she was in his arms, sheltered and protected by him in the way she had always wanted to be. For a long moment he held her close and then at arm's length. 'Well, Rhiannon?' His words now were for her alone. 'I love you and want to marry you. Are you going to give me an answer?'

'Oh, Bull, if you really want me of course I'll marry you. I love you so much, I've always loved you and . . .' She fell silent as Bull put a gentle finger over her lips.

'I know, my darling, there's no need for any more words.' He drew her close to him and kissed her hair, and she felt his warmth, and knew that this was meant to be. It was written in the stars that she and Bull were to be together.

It was Eynon Morton-Edwards who started the cheering, then the servants, who had gathered in the doorway, were clapping, shouting congratulations, and soon the whole room was applauding.

Bull took her hand and led her through the crowd of smiling faces and out into the cool of the evening air. She heard the band strike up in the ballroom, saw the lights shining from the hotel windows, and felt that Mrs Paisley was up in the heavens looking down at her in approval.

Rhiannon's heart was full of joy, love and hope

351

because here, in her arms, was the greatest prize of all: her beloved Bull Beynon. Then everything was blotted out as his lips claimed hers and she lost herself in the wonder of his kiss.